Geoffrey Ward
STATUTES OF LIBERTY
The New York School of Poets

Moustapha Safouan
JACQUES LACAN AND THE QUESTION OF PSYCHOANALYTIC TRAINING
(*Translated and introduced by Jacqueline Rose*)

Stanley Shostak
THE DEATH OF LIFE
The Legacy of Molecular Biology

Elizabeth Cowie
REPRESENTING THE WOMAN
Cinema and Psychoanalysis

Raymond Tallis
NOT SAUSSURE
A Critique of Post-Saussurean Literary Theory

Laura Mulvey
VISUAL AND OTHER PLEASURES

Ian Hunter
CULTURE AND GOVERNMENT
The Emergence of Literary Education

Denise Riley
'AM I THAT NAME?'
Feminism and the Category of 'Women' in History

Mary Ann Doane
THE DESIRE TO DESIRE
The Woman's Film of the 1940s

Language, Discourse, Society
Series Standing Order ISBN 0–333–71482–2
(*outside North America only*)

You can receive future titles in this series as they are published by placing a standing order. Please contact your bookseller or, in case of difficulty, write to us at the address below with your name and address, the title of the series and the ISBN quoted above.

Customer Services Department, Macmillan Distribution Ltd, Houndmills, Basingstoke, Hampshire RG21 6XS, England

Romancing Jane Austen

**Narrative, Realism, and
the Possibility of a Happy Ending**

Ashley Tauchert
University of Exeter

palgrave
macmillan

First published in 2005 by
PALGRAVE MACMILLAN
Houndmills, Basingstoke, Hampshire RG21 6XS and
175 Fifth Avenue, New York, N.Y. 10010
Companies and representatives throughout the world.

PALGRAVE MACMILLAN is the global academic imprint of the Palgrave Macmillan division of St. Martin's Press, LLC and of Palgrave Macmillan Ltd. Macmillan® is a registered trademark in the United States, United Kingdom and other countries. Palgrave is a registered trademark in the European Union and other countries.

ISBN-13: 978–1–4039–9747–0 hardback
ISBN-10: 1–4039–9747–0 hardback

This book is printed on paper suitable for recycling and made from fully managed and sustained forest sources.

A catalogue record for this book is available from the British Library.

Library of Congress Cataloging-in-Publication Data

Tauchert, Ashley.
    Romancing Jane Austen : narrative, realism, and the possibility of a happy ending / Ashley Tauchert.
        p. cm.—(Language, discourse, society)
    Includes bibliographical references (p.) and index.
    ISBN 1–4039–9747–0
    1. Austen, Jane, 1775–1817 – Criticism and interpretation. 2. Women and literature–England – History – 18th and 19th century. 3. Narration (Rhetoric)– History –19th century. 4. Love stories, English – History and criticism. 5. Closure (Rhetoric) – History – 18th and 19th century. 6. Happiness in literature. 7. Realism in literature. I. Title. II. Language, discourse, society (Palgrave Macmillan (Firm))

PR4037.T385 2005   2005049831
823'.7—dc22

10 9 8 7 6 5 4 3 2 1
14 13 12 11 10 09 08 07 06 05

Transferred to Digital Printing in 2005

Dedicated with love to Chris, who continually reminds me of the possibility of a happy ending in spite of overwhelming odds to the contrary.

Contents

Acknowledgements

This work would not have been possible without the time and labour of the following people: Gill Howie, for understanding the nature of the quest; Jane Spencer, who knows more than most how to do this kind of thing properly, and still encourages me to do it in my own way; Margaretta Jolly, for trawling through early (and very late) drafts and asking all the right questions; Helen Taylor, for embodying critical and challenging leadership; Colin MacCabe for provoking thought and 'putting his money where his mouth is'; Helen Hanson, for understanding something very important about being a heroine; Min Wild, for being a passionate and constructive reader; Regenia Gagnier for telling me what my question *really* was early in the project, and for complimenting my writing at just the right moment. Warm thanks are due to everyone in the School of English at Exeter for being patient with me while this has been on my mind. Finally, I'd like to acknowledge all the vibrant and passionate students who took the level 3 'Colin Firth' module in 2005 ...

I am indebted to my lovely family for laughing at me when I am distracted, for making me laugh when I have become too serious, and for reminding me of the importance of domestic comfort above all else. Thanks to Mark Tauchert and Becky Peters, Gemma, Joseph and Zak for being there, and to my dad for showing me how to make an argument. Thanks to Craig for the inspiring photos of Upton Pyne. Love to Valerie Callaghan for being such a positive role model. I am particularly grateful to Jack, Alice and Georgie for making my life so happy, and for being so easy to love.

An early version of the argument made here appears as 'Mary Wollstonecraft and Jane Austen: "Rape" and "Love" as (Feminist) Social Realism and Romance', in *Women: A Cultural Review*, 14, 2 (1993): 144–58.

Preface

'If love is a conspiracy, it is much older than the age of "bourgeois individualism" in which some historians tend to locate it.'

Margaret Doody, *The True Story of the Novel*[1]

'The articulation of a feminist standpoint based on women's self-definition and activity ... embodies a distress which requires a solution. The experience of continuity and relation – with others, with the natural world, of mind with body – provides an ontological base for developing a non-problematic social synthesis, a social synthesis which need not operate through the denial of the body, the attack on nature, or the death struggle between the self and other, a social synthesis which does not depend on any of the forms taken by abstract masculinity.'

Nancy M.C. Hartsock, *The Feminist Standpoint*[2]

'A woman with the misfortune of knowing any thing, should conceal it as well as she can.'

Jane Austen, *Northanger Abbey*[3]

Following on from the publication of *Mary Wollstonecraft and the Accent of the Feminine* (Palgrave, 2002), this study closes a research cycle which initiated in a desire to participate in contemporary debates concerning the dawn and daybreak of women's Anglophone literary history. Taken together, these two books offer a revised account of Wollstonecraft and Austen as peculiarly resonant figures in that documented history, through engagement with contemporary critical questions concerning femininity, subjectivity and writing. *Accent of the Feminine* tested the arguments of the 'equality/difference' debate raised in recent feminist philosophy against the textual evidence of Mary Wollstonecraft's interventions in late eighteenth-century political theory. My key focus there concerned the anachronistic implications of a resonance between the eighteenth-century feminist polemic of Mary Wollstonecraft and the twentieth- century 'feminine philosophy' of Luce Irigaray. *Romancing Jane Austen* considers the Jane Austen cultural phenomenon through the strong lenses available from accounts of the romance as a narrative mode. It is both an attempt to make conscious the complex and sometimes contradictory network of associations centred on the romance, and to offer yet another account of Austen as the first female writer who seems to have transcended her social coordinates as a narrative artist.

Austen has been traditionally understood as a 'high' realist writer, but one who was limited to the representation of feminised zones, further curtailed by her identity as a product of the lower gentry and clergy. She has also become a successful English brand: the increasingly popular, and culturally valuable, mother of the popular 'feminine romance'. Narrative romance has come into focus as a distinctive literary mode in the defining antinomy that characterises the history of narrative writing: 'Romances oppose reality'.[4] Critical interest in the romance is split between a feminist literary history that locates Austen as a key figure in the history of the realist novel, and a Marxist-inflected narrative theory that has largely overlooked her work.[5] I want to consider a number of significant structural parallels between romance as narrative expression of a pre-capitalist 'mythic' form, and romance as a debased 'feminine' genre, both of which can be apprehended in Austen's famous body of work. This study approaches Austen as a missing link between otherwise strongly diverging strands of the 'mythic' and 'feminine' romance. It considers the epistemology of romance – and its tendencies to accommodate femininity, irony and the comic – as focused through Austen's accomplished narrative romances.

The discussion starts from a hypothesis that Austen's six famous novels can be read productively as late adaptations of romance narrative, which, according to Erich Auerbach, has an exacting 'relationship to the objective world of reality'.[6] This relationship is captured in the structural necessity of the series of *avantures* undertaken by the courtly hero: 'trial through adventure is the real meaning of the knight's ideal existence'. Furthermore, 'the most significant actions are performed primarily for the sake of a lady's favor'.[7] That lady, in the hands of critics as diverse as Northrop Frye and Margaret Doody, can be read for tropes of what has recently been described as the 'feminine divine'. This makes Austen's work particularly interesting to ongoing attempts to develop a 'feminist standpoint', and her work can be taken as audacious evidence for our understanding of an otherwise culturally belittled feminine agency.

The romance – whether feminised or not – is a narrative formation centred on the possibility of salvation. Austen's work captures, under conditions of meticulous realism, the narrative formula of the feminine subject of romance. This is not necessarily a new figure, in fact by definition archaic if not archetypal, but expressed and represented under new conditions. With reference to the powerful Marxian critical frame, as received through Fredric Jameson's analysis of the 'ideology of form',

I am particularly interested in a structural analogy available between the feminine romance, the salvational narrative quest, and the problem that is feminine subjectivity in the narrative of history. Austen's narrative fiction, from this perspective, provides evidence that feminine subjectivity might yet have a role in salvational historicity.

Since starting this project I have learnt that 'romance' resists definitive closure. At the point of finishing the book, I am still uncertain of what it is that the term names. I am inclined to think that it might indicate something no longer, or not yet, within our range of consciousness. Raymond Williams noted some problems with defining 'romantic' that point to the inherent ambiguity of 'romance':

> Romantic is a complex word because it takes its modern senses from two distinguishable contexts: the content and character of romances, and the content and character of the Romantic Movement.

'Romance', he notes, was already changing when it appeared in English from 1650: 'The word in varying forms, *romanz, romaunz, roman, romant,* etc., had come through oF and Provençal from *romanice*, mL – "in the Romantic tongue": that is to say, in the neo-Latin vernacular languages.'[8] I am not equipped to offer a complete formal study of the origins and directions of 'romance' beyond the ordinary awareness, available from many sources including Williams, that narratives which attract this label tend to be defined in distinction to what has come to be recognised as the literary 'realism' characteristic of 'the novel'. What I intend to offer instead is a meditation on the peculiar tendencies of romance in the here and now, refracted through Austen, to denote two quite distinct literary phenomena: one best captured by Marxian analysis of the dialectical history of 'realism'; the other crystallised more immediately in the resolutely feminised realm of the love story.

Jane Spencer has already noted that romance held 'an especially strong appeal for women', and played a significant part in the development of women's writing through the eighteenth century.[9] I would add that this powerful hold continues, as evidenced by the phenomenal contemporary interest in popular romance narrative in general and Austen adaptations in particular. My argument is simply that there is a structural – or formal – relation between the two critical connotations of the romance, as salvational narrative and as heterosexual love story, which suggests something interesting about what we are now beginning to understand as feminine subjectivity. Furthermore, I think that Austen was conscious of what she was doing when she brought these strands into peaceful relationship in her six key works.

If romance can now be said to *be* anything at all, it seems most likely to refer to a fantasy formation that still has a central place in the emotional lives of women. My local charity shop is large enough to set aside a separate room for books. Those books are organised around bold categories that fit the reading habits of a mixed socio-economic demographic: 'Thrillers', 'Gardening', 'Education', 'Children's', 'Miscellaneous' and 'Romance'. 'Romance' is by far the largest section, crowding a wall of shelves usually populated by women browsers. The local library, with its more sophisticated referencing system, also highlights the category of the 'Romance', in which section Austen is sometimes found sitting unobtrusively alongside reams of paperback bodice-rippers. Whether we choose to understand this persistent narrative phenomenon as a cultural symptom of the powerful ideology of 'heteronormativity', or as the natural expression of inherent and instinctive feminine desires, is not my immediate concern here. Women as a genus crave romance. Romance structures femininity in a way that demands attention. That kind of craving calls on the language of psychoanalysis, which comes readily to hand:

> The issue of female sexuality always brings us back to the question of how the human subject is constituted. In the theories of Freud that Lacan redeploys, the distinction between the sexes brought about by the castration complex and the different positions that must subsequently be taken up, confirms that the subject is split and the object is lost. This is the difficulty at the heart of being human to which psychoanalysis and the objects of its enquiry – the unconscious and sexuality – bear witness.[10]

This is also the difficulty at the heart of Austen's feminised romance narratives. Exemplified by Austen at its aesthetic high-point, the feminine romance can be read as a kind of cultural day-dreaming common to women. That daydream concerns the splitting of the subject and quest for the object, focalised through the feminine subject of narrative. Whether we, as academically trained readers, revel in or resist that daydreaming tendency is not the point. Everyone reading this book will have indulged to some extent in the compelling romance fantasy available through Austen's narrative performances. Some might raise an eyebrow at its ironic reincarnation in the *Bridget Jones* phenomenon, or its postcolonial recasting as *Bride and Prejudice*. We would probably share a smirk at the innumerable popular examples revealing the structure of the fantasy in all its literal infelicities, and stripped of all pretensions to critical consciousness:

> She jumped, her eyes going wide and startled. Then as her gaze flashed to his, she saw his control shatter in an explosion of raw need that stunned every sense she possessed. His face went hard, his eyes fierce, blazing, almost savage in their passionate hunger. He looked primitive, as if polite society had barely touched him.
>
> Fear, sheer primal female fear, streaked through her, urging flight, but at the same time she was paralysed, completely and helplessly fascinated.[11]

This may seem trivial material, until we recall that 95 per cent of Hollywood films have been defined as containing dominant or secondary romance narratives.[12] One of the things that makes Austen so astonishingly successful as a writer is also the thing that associates her work with the basest of feminine fantasies: she narrates the daydream of the heroine's persistent desire to be *somehow* saved by an ideal gentleman: a common desire to be rescued from 'all this', and to live 'happily ever after'. The 'somehow' seems to involve a feminine power to transform an animalistic masculine desire into civility, or gentlemanly action.

It seems a double-bind, then, on turning to feminist criticism for an account of this structurally persistent daydream, to find the romance is widely denounced as a dangerous lure towards a cultural 'idealization of heterosexual romance and marriage' which should be resisted by the conscious woman.[13] Alison Light notes this tendency in her positive reconstruction of romance reading for feminist literary politics:

> [Romance is] seen as coercive and stereotyping narratives which invite the reader to identify with a passive heroine who only finds true happiness in submitting to a masterful male. What happens to women readers is then compared to certain Marxist descriptions of the positioning of all human subjects under capitalism. Romance thus emerges as a form of oppressive ideology, which works to keep women in their socially and sexually subordinate place.[14]

A recent comment on the character of Dawn in *The Office* gives a grumbling account of her 'passive' characteristics, aligned with the romantic Austen heroine:

> She's been instilled from birth with that great feminine virtue of forbearance. ... The really chilling thing about Dawn is that her character would sit as easily in a Jane Austen novel as it does in the 21st-century office; despite 150-odd years in the advance of

women's education and professional achievement, the same contours are visible of female subservience to male ego.

Dawn, like Lizzy, still suffers the 'fantasy of being discovered, of someone else stepping in to make their destiny – a man, a talent scout or a head-hunter'.[15] Maybe this is because the moderately educated Dawn might plausibly be imagined reading Austen in her quiet moments. Psychoanalysis offers a vocabulary to think through the fact of this persistent daydream as a structuring principle of feminine subjectivity, recognisable under historical conditions as palpably different as the pre-industrial Regency and the post-industrial wasteland in which Austen's romance still flourishes.

Jungian psychoanalysis makes strong claims for the existence of 'patterns of functioning', or 'primordial images', which 'are present in every psyche'. The persistence of romance implies just such a primordial image, but it is important to distinguish between the form and the content of this image:

> A primordial image is determined as to its content only when it has become conscious and is therefore filled out with the material of conscious experience. Its form, however, as I have explained elsewhere, might perhaps be compared to the axial system of a crystal, which, as it were, preforms the crystalline structure in the mother liquid, although it has no material existence of its own.[16]

The 'form' of romance, taken as an 'axial system', expresses a very human desire for salvation. Its content under conditions of narrative realism has become inextricably entwined with feminine fantasy in the name of love.

While psychoanalysis offers an available vocabulary for thinking through romance as a persistent subjective fantasy, late Marxian analysis offers an equally advanced vocabulary for thinking through the cultural function of romance as 'ideologeme'. In these discussions, the romance operates as a covert narrative mode in dialectical relation with the overt tendency of the historical moment in which it arises. I find Frederic Jameson's account of the 'political unconscious' particularly productive for considering the historical significance of Austen's successful mediation of romance and realism, expressed through feminine narrative consciousness. Austen's foregrounding of Providence in the working out of her narrative equations can be read as an example of 'adequate theoretical mediation between the salvational logic of the romance narrative and the nascent sense of historicity imposed by the social dynamic of capitalism'.[17] Mode and archetype are equally abstract principles of a structural causality, and I think we need both concepts to understand the forces at work in Austen's exquisite narrative performances.

Vladimir Propp's formulation of narrative 'functions' as 'stable, constant elements in a tale, independent of how and by whom they are fulfilled' exposes the 'problem of the character' in 'its incapacity to make a place for the subject'.[18] In short, narrative functions exceed the role of individual characters, much as heroic actions exceed the role of individual actors in the example offered by cinema. The supplements of stuntman and special effects bridge the gap between the individual's range of possible actions and the 'Action' demanded by narrative function. Alex Woloch notices this 'strange doubling' at work in *Pride and Prejudice*:

> Darcy quickly substitutes a servant for himself, transforming what would have been an action growing out of and elaborating the novel's emotional center into a mundane, meaningless duty. The strange doubling – 'let me, or let the servant' – reveals a sudden similarity between the two characters who exist at the poles of the narrative's asymmetric structure. In this brief moment we can see what the system of characterization usually distorts but ultimately relies on: the radical continuity, or similarity, of all human agents.[19]

Beyond the 'story of "individuals" ' or 'the chronicle of generations and their destinies', Jameson asks us to consider narrative 'rather as an impersonal process, a semic transformation', which performs itself through a series of transformational relations between paired characters.[20] What I find interesting when applying this thought to Austen is that it allows us to regard the powerful feminine agency of her heroines as one yielding to narrative providence. This yielding agency, represented through key characteristics of patience, humility, gentleness, civility and forbearance, and expressed through the determinants of actions available to realist subjects, calls on a faith and hope in futurity that is now very difficult to imagine possible. Perhaps we still read and care about Austen because she imagines it for us, and allows us at least temporarily to suspend our belief in the inevitability of suffering. That may well seem a tall order for 'Dear Jane', unless we recognise in her a woman with the 'misfortune of knowing' something we have since largely forgotten, and who concealed it as well as she could.

ASHLEY TAUCHERT,
University of Exeter

Introduction: The Persistence of Jane Austen's Romance

Every universalizing approach, whether the phenomenological or the semiotic, will from the dialectical point of view be found to conceal its own contradictions and repress its own historicity by strategically framing its perspective so as to omit the negative, absence, contradiction, repression, the *non-dit*, or the *impensé*. To restore the latter requires that abrupt and paradoxical dialectical restructuration of the basic problematic which has often seemed to be the most characteristic gesture and style of dialectical method in general, keeping the terms but standing the problem on its head.

Fredric Jameson, *Political Unconscious:*
Narrative as a Socially Symbolic Act[21]

A critique of ideology has thus to proceed in two moves. First, of course, it has to follow Jameson's well-known injunction 'Historicize!', and to discern in an apparently universal unchangeable limitation the ideological 'reification' and absolutization of a certain contingent historical constellation. ... The second move then, in a kind of reflective turn, compels us to conceive this explanatory reference to concrete historical circumstances itself as a 'false', ideological attempt to circumvent the traumatic kernel of the Real (the death drive, the non-existence of sexual relationship), to explain it away and thus render invisible its structural necessity.

Slavoj Žižek, 'There is no Sexual Relationship'[22]

She had been forced into prudence in her youth, she learned romance as she grew older – the natural sequel of an unnatural beginning.[23]

Jane Austen, *Persuasion*

1

If the English eighteenth century is understood as a period of social and material reform on an unprecedented scale, characterised by discourses of individual 'rights' and 'egalitarianism', of 'rationality' and 'liberty', wrought through struggles between traditionally oppressive social structures and emergent forms of individual consciousness, then Jane Austen seems a rather arbitrary literary expression of English enlightenment. To receive her six famous novels from this perspective, we would expect to find tropes that herald the great political, social, material, philosophical and economic changes taking place in her lifetime, and the lifetime of her narratives; echoes or displaced imprints of the calls for – or resistances to – freedom from accrued tradition, and increased demand for liberty of thought. One of the most overwhelming facts about these six novels, however, remains their overt indifference at the level of content in the great social, economic, political or material events forming their immediate context. This has always been an interesting absence, given the author's credentials as an intelligent and literate woman. The absence becomes more visible when we remember the naval brothers who had seen action against the French, chased real pirates, carried bullion for the East India Company, and just missed the Battle of Trafalgar; or the cousin married to a French aristocrat guillotined in 1794.[24]

Austen's novels famously prefer to turn their gaze from a potentially vivid window onto the violent social upheavals which marked the culmination of a century or so of 'European Enlightenment', towards the microcosmic intensities of the drawing room at its domestic heart. Austen's signature is visible in the work's uninterrupted focus on the minutiae of a dozen or so mostly rural English families drawn from the clergy and the gentry, documenting their courtships, foibles, dramas, domestic habits, and manners. This interior turn is a characteristically feminine move; to draw the curtains, light the fire, and keep loved ones close to home in times of trouble. These famous and much-loved novels are unavoidably feminocentric, attending quietly to the detail of spoilt dresses, pretty bonnets, secret love notes, long walks reading letters, sisterly love, and the private dramas of uncertain courtship. They hail women readers in their offer of the consolations of romance. This interior turn, feminised and courteous, is an example of what Fredric Jameson has effectively analysed as the historical consciousness of a literary act, keeping the terms expressive of its determinate moment, but standing the problem on its head.

In this study I aim to make conscious what strikes me as the puzzle of Austen's status in English literary history. The discussion thread

I am following here can be summarised as follows:

1. In the context of feminist cultural criticism, our understanding of women's writing follows from the fact of women's historical oppression.
2. Women come to writing later, they 'enter' a literary tradition long-established, and 'struggle' to find space for their particular literary expression in the emerging market.
3. If they get through this cultural glass ceiling, they are soon forgotten by a tradition of criticism that has assigned aesthetic value according to the terms pre-set by the work of men.
4. The resulting absence of women from the literary 'canon' is then taken as evidence for their aesthetic failure as a 'class'.
5. The absence of a common ground for feminine self-representation leaves feminine subjectivity derelict of a cultural imaginary, thus denying women autonomous self-expression.

This argument, made impressively across a large body of critical work resulting from the introduction of a feminist perspective to the study of women's writing and the canon, works beautifully to explain the 'negative, absence, contradiction, repression' of English women's literary production:

> Men set the pace in societies where women are subordinated. Male paradigms drove literary practice just as they have driven literary history. Men's writings, men's sociable interaction and rivalries, their cultural and political disputes as well as their ventures in publishing led the way. Though there were many women writers, men had social, political, economic and literary power. Literary recognition could only be fully provided by men. Few (perhaps no) women were able to succeed as writers without the support of men.[25]

That is, it works beautifully until it comes to Austen. Austen produced aesthetically accomplished narrative work that challenged and completed a particular strand of the English literary tradition; work that not only soon found a respected place in that tradition, but also consolidated and reinterpreted it for futurity, and seems set to continue to do so.

Austen is doing something notably different when compared to *any* writers preceding her, and that difference produces a very different outcome in terms of her reception, a reception which spans professional criticism and popular culture. The work in which she does this is centred on a common narrative formula that represents a feminine subject achieving a happy ending after all, in spite of the carefully specified plausible reasons for her final suffering. Austen turns the tragic possibilities of meticulous realism into the comic resolutions of romance, and she concretises the unarguably universal desire for an empirically implausible happy ending in an image of ideal heterosexual love. She does all this with a wink and a smile that manages to make it all look very light.

There is simply something uncanny about Austen's work: the familiarity of her plots and characters, still recognisable as 'true' to modern readers; the way the works continue to draw new waves of professional and lay audiences; the way it has seeped deep into the fabric of an imaginary lost Englishness, now associated with the Regency period; and the way it continues to circulate as highly valuable cultural material long after the specific conditions producing the narrative dramas have passed out of practice. Austen writes in a way that no one before her was writing: her writing establishes the immediate conditions for the empirical realism that comes to dominate nineteenth-century narrative. She was clearly building on possibilities available from accomplished predecessors such as Samuel Richardson and Frances Burney, but something surprisingly new (and possibly unrepeated since) is achieved through her work which has allowed these novels to lift off from their immediate context and apparently transcend the conditions of their production.

Austen's work challenges the hard-won case of women's historical oppression: she was only the daughter of a clergyman and tutor, seventh of eight children, with no formal education to speak of. Out of an apparently open access to her Oxford-educated father's and brothers' books, and a mother's talent for versification, this otherwise unremarkable young woman carved powerful and lasting narrative art works for futurity. The work testifies to the expression of what we might call a specifically *feminine* enlightenment.

Tony Tanner remarks in one of his four awed footnotes to *Pride and Prejudice*, that although the narrator mentions 'peace' towards the end of this novel, it is uncertain whether this refers specifically to the Treaty of Amiens of 1802, which might otherwise be grasped as a concrete historical referent for the narrative's immediate context: 'As for Wickham and Lydia ... Their manner of living, even when the restoration of peace dismissed them to a home, was unsettled in the extreme.'[26] His analysis of this uncertain reference situates any uncertainty firmly in the mind of the critical reader: 'If Jane Austen wanted to bring anything into clear focus she was well able to: and where she has been content to leave a matter as absolutely peripheral to her particular action and fiction, then so should we.'[27]

But we have not. Austen's apparent indifference to concrete historical markers makes academics squirm, and quickly reach for the concept of 'ideology' to explain away an uncomfortable contradiction represented by the work. On the one hand we face the fact that Austen's writing has had a profound and lasting influence on the cultural evolution of narrative realism: she apparently inaugurates *free indirect discourse* as well as capturing recognisable human types in plausible narratives that reveal a pre-industrial world long-since lost to our immediate experience. On the other hand, she works only from scraps of material close at hand, as one might have constructed a smart new dress from discarded fabric. This makes the novels unmistakably the work of a woman, since their content embroiders minute experiences of the world from a particular woman's perspective. But women's work, like women's subjectivity, does not normally transcend. Nancy M. Hartsock illuminates this important argument well:

> Dualism, along with the dominance of one side of the dichotomy over the other, marks phallocentric society and social theory. These dualisms appear in a variety of forms – in philosophy, technology, political theory, and the organization of class society itself. One can, for example, see them very clearly worked out in Plato, although they appear in many other forms. There, the concrete/abstract duality takes the form of an opposition of material to ideal, and a denial of the relevance of the material world to the attainment of what is of fundamental importance: love of knowledge, or philosophy (masculinity). The duality between nature and culture takes the form of a devaluation of work or necessity, and the primacy instead of purely social interaction for the attainment of undying fame. Philosophy itself is separate from nature, and indeed, exists only on the basis of the domination of (at least some) of the philosopher's own nature. Abstract masculinity, then, can be seen to have structured Western social relations and the modes of thought to which these relations give rise at least since the founding of the *polis*.[28]

Attempting to follow the contradiction – between the feminocentric material of Austen's literary work and its phenomenal reception as great art – to a reasonable resolution, has brought the argument made in this study to a conclusion I did not expect at the start. Each chapter considers one of Austen's novels through a synthesis of feminist and structural narrative analysis in search of the elusive key to her happy endings. From here it is short step into the Marxian arguments concerning literary and economic modes, which take the narrative model as analogous to the problem of structure and agency at the level of history. Austen's work, read from this perspective, reveals a narrative agency associated with femininity that harmonises discordant elements into providentially realised happy endings of individual, dyadic and social concord.

Paul Riceour's narrative philosophy helps to reconceive the eighteenth-century English 'rise of the novel' as a manifestation under new conditions of an ancient cultural form expressive of the relationship between time and eternity on a human scale. The problem of Austen's happy endings in relation to her otherwise unremitting realism takes the discussion into the recesses of the writing subject to face the question of feminine agency, and all the time haunted by the idea of the archetype that seems to be mobilised in the romance as narrative genre. Anyone who has ever 'got' Austen, will recognise that there is something fundamentally transformative in her work. The closer this argument has come to understanding the narrative transformation it offers, the more it has found itself transformed. The result is an admittedly romantic argument, expressing *this* writer's desire for a happy ending in spite of the deluge of empirical evidence testifying to its impossibility.

Austen's historical indifference has already been thoughtfully engaged by critics in a number of ways: as an 'innocent' decorative interlude; as a moderately conservative resistance to the winds of change; or as a subtle 'critique' of the politicised micro-context for her writing. The ambiguity of the 'peace' that breaks out towards the end of *Pride and Prejudice*, for instance, might record a simple vagueness about concrete historical data; a covert encoding of distanced awareness of the historical data; or a knowing wink at the historical irony of her courtship dramas. We might want the 'peace' to be a historical reference, but it also refers to the return of a domestic peace following the family's upheavals that form the material of the narrative.

John Skinner equivocates over the point of Austen's historical and political indifference, noting that many critics are 'unconvinced' by the argument that this writer had 'much more material at her disposal, but chose to ignore it'.[29] Andrew Sanders decides that although Austen's work 'may seem to stand apart from the preoccupations of many of her literary contemporaries ... it remains very much of its time'.[30] She is taken to be advancing 'Christian conservative, but not necessarily reactionary, terms against current radical enthusiasms', while also recognised as satirising those very values.[31]

Edward Said has resolved the deep historical ambiguity of Austen's writing differently, by grounding *Mansfield Park* in a displaced, rather than conscious, historical realism, which encodes awareness of the late eighteenth-century slave economy propping up the aesthetic and social mannerisms of the 'Park' itself.[32] Marilyn Butler, Margaret Kirkham, Isobel Armstrong, and Claudia Johnson have demonstrated in persuasive detail different aspects of the politically embedded vicissitudes of Austen's narrative position, to argue for a critically aware but highly ambiguous Austen, who subtly negotiates a complex position in the debates concerning female rights, duties, and education flooding late eighteenth-century and early nineteenth-century England.[33] Tony Tanner recognises a critically conscious Austen in his claim that 'she was certainly aware – or made cognizant of – more than appears in her fiction'.[34]

These arguments are valuable and convincing, and inform my discussion throughout. I do not aim to contend any of them as much as to suggest that something interesting might have been neglected in the need to define Austen's relationship to her immediate context. This 'something', when held to account, reveals an intriguing narrative claim for feminine agency. It only seems to become visible when we remember that Austen is working her extraordinarily plausible realism through the magical framework of romance. She does not attempt to represent objective history, perhaps, because she had already noticed there were bigger fish to fry.

Austen was conscious of her distancing of objective history. Two authorial moments are worth considering: Catherine Morland's anti-history speech in *Northanger Abbey* and Austen's genuinely hilarious early parody of Goldsmith's *The History of England from the Earliest Times to the Death of George II*.[35] Catherine, in an exchange with her future husband over taste in reading, asserts that she reads history only 'as a duty, but it tells me nothing that does not either vex or weary me … hardly any women at all – it is very tiresome; and yet I often think it odd that it should be so dull, for a great deal of it must be invention'.[36] Austen's juvenile *History of England*, as Antoinette Burton reminds us, laughs out of court any attempt at achieving an objective account of historical events, contains only three specific dates, and consistently foregrounds an avowedly subjective and necessarily limited grasp of the order and meaning of events: 'It is to be supposed that Henry was married, since he certainly had four sons, but it is not in my power to inform the reader who was his wife.'[37]

Burton finds in these examples a disengagement from objective social history, revealing a consciously proto-feminist Austen. This is an Austen aware of, and resisting, claims to objective history by deliberately rewriting the received narrative of English history to emphasise a 'power struggle between two women' (Elizabeth and Mary), and insisting that – whatever the more orthodox historians may believe – Mary was always in the right. Burton concludes that Austen's 'own consciousness as a resistant female reader in the present is the product of critical engagement with women's condition in the historical past'.[38] Perhaps so, but how far we can read Austen's 'consciousness as a resistant female reader' into direct remarks by her pseudo-gothic heroine, or her playful parody of Goldsmith, is notoriously complicated by precisely that studied authorial distance Burton finds at play in Austen's tendency to parody.

It is in this parodic, 'slanted', view of history that we meet the critically conscious Austen, intervening in politicised debate as a self-aware woman writer. Claudia Johnson argues convincingly that: 'for a woman novelist writing at the end of the eighteenth century, the issue of gender affected more than choices of characterization, and indeed it eventually called into question the act of authorship itself'.[39] A woman writing at this time could be *expected* to 'smuggle in their social criticism ... through various means of indirection – irony, antithetical pairing, double plotting, the testing or subverting of overt, typically doctrinaire statement with contrasting dramatic incident'.[40] Hence Judith Lowder Newton celebrates Elizabeth Bennet's 'refreshing self-direction', but finds this stance is then 'qualified by her defensive ironies':

> She may speak her mind to Darcy, may finally change him, and the reader is allowed to enjoy her daring, but at the same time we are continually reminded that Elizabeth is wrong about Wickham and wrong about Darcy and that she is controlled by her desire to please both. ... Elizabeth Bennet, though her own woman to the end, still dwindles by degrees into the moral balance required in Darcy's wife.[41]

Austen is praised for demystifying her contextual moment effectively, through accented mimicry of the formal terms of 'conservative' novelisation available. I focus here on the fact that she also, at the same time, performs near-perfect examples of the romantic myth in question, precisely by *giving* all her mature heroines a romance-centred happy ending. We might not want to believe in the myth of romance she represents, but that is what draws us to these narratives in the first place.

The difficult relationship between history and myth is central to this assessment of Austen, but opens a discussion that calls into question the reader's own beliefs. How we read Austen seems to depend on what we think writing is *for*. Jameson notes that we have experienced a critical shift from the question of *what* literary works *mean* to the question of *how* they *work*.[42] I am interested in the purpose of literary works: what are they *for*? When we read Austen we have to decide whether we are prepared to accept romance as anything other than myth in the Barthesian sense of something historical made to appear natural and universal: the part misrepresenting itself as the whole. We should perhaps also consider Austen's work as representing something natural and universal through the most subjective material available: the whole represented in the part.

The six novels which have constituted Austen's claim to serious authorship over the last two centuries offer clear evidence that 'history', as read in Goldsmith's materially and stylistically weighty volumes, is simply not her immediate concern as a writer. It has been convincingly demonstrated that we cannot claim this as symptomatic of the writer's ignorance of, or indifference to, the serious events through which she was writing. Neither do her novels suffer aesthetically from traces of a conscious, if subtle, erasure of historical specificity. It is an interesting reflection on contemporary critical determination that we find this internal evidence difficult to digest raw, and want to season it with historicist frameworks necessary to account for contextual factors that must, *at some level*, drive Austen's narrative consciousness, if not that of her characters. Perhaps we start to want Jane Austen to be a radical, or at least a critical, writer, as soon as we are no longer – for whatever reason – comfortable with her as simply a 'Great Novelist'. Nevertheless, Austen as radical or critical writer can only ever be indirectly argued, by close reading *against* the grain of the a-historical romance narratives which lead us to be interested in her in the first place. At the same time, popular Austen continues to be promoted by a culture industry that has appropriated the novels for English heritage, reproducing in fetishised detail the 'lost' graces of pre-industrial England for an audience still hungry for Austen's incarnation of the romance.

We might say that Austen's work has effectively resisted the desired formulas of radical critical methodologies, while remaining a valued literary artefact within them. This ambiguous status sustains her presence in the field of interpretation and avoids any foreclosure of the debate as to her status within, and meaning for, literary history. She remains, however discretely, centre stage to ongoing discussions of the complex evolution of 'the novel' out of the various strands of early narrative fiction into the polyvocal form that grounds on the literary plane the nascent subject of capitalism in social realism.

Gregory L. Lucente identifies the literary symptom of 'the rise of competitive capitalism' in the realist narrative phenomenon of 'solitary, apparently self-sufficient individuals'. Realism as a narrative project leads both to 'self-consciousness and to self-doubt, instilling in realistic narrative the epistemological disturbance of irony'.[43] Anthony Easthope has argued that English realism is an expression of a particular relationship to reality as cohered in the idiom of English empiricism, which constructs the object of reality in the same terms that it constructs a knowing subject:

> The priority of reality (over language, over reason) is constituted on the basis of the everyday world of common sense as perceived by the empirical individual, who, in the act of indicating a given reality ... reciprocally defines his or her own givenness.[44]

He finds 'an informal empiricist discourse working at a deeper level than an explicit ideology (as Edward Thompson suggested)'. This discourse can be identified by the following tendencies, which also characterise English narrative realism:

1. The object is assumed to exist in a reality which is supposedly pregiven. All you have to do is observe reality 'objectively', that is, without prejudgement or self-deception, and reality will yield knowledge of itself (the English seem to be obsessed with reality.)
2. The means of representation by which the object is represented to the subject is presumed not to interfere – or to intervene only minimally – with the subject's access to reality. In principle, discourse is transparent so that the only problem for knowledge is, as it were, to go and look and see what things are *there*.
3. In an epistemological scenario, subject and object always correspond to each other. If, according to the empiricist conception, reality is thought of as simply autonomous, given, then reciprocally the English subject is envisaged not as the effect of a process of construction but as always already merely *there* as the subject of or for knowledge/ experience. (A specially English version of morality inheres in this structure of subject, object, and knowledge.)[45]

Austen clearly bats for the empiricists, building her work on the transformative potential of experience, and widely recognised as 'the key figure in the early nineteenth-century consolidation of the novel', even though '[h]er contemporaries may have believed that the future belonged to Sir Walter Scott and the historical romance'.[46] At the same time, her refusal of a final cut between realism and romance makes these works radically ambiguous. This explains how she has come to be subsequently claimed by identifiably conservative and radical methodologies, and subsumed within neither. Austen's narrative presents a literary object of mediation between otherwise divergent critical world views. Jameson defines the concept of *mediation* as 'the relationship between the levels or instances, and the possibility of adapting analyses and findings from one level to another':

> Starting from this point, the analysis of mediations aims to demonstrate what is not evident in the appearance of things, but rather in their underlying reality.[47]

It is interesting, then, that Austen's key works offer internal evidence of a narrative mediation of the generic strands that coalesce in the eighteenth-century novel.

According to Robert Miles, '[t]he novel has always been a hybrid form, a mix of many pre-existing genres: Austen takes full advantage of this hybridity'.[48] Her meticulous novelistic 'realism', he suggests, is one of her 'shrewd decisions as an aspirant professional writer'. At the same time, the narratives incorporate aspects of (already outmoded) romance figures: 'Thematically, stymied love represents social disharmony; the marriage ... accordingly restores the social order to what it should be. Austen's six major novels are all variations on this pattern'.[49]

Austen's realism dovetails with comedic romance, both in the sense of feminine 'love story' and archetypal narrative mode. Her realism is always already ironic:

> Classic irony, if it succeeds, produces the effect of referring to reality almost as surely as does transparent discourse. But it is not equivalent to direct statement because the interpreter has to respond to both the meanings, 'apparent' and 'real', and irony is the effect of both.[50]

Michael McKeon has made an important argument that romance as a literary category emerges as the 'antithetical' term in the dialectical production of the novel as the dominant mode of plausible 'realism' at the end of a long 'epistemic' battle over history and representation. The account goes that under the emerging conditions of print culture, the 'romance' is captured as 'that which the present age – the framing counterpart of the classical past – defines itself against'. Romance becomes 'the locus of strictly "romance" elements that have been separated out from the documentary objectivity of "history" and of print'. In the English eighteenth century, romance was effectively defined as 'antithetical' to the realist novel and all it represents.[51] Nineteenth-century narrative realism follows on from the trajectory of that 'particularised epistemological perspective' of eighteenth-century British empirical philosophy.[52]

Austen seems to fit nicely into this story, and can be read as a progressive step in the direction of a broader cultural shift towards the 'democratic impulse of realism' and against the 'courtly form of romance', where 'idealised knights and ladies meet with fantastic adventures in enchanted landscapes, peopled by magic figures of good and evil'.[53] Austen's work is constructed around an empiricist vision in accordance with contemporary plausibility. She is found prioritising realist plausibility in her critical feedback to a neice's draft novel:

> Lyme will not do. Lyme is towards 40 miles distance from Dawlish *and* would not be talked of there. – I have put Starcross [instead]. If you prefer *Exeter*, that must always be safe.[54]

However, in her own work she retained aspects of a romance narrative paradigm to structure, and finally resolve, her 'realist' representational content. This is a significant move at the culmination of a literary evolution that has marked 'the category of romance' as 'a simple abstraction, in definitive opposition to the notion of "true history" '.[55]

Austen's realist-romance narratives, then, offer distinct epistemological possibilities foreclosed in the claims to 'true [or at least plausible] history' expressed through 'social realism'. She gives us access to the very material that the story of 'European Enlightenment' we have inherited omits as incredible, unreasonable, irrational, implausible, or impossible. Alex Woloch has recently analysed Austen's asymmetrical characterisation as evidence of her thorough grasp of 'the emergent structure of modern capitalism':

> Beneath the fragmentation and dispersion inherent in Austen's asymmetry is a controlling vision of human equality, without which the poetics of the narrative system would not coalesce.

He finds in *Pride and Prejudice* a representational structure linking characters 'within a common, although asymmetrical structure', which illuminates the 'complicated relationship between the form of Austen's novel and the emergent social structure that is both a source and end point of this narrative form'.[56] According to McKeon, the epistemology of romance connotes the presence of an 'invisible principle, rhetorical or theological, the intuition of whose authoritative workings is necessary to render complete that which only appears partial'.[57]

Austen is writing at the culmination of a long period of intensive rationalisation of knowledge, in which 'truth' is increasingly externalised and objectified as empirical data:

> The more the mediation of essential truth is objectified and concretized, the more narrative epistemology is implicated in a shift from qualitative to quantitative standards of completeness.[58]

Her insistence on resolving realist problems through the formal conventions of romance reverses this apparently inevitable tendency. Ruth Salvaggio's work has opened up the related question of the displacement of femaleness and the feminine in this historical narrative: "[i]t is not the Enlightened mind that rescues woman from her historical obscurity, but rather the suppression of woman and all her feminine associations that allows Enlightenment to thrive'.[59] It is in the light of Austen's reverse gesture – where 'woman and all her feminine associations' take centre stage – that I will consider her six rational-feminine heroines and their combined narrative achievement as agents of transformation and healing.

Austen's refusal to leave the romance behind positions her work differently in relation to the questions of history and representation raised earlier. Susan Sontag has argued that the 'arrogance of interpretation' is produced by the 'tyranny of content': 'If excessive stress on *content* provokes the arrogance of interpretation, more extended and more thorough descriptions of *form* would silence'.[60] She notes that preoccupation with content occurs at times of 'scientific enlightenment', in acknowledgement of a 'realism' at odds with 'the power and credibility of myth':

> Once the question that haunts post-mythic consciousness – that of the *seemliness* of religious symbols – had been asked, the ancient texts were, in their pristine form, no longer acceptable ... interpretation was summoned, to reconcile the ancient texts to 'modern' demands. ... It is the revenge of the intellect upon the world. To interpret is to impoverish, to deplete the world – in order to set up a shadow world

of 'meanings'. It is to turn *the* world into *this* world. ('This world'! As if there were any other.)

Equally powerful and credible is Margaret Doody's striking account of the *True Story of the Novel*, which identifies novelisation itself with a cultural ritual far older and wiser than the narrative objects of middle-class expression arising as a 'new' feature of the eighteenth-century English literary landscape. She understands novelisation as a process of narrative entroping that persistently resists the 'Puritanism' of a 'Prescriptive Realism', which 'cuts out fantasy and experimentation, and severely limits certain forms of psychic and social questioning'.[61] Austen is a key figure in the adaptation of novelisation into modern English literature:

> The Novel must have its foes because it is the Great Alternative (which is another way of saying 'under the Goddess'). It is the repository of our hope in something that can be stated as 'feminine' if the State and Establishment are thought of as 'masculine', under the sign of the Phallus.[62]

While Doody rejects the conceptual distinction between 'romance' and 'novel' central to the critical account of narrative forms under developing capitalism, I want to centre this analysis on the romance to argue for Austen's consciousness of her own creative insolence at a pivotal stage in that history. Doody finds seven core 'tropes of the novel' persisting through its various incarnations:

(1) breaking and entering;
(2) marshes, shores, and muddy margins;
(3) tomb, cave, and labyrinth;
(4) Eros;
(5) Ekphrasis: Looking at the Picture;
(6) Ekphrasis: dreams and floods;
(7) The Goddess.

The arrival of the 'Goddess' is discussed in Chapter 6, and associated with the sexual blossoming of the heroine in the romance.

This account of Austen aims to illuminate and explore a narrative mediation between empirical-realist content and a striking formal intelligence in which can be found evidence of structural symbols exploring something parallel to Sontag's question of the relationship between '*the* world' and '*this* world'. Austen's representational 'realism' is evident in the work's encoding of the most immediate subjective content, and the close attention paid to plausibility in its expression of narrative causality. This realist aesthetic makes representational demands in negation of romance epistemology, which nonetheless underpins her narrative conclusions.

Romance imagines the harmonising of individual, dyadic, and social discord; and this is barred as inherently absurd under the conditions of what Doody calls 'Prescriptive Realism', which seems to insist on witnessing to the impossibility of synthesis. The profound ambiguity presented by Austen's work can be read both ways, and this is what we tend to call her 'irony'. She presents a covert critique of 'established forms and the attractive men who embody them'.[63] At the same time she indicates the possibility of a romance reversal, which takes on the causal inevitabilities of empirical realism, and suggests these to be transcend-able under certain conditions.

Those conditions are not terribly mysterious, and are carefully specified within the terms of each novel: a transformative break in feminine consciousness, or comedic *anagnorisis*, is central to the abstract narrative 'solution' to the six key novels in Austen's mature work. Elinor and Marianne Dashwood, Catherine Morland, Elizabeth Bennet, Emma Woodhouse, Fanny Price, and Anne Elliot are shown to be the key agents in resolving the individual and social contradictions raised by the narratives in which they feature; brought by their plausible experiences to crucial moments of 'recognition and reversal' which lead to the harmonious marriages that 'solve' the narrative equations these works have brought into focus.[64]

This analysis of Austen accommodates her characteristic 'irony', her development of *free indirect discourse*, and her abiding popularity with specialist and lay audiences as aspects of a remarkable propensity in the work itself towards 'narrative mediation'. These narratives offer examples of *conceivable* mediation between otherwise incommensurable 'worlds'; of men and women; of realism and romance; of art and popular culture (which expresses itself since the twentieth century as a new film audience for her narratives); and finally of the material and ideational (or spiritual) contexts for understanding literature itself. Narrative mediation is one of the tendencies of all narratives: to imagine models for how things *might* change, since '[a]ll plots in their nature raise questions about agency and causality: what, or who, makes things happen?'[65]

What actually happens in Austen's plots is in the most general sense the achievement of a narratively realised happy-ever-after in spite of all the empirically specified odds. *How* this is shown to happen, given that

Austen's work is generally acknowledged as representing a complex and plausible empiricist realism, is studied in detail in relation to each of the six mature novels in the following chapters. In each case, but expressed differently, the 'recognition and reversal' familiar from tragedy is transmuted with a wink into a transformative experience of comedic enlightenment in the feminine consciousness that centres the narrative focus.

The comedic resolution of harmonious marriage, redolent of the spring/summer quarter of cyclical myth, becomes the object of feminine desire, and is achieved through specifically feminine modes of heroic agency or 'virtue' (modesty, passivity, restraint, negativity). These striking features of romance are reintroduced by Austen into the novel market at the turning point between Regency and Industrial England in such a way as to be read as exemplary, if feminised, plausible realism. Her otherwise troublesome turning aside from 'history' implies a mythic consciousness at work in her aesthetic choices: eternal forms presented through passing shadows.

This return to the admittedly rather unsettling terms of Northrop Frye's analysis of 'The Archetypes of Literature' offers a way to recontextualise Austen in her own field of consciousness; one which, as the daughter of a hard-working country parsonage, was fundamentally preoccupied with the very real question of salvation in a long-fallen world. Frye's identification of the quest-myth as the 'central myth of literature' understands the arch-object of the mythic quest as 'the vision of the end of social effort, the innocent world of fulfilled desires, the free human society'.[66] For this reason he asserts that 'religious conceptions of the final cause of human efforts are as relevant as any others to criticism'. The figure of feminine enlightenment central to Austen's turn from tragic conditions to comic resolutions can be understood as a shift in narrative consciousness. There seem to be two vocabularies available to capture this figure: the religious experience of 'awakening' to the 'truth', and the Marxian dialectic as 'thought to the second power'. Austen's work calls on both.

This experience of feminine enlightenment tends to be represented as a profound crisis of judgement:

> 'Till this moment, I never knew myself ...'
> 'The truth rushed on her'
> 'she found every doubt, every solicitude removed'
> 'The revolution which one instant had made in Anne, was almost beyond expression'

'Emma's mind was most busy, and, with all the wonderful velocity of thought, had been able – and yet without losing a word – to catch and comprehend the exact truth of the whole'.[67]

These moments become crucial points of conversion which produce, or reflect, a new relationship between the heroine's desire and its object. The synthesis which follows seems to radiate out from the central dyad into the social world that remains its context. Occurring as the result of extended – sometimes bordering on excessive – introspection, some-times from the shock of recognising what has already changed in accor-dance with her desire, Austen's heroines' subjective enlightenments act as instances of 'pure significance' redolent of the formal archetype: 'fragments of significance are oracular in origin, and derive from the epiphanic moment, the flash of instantaneous comprehension with no direct reference to time'.[68] The novels offer a form of communica-tion for this 'incommunicable state of consciousness', since 'communi-cation begins by constructing narrative'. Austen seems conscious that such an experience is possible: referring rather casually to 'those extraor-dinary bursts of mind which do sometimes occur' and the possibility of a 'sudden illumination' of mind.[69] The narrative result of 'illumination' tends to be an experience of 'love' associated with a 'truth' previously considered impossible in the narrative's own terms. But what's love got to do with it?

'Love' is the key figure in defining the feminine romance: the romance narrative represents the feminine subject's quest to identify and secure 'true' love. But romance is a difficult term to inherit, connoting a num-ber of now quite discrete objects, which are related but treated differently in most definitions:

- Medieval fantasy literature
- Chivalrous stories
- Improbable, magical stories (mythic)
- 'Quest' narratives
- The specific, if diverse, cultural-linguistic formation (vernacular Romance languages) in which 'romance' tales were traditionally written (French, Italian, Spanish, Portugeuese)
- That which is fictional prose narrative but not properly The Novel (especially since the eighteenth century)
- An out-moded prose-rooted 'Romantic' literature, that is aesthetically inferior to the poetics of 'Romanticism' proper
- Working class (folk culture, or popular culture rather than High Culture)

- Feminised story-telling (women's stories, women's films, not serious, degraded wish-fulfilment, feminine escapist pulp)
- Not realism – stories involving implausible outcomes and dodgy causality
- Ur-text for individual and historical processes of engendering the subject (Freud's 'Family Romance')
- Sentimentalised or slushy Love
- A dangerous myth constructed and perpetuated by Institutional Heterosexuality (evidencing feminine false consciousness and tending towards rape fantasy)
- 'Category literature' feeding constructed appetite for the above – unreflexively ideological and critically despised.

The remarkable refraction of the concept of 'romance', particularly between its ancient (heroic-mythic) senses and its contemporary (feminised-sexualised-commercialised) senses, can be overcome when both forms are recognised as centred on the narrative quest, focalised differently through a masculine or feminine imaginary. Taken together, we can understand romance as a narrative expression of a desire for salvation, the end of evil, or the achievement of freedom out of necessity in the more materialist register.

Late twentieth-century feminist criticism has pointed out that the 'fairy-tale' heterosexual love endings of Austen's novels are 'politically suspect', and fail to follow through the sharp critique of the real 'social problems' facing her heroines.[70] Janice Radway's work on the 'institutional matrix' of Twentieth-century romance attempts to understand the marked compulsion of women readers towards heterosexual-romance narratives which runs parallel to a history of feminist criticism and activism:

> While American college students were beginning to protest American involvement in Vietnam and a gradually increasing number of feminists vociferously challenged female oppression, more and more women purchased novels whose plots centred about developing love relationships between wealthy, handsome men and 'spunky' but vulnerable women.[71]

Radway takes issue with the notion that 'changes in textual features or generic popularity must be the simple and direct result of ideological shifts in the surrounding culture' which would evidence in the heightened popularity of women's romance 'a new and developing backlash against feminism'. The argument here is that the modern heterosexual romance is a mode of 'formulaic literature' defined through 'its standard reliance on a recipe that dictates the essential ingredients to be included in each new version of the form'.[72] In 2002, 93 per cent of popular romance consumers in the United States were women, and this readership accounts for approximately 48.6 per cent of the multi-million dollar paperback book market.[73] Radway equally acknowledges that 'category literature is *also* characterized by its *consistent appeal to a regular audience*'.[74] The template for women's 'pulp' romance narratives of the twentieth century ('plots centred about developing love relationships between wealthy, handsome men and "spunky" but vulnerable women') is available in Austen's famous works of 'democratic realism', produced long before the specific material conditions for 'category literature' were in place.

This tradition has since turned back on itself, now Austen tends to be credited by contemporary popular 'Romance' readers as the 'founder' of the sub-genre of 'Regencies' (or 'Historicals'). *Pride and Prejudice* came thirteenth in the 'Y2K Romance Readers' Top 100 Romances', and topped the 2005 poll for the 'Romance Writer's favourite Romance'.[75] Austen's compulsion towards a romantic 'happy ending', centred in implausibly ideal marriages that *somehow* resolve real (social) contradictions for her heroines and their communities, is an epistemic as well as an aesthetic issue. Furthermore, it is an epistemic issue expressed through feminine consciousness.

In spite of their studied avoidance of explicit historical anchorage, Austen's 'timeless' narratives emerge within, and could be expected to incorporate, a number of cultural metanarratives: the self-awareness of an indisputably masculine genealogy of 'great' writing; the consolidation of 'the Novel' as a specific literary mode central to the exponential development of the systems and subjects of capitalism; the more demotic genealogy of female-authored, feminocentric prose narratives following from Aphra Behn and Eliza Haywood; the emergence into historical consciousness of proto-feminism; the refinement of 'middle'-class social hegemony in England; the backdrop of a new national consciousness following the French revolution and wars.

Critics frustrated by the absence of what Austen *might* have been telling us, given her eye for living detail, have in recent years brought the appropriately elusive concept of 'ideology' to bear in resolving the deep paradox these works offer to contemporary critical consciousness. Terry Eagleton leads the field here: 'It is not that Jane Austen's fiction presents us merely with ideological delusion; on the contrary, it also offers us a version of contemporary history which is considerably more revealing than much historiography.' This is because her novels are 'the product of certain ideological codes which, in permitting us access to certain values, forces and relations, yield us a sort of historical knowledge. This is not 'knowledge in the strict scientific sense' but neither is it 'sheer illusion'. Ultimately, the value of Austen's work 'thrives quite as much on its ignorance as on its insight':

> it is because there is so much the novels cannot possibly know that they know what they do, and in the *form* that they do. It is true that Austen, because she does not *know*, only 'knows'; but what she 'knows' is not thereby nothing at all.[76]

So Austen is 'valuable', then, precisely because she does not *know* the raw and bloody abstract material forces combining to determine the lace-work of her narratives. What she *does* 'know', and therefore *can* faithfully record, are the intricate minutiae of private, domestic, intimate patterns of gesture and voice between her characters, through which the slightest vibrations in the otherwise static being of pre-social women are crystallised. More to the point, these narratives are *particularly* 'valuable' *now* (more valuable than contemporaneous narratives) precisely because this is *all* they 'know'. Austen's value as a novelist is in inverse relation to her knowledge and understanding of the 'real' (material) conditions determining her life and her writing. Since she was at least economically related (via her cousin, 'Eliza' Hancock) to Warren Hastings, Governor of the East India Company and – eventually – of Bengal, Austen's informal stream of 'knowledge' might in fact have been unusually explicit and detailed.[77]

Isobel Grundy remarks on a shift in approaches to interpreting Austen's work: 'We no longer find it easy to believe Austen's claim to be the "most unlearned, & uninformed Female who ever dared to be an Authoress".'[78] The innocent Austen, beloved of gentlemen scholars and educated housewives, and invoked by Austen herself earlier, has more recently given way to a knowing Austen, one who smirks in anticipation of a suitably duplicitous audience. Following Harding's Leavisite apprehension of a subversive Austen manifesting 'regulated hatred' for the society she also represents as 'literary classic of her time', Austen's work – and to some degree also her character – have been subject to the minute gaze of the radical critic, seeking for evidence of cultural subversion of dominant social modes: 'her books are, as she meant them to be, read and enjoyed by precisely the sort of people whom she disliked; she is a literary classic of the society which attitudes like hers, held widely enough, would undermine'.[79] This work has never been completely assimilated to the radical critical agenda, and is still received as moral realism at the same time that it functions as 'stealth' radical feminism. Austen has effectively undermined the very social categories she has also been understood rather problematically to champion: marriage, feminine virtue, constancy, propriety, humility, domesticity, modesty, gentility, proper hierarchy. She features happily on overtly Christian reading lists for 'the Novel', while one of her novels is clearly recognised as bearing 'incestutous permutations' in its marriage resolution.[80]

Mary Wollstonecraft becomes under this analysis *less* valuable as a historical writer, since her writing grasps with desperation the sheer trauma of women's being under developing capitalism, and offers an overt political analysis of the conditions determining her life and her writing. Austen's narratives choose their focus with more discretion, and settle on the middle-distance, temporally arranged to engage that short but turbulent interval between a young woman's identification as 'daughter-of-the-father' and as 'wife-of-the-husband'. This space is foreclosed in Wollstonecraft's 'hysterical' narrative work as the 'chimera' of 'romance' which threatens to distract the imprisoned feminine subject from her plot of escape.[81] And it is (perhaps coincidentally) in just this private and a-social state which charts the precise modulations of the troubled waters of female courtship, that women's lives are most transparently over-determined by structural forces. We *still* value Austen because: (a) she offers data for understanding something concrete of the abstract historical fusion between patriarchy and capitalism; and (b) she does it so well.

McKeon understands 'the Romance' primarily as the aesthetic mode of the defeated party in the 'early modern epistemological revolution' manifested in and through the eighteenth-century triumph of 'the Novel'.[82] It is a fair point, but if romance is only a mode of literature, expressive of a quite literally outmoded past, why do more people (and especially women) *voluntarily* read Austen than Scott, Fielding, Defoe, Richardson or Burney under very late conditions of capitalism? Austen's 'politically disappointing' *Pride and Prejudice* was the most popular piece of literature by a female writer according to the 6000 votes polled in the 2003 Orange annual prize, and came second in the BBC poll for the 'Nation's Favourite Read' without Peter Jackson's help.[83] We still seem to read Austen for pleasure, while we continue to read her peers and predecessors because they are on the syllabus.

The answer to the Austen puzzle might lie in the odd fact that romance is also a specific kind of narrative of the desiring subject and its objects. Narrative is 'the most elaborate kind of attempt, on the part of the speaking subject, after syntactic competence, to situate his or her self among his or her desires'.[84] Women's literary tradition really takes off with the emergence of female-authored narrative prose 'amatory romances' (especially in the hands of Aphra Behn and Eliza Haywood) that prefigure the novel as we come to recognise it.[85] I have argued elsewhere that these early incarnations of women's narrative in English tend to iterate a number of core figures for feminine subjectivity: including maternal severance and the Athenic foreclosure of femininity; and sexual difference as represented by opposing discourses of 'Love'.[86] Romance offers a literary mode peculiarly suited to represent feminine wish-fulfilment in narrative.

Romance is argued by Northrop Frye as well as by Fredric Jameson to carry traces of an original genre that pre-figures and contains all later modes of narrative.[87] Clara Reeve in 1784 had already made this argument: that the 'progress' of romance included its incorporation of the modern novel, which had 'sprung up out of its ruins'.[88] The critical question posed by the persistence of romance is whether the marked shift, documented by the history of literary narrative, from origins in the 'romance' narrative mode towards novelistic 'realism' as the 'successful' aesthetic of verisimilitude, is a marker of some kind of real progress. Since all 'modes of production' coexist at any one time in muted and dominant forms, this account goes some way to explain the polyvocal, heterogeneous nature of 'the Novel', as well as Austen's uncanny capacity for mediating between the 'democratic realism' descriptive of emergent capitalism and the 'romance' paradigm redolent of mythic (now in the sense of pre-social) consciousness.

Romance is now widely received as the rump of an aristocratic fantasy, where idealised heterosexual love still offers the illusion of a 'happy-ever-after' in spite of a deluge of empirical evidence to the contrary; and in this sense is denigrated as performative of a powerful sexual ideology central to continuing economic domination. Doody notes that this argument makes the dream of ideal heterosexual love 'an aspect of a kind of conspiracy against women', in which 'the novel that developed to promote it encouraged women in isolation and fantasy'.[89] Romance is aesthetically, politically, and historically redundant, but remains resolutely 'popular'. Its immense popularity seems to suggest an essential false consciousness at work; only the uneducated masses, women, and children could still possibly cling to a belief in the possibility of a happy ending.

That romance would have been feminised as a side effect of a developing capitalism which centred itself through representational novelistic realism, is a productive way to approach this structural associ- ation between narratives of specifically feminine desire and epistemic failure. Recognising that women and men have a distinctive relation- ship to labour under the economic mode of capitalism leads us to the questions associated with feminist epistemology.[90] Jane Flax has defined the 'task of feminist epistemology': 'to uncover how patriarchy has permeated both our concept of knowledge and the concrete content of bodies of knowledge'. This is important work because '[w]ithout adequate knowledge of the world and our history within it (and this includes knowing how to know), we cannot develop a more adequate social practice.'

The questions central to feminist epistemology are tested in Austen's narrative studies of feminine desire and its imagined fulfilment:

> Separation-individuation cannot be completed and true reciprocity emerge if the 'other' must be dominated and/or repressed rather than incorporated into the self while simultaneously acknowledging dif- ference. An unhealthy self projects its own dilemmas on the world and posits them as the 'human condition'.[91]

Woloch shows how Austen's narrative work brings into relief the 'alien- ating nature of the structure she is depicting', a structure which 'makes the notion of equality invisible, persisting only as the receding assump- tion of an ineluctably human quality'.[92] The question of sexual equality is played out most famously in Elizabeth Bennet's relationship with Mr Darcy, but reiterated through the many layers of 'the larger conflict between singularity and multiplicity that is governing the structure of this text as a whole'.[93] The Elizabeth-Darcy romance plot displaces the more 'realist' marriages represented in the first half of *Pride and Prejudice*: 'romance conventions ... displace complexities raised by the introduc- tion of realistic social and psychological details'.[94] The romance plot is widely received as a purely symbolic resolution of material problems, and Austen's insistence on idealised marriage as narrative resolution is read as an illusory foreclosure of real questions: 'The closure of *Pride and Prejudice* is thus aesthetically successful, but whether it ensures a comparable ideological resolution is doubtful.'[95]

We still seem to want our Mr Darcy, however, in spite of having plentiful critical tools with which to demystify this illusory object of an outmoded romantic desire. Mr Darcy was voted by women to be the most 'desirable' fictional figure in a BBC poll in 2003. This 'desire' has somehow survived decades of the fundamental deconstruction of heterosexuality as a key condition for the institutionalisation of normative feminine subjectivity under capitalism, and remains a sticking-point in our aesthetic and cultural understanding of Austen. The abiding desire for a 'Mr Darcy' seems to evidence both Austen's own neo-conservative dream of being *somehow* rescued from the 'real' contradictions structuring women's lives under capitalism, and the persistence of this day-dream in the reading and viewing tastes of her contemporary mass audience.

If the heterosexual-romance narrative is only an illusory consolation for real social contradictions, the feminine desire represented in Austen's romantic novels is only the appendix of a redundant 'wish-fulfilment', once feminine will has been eradicated from the historical narrative. Austen's work at one level embodies pure escapism in the most dangerously subjective sense, bordering on the pornographic in its invitation to repeat consumption. Yet something more hopeful occurs when, led by Austen, we begin to weave the diverging strands of 'romance' as feminine wish-fulfilment and as out-moded literary aesthetic together.

Romance at its most abstract is claimed by theorists of the novel as the source text for all narrative forms; the paradigmatic expression of a now unconscious ideal mode of relations, apprehended in myth, and persisting through the novel's various particularities of 'social realism' like a Magic Eye photo-image. The 'Romance paradigm', for Jameson, offers a 'salvational or redemptive perspective of some secure future'.[96] Romance approaches Utopia, but with a particular relation to the conditional terms in which it is set, and the perspective (or 'stand-point') from which it is viewed. In the context of 'the gradual reification of realism in late capitalism', romance offers the possibility of 'narrative heterogeneity and of freedom from that reality principle to which a now oppressive realistic representation is the hostage'.[97]

Austen's realist-romances offer a peek round the edge of an otherwise largely inescapable, all-determining 'mode', that seems to have passed itself off as historical and social inevitability. The *feminine* romance is a particular expression of a more general representational freedom, a seeing otherwise: 'Romance now again seems to offer the possibility of sensing other historical rhythms, and of demonic or Utopian transformations of a real now unshakably set in place.' Or, as Jane Spencer puts it: 'It depends who decides what reality is.'[98]

I argue through the following chapters that Austen's very particular realist-romances evidence a narrative mediation between an abstract apprehension of feminine desire and the already outmoded, culturally debased, terms of romance as mode. Since Jameson would claim that these represent 'syllables and broken fragments of some single immense story' which has as its 'fundamental theme' a 'collective struggle to wrest a realm of Freedom from a realm of Necessity', the argument seems worth the risks I am conscious are associated with making it.[99]

The romance, as the core narrative form for feminine wish-fulfilment, corresponds to a muted and displaced epistemology, *no longer – if ever – aligned with the credible* (and by making this claim I have already nudged my own argument onto the side of the incredible.) If this claim is shown to hold, what is to be made of the feminist critique of 'heteronormativity' as a specific ideological form of feminine false consciousness? We can begin to answer this question when we consider that it might result from swallowing whole what Frye calls the 'representational fallacy' of 'democratic realism'.[100] Austen's romances offer distinctly credible evidence of feminine knowledge in narrative. That claim to significant knowledge *does* seem incredible when considered against the objective history of women's apparent exclusion from institutions and forms of higher knowledge. Anne Elliot reminds us: 'Men have had every advantage of us in telling their own story. Education has been theirs in so much higher a degree; the pen has been in their hands.'[101]

We identify with this incredulity if we are tempted to write off Austen's dodgy endings as an aesthetic cop-out, or ironic deflation of the highly credible realism otherwise claimed by the works:

> Unless we can somehow incorporate something like an ironic vision of the ending – even while pretending not to, even when enjoying the fairy tale to the full – we are indeed confirming its capacity to implant a *harmful* vision of the sexes.[102]

It is this potentially 'harmful' romance plot, the possibility of a happy ending represented through the providential marriage, and the achievement of freedom out of necessity this implies, that continues to engage the desire of innumerable readers and viewers of Austen's narratives. This compelling cultural evidence arises at the end of a long century or two of 'scientific enlightenment' and implies that the knowledge of which it quietly speaks is precisely that which has been disavowed by an increasingly 'instrumental' rationality: feminine, native, irrational, fantastic, false consciousness, pre-social, and incredible (mythic). Romance persists as a now largely feminised 'abstract category' in dialectical relation to the more sensible novel of plausible realism, but can be seen to have contained – at some time, in some of its contexts – all of these foreclosed knowledges and their modes of expression.

> Western Enlightenment may be grasped as part of a properly bourgeois cultural revolution, in which the values and the discourses, the habits and the daily space, of the *ancient regime* were systematically dismantled so that in their place could be set the new conceptualities, habits and life forms, and value systems of a capitalist market society. This process clearly involved a vaster historical rhythm than such punctual historical events as the French Revolution or the Industrial Revolution.[103]

The lingering question posed by the persistence of Austen's romance concerns the possibility of salvation in an empirically fallen world, expressed through the final triumph of (usually pastoral) comedy over (usually social) tragedy. Perhaps Jane Austen is not such a serendipitous cultural expression of the long process of 'eighteenth-century' rationalisation after all. The tragic foreclosure of mythic consciousness that is the hallmark of the instrumentalising tendencies of the mode of capitalism might indeed be expected to have produced a comedic counter-point in the remarkable literary work of an otherwise rather ordinary woman.

1
Northanger Abbey: 'hastening together to perfect felicity'

We tend to underestimate the extent to which the cultural tradition is not only a selection but also an interpretation. We see most past work through our own experience, without even making the effort to see it in something like its original terms. What analysis can do is not so much to reverse this, returning a work to its period, as to make the interpretation conscious, by showing historical alternatives; to relate the interpretation to the particular contemporary values on which it rests; and, by exploring the real patterns of the work, confront us with the real nature of the choices we are making.

Raymond Williams, *The Long Revolution*[104]

How to analyse the part as part when the whole is not only no longer visible but even inconceivable?

Fredric Jameson, *Marxism and Form*[105]

To say that a theory is mythic is hardly to diminish its authority for interpreting culture.

Margaret Homans, *Bearing the Word: Language and Female Experience in Nineteenth-century Women Writing*[106]

Laura Mooneyham White makes a strong claim that the 'persistence' of the marriage plot, particularly 'in popular culture' and in the context of 'our culture's well-founded suspicions of marriage', is 'very odd indeed'. She nudges us to consider the marriage that resolves Austen's novels less as 'particular historical and social practice' and more as an imaginary encounter with one of the 'elementals of human experience'.[107] White notes, however, that there is an unresolved problem with thinking of marriage as central to narrative completion: 'How could one suggest that the movement to heterosexual pairing is *the* central narrative experience when heterosexual pairing is so clearly not a part of so many people's lives?'[108] This is only the case when we forget the necessary conditions of our own birth. Heterosexual pairing remains fundamental to human existence, however difficult it has become to reconcile the social conventions of marriage. But since it is difficult to say anything directly about the 'elementals' of human experience without universalising one's own experience, it is probably best to approach them indirectly, and Austen's *Northanger Abbey* is a good place to start.

Following White's suggestion, this discussion takes up Northrop Frye's attempt to apprehend something equally 'elemental' in romance narrative, to reflect on the way in which Austen's narratives make heterosexual union a fundamental desire for the readers of her work. Fredric Jameson's revision of Frye's archetypes in terms of signifying modes involves us in an argument concerning narrative agency and structure, which helps to understand the feminine agency at work in Austen's narratives. Through Jameson's frame of reference it is possible to read this work in particular as a dialectical expression of its moment. Woloch has demonstrated that we can read Austen's work not so much as an example of 'the moment when the text turns away from material reality or inscribes its own evasions', but rather as a register on the literary plane of 'the derealization, the dehumanization inherent to Austen's world, and inherent to the economic modalities that structure this world.'[109] We can take the point further if we consider Austen's heroines and their encounters with their desired objects as a literary expression of an analogous relationship between feminine subjectivity and history. To make this argument properly, it is necessary to take quite a lengthy detour through archetypal, structuralist and Marxian theory.

Frye's account of romance begins from a primary distinction between 'fragments of significance' abiding in the 'verbal structure' of a literary work and tending towards the archetype, and 'narrative' which acts as the 'rhythm of literature' and tends towards the chronological or cyclical. This account of a fundamental duality inherent in the literary work implies two distinct axes of understanding for our experience of literature in general, and Austen in particular. These axes (abstract 'timeless' significance and the patterns of narrative temporality) are argued by Frye to intersect in a specific literary text, and are commonly apprehended at the level of form and content; when 'form' denotes the (abstract) 'shape' of the work, and 'content' denotes the (historical) material that is shaped. In literature, 'the art is the form, and the nature which the art imitates is the content, so in literature art imitates nature by containing it internally.'[110]

Gregory L. Lucente has more recently argued that literary 'form' can be understood as the articulation of 'mythic components' which 'affect the plots of even the most realist narratives'; a codification of 'transcendent fullness' which 'locates its significance not in the world of time and matter, but in a realm beyond temporal and spatial limitation.'[111] These 'repeating elements of narrative ... at their core involve unified and idealized figures' which 'establish and depend upon a relationship of unquestioning belief', in contrast to 'those elements that claim a clear and definite position in space and time (and so in culture), that involve figures whose relation to experience is not idealized and that invite an attitude of analysis or even scepticism rather than immediate faith', pertaining to 'realism'.[112] Form, symptomatic of 'the logical possibilities preceding narrative', is more widely recognised as that which produces 'an aura of unified necessity rather than randomness or contingency'.[113]

Form tends towards 'genre', and the 'happy ending' inherent in romantic comedy is one aspect of its essential 'form', in the sense of 'intrinsic laws'.[114]

> When we speak of the form of a literary work we refer to its shape and structure and to the manner in which it is made ... – as opposed to its substance or what it is about. Form and substance are inseparable, but they may be analysed and assessed separately.[115]

Therefore we can talk about literary form as an aspect of the work that refers to a world of forms: 'work *in* a given form, or *against* a given form, in a context in which the various genres are felt to coexist at fixed distances from each other in relatively systematic complexes which can themselves form an object of study in their historical coexistence or succession'.[116] Form is taken to point towards something beyond content describable in terms of a 'mythic consciousness', or a 'transcendent realm', or even the 'final determinant', recoding 'on an idealized level what realist representation codes on the material one'.[117]

Frye's romance 'archetypes' function in this way; accounting for the 'technical devices of storytelling' as 'the result of working within a certain kind of mythological framework'.[118] He apprehends romance as the 'normal containing form' of *all* literary narratives, and identifies 'devices' recurring in the multitude of specific narrative texts which lead to a recognition of 'the novel' as 'a realistic displacement of romance', with 'few features peculiar to itself'. Romance is 'the structural core of all fiction', which ultimately externalises 'man's vision of his own life as a quest'. The 'central element' of romance manifests as 'a love story', with 'exciting adventures' offering a kind of 'foreplay' for the figure of 'sexual union' as closure and resolution.[119]

Doody reaches a parallel conclusion through her monumental study of examples of literary narrative predating the putative 'rise' of 'the Novel' in the eighteenth century while Frye intuits the structural laws governing its recurrence. Both studies imply a continuum of 'mythic' narrative tropes throughout literary history:

> If you contemplate the Novel for a long time, and still more certainly if you undertake the writing of novels, you will eventually realize that it is impossible not to write History (no matter how fantastic your story may be). It is equally impossible not to write Myth (no matter how grimly realistic your prosaic narrative). The Novel represents the union between history and myth.[120]

Austen's narratives offer a particular union between history and myth, where we might indeed expect to find 'an Augustinian strategy of mediating an essential truth by contingent means'.[121] By wedding 'realism to romance', we can read Austen as offering a particular narrative 'form capable of measuring what *is* against what *should be*'.[122]

Lucente has usefully described Jung's archetypes as 'a psychoanalytic version of Hegelian dialectics, with the archetypes providing the charged transition between creation and aesthetic perception' or between 'formal art and social life'.[123] Form is for Frye 'something more like that shaping spirit, the power of ordering which seems so mysterious'; and 'content' becomes 'the sense of otherness, the resistance of the material, the feeling that there is something to be overcome, or at least struggled with'. An archetype is a simple formulaic unit; and realist narrative has adapted 'formulaic units' to the resistance of 'a world which is separate', through 'displacement'. Austen's *Northanger Abbey* (1818) offers a clear expression of such a 'tension' between 'the shape of her stories' and 'the outlines of the story into which they are obliged to fit'. This tension is particularly visible in the 'endings', which achieve through 'adjustments' the conditions for idealised romance consummation; 'although the inherent unlikelihood of these unions has been the main theme of the story'.[124] Jameson might ask us to consider this kind of literary work 'less as an example than as a kind of immanent critique of romance in its restructuration of the form'.[125]

While Frye highlights 'the displacement of romance from one mimetic level or "style" (high, low, mixed) to another', Jameson argues that 'the problem raised by the persistence of romance' is that of 'substitutions, adaptations, and appropriations'. This approach allows us to look for 'what, under wholly altered historical circumstances, can have been found to replace the raw materials of magic and Otherness which medieval romance found ready to hand in its socioeconomic environment'.[126] Under 'the increasingly secularised and rationalized world that emerges from the collapse of feudalism', 'substitute codes and raw materials' seem to have been 'pressed into service to replace the older magical categories of Otherness which have now become so many dead languages'.

Frye's 'displacement' is further understood by Jameson as 'a conflict between the older deep-structural form' of romance, and 'the contemporary materials and generic systems in which it seeks to inscribe and reassert itself'.[127] Austen's realist adaptations of romance create 'a verisimilitude capable of observing probability' and 'omitting miracles or coincidences that obscure the workings of natural law'. Since *aventura* denote unexpected or accidental experiences, 'events that come to one from without', the relative powerlessness of her heroines becomes a condition of their quest.[128]

Frye characterises the core 'units' of romance narrative under the following broad classifications:

- Love – Quest (containing variations of 'adventure', 'desire', etc.)
- Threat of Incest overcome
- Illusion (as absence of identity) in opposition to Reality (as regaining of identity)
- Descent into a nightmare world (as separation, alienation) in opposition to Ascent to idyllic world (as marriage, union)
- Violence overcome by Cunning
- Female Victim (of rape, death) transformed into Female Heroine (agent of healing)

The romance narrative begins with 'a sharp descent in social status, from riches to poverty, from privilege to a struggle to survive and even slavery' (epitomised by Fanny Price and Anne Elliot as well as in milder forms by the Dashwood sisters and Catherine Morland). Separation occurs, usually marked by the breaking up of initial family or community (epitomised in different ways especially by Emma Woodhouse, Elinor and Marianne Dashwood, and Catherine Morland). At the 'structural core' is 'the individual loss or confusion or break in the continuity of identity', analogous to 'falling asleep and entering a dream world' (epitomised by Emma Woodhouse and Elizabeth Bennet as well as the Dashwood sisters on entering Devon and Catherine on entering the Abbey).[129]

'Loss of identity' is further identified as the 'condition for narrative', so that the regaining of identity coincides with narrative conclusion; since 'full' identity indicates, among other things, 'a state of existence in which there is nothing to write about'.[130] White has already indicated that the marriage unions which uniformly mark the happy ending of Austen's major narratives also mark the psychic condition of 'full identity': 'the movement to a wedding in fiction represents the achievement of psychic identity'. This 'psychodrama's logic persists even when (as always) particular cultural and historical expressions of the relationships between men and women fall into question'.[131]

Austen's work performs a mediation of 'romance' functions (expressed at the level of form in particular), and realist 'raw materials' (expressed at the level of represented content). As a result we do find, as Frye notes, 'resistance' to 'social conditions governing the place of women in her time', but not at the level of social reference as much as through the persistence of the romance form in spite of careful adherence to mimetic accuracy and causal plausibility: 'it is the romantic convention she is using that expresses the resistance'.[132] Austen's most politically charged move was perhaps her insistence on representing this final vision of romance, and its feminisation, in spite of the apparent resistance of the 'raw materials' available to empirical realism: 'But so it was.'[133] *Her* resistance is displayed precisely in the works' denial of the developing contextual antinomy between realism and romance.

Jameson's materialist revision of Frye's literary typology identifies three distinct 'horizons' of critical apprehension:

1. The 'narrowly political or historical': where 'the "text," the object of study, is still more or less construed as coinciding with the individual literary work or utterance ... grasped as a *symbolic act*'.
2. Where the 'semantic horizon in which we grasp a cultural object has widened to include the social order' and 'the very object of our analysis has itself been thereby dialectically transformed' so that 'it is no longer construed as an individual "text" or work in the narrow sense, but has been reconstituted in the form of the great collective and class discourses of which a text is little more than an individual *parole* or utterance'.

3. The 'ultimate horizon of human history as a whole': where 'the individual text and its ideologemes ... must be read in terms of what I will call the *ideology of form*'.[134]

Under the first horizon 'history is reduced to a series of punctual events and crises in time, to the diachronic agitation of the year-to-year, the chroniclelike annals of the rise and fall of political regimes and social fashions, and the passionate immediacy of struggles between historical individuals'.[135] Literary objects are here received as 'resolutions of determinate contradictions', and taken to 'reflect' their 'social background'.[136] The 'political allegory' of 'a sometimes repressed ur-narrative or master fantasy about the interaction of collective subjects' borders on the 'second horizon', in which 'what we formerly regarded as individual texts are grasped as "utterances" in an essentially collective or class discourse'.[137] This horizon is demonstrated by the emphasis of Bakhtin on the 'dialogic', as 'the dialogue of class struggle is one in which two opposing discourses fight it out within the general unity of a shared code'. The dialogic, for Jameson, is the discourse of 'the irreconcilable demands and positions of antagonistic classes'. The 'ideologeme' is a minimal unit in 'class *langue*', which can be read as both 'a conceptual description and a narrative manifestation'.

The apprehension of the 'new object' of 'code, sign system, or system of the production of signs and codes' which emerges as 'an index of study' for the second horizon, transcends the 'narrowly political' and 'the social' as contexts for the literary work, and indicates 'the historical in the larger sense of this word'. Under the third horizon, we apprehend the *ideology of form* as 'symbolic messages transmitted to us by the coexistence of various sign systems which are themselves traces or anticipations of modes of production'.[138]

Now, a 'mode of production' describes a 'stage' in 'human society'. These stages are named as follows:

- 'primitive communism' associated with 'the horde';
- 'hierarchical kinship societies' associated with the 'neolithic';
- 'Asiatic' associated with 'Oriental despotism';
- 'the *polis*' associated with 'oligarchical slaveholding society';
- 'feudalism';
- 'capitalism';
- 'communism'.

Each 'mode' is understood to be governed by 'a cultural dominant or form of ideological coding specific to each mode of production,' and 'modes' seem to be in some sense preceded by and tending towards 'fully developed forms of collective or communal association'. The 'mode of production' is, in 'properly Marxian' terms, 'all-embracing and all-structuring'; apprehended otherwise as ' "total system" in which the various elements or levels of social life are programmed in some increasingly constricting way'. These 'horizons' of possible interpretation together mark a shift from the diachronic towards the synchronic apprehension of the 'text' in 'history'.[139] It is within the third scene of interpretation that I want to present Austen's narrative works for the duration of this discussion. Modes, as I understand the term, refer to structuring possibilities determining the scope of relationship between two individuals, and between self and world.

It is important for this analysis to understand that this increasingly 'synchronic' apprehension of 'mode of production' as 'total structure' brings into view the classic Marxist problem of structure and agency. In terms of synchronic analysis, 'change and development' are relegated to the merely 'diachronic'; 'the contingent or the rigorously nonmeaningful'.[140] The sheer 'level of abstraction of the concept of mode of production' allows us to consider that,

> every social formation or historically existing society has in fact consisted in the overlay and structural coexistence of *several* modes of production all at once, including vestiges and survivals of older modes of production ... as well as anticipatory tendencies which are potentially inconsistent with the existing system but have not yet generated an autonomous space of their own.

The literary work now comes into focus as an object 'crisscrossed and intersected by a variety of impulses from contradictory modes', and draws attention to itself as emblematic of 'that moment in which the coexistence of various modes of production becomes visibly antagonistic.' Jameson highlights the 'properly Marxian' tension between a 'synchronic' apprehension of a 'given system', and the 'diachronic' narrative of history as 'the passage from one system to another'. He aligns the synchronic with the diachronic by the following proposal:

> overtly 'transitional' moments of cultural revolution are themselves but the passage to the surface of a permanent process in human societies, of a permanent struggle between the various existing modes of production.

This offers a beautiful solution, and one which finds strong resonance in Austen's dovetailing of realism and romance in narratives of feminine wish-fulfilment. It leads us to the suggestion that a 'mode' of literature, such as the realist novel which makes its 'passage to the surface' through the eighteenth century, can also be considered as 'a synchronic unity of structurally contradictory or heterogeneous elements, generic patterns and discourses' in a way which implies 'the coexistence or tension between several generic modes or strands'.[141] Austen negotiates those 'modes' in a distinctive way. In doing so successfully, she also holds up a model of the possibilities available to feminine agency in the historical narrative.

Frye's central distinction between 'significance' and 'rhythm' is parallel to Jameson's synchronic–diachronic model. Here significance is a property of the total (synchronic) 'structure', which we 'grasp' as meaning; rhythm is the property of the mediated (diachronic) temporal condition for communication of that meaning. While 'pure narrative would be unconscious', 'pure significance would be an incommunicable state of consciousness'.[142] A further parallel can be identified in the polarity between metaphoric and metonymic modes of signification, which again lines up with the core unconscious processes identified as 'condensation' and 'displacement' respectively.[143] This primary distinction is famously articulated by Jakobson as the 'paradigmatic' and 'syntagmatic' sequences. The literary modes we identify as realism and romance align with these axes of signification.

Romance is understood to be governed by the 'metaphoric' or 'paradigmatic', while realism is understood to be governed by the 'metonymic' or 'syntagmatic'. Austen's work, most generally received as genteel realism, tends to be received metonymically. Interestingly, Miles notes that this debate is internalised in *Northanger Abbey*:

> If there is, after all, a kind of Gothic reality in what is happening to Catherine, in being abducted to an abbey by a patriarchal tyrant intent on cementing a marriage of alliance, it is something she cannot see, because she has read too many Gothic romances: she insists on reading metaphorically, rather than metonymically.[144]

Had she read her own experiences as a metonymic sequence, she would have seen her way through the plot more effectively. But her 'metaphoric' assessments are nonetheless resonant with what turns out to be the truth. While Henry's father did not literally murder his wife, we are led to wonder at her treatment during life: 'He loved her, I am persuaded, as well as it was possible for him to – We have not all, you know, the same tenderness of disposition – and I will not pretend to say that while she lived, she might not often have had much to bear.'[145]

Catherine's specific quest, from this perspective, concerns her aesthetic as much as her ethical judgement, as myth and realism tend to adopt 'a favored trope'. But since '[m]ythic and realistic discourse' also coincide diachronically with crudely recognisable periods of 'cultural history', Austen's internalisation of the struggle between metaphor and metonymy at the level of the subject's perception of her world and its characters turns out to be innately historical.[146] Lucente, Frye, McKeon and Jameson broadly locate the cultural highpoint of 'myth' and its expression as narrative 'romance' in pre-capitalist stages of history: 'the early stages of social communion'. English realism makes its 'passage to the surface' in the eighteenth century, and becomes dominant in the nineteenth century; parallel to the consolidation of the industrial-capitalist mode in the West.

Austen's *Northanger Abbey* is taken here as a narrative example seeded in a late moment of transition between old and new forms of social organization: 'mythic discourse and realistic interpretation are considered as distinct but not fully contradictory operations carried out at two historical moments of perception'.[147] Catherine's understanding of the events which meet her in Bath and at Northanger Abbey, and – more precisely – the narratively staged oscillation between her 'romantic' misperceptions and Henry's realist demystifications, are finally rooted in a fundamental disjunction between metaphoric and metonymic ways of knowing. This is an internalised expression of a tension between empirical-metonymic versus analogic-metaphoric epistemologies at play in the narrative's context.

For Roland Barthes, any given narrative acts as a 'message' generated from, and meaningful within, a perceivable 'code' or 'structure' operating according to the terms of signification understood to govern language generally.[148] Narrative is also 'the principle instrumentality by which society fashions the narcissistic, infantile consciousness into a "subjectivity" capable of bearing the "responsibilities" of an "object" of the law in all its forms'.[149] Austen's narrative work emerges from one of Jameson's ' "transitional" moments of cultural revolution' when 'a permanent struggle between the various existing modes of production' crystallises. It can be read, then, for a micro-struggle between recognisable literary modes of 'romance' and 'realism' analogous to a macro-struggle between metaphoric and metonymic 'modes'.

From 1793–1815 thousands of Enclosure Acts were passed through the British Parliament.[150] The rapid enclosure of communally farmed land, and of common land by larger land-owners, could be easily justified under the rationalist terms of 'capitalist enterprise' which valued economic efficiency above 'waste': 'The capitalist farm and the common fields thereby became parables of industry and idleness respectively.'[151] Brookes's Gazetteer recorded in 1815 that Austen's home county of Hampshire was 'excellent land', and 'one of the most fertile and populous counties in England', where 'are fed plenty of sheep', although 'the stock is considerably decreased, owing to enclosures'.[152] Roy Porter has already noted what was at stake in the avalanche of land enclosure characteristic of the later eighteenth century. The traditional 'common land and grazing rights' overtaken by the advancing rationalization of the land was rooted in an 'ancient piety that, everyone being the son of Adam, all were entitled to some access to God's soil'.[153] Enclosure of common land is only one concrete example of the 'transition' between romance and realist epistemologies, but it is one that helps to frame our heroine's subjective crisis as all the more expressive of its moment. It also implies an immanent dialectical awareness at work in Austen's art.

Catherine, in spite of having nothing to recommend her in her infancy as one 'born to be a heroine', starts at fifteen to be 'in training for a heroine' and has by the age of seventeen 'read all such works as heroines must read to supply their memories with those quotations which are so serviceable and so soothing in the vicissitudes of their eventful lives'.[154] As one of Austen's early-mature works, *Northanger Abbey* reveals by negation the dimensions of the heroine as measured by romance literature:

> She had reached the age of seventeen, without having seen one amiable youth who could call forth her sensibility; without having inspired one real passion, and without having excited even any admiration but what was very moderate and very transient. This was very strange indeed! But strange things may be generally accounted for if their cause be fairly searched out. There was not one lord in the neighbourhood; no – not even a baronet. There was not one family among their acquaintance who had reared and supported a boy accidentally found at their door – not one young man whose origin was unknown. Her father had no ward, and the squire of the parish no children.[155]

Catherine's destined romance quest is quickly deflated to the more realist dimensions of a 'six weeks' residence in Bath', but revived again in her sudden 'abduction' to a *real* Abbey, by a wilful paternal figure who means to marry her to his son. This new sequence of potential romance material is again deflated when Catherine is brought to realise that the empirical reality of the Abbey is more prosaic than her Gothic romance of a mother murdered: 'What have you been judging from?' Following Henry's realist injunction to Catherine to 'remember the country and the age in which we live ... that we are English, that we are Christians', her 'visions of romance are over' and she is described as now 'completely awakened'. English Christians do not murder their wives. Her 'self-created delusion' is ascribed to 'the influence of that sort of reading which she had there indulged'.[156] There it may have rested, but the heroine suffers a further awakening: to the genuinely devious Miss Thorpe's manifold seductions, and to the General's brutal decision to eject her suddenly from the hospitality of the Abbey to the very real dangers of 'a journey of seventy miles to be taken post by you, at your age, alone, unattended'![157]

Catherine's projections of romance are demystified, then, while the empirical judgements which displace the former are subject to further revision, and this romance-realism dialectic only closes once we accept a 'new circumstance in romance' which seems to align the two poles: Catherine's pre-emptive desire for Henry, which we might read in terms of feminine wish-fulfilment. It is Catherine's desire that the narrator foregrounds as the key causal agent in the successful resolution: 'I must confess that his affection originated in nothing better than gratitude; or, in other words, that a persuasion of her partiality for him had been the only cause of giving her a serious thought.'[158] Moreover, the General's 'cruelty' and 'unjust interference' is claimed finally as 'far from being really injurious to their felicity' and 'perhaps rather conducive to it, by improving their knowledge of each other, and adding strength to their attachment.' The work itself may, in the words of the narrator, either recommend 'parental tyranny' or reward 'filial disobedience'.[159]

Since everything turns out perfect ('Henry and Catherine were married, the bells rang, and everybody smiled' within 'a twelvemonth from the first day of their meeting'), all the various (and quite plausible) obstacles and incidents experienced on the way are revealed to have been nothing more than interludes, exercising the reader's desire for the inevitable.[160] The work's disavowed romance form presupposes the happy ending that its self-conscious delays, and realist interjections, makes more than usually visible. This takes place in a narrative style very conscious of its own oscillation, and final collapse, between formulas of 'romance' and realist representation: 'It is a new circumstance in romance,

I acknowledge, and dreadfully derogatory of an heroine's dignity; but if it be as new in common life, the credit of a wild imagination will at least be all my own.'[161]

Catherine is, in spite of all available evidence to the contrary, '*born* to be a heroine'. The realist undermining of the code of mythic inevitability initiated by her simply *being* a heroine from the first page is itself finally undermined by the disclosure that the happy ending has nevertheless been quite safe all along: 'The anxiety, which in this state of their attachment must be the portion of Henry and Catherine, and of all who loved either, as to its final event, can hardly extend, I fear, to the bosom of my reader, who will see in the tell-tale compression of the pages before them, that we are all hastening together to perfect felicity.'[162]

This impressively swift narrative reversal of the obstacles to 'perfect felicity' via a series of structural transformations takes place in a strikingly condensed and self-aware last chapter. The final 'obstacle' is identified as 'such a change in the General, as each believed impossible'. This 'impossible' change is nonetheless 'speedily' achieved through a series of economic re-valuations: the sudden and happy marriage of Henry's sister, Elinor, to a Viscount; the General's enlightenment as to Catherine's true value of 'three thousand pounds'; and the availability of the Fullerton estate to 'greedy speculation'.[163] Henry is finally designated 'the bearer of his [father's] consent', releasing the agent of the happy ending to full effect. This tension between the 'formulaic' – and hence narratively inevitable – conclusion and the 'realist' obstacles which appear to delay its coming, retraces the relation between mythic and empirical knowledges that marks the social context in which this work is rooted. Blanford Parker has noted that the shock of the early eighteenth-century poets was precisely the sudden introduction of the 'empirical field' illuminated by Newton's 'new enclosed and intelligible system of Nature': 'Nothing is more surprising to a culture habituated to metaphysical design than an empirical field.'[164] When it comes to Austen this point can be reversed.

What is particularly interesting for this analysis, however, is precisely what happens to such arguments 'when it comes to Austen'. While Frye notes her striking awareness of romance narrative tropes, he criticises the early 'burlesques' in which this knowledge is practised for 'a regrettable tendency to humor, which might have been of some disadvantage to her if she had continued with this genre'.[165] '*Love and Freindship*' contains my favourite example of this regrettable tendency: 'Run mad as often as you choose; but do not faint.'[166] She did of course continue with this genre, and continued to laugh at her readers' participation in a romantic desire for a happy ending. Austen's mature works incorporate realist credentials and historical content to an extent that veils the act of adaptation itself. The governing romance conventions are openly avowed in the relatively early *Northanger Abbey*. It seems that Austen's 'displacement' of romance tropes into recognisably realist content is highly conscious, and hence invisible, until the final alignment of idealised closure and realist content.

Eleanor Tilney's wonderfully convenient and structurally essential husband turns out to be 'really deserving of her; independent of his peerage, his wealth, and his attachment, being to a precision the most charming young man in the world':

> Any further definition of his merits must be unnecessary; the most charming young man in the world is instantly before the imagination of us all. Concerning the one in question therefore I have only to add – (aware that the rules of composition forbid the introduction of a character not connected with my fable) – that this was the very gentleman whose negligent servant left behind him that collection of washing-bills, resulting from a long visit at Northanger, by which my heroine was involved in one of her most alarming adventures.[167]

This conscious display of the implications of romance adaptation available in *Northanger Abbey* is on a par with the recent film, *Adaptation*, where the screenwriter's struggle to adapt a book about orchids into a narrative film exposes the generic conventions by which a successful narrative film is governed.[168]

For Frye, it is precisely the readerly experience of 'jarring' between the plausible and the actual outcomes that testifies to the 'revolutionary quality' of romance literature; 'however conservative the individual stories may be'. Romance is finally understood by Frye as the struggle between two polarized world views: 'one desirable [transcendent] and the other hateful [fallen]'.[169] It is only possible to make a choice between world views once the directions in which they lead are made quite clear by contrast. In the tension between romance and realism brought into consciousness by Austen's happy-ending-against-all-empirical-odds, we find an 'opposition between truth and falsehood': 'a means of organizing a version of truth which claims to be worldly and transcendent, empirical and imaginative, equally capable of reflecting and generating meaning'.[170] Frye's 'revolutionary' potential of romance 'jarring' is precisely embodied in Austen's most problematic heroine, Marianne, who most deeply experiences, but miraculously survives, the dangers of simply *being* a romance heroine.[171]

The particular resolution of *Northanger Abbey* holds apart and in tension the twin cords which otherwise bind to form a fundamental narrative condition for Austen's romance resolutions: the heroine's experience of desire and the determinants of her value as a desirable object in turn. It is only once her 'subjective' perspective and her 'objective' status are in alignment that the ending be a happy one. The narrator underlines the sheer literariness of this unificatory force. The reader's desire for a happy ending is openly greeted by the narrator's reassurance as to its inevitability: in spite of the work's careful and comic demystification of romance narrative formula, it remains a romance, and displays a casual consciousness of the implications of this final reversal.

In *Northanger Abbey*, then, we find evidence of Austen's narrative dialectic between realism and romance, working with elements of each mode to produce a conclusion that draws attention to its literary conditions as the convergence of narrative, readerly, and subjective desire with objective correlatives operating at the level of empirical-realism. The ending is both entirely plausible and utterly staged, with the formal machinations of the romance literary mode on which it depends happily exposed to the reader. At the break of the new realist wave, in the broader context of the historical consolidation of English empiricism, this exposure of a romance epistemology as implicated within a thoroughly redeemable verisimilitude (particularly expressed through economic markers) seems Hegelian in its scope. But since the author is known not to have read Hegel, we can only conclude that her dialectical awareness is truly phenomenological.

The notion of 'form' as abstract a-historical pattern (synchronic – the complete 'verbal *structure*') and 'substance' as detailed, historicised material (diachronic – the specific referential content), is challenged by the tendency of 'form' to register external, superficial, and extrinsic qualities, while 'substance' (or 'content') can be taken to indicate the more essential qualities inherent in the literary object itself. Raymond Williams calls attention to a strong ambivalence in our understanding of 'form', revealed by the history of literary 'Formalism': 'There was a simple opposition (bringing into play a received distinction between *form* (i) and *content*) between a formalism limited to "purely" aesthetic interests and a *Marxism* concerned with social content and ideological tendency'. Hard 'Formalism', he implies, defined itself against the 'relevance of "social content" or "social meaning" at *any* stage [of the critical process]', at least partly because it defined itself against the instrumentalist tendencies of 'mimetic' social(ist) realism.

Williams describes the 'more interesting' and 'extremely difficult' notion of 'form (ii)' as a 'shaping principle', which overlaps with our perception of 'genre' and at a more local level denotes 'a discoverable organizing principle within a work (cf. "no work of true genius dares want its appropriate form," Coleridge)'. When 'form (ii)' is intended, we can 'reasonably' talk about 'a formalism of content', so that 'different questions could be asked' about the methodological polarisation of 'form' and 'content'. These questions involve the intended analysis of what Williams calls the 'real formation' of a work. Form (ii) 'requires specific analysis of its elements in a particular organization', and allows for 'extension from the specific form to wider forms, and to forms of consciousness and relationship (*society*)', hence 'social formalism'.[172]

Williams's concept of a 'structure of feeling' indicates the operation of something as 'firm and definite as "structure" ' in the 'most delicate and least tangible parts of our activity'.[173] It is in 'the arts of a period', and particularly the 'documentary' arts, that we should expect to find such 'characteristic approaches and tones in argument' expressed 'often not consciously'. A 'structure of feeling' manifests itself through the work, but 'will not appear to have come "from" anywhere', and can be taken as evidence of 'the changing organization ... enacted in the organism'. The literary work, then, can be read for a micro-sequence, or logical unit, that grasps an essential, and *otherwise transparent*, quality inherent in the social moment of its production. This approach avoids what Jameson understands as the over-simple account of the 'ideologeme's' passive 'reflection' of historical data under the first horizon of interpretation, or what Frye terms the 'representational fallacy': 'The ideologeme' is not simply a 'reflex or reduplication of its situational context', but also the 'imaginary resolution of the objective contradictions to which it thus constitutes an active response'.[174]

For this reason, the *literary* problem of structure and agency, revealed by Formalist analysis of narrative in particular, parallels the social question posed by Marxist philosophy. If art *is* the 'imaginary resolution of real contradiction', we should be able to distinguish between different kinds of imagined resolution, and consider the analogy between economic and literary modes as co-penetrative as well as co-determining. Jameson invites us to remember that while 'there exist social contradictions which are structurally insoluble', we must *also* face the 'fact of successful revolutions'. Some art-forms must be considered 'prophetic rather than fantasy-oriented', and as a result will offer 'genuine solutions underway rather than projecting formal substitutions for impossible ones'.[175] When Austen's narrator informs us we are 'all hastening together to perfect felicity' as she brings the suspense concerning Catherine and Henry's destiny to a satisfactory narrative closure ('perfect happiness'), it is just possible that she believes it in a way that it is now difficult to reconstruct.

The question of structure and agency can be summarised as an uncertainty concerning final determination. Torfing raises the problem in an account of Althusser's structural Marxism: 'By exercising its hegemony over and in the ideological state apparatuses the dominance of the ruling classes becomes almost total, and the possibility of historical change, therefore, becomes almost entirely dependent upon class struggle at the level of ideology.' The logic of this analysis implies the eventual 'omnipotence' of 'dominant ideology', and essentialises class identity, by reducing 'politics to the role of realizing the structurally determined interests of the subaltern classes'. Since classes are 'bearers of the structure', their struggle is defined by and contained within terms pre-established by the structure itself and their position within it.[176] The determinant 'mode of production' finally cancels out consciousness and subjective or class agency beyond its own terms:

> The ultimate paradox of the notion of 'class struggle' is that society is 'held together' by the very antagonism, splitting, that for ever prevents its closure as harmonious, transparent, rational Whole – by the very impediment that undermines every rational totalization.[177]

And as a result we should expect 'the collective consciousness' gradually to lose 'all active reality' and 'become a mere reflection of the economic life and, ultimately, to disappear'.[178] This, coupled with the fact that we have no idea how far along the line of this inevitable trajectory we find ourselves, is the social problem.

The question of agency and structure inevitably recurs in the structural analysis of narrative. Roland Barthes reviews the *'problem of the subject'* in his definitive 'Structural Analysis of Narrative' as centred on 'the characters of narrative':

> Greimas has proposed to describe and classify the characters of narrative not according to what they are but according to what they do (whence the name *actants*), inasmuch as they participate in three main semantic axes (also found in the sentence: subject, object, indirect object, adjunct) which are communication, desire (or quest),

and ordeal. Since this participation is ordered in couples, the infinite world of characters is ... bound by a paradigmatic structure (*Subject/object, Donor/Receiver, Helper/Opponent*) which is projected along the narrative; and since an actant defines a class, it can be filled by different actors, mobilized according to rules of multiplication, substitution, or replacement.[179]

The 'action' of characters for narrative analysis is 'not to be understood in the sense of the trifling acts which form the tissue of the first level [of discourse], but in that of the major articulations of *praxis* (desire, communication, struggle)'. Once narrative has been analysed as an 'actantial matrix', the 'real difficulty' is in locating the 'place (and hence the existence) of the *subject*' itself. While we are accustomed to the novel's privileging of action through a single character, itself a cultural symptom of fetishised individuation characteristic of the social context in which the novel 'arises', 'such privileging is far from extending over the whole of narrative literature'. Barthes's important suggestion was that rather than the 'psychological' person as 'the subject of the quest, or of the desire, of the action', we might consider the 'grammatical' person 'accessible in our pronouns' as the proper location of narrative agency.

The Hegelian subject–object determinant is here reduced to its lowest common denominator in exchange, acted at the level of narration and variously displaced and delayed by the resistance of the material. It is in this sense that the agency-structure problem reveals itself to be both a literary and a social one; whether considered in terms of Hegelian 'objective realism', in which 'all experience is a function of a subject–object structure of a determinate kind'; or 'in the Marxist sense in which the external world is the product of human labor and human history so completely that the human producer is himself the product of that history'.[180]

The writer as 'producer' is both subject and object, or 'product', of history. A *female* writer might be said to have had a quite distinctive relationship both to 'human labor' and to 'human history':

The male worker in the process of production, is involved in contact with necessity, and interchange with nature as well as with other human beings but the process of production or work does not consume his whole life. The activity of a woman in the home as well as the work she does for wages keeps her continually in contact with a world of qualities and change. Her immersion in the world of use – in concrete, many-qualitied, changing, material processes – is more complete than his. And if life itself consists of sensuous activity, the vantage point available to women on the basis of their contribution to subsistence represents an intensification and deepening of the materialist world view and consciousness available to the producers of commodities in capitalism, an intensification of class consciousness.[181]

A narrative form conducive to feminine wish-fulfilment is analogous to a narrative form expressive of a 'mythic' (pre-capitalist) modality. At this point we come face to face with Barthes's apprehension, via Lévi Strauss, of narrative's conjunction between historical specificity and timelessness: 'the order of chronological succession is absorbed in an atemporal matrix structure'.[182] Or, to adopt Lucente's terms, Austen successfully mediates between empirical and metaphysical realism, weaving a plausible representation of the former into a narrative performance of the latter: 'the transcendence of everyday particulars, pointing to a system held to be truly universal and so more "real" '. While empirical realism privileges 'subject–object relationships'; metaphysical realism realigns the 'existential position of both subject and object in regard to an external source of meaning'.[183]

Put another way, Austen's consciousness of romance causality at the level of form, tending to the metaphorics of 'being' ('*born* to be a heroine'), expresses itself through the metonymic terms of the relatively new 'empirical realism' of late eighteenth- and early nineteenth-century novelisation. Following Lévi-Strauss further, 'the poles of metaphorical ... and metonymic ... conceptualization' have in the last century been 'reevaluated, in an open attempt to counter the pervasive prejudice in favor of rational discourse since the eighteenth century (despite periodic Romantic reactions.)'[184] This re-evaluation has largely involved a shift towards synchronic analysis, which allows us to recognise that precapitalist 'modes' are not necessarily any less mature or complete, as they inevitably appear on a diachronic scale. 'The progress of knowledge and the creation of new sciences take place through the generation of anti-histories which show that a certain order which is possible only on one [chronological] plane ceases to be so on another.'[185] The insistence of Austen's romance conclusions might now be considered to express 'a specifically organized, though not autonomous, body of knowledge', or 'a mode of thought with a distinct relation to the history of ideologies', rather than a failure of verisimilitude or the residue of 'an immature genre'.[186]

That recognisable 'mode of thought', apparently common to the formulas of feminine-romance and mythic-romance, has been taken as evidence of women's 'late' coming to literary writing, their 'immature' aesthetic vision, or their 'failure' to transcend local subjective determinants. I am asking the reader to consider it rather as the key to Austen's unprecedented literary canonisation, at the same time as her exponential popularity with a culturally 'immature' reading and viewing audience. It is *precisely* this alignment of a specifically feminine subjective desire and the objective determinants of exchange value – expressed economically – which allows the formally inevitable harmonious ending of *Northanger Abbey* to be plausible.

For Marxism 'the emergence of the economic, the coming into view of the infrastructure itself, is simply the sign of the approach of the concrete'. Austen's exposure of the economic infrastructure of the happy ending offers an unflinching answer to Jameson's compelling questions:

> How to analyse the part as part when the whole is not only no longer visible but even inconceivable? How to continue to use the terms subject and object as opposites which presuppose, in order to be meaningful, some possible synthesis, when there is no synthesis even imaginable, let alone present anywhere in concrete experience? What language to use to describe an alienated language, to what systems of reference to appeal when all systems of reference have been assimilated into the dominant system itself?[187]

We might, with the King of Rohan surveying the breach of Helm's Deep, ask more succinctly: 'how did it come to this?' That Austen's answer coincides with Sam's (the earthy, also-ran hobbit who accompanies the structurally more heroic, if unconsciously motivated, Frodo), is also revealing: 'It's like what you read in the old stories, you know, the ones that really matter ... there is some good in this world, and it is worth fighting for.'

The conscious display – first debunked then reinstated at a higher level – of narrative as formulaic, and into which one is also inserted at the level of history, is itself a marked characteristic of the romance mode, and tends to irony under conditions of realism: 'To begin perfect happiness at the respective ages of twenty-six and eighteen, is to do pretty well.'[188] As readers we have to question whether the 'perfect happiness' explicitly promised is an authorial wish-fulfilment, in which case Austen makes a naïve display of her own lack of 'realism'; or an expression of irony, in which case we are left with the bitter laugh of the spinster. Alternatively, we can follow the point made by Deborah Ross, that 'if one accepts McKeon's theory that the novel appeared only after a painstaking process whereby readers became able to understand a work of fiction as "realistic" rather than true or false, then women's position may have given them a shorthand to this understanding'.[189] In this case, Austen may simply be reminding her readers – and herself – of the role of feminine desire in the historical equation.

Jameson offers a dynamic equation between form and content: 'The content of a work of art stands judged by its form' since 'the realized form of the work ... offers the surest key to the vital possibilities of that determinate social moment from which it springs'.[190] The dialectic, as 'thought to the second power' is aimed 'not so much at solving the particular dilemmas in question, as at converting those problems into their own solutions on a higher level'. Austen's determinedly happy endings, then, might best be understood as discrete performances of dialectical thought, where,

> an entire complex of thought is hoisted through a kind of inner leverage one floor higher, in which the mind, in a kind of shifting of gears, now finds itself willing to take what had been a question for an answer, standing outside its previous exertions in such a way that it reckons itself into the problem, understanding the dilemma not as a resistance of the object alone, but also as the result of a subject-pole deployed and disposed against it in a strategic fashion – in short, as the function of a determinate subject–object relationship.[191]

The trope of 'reversal' central to the dialectic's apprehension of the 'interrelationship of phenomena', implies that completion of dialectical movement presupposes a 'diachronic framework' as 'a necessary condition' of its 'articulation'. This characteristic 'reversal' of an initiating thought can be perceived as 'a moment or single interlocking section in a single articulated process'.[192] And it is this, in terms of the 'logical unit' of functional sequences, which becomes central to Barthes' structural analysis of narrative.

Jameson notes that attempts to understand literary works historically leads the 'object of study' (a work, or a character, or an action) to be articulated 'into a succession of alternative structural realizations which we have called the diachronic sequence or construct.' This apprehension of temporality as a succession of discrete synchronic moments is 'expressed as a contradiction between a form and its content.' 'New' forms are to 'old' forms 'as latent content working its way to the surface to displace a form henceforth obsolete'. Historical as well as narrative patterns of 'change' can be understood as 'a function of content seeking its adequate expression in form'.[193] An act of pure consciousness, or 'awakening', occurs in response to unresolvable contradictions revealed when two mutually negating modes are seen to coincide.

Each of Austen's heroines experience an 'awakening' which, in changing her understanding of her subjective desire *and* objective value, produces narrative transformations. The 'awakening' of key characters, leading to their successful unions in-spite-of-all-empirical-odds, is a common denominator for the six novels. These unions are represented through a desired and desirable marriage between the central female character and her providential male partner, but they also represent unification at the level of romance quest. Deborah Ross makes this point well:

> Marriage in Austen's novels is not only the 'career' most real women of the time had to look forward to. Rather it is a way of grounding in familiar reality a powerful old romantic and religious symbol. In romance it is not only the heroine and hero who marry, but ... self and society. In Austen's novels many other seemingly opposed principles are wed as well, including humanity and God.[194]

Austen's polite insistence on wedding realism to romance represents a narrative mediation of incommensurate modes. The recognition and healing of social antinomies centres the work, and the agency for such healing is focalised through the 'awakening' of a feminine consciousness. The narrative dialectic between realism and romance which traverses the six works for which we remember Austen is articulated by her in such a way as to ask the question of what women know, how they come to their knowledge, and what difference this knowledge might make – given the necessary conditions for its full expression. Read through the Marxian account of economic and literary 'modes', this achievement has implications for what we make of feminine subjectivity in the narrative of history.

2
Sense and Sensibility: 'her opinions are all romantic'

Therein consists the alternative between positing and external reflection: do people create the world they live in from within themselves, autonomously, or does their activity result from external circumstances?

Slavoj Žižek, 'From "In-itself" to "For-itself" '[195]

In entering the Novel, we break the umbilical cord, we are cast into a birth, which is repeated as rebirth or new birth at one or more intervals along the way. We begin by gazing at facades and interfaces, noting the combining of wet and dry. As we progress, we come upon mud and slime, marshy passages of possibility. Renewed contact with the earth and all its dirt is here sacred to us and to our purposes.

Margaret Doody, *The True Story of the Novel*[196]

He was released without any reproach to himself, from an entanglement which had long formed his misery, from a woman whom he had long ceased to love; – and elevated at once to that security with another, which he must have thought of almost with despair, as soon as he had learnt to consider it with desire. He was brought, not from doubt or suspense, but from misery to happiness.

Jane Austen, *Sense and Sensibility*[197]

Sense and Sensibility draws to our attention a strong narrative tension between the empirical odds stacked against the possibility of a 'happy ending' (characteristic of realism), and the realisation of this ending nonetheless (characteristic of romance). The discrete happiness of the entwined double plots emphasises a dialectical 'conversion' of the two sisters. The hitherto 'romantic' Marianne's final happiness is quiet, slow-burning, and discrete: 'her joy, though sincere as her love for her sister, was of a kind to give neither spirits nor language.' The hitherto 'cool' Elinor's is passionate and extreme: 'she found every doubt, every solicitude removed, compared her situation with what so lately it had been ... she was overcome by her own felicity; – and happily disposed as is the human mind to be easily familiarized with any change for the better, it required several hours to give sedateness to her spirits, or any degree of tranquillity to her heart'.[198]

Structuralist literary analysis, by reproducing the final determinant of an abstract 'mode of production', addresses the problem of structure and agency at the level of literary narrative. The homology forwarded by Barthes, between the sentence as 'the smallest segment that is perfectly and wholly representative of discourse', and 'discourse' itself as 'the message of another language, one operating at a higher level than the language of the linguists' is intuited through 'the purely formal nature of the correspondences': 'insofar as it is likely that a similar formal organization orders all semiotic systems, whatever their substances and dimensions'.[199] In this approach, an individual narrative, such as *Sense and Sensibility*, 'receives its final meaning from the fact that it is narrated, entrusted to a discourse which possesses its own code'.

Characters, as 'subjects' of the narrative (e.g. Elinor and Marianne Dashwood) can be seen to 'yield to the sentence model' of linguistics, so that 'the actantial typology' operates according to the 'elementary functions of grammatical analysis'.[200] The narrative work combines three 'levels of description', and 'these three levels are bound together according to a mode of progressive integration', receiving their 'final meaning' from the very fact of narration, which 'intall[s] in us, all at once and in its entirety, the narrative code we are going to need' to receive it properly.[201] Narrative is 'isotropic', completing itself along a vertical index with reference to a 'unity of meaning' which 'impregnates' both sign and context through 'integration'; and distributional along a horizontal index, which coincides with the 'realist illusion' of chronology.[202]

The three levels of narrative structure are 'Functions', 'Action', and 'Narration'. Functions are defined as 'the seed' which plants 'an element that will come to fruition later'. 'Cardinal' functions are nuclei of sequences which refer to 'a complementary and consequential act', distinguished from 'indices' (referring to 'a more or less diffuse concept which is nevertheless necessary to the meaning of the story').[203] Cardinal functions are primarily distributional, while indices are primarily integrational, since the 'ratification of indices is "higher up." Functions refer us "further on" for their completion (hence distributional) while indices refer us to a "paradigmatic ratification" '. This distinction again turns on the recognition of a duality in the conditions for narrative: *'Functions* and *indices* thus overlay another classic distinction: functions involve metonymic relata, indices metaphoric relata; the former correspond to a functionality of doing, the latter to a functionality of being.' Cardinal functions will 'inaugurate or conclude an uncertainty'.

A number of functions combine to produce a 'sequence': 'the sequence opens when one of its terms has no solidary antecedent and closes when another of its terms has no consequent'.[204] A sequence of functions is itself a unit in the 'next level' of significance, 'Actions'; and it is here that we encounter a version of the question of structure and agency at the level of narrative. The final point of reference in the articulated 'pyramid' structure of narrative is that of 'Narration': the fact of being narrated, the sending and receiving of the message 'of another language, one operating at a higher level than the language of the linguists'.[205] Barthes's terms offer a distinctive approach to the question of structure and agency ('how did it come to this', and – perhaps more to the point – 'how do we get a happy ending from here'), when applied to Austen's *Sense and Sensibility*.

The 'logical sequence' that is the concern of *Sense and Sensibility* is specifically inaugurated through a description of the inheritance complex of the 'family of Dashwood'. An early reviewer complained of 'a little perplexity in the genealogy of the first chapter, and the reader is somewhat bewildered among half-sisters, cousins, and so forth'.[206] The film adaptation of 1996 cuts the tangled genealogical detail of the novel's opening pages and has Elinor explain with a sigh to the young Margaret that they must leave Norland because women simply don't inherit property.[207] Austen herself is careful to pose this question precisely, and sets the disinheritance of the Dashwood women in contrast to the power to bequeath of the mysterious 'Mrs Smith' who owns Allenham Court and temporarily disinherits Willoughby; the surly Mrs Ferrars, on whose 'will' her son's fortune depends; and even the jovial Mrs Jennings ('a widow with an ample jointure').[208] The Dashwood's 'long settled' inhabitation of the 'large' estate, centred on the 'property' of Norland Park, who for 'many generations' continue in peace and prosperity in 'the general good opinion of their surrounding acquaintance', becomes 'uncertain' as a direct result of the fact that the 'late owner of this estate' died a 'single man'.[209]

More precisely, peace holds until the death of his 'constant companion and housekeeper ... sister', which 'produced a great alteration in his home': namely, the invitation to the estate of his nephew, Henry Dashwood, who is initially overdetermined as its future incumbent: 'the legal inheritor of the Norland estate, and the person to whom [the old gentleman] intended to bequeath it'. Henry Dashwood brings a wife and three daughters, but has a pre-existing son from a 'former marriage'. That son (John Dashwood) has already inherited 'the fortune of his mother, which had been large' and 'added to his wealth' by marriage to Fanny Ferrars, daughter to a man who 'had died very rich' and a mother who is later described as embodying the 'old, well-established grievance of duty against will, parent against child'.[210]

It is explicitly noted in the opening passages that the 'succession to the Norland estate was not so really important' to this son as to 'his sisters': 'for their fortune, independent of what might arise to them from their father's inheriting that property, could be but small,' since 'their mother had nothing'.[211] Once the 'old gentleman died', and his 'will was read', the 'cardinal' narrative function of the work reveals itself in its first moment of self-consciousness:

> He was neither so unjust, nor so ungrateful, as to leave his estate from his nephew; but he left it to him on such terms as destroyed half the value of the bequest. Mr. Dashwood had wished it more for the sake of his wife and daughters than for himself or his son: but to his son, and his son's son, a child of four years old, it was secured, in such a way as to leave himself no power of providing for those who were most dear to him, and who most needed a provision, by any charge on the estate, or by sale of any of its valuable woods.[212]

This effective disinheritance of a mother and daughters (the girls receive 1000 pounds each), in favour of the son of a nephew's son, is the striking chord of the fugue between matrilineal and patrilineal claims played out through this narrative, until resolved by the double marriages with which it closes. A similar functional chord founds *Pride and Prejudice*, centred on a family of five daughters and their 'entailed' estate. *Sense and Sensibility* is particularly distinguished by an insistence upon doubling: between first and second wives; son and nephew; mother of daughters and father of sons; brothers (Edward and Robert); competing suitors (Brandon and Willoughby, Lucy and Elinor); sisters (Marianne and Elinor).

In *Pride and Prejudice*, the doubling of functions has been muted to produce a major and minor sequence (Elizabeth–Darcy and Jane–Bingley). Barthes notes the function of doubling as itself 'a common archaic form' of narrative: 'Many narratives, for example, set two adversaries in conflict over some stake; the subject is then truly double, not reducible further by substitution. Indeed, this is even perhaps a common archaic form, as though narrative, after the fashion of certain languages, had also known a *dual* of persons.'[213] In *Sense and Sensibility* the function of doubling is itself abstracted in the inessential relation between will and law (or 'duty') which determines the inheritance of Norland prior to the old gentleman's death, and which ultimately divides possible and actual outcomes between his 'intent[ion] to bequeath' and the 'legal' right of the inheritor.

An index for the 'logical anxiety' of this functional sequence is hinted at in the given reasons for the change of will: the old gentleman is said to have 'tied up' the 'whole' of his estate for the future enjoyment of a toddler (his nephew's grandson). This child is both indistinguishable to all other children, notable for 'such attractions as are by no means unusual in children of two or three years', and drastically over-valued by the old man in comparison to the 'value of all the attention which, for years, he had received from his niece and her daughters'.[214] The nature of the split designated in these various doublings is given a 'higher' index in this example between the concrete and the abstract, or the singular and the universal. The particularity of the old gentleman's will conflates the abstract 'right' of inheritance by a male child representing the most abstract of qualities (characteristics shared by all children of that age).

The old gentleman's will overlooks the 'value' of the ethic of particular relationship represented by the disinherited – and subsequently exiled – mother and daughters. In the process the estate is preserved whole for an abstract patrilineal inheritance; the particular 'claims' of a mother and her daughters leapfrogged in favour of the son of the son of a nephew. An anxiety over the 'wholeness' of the estate returns in *Persuasion*: 'The Kellynch estate should be transmitted whole and entire, as he had received it.'[215] In both cases the anxiety is not the centre of the action, but its catalyst: a cover for a logical anxiety concerning the relationship between the part and the whole, or the singular and the universal.

Since Henry Dashwood (Elinor and Marianne's father) dies only a year after the old gentleman, this bifurcation of particular human *will* and abstract legal *right* initiates and is answered in a discrete 'complementary and consequential act': the deathbed promise spoken by John Dashwood (son of Henry Dashwood, the old man's great-nephew, father of the inheriting toddler, step-brother to Elinor and Marianne, and now holder of the estate): to 'do every thing *in his power* to make [Marianne, Elinor and their sister and mother] comfortable'.[216] This verbal assertion of a 'solemn promise', unwitnessed, has no legal standing, and is limited to the will, or 'power', of the promiser.[217] His 'power' is at first considered enough to respond with generosity, and given 'leisure to consider how much there might prudently be in his power', he 'would give them three thousand pounds' – equivalent to the value placed on them by the old gentleman's will.[218]

Once Fanny Dashwood arrives on the scene, this understanding of the 'promise' is soon halved, and then completely degraded to a general intention to provide 'neighbourly acts' as might help the bereaved women start a new life in a different home: 'looking out for a comfortable small house for them, helping them to move their things, and sending them presents of fish and game, and so forth, whenever they are in season'.[219] The grounds for the sudden and severe degrading of the 'solemn promise' on which the future welfare of Elinor and Marianne now depends, are disclosed in the course of a conversation between John Dashwood and his wife as a 'universal' opinion concerning relationship between a son and his 'half-sisters': 'It was very well known that no affection was ever supposed to exist between the children of any man by different marriages.'[220] The claims of a 'half-blood' kinship with 'the widow and children of his father' are measured against the less ambiguous claims of their 'dear little boy', and in the course of a reasonable conversation found to be first 'half' then 'nothing' (reiterating the core terms of the inheritance problematic that founds the narrative).

Barthes's structural analysis is directed at capturing something of the 'atemporal logic lying behind the temporality of narrative,' following Lévi Strauss's apprehension of 'an atemporal matrix structure' existing above and beyond the 'chronological succession' of narrative. What we think of as literary form, then, can be said to indicate a particular narrative's imbrication in this 'atemporal matrix', allowing access to consciousness of the 'message' of the particular narrative in relation to its encoding frame. The 'chronological illusion' of realist narrative is contained within this super-narrative (or 'metasynchronic') system of meaning, which pre-exists and remains unchanged by particular instances:

> Time belongs not to discourse strictly speaking but to the referent; both narrative and language know only a semiotic time, 'true' time being a 'realist,' referential illusion.[221]

This inaugurating sequence is, according to structural analysis, 'governed by a logic ... at once necessary and sufficient'. And in this 'framework' offered by 'finite sets grouping a small number of terms', we should expect to find the blueprint, or archetype, of 'other units [which] fill it out according to a mode of proliferation in principle infinite'.[222]

The initial, pre-narrative split initiating the narrative of *Sense and Sensibility* is between the old gentleman's will and the will-lessness of his 'sister', which remains fundamentally unspoken. This pre-narrative split fractures the sequence which follows: a family 'split' by two marriages – same father, different mothers – is organised through the enacting of the 'will' of the patrilineal line, and the silencing, or displacement, of the claims of the matrilineal line. But the point does not rest there. John Dashwood's splitting of his 'solemn promise' between 'prudence' and 'power' is resolved through the claim of the full son compared to only 'half-blood' (maternal sisters). 'Half-blood' is no blood at all, so the maternal line is returned almost 'nothing' to add to the 'nothing' it brings to inheritance.

The specific argument for this 'nothing' is, however, repeated differently in the grounds asserted for the infant son's full inheritance. As the son of the son of a nephew, he is already an *indirect* recipient of the gift of the estate: also less than 'full' blood. Henry Dashwood's father, we are to conclude, was the younger brother of the 'old gentleman' and his 'housekeeper … sister', and – in contrast to the 'old gentleman' – was by no means 'single'. Yet, had the estate *remained* the full inheritance of Henry Dashwood (son of the younger brother, and legal – if indirect – patrilineal inheritor) this inaugurating split would have been quickly answered by recognition of the claims of a 'second marriage', and there would have been little of interest to tell. The split is by contrast *doubled* when the will of the 'old gentleman' values the male issue of a first marriage over and above the female issue of a 'second' marriage. And it is this which allows for the arrival of John and Fanny Dashwood, and the resulting introduction between Elinor and Edward. The subsequent move to Devon, also initiated by the pre-narrative split, opens the important micro-romance between Marianne and Willoughby, as well as introducing Colonel Brandon, fundamental to its conclusion.

It is, therefore, especially significant that both Marianne and Elinor turn out to be 'second' attachments to their respective partners: Edward is secretly pre-engaged to Lucy Steele, and Colonel Brandon is heart-broken as a young man by the loss of his first love (Eliza) to his older brother. Marianne learns to appreciate the value of her own 'second' attachment, following the public fall of Willoughby and his immersion in a mercenary marriage, and finds that she was (at least) a second attachment to *him*, following his prior seduction and abandonment of the second Eliza (daughter of the first). Colonel Brandon's capacity for a second attachment, furthermore, is what finally saves Marianne from the exponential proliferation of attachments characteristic of the fallen woman, and is enabled by the striking resemblance between Brandon's Eliza and Marianne.

This branch of the narrative indicates an abstract index for the significance of these variations on 'second': one thing when compared to a singular attachment, and quite another when compared to the innumerable attachments of the 'libertine'. Colonel Brandon expresses this narrative preoccupation between singularity and innumerability by his parallel desire for the structurally similar Marianne and Eliza. In a discussion with Elinor regarding Marianne's 'objections against a second attachment', he sees that her false logic 'cannot hold', but fears the consequences of her attachment to singularity giving way on 'a better acquaintance with the world':

> But a change, a total change of sentiments – No, no, do not desire it, – for when the romantic refinements of a young mind are obliged to give way, how frequently are they succeeded by such opinions as are but too common, and too dangerous! I speak from experience. I once knew a lady … [223]

Generalised, this would again take us to the higher index of the singular and the universal, and sexualises a 'logical anxiety' concerning the decimation of totality.

Metonymic-realism is in the most general terms a decimation of totality into dissociated parts. This seems terribly abstract until we recall that the late eighteenth and early nineteenth century was marked by a very clear experience of the decimation of a totality in two forms related to land and property: (1) the landed class's anxiety over the breaking up of the 'whole' estate before its inheritance, or the loss of the inherited estate to 'new' money, answered in the entail; (2) the legitimate transformation of 'common' land into personal property. *Sense and Sensibility* refers directly to both anxieties: (1) in the odd form of patrilineal inheritance described so casually in the narrator's opening passages; (2) when John and Fanny Dashwood, on inheriting the estate on behalf of their son, quickly move to enclose the local common:

> The enclosure of Norland Common, now carrying on, is a most serious drain. And then I have made a little purchase within this half year; East Kingham Farm, you must remember the place, where old Gibson used to live. The land was so very desirable for me in every

respect, so immediately adjoining my own property, that I felt it my duty to buy it.[224]

The John Dashwoods are closely associated with what Roy Porter has encapsulated as the new 'political economy' of English Enlightenment: 'which laid claim to a superior rationale, a scientific grasp of wealth creation and the satisfaction of wants'.[225] They are also the characters most clearly at odds with the narrator's ethical judgement. Even Willoughby is ultimately 'forgiven'; but not the economically acquisitive John Dashwoods.

The first Eliza is Colonel Brandon's 'unfortunate [adopted] sister', who in spite of a young and passionate reciprocal attachment to the Colonel, is married 'against her inclination' to his older brother: 'This lady was one of my nearest relations, an orphan from her infancy, and under the guardianship of my father.'[226] Colonel Brandon's father is 'at once her uncle and guardian', positioning Brandon himself as cousin and brother (a kinship tension returning in the figure of Edmund in *Mansfield Park*). Since, although an orphan, Eliza's 'fortune was large' and the Brandon 'family estate encumbered', the marriage to the first brother is forced by the estate holder, and the misery of the attachment leads to Eliza's eventual 'fall' and 'divorce'.[227] She is quite literally 'lost' to Brandon: 'I could not trace her beyond her first seducer.'

Given the multiple kinship between Brandon and Eliza (she is orphan, cousin, sister, lover, near-wife), we can 'name' this functional series as the question of over/undervaluing relations (turning on claims to 'blood') found in the inaugurating terms of the narrative. The 'old gentleman' of Norland estate *under*-values his female blood relations, and his undervaluing is compounded by John Dashwood's further devaluing of 'half blood' sisters; 'no relation at all', since children of different *mothers*. Brandon reverses the gesture by somewhat *over*-valuing his 'half-blood' 'sister'. This overvaluing leads him to return to find her following her 'fall', and we see a second 'solemn' deathbed promise, when Eliza's 'only child, a little girl, the offspring of her first guilty connection, who was then about three years old' is given to his care.[228] Brandon initiates the 'complementary' act for the sequence of under-valuing half-blood relations, then, by continuing the over-valuation of its origin: Eliza (ii) becomes a displaced 'value'; 'a precious trust'.

So it turns out that Brandon is himself a 'second' brother, now structurally aligned with Elinor and Marianne's paternal grandfather and – later – with Edmund's demotion. Since Mrs Dashwood 'had nothing', they become effectively dependent on the will of their paternal grandfather's older brother; as 'second' brother, their paternal grandfather only seems to have left his son with 7000 pounds 'at his disposal', and their father's first wife's fortune is already entailed to their half-brother.

Brandon is more fortunate in the death of his morally reprehensible older brother, and soon comes to possess the 'family property'; now in an inverse relation to Edward's demotion from first to second son. Brandon has misrepresented the second Eliza as a 'distant relation', but is 'suspected of a much nearer connection with her'.[229] The truth lies somewhere in between. Mrs Jennings describes Eliza (ii) as Brandon's 'natural' daughter, although there is no 'blood' relationship to be claimed.[230] Brandon's respect of the deathbed promise of his childhood love rests entirely on his own will, rather than paternal 'duty'. She is a purely matrilineal (hence purely illegitimate) daughter of a divorced mother, and Brandon comments on the 'unhappy resemblance between the fate of mother and daughter'. Since he eventually finds Eliza (ii) 'near her delivery', a new generation – Willoughby's illegitimate offspring – now stands to be valued by the Colonel.[231] Moreover, this line of pure matrilineality is illegitimate – deserving of 'nothing' – because it can claim *only* blood relation.

At this point it is worth wondering what happened to Eliza (i)'s large 'fortune', following the death of her ex-husband. The estate, which eventually passes to Brandon on the death of his older brother, is no longer 'encumbered' it seems; but Elizas (i) and (ii) have no direct claim on it, in spite of – and because of – their inheritance claim as pure 'matrinome'. The Elizas' misdirected fortune is structurally essential to Marianne's particular happy ending as 'Mrs. Brandon', in an economic closure of the narrative insistence on the structural resemblance between Marianne and the Elizas. Mrs Jenning's earlier sly comment that Brandon is likely to 'leave [Eliza] all his fortune' is, then, more pointed than it seems.[232]

Marianne is said to be reminiscent of Eliza (i), and – as she notes – is of an age to be Brandon's daughter, parallel with Eliza (ii). Willoughby, seducer of Eliza (ii), is clearly drawn to Marianne for the same reasons he was drawn to Eliza (ii), describing the former's 'affection for me' as '*scarcely less warm*' than the fast-fallen Eliza's. Eliza (ii) was about 17 when seduced (in Bath) by Willoughby, shortly before he arrives in Devon and on the scene of Marianne's 'romance'. Their illegitimate offspring is born shortly after Brandon leaves Barton for London on the day of the planned visit to Whitwell: the very day that Marianne 'never spent a pleasanter morning in [her] life', being taken round the house that 'will one day be Mr Willoughby's'.[233] Marianne's 'romance' with Willoughby is gestated in the nine months intervening between his seduction of Eliza (ii) and the birth of their child.

Eliza (ii) is considered, by Willoughby as well as Brandon, as like her mother in more than appearance. Willoughby asks Elinor to consider whether 'because *I* was a libertine *she* must be a saint'. He contrasts the 'violence of her passions' with 'the weakness of her understanding' as context for a mutual seduction, in terms that win 'compassion' for his own suffering from Elinor's 'strength of understanding, and coolness of judgment'.[234] The 'complementary consequence' thesis begs the question: what is it, given the extent to which Eliza (ii) and Marianne share the signature of the function of violent passion, that has saved Marianne from a similar, or worse, fate? Both daughters of second 'attachments' (in the most abstract sense); both attached with violent and open passion to the same man (Willoughby); both loved and protected by the same man (Brandon); and both markedly similar to their mothers: 'The resemblance between [Marianne] and her mother was strikingly great', and Brandon comments with reference to the Elizas on the 'unhappy resemblance between the fate of mother and daughter'![235]

Mrs Dashwood embodies a 'violence' of feeling, which shatters all gradation and differentiation: 'I can feel no sentiment of approbation inferior to love ... I have never yet known what it was to separate esteem and love.'[236] This 'eagerness of mind', shared by Marianne and her mother, is contrasted with Elinor's more balanced composition, where 'strong' feelings could nonetheless be 'govern[ed]'.[237] We must conclude that Elinor has more of her father in her, for 'his temper was cheerful and sanguine'.

John Dashwood, son of this father, 'had not the strong feelings of the rest of the family', is 'rather cold-hearted, and rather selfish', and further influenced by a wife 'more narrow-minded and selfish' than himself.[238] This wife, as daughter of the dreadful Mrs Ferrars, and sister to Edward Ferrars (Elinor's eventual husband), offers a further distinction between matrilineal and patrilineal inheritance. Fanny is seen to have inherited the 'serious[ness], even to sourness', and 'strong characters of pride and ill-nature' of her mother's 'aspect'. Edward, on the other hand, has 'an innate propriety and simplicity of taste', and is markedly unambitious. The first brother, Robert, is all 'conceit' to Edward's 'modesty and worth'. Robert explains these differences, to Edward's discredit, in terms of his own 'public' education in contrast to Edward's 'private' tuition.[239] And the perverting tendencies of a misconceived (worldly) education are offered again by Elinor to explain to herself Willoughby's moral downfall:

> the irreparable injury which too early an independence and its consequent habits of idleness, dissipation, and luxury, had made in the mind, the character, the happiness, of a man who, to every advantage of person and talents, united a disposition naturally open and honest, and a feeling, affectionate temper. The world had made him extravagant and vain – Extravagance and vanity had made him cold-hearted and selfish.[240]

However, the same 'world' that has made him 'extravagant and vain' also structures his 'punishment': 'Vanity, while seeking its own guilty triumph at the expense of another, had involved him in a real attachment, which extravagance, or at least its offspring, necessity, had required to be sacrificed. Each faulty propensity in leading him to evil, had led him likewise to be punished'.[241] His due punishment consists of the loveless marriage of convenience: 'Domestic happiness is out of the question.' His 'evil' is specifically given: 'To avoid a comparative poverty, which [Marianne's] affection and her society would have deprived of all its horrors, I have, by raising myself to affluence, lost everything that could make it a blessing.'[242]

Willoughby's contextual vindication offers a discrete perspectival narrative, framed by its 'complementary' closure of the dialectical logic inherent in this narrative work. This succinct message of an inversion between 'love' and 'prudence' speaks back at the romance reader's polarisation of Willoughy as either hero or villain: this 'extraordinary conversation' allows the reader, with Elinor, to 'forg[i]ve', by setting his actions in a context of broader explanation.

What is at stake in this conversation, and in Elinor's forgiveness, is the responsibility for individual agency in a now quite explicitly social context. His reply to Elinor's claim that she has already 'heard it all' regarding Willoughby's 'part' in the 'dreadful business' of Eliza's seduction raises the related question of partiality: 'Remember ... from whom you received the account. Could it be an impartial one'?[243] One might now wonder at Brandon's description of his own attempt to 'elope' with the first Eliza: a 'romantic', passionate bid for freedom or another mode of illicit seduction? Brandon describes Willoughby as fundamentally unfeeling, a man who had 'done that, which no man who *can* feel for another, would do'.[244]

Willoughby admits that his intentions towards Marianne were founded in pure 'vanity': 'thinking only of my own amusement, giving way to feelings which I had always been too much in the habit of indulging, I endeavoured, by every means in my power, to make myself pleasing to her, without any design of returning her affection'. His justification is that he 'did not *then* know what it was to love'. Finding himself attached to her 'by insensible degrees', however, he delays making his intentions public 'from an unwillingness to enter into an engagement while my circumstances were so greatly embarrassed.' The intended proposal never occurs, due to the karmic backlash unleashed by his earlier treatment of Eliza (ii): 'in the interim of the very few hours that were to pass before I could have an opportunity of speaking with her in private – a circumstance occurred – an unlucky circumstance, to ruin all my resolution, and with it all my comfort'. He is disinherited by his female benefactor (the mysterious Mrs Smith), and 'nothing else in common prudence remained for me to do', but 'address' the woman 'of fortune', 'whose money' had now become 'necessary to me'.[245]

This striking disinheritance of a male heir by a property-holding female relative, on the grounds of his seduction and abandonment of a young woman, and its 'ironic' reinstatement after the fact, inverts and closes the inaugural sequence of the narrative, as well as the sequence of matrilineal disinheritances embodied by the Elizas. Willoughby's effective disinheritance, Brandon's 'second' inheritance, Edward's demotion from the distinctions and income of 'elder' to the pastoral happiness entailed by 'second' brother (insisted upon in the misunderstanding of news that 'Mr Ferrars is married')[246], as well as the 'second' attachments inherent in the narrative completion, collectively recapitulate the under-valuing of the 'second' marriage of Henry Dashwood that inaugurates the narrative sequence.

The only attachment that remains truly singular is that of the unromantic Elinor; who achieves her original desire in spite of its object's prior promise to marry another. A hidden parallel between Edward and Willoughby, however, surfaces in a common discrepancy between 'faith' and 'honour'. Willoughby accepts that he was to blame for 'scrupling to engage my faith where my honour was already bound'. Edward admits that he 'was simple enough to think, that because my *faith* was plighted to another, there could be no danger in my being with [Elinor]': 'the consciousness of my engagement [to Lucy] was to keep my heart as safe and sacred as my honour'.[247] Barthes would explain this through the 'doubly implicative' relations between cardinal functions.[248]

The function of 'second marriages' is explored through the sequence represented by Marianne's 'romantic' disapproval of 'second attachments'.[249] The summary of Marianne's fate in the closure of the narrative makes a self-conscious display of her particular actantial status, and leads us to a clear index for significance. This recognisable functional signature can be raised to the 'higher' level of 'Actions', with its integrational completion of a logic of origins and ontology:

> Marianne Dashwood was born to an extraordinary fate. She was born to discover the falsehood of her own opinions, and to counteract, by her conduct, her most favourite maxims. She was born to overcome an affection formed so late in life as at seventeen, and with no sentiment superior to strong esteem and lively friendship, voluntarily to give her hand to another! – and *that* other, a man who had suffered no less than herself under the event of a former attachment, whom, two years before, she had considered too old to be married, – and who still sought the constitutional safeguard of a flannel waistcoat!

The gesture is complete when we learn that 'Marianne could never love by halves ... her whole heart became, in time, as much devoted to her husband as it had once been to Willoughby.'[250]

Marianne's pure romance function (born to suffer dialectical reversal) overcomes her more predictable function, which would have made her share the outcome of the Elizas, reserved for women who indulge feelings over reason in both fiction and life. The 'polarization' identified in her 'mind' by Frye as a 'clue' to the revolutionary potential of romance, is finally a polarization between subjective experience (feelings) and objective value (reason). Her awakening is initiated in recognition of the illusory nature of her precious 'feelings' as ultimately 'selfish'. She learns, among other things, to stick to the common paths, having almost died from a fever brought on by walking 'not merely on the dry gravel of the shrubbery, but all over the grounds, and especially in the most distant parts of them, where there was something more of wildness than in the rest, where the trees were the oldest, and the grass the longest and wettest'.[251]

On recovery, she reflects that her 'peace of mind' had been 'doubly involved' in Willoughby's betrayal of Eliza (ii): 'for not only is it horrible to suspect a person, who has been what *he* has been to *me*, of such designs, but what must it make me appear to *myself*? What, in a situation like mine, but a most shamefully unguarded affection could expose me to – '. The blank covers the shame of her structural relation to Eliza's fate, unspeakable in itself. She claims her illness to have been 'entirely brought on by myself' and her near-death as a case of 'self-destruction'. Her 'desire to live' is characterised as wanting 'time for atonement to my God, and to you all'. And she resolves to live 'solely for my family', checking her 'feelings' with 'religion', 'reason', and 'constant employment'.[252]

In case we had not yet got the point, the narrative conclusion further draws out the contrast between Marianne's plausible (realist) end, and her actual (romance) end:

> Instead of falling a sacrifice to an irresistible passion, as once she had fondly flattered herself with expecting, – instead of remaining even for ever with her mother, and finding her only pleasures in retirement and study, as afterwards in her more calm and sober judgment she had determined on, – she found herself at nineteen, submitting to new attachments, entering on new duties, placed in a new home, a wife, the mistress of a family, and the patroness of a village.[253]

Neither dead, nor lost, nor spinstered: Marianne achieves one of the most startling happy endings of all Austen's heroines.

The insistence on the different characteristic qualities carried by Marianne and Elinor, as compared to their half-brother John, offers a further statement of integral significance beyond the chronological sequence of actions and consequences. Are women daughters of their mothers only, and what does this particular 'blood' relationship entail, given that it seems to stand for 'nothing' in the face of the Name-of-the-Father, which is functioned through the variations on inheritance, and asserted in the convergence of 'will' and 'duty' in patrilineal inheritance. Lack of distinction between mother and daughter, as revealed in the pairings of Marianne and Mrs Dashwood, Fanny and Mrs Ferrars, and the indistinguishable Elizas, counters the splitting (or halving) of a whole on degrees of 'blood' and 'name'. Mothers and daughters in this narrative suffer indeed from 'unhappy resemblance', unless differentiated, usually by association with contrasting functions in their male partners or fathers.

Sometimes oppositional pairings are shown to reinforce weaknesses, as in the case of Mr and Mrs Palmer. Marianne and Willoughby's misery is also caused at least in part by their *sameness* in taste and disposition, both inclined to regard 'sensibility' (in the 'violence' of passion) over and above 'sense' (cool judgment, strong reasoning). The 'violent passion' of a Willoughby, in combination with a 'worldly' education resulting in 'vanity' and an inability to '*feel* for another', produces a libertine, who acts narcissistically to indulge his own passions at the expense of the young women involved.

Elinor's remarkable 'forgiveness' of Willoughby parallels Marianne's, but is set 'on more reasonable grounds'. These grounds turn out to demand a fuller explication of his actions, in wider and wider circles of context, finally raising the question of agency and structure as focused through the actant.[254] In place of the imputed 'diabolical motive' of romantic seducers, Willoughby's immoral actions are set in a (social) structure which rewards self-interest, and which tends to make them inevitable. The 'violent passion' of an Eliza, in combination with the absence of true parentage (she is an 'orphan'), results in the multiple attachments and illegitimacy of the fallen heroine. The 'violent passion' of a Marianne, in combination with the more 'reasonable' tendencies of her sister, and a 'superior' mind, result in a dramatic and painful process of learning, and more gradual acceptance of domestic happiness over and above 'violent passion'. She gains the 'sense' to love that which protects and esteems her; rather than protecting and esteeming that which her 'sensibility' has selected to love.

'Sensibility', through association with 'violent passion', implies an overindulgence of subjective feeling. The relationship between sense and sensibility is broadly analogous to the relationship between mind and body: sensibility arises as a literary concept out of the Lockean notion of human understanding as the retroactively organised accumulation of sense impressions; the seventeenth-century 'empirical turn'. But sensory involvement with the world is itself the basis for a 'higher' knowledge, and ultimately attunes us to 'natural law', according to Rousseau. 'Sense', on the other hand, is a process of mind that implies a higher pre-ordering of sense-impressions. The ability to 'sense' the world through our 'senses', which tends to the capacity for intuitive knowledge implied by heightened 'sensibility', finally collapses into the ability to 'make sense' (after reasoned reflection) of the deluge of sensory information received through the 'senses'.[255]

Sense can function as an organising principle in itself, while sensibility takes on – and amplifies – attributes of empirical epistemology. But sensibility is at the same time a route to apprehend the 'organizing principle' (or 'sense' as 'meaning') inherent in empirical data. Lucente identifies just this as the transformative moment in the dialectic between 'realism' and 'myth': wherein the turn from a 'mythic' locus of knowledge towards 'the objective accumulation of data' tends towards discovering 'the set of laws that organized the existing environment'.[256] The agency for salvation in this narrative is situated beyond the limited vision of any single character, belonging to a series of narrative alternatives centred on a fundamantal reversibility between outcomes productive of 'misery' and 'hope'. It seems to depend on the *interpretation* of evidence available to our senses.

The otherwise productive dialectic between sense and sensibility, is foreclosed both by Marianne's dangerous 'excess of sensibility', and by Fanny Dashwood's equally perverse lack of it: 'Mrs John Dashwood had never been a favourite with any of her husband's family; but she had had no opportunity, till the present, of shewing them with how little attention to the comfort of other people she could act when occasion required it.'[257] The inverted propriety of Fanny and Mrs Ferrars (the latter driven by fear of 'the reproach of being too amiable') is situated on the side of unfeeling, self-motivated, vanity; and bears a precise inability to '*feel*' for others as marked as Willoughby's.[258] An excess of 'sense' – as exhibited in the reasoning of Fanny and John Dashwood regarding the claims of 'half-blood' on the Dashwood estate – is as ridiculous, and socially dangerous, as an excess of 'sensibility'. And we might return this point to the will of the 'old gentleman', whose excess of sensibility leads him to be over-fond of a child, indistinguishable from all other children of the same age. The interesting Mr Palmer is said to hold a

> common, but unfatherly opinion among his sex, of all infants being alike; and though [Mrs Jennings] could plainly perceive at different times, the most striking resemblance between this baby and every one of his relations on both sides, there was no convincing his father of it; no persuading him to believe that it was not exactly like every other baby of the same age; nor could he even be brought to acknowledge the simple proposition of its being the finest child in the world.[259]

Lady Middleton 'did not really like [Elinor and Marianne] at all' because they 'neither flattered herself nor her children'. An incidental scene describes the 'ladies' discussing 'the comparative heights of Harry Dashwood and Lady Middleton's second son William, who were nearly of the same age'. Since the 'affair might have been determined too easily by measuring them at once', the scene takes on the impression of a further example of overvaluing blood relations over and above more objective, empirical, evidence. Lady Middleton's preference for her own offspring is always in evidence, but this over-valuing of blood-kin is further revealed as a universal maternal trait: 'Mrs Jennings considered that Marianne might probably be to [her mother] what [her own daughter] was to herself', and as a result 'her sympathy in *her* sufferings was very sincere'.[260]

Cumulatively, *Sense and Sensibility* proposes a series of reversals: indiscriminability between children of the same or similar age alongside the differentiation between children according to which parent they most resemble; the common characteristics of all individuals alongside the specific impact of education and experience on differentiating individuals, and particularly the singling out of first-born males (primogeniture) over 'second' sons, and over all daughters. If all children are the same at birth, how do different people emerge with different 'claims'? What differentiates (splits) identity? How, for example, does a Mrs Jennings produce daughters such as Lady Middleton and Mrs Palmer? One all 'cold', insipid, self-absorption, relieved only by 'spoiling' her children; the other all surface chatter, gossip and drollery. We might consider this question of sameness and difference, equality and differentiation, as the work's 'inner metalanguage for the reader (or listener) who can grasp every logical succession of actions as a nominal whole'.[261]

There are four striking scenes of surprised or mistaken arrival or reception, which substitute an unexpected message for an expected one. Marianne expects Willoughby to be approaching, but finds Edward walking over the downs towards them; Marianne expects a proposal from Willoughby that will finally unite them, and is parted from him instead; Marianne expects a letter from Willoughby, but receives one from her mother; Elinor expects her mother's carriage, but is surprised by Willoughby's sudden arrival and explanation. These misrecognised arrivals imply a 'higher' misrecognition at the level of narration itself: one which leads the reader to expect one thing, and delivers another. The romance/realism axes, to return to Frye, indicate contradictory modes of signification: the timeless and the temporal, or the universal and the singular.

We expect Marianne to end badly, but she is saved. We expect Edward to marry Lucy out of 'duty', but he and Elinor are nonetheless blamelessly united. Marianne might reasonably have suffered the fate of both Elizas, while Elinor might reasonably have ended as a repeat figure for the pre-narrative 'sister housekeeper', whose death initiates the narrative movement. Interestingly, Elinor turns out to be the *only* character to enjoy the successful conclusion of a first attachment, even when her object is secretly 'promised' to another. Where we are led to expect a 'realist' outcome, we are given a romance union; and where we expected romance union, we find a salvational transformation.

At the beginning I expected this analysis to yield a clear version of the patrilineal/matrilineal tension that would show a consciousness of the elision of feminine will from the historical narrative. In place of this, or rather alongside it, I found something else at work. The final narrative message emerges: If the Dashwoods had not found themselves evicted from Norland, they would not have achieved their peculiarly happy outcomes. This late reversal underlines Austen's successful mediation between realist and romance epistemologies. It is a truth that can only be experienced narratively.

The narrative forks taken to achieve the 'happy ending' of *Sense and Sensibility* deserve particular attention. To summarise brutally: following the death of their father, the sisters and their mother are evicted from their family home and undertake a long journey to a new existence as relative strangers in a different kind of house and context. The move from Norland to Barton signifies an exile, a loss of privilege and property, corresponding to the 'descent' cycle of the romance frame. Marianne speaks this loss in the last words uttered before they undertake their journey: ' "Dear, dear Norland!" said Marianne, as she wandered alone before the house, on the last evening of their being there; "when shall I cease to regret you! – when learn to feel a home elsewhere! – Oh! Happy house, could you know what I suffer in now viewing you from this spot, from whence perhaps I may view you no more!" '[262] Elinor is silently separated by the move from her potential love interest. The journey marks a break between the different scenes of action, registered in a shift from the formal interiors of Norland House to the pastoral scene of the Devon cottage:

> The first part of their journey was performed in too melancholy a disposition to be otherwise than tedious and unpleasant. But as they drew towards the end of it, their interest in the appearance of a country which they were to inhabit overcame their dejection, and a view of Barton Valley as they entered it gave them cheerfulness. It was a pleasant fertile spot, well wooded, and rich in pasture. After winding along it for more than a mile, they reached their own house. A small green court was the whole of its demesne in front; and a neat wicket gate admitted them into it.[263]

Having settled into their new home, and been introduced to the new characters based at Barton Park, the 'memorable morning' arrives when Marianne decides to take Margaret for a walk on the downs. Turned back by 'a driving rain', they take 'consolation' in 'running with all possible speed down the steep side of the hill which led immediately to their garden gate.' A 'false step' brings Marianne to the ground, while Margaret 'unable to stop' keeps going to the bottom. At that moment, Willoughby is introduced:

> A gentleman carrying a gun, with two pointers playing round him, was passing up the hill and within a few yards of Marianne, when her accident happened. He put down his gun and ran to her assistance. She had raised herself from the ground, but her foot had been twisted in her fall, and she was scarcely able to stand. The gentleman offered his services, and perceiving that her modesty declined what her situation rendered necessary, took her up in his arms without farther delay, and carried her down the hill. Then passing through the garden, the gate of which had been left open by Margaret, he bore her directly into the house, whither Margaret was just arrived, and quitted not his hold till he had seated her in a chair in the parlour.[264]

Following her literal 'fall' in the mud, Marianne then falls in love with Willoughby, and spurns the older, wiser and sadder Colonel Brandon ('thirty-five has nothing to do with matrimony') who nonetheless falls in love with her just as fast ('he has loved her ... ever since the first moment of seeing her.')[265] Elinor's love interest turns out to be long pre-engaged to another (coincidentally related to the Middletons who inhabit Barton park).

During an extended stay in London, the characters (minus the mother and younger sister) recombine in ways that expose the narrative's probable outcome as 'consciousness of misery'.[266] Willoughby turns out to have seduced and abandoned Colonel Brandon's ward shortly before encountering Marianne on the hill, and – after privately and publicly rejecting her – marries yet another woman for her fortune. Elinor gives up all hope of Edward, now perceived as 'a second Willoughby', and evil seems to triumph:

> 'Poor Marianne!' said her brother to Colonel Brandon in a low voice, as soon as he could secure his attention, – 'She has not so much good health as her sister, – she is very nervous, – she has not Elinor's constitution; – and one must allow that there is something very trying to a young woman who *has been* a beauty, in the loss of her personal attractions. You would not think it perhaps, but Marianne *was* remarkably handsome a few months ago; quite as handsome as Elinor. – Now you see it is all gone'.[267]

The exposure of Edward's secret engagement to Lucy Steele enrages his wealthy and ambitious mother, who disinherits him, giving all the privileges of the first son to his younger and more 'worldly' brother, Robert. Colonel Brandon steps in to offer Edward the 'Delaford living' as a favour to Elinor, which makes the undesired wedding to Lucy Steele all the more inevitable. In a further twist, Elinor is given the role of communicating this news to Edward in person: ' "When I see him again," said Elinor to herself, as the door shut him out, "I shall see him the husband of Lucy".'[268] Marianne almost dies of a chill brought on by her self-indulgence in suffering. The narrative's darkest moment arrives as Elinor sits watching her apparently dying sister all night and into the following morning:

> She was calm, except when she thought of her mother, but she was almost hopeless; and in this state she continued till noon, scarcely stirring from her sister's bed, her thoughts wandering from one image of grief, one suffering friend to another.[269]

At noon, the scene shifts unexpectedly to one of recovery, and from here the narrative turns on the seeds of 'hope' which emerge in the midst of Elinor's hopelessness:

> About noon, however, she began – but with a caution – a dread of disappointment, which for some time kept her silent, even to her friend – to fancy, to hope she could perceive a slight amendment to her sister's pulse ... Anxiety and hope now oppressed her in equal degrees, and left her no moment of tranquillity till the arrival of Mr. Harris at four o'clock; – when his assurances, his felicitations on a recovery in her sister even surpassing his expectation, gave her confidence, comfort, and tears of joy.[270]

A number of things happen following this sudden and (on first reading at least) unexpected swerve from the demise of Marianne to her recovery, represented through Elinor's shift from 'misery' to 'hope'. First, Willoughby arrives equally unexpectedly to offer a contextual explanation for his previous behaviour and is forgiven by Elinor as well as Marianne and her mother: 'Elinor's heart was full. The past, the present, the future, Willoughby's visit, Marianne's safety, and her mother's expected arrival'.[271] Then Colonel Brandon arrives with Mrs Dashwood, to the news of Marianne's 'safety', and everyone rejoices in 'the bliss of the moment'. When they have returned to Barton, we hear the fateful news from their 'man-servant' on return from business in Exeter: 'I suppose you know, ma'am, that Mr. Ferrars is married.' We are then given an account of Elinor's hitherto unconscious 'hope':

> Elinor now found the difference between the expectation of an
> unpleasant event, however certain the mind may be told to consider
> it, and certainty itself. She now found, that in spite of herself, she had
> always admitted a hope, while Edward remained single, that some-
> thing would occur to prevent his marrying Lucy; that some resolu-
> tion of his own, some mediation of friends, or some more eligible
> opportunity of establishment for the lady, would arise to assist the
> happiness of them all. But he was now married, and she condemned
> her heart for the lurking flattery, which so much heightened the pain
> of the intelligence.

Then we have a final mistaken arrival: 'the figure of a man on horseback
drew her eyes to the window. He stopt at their gate. It was a gentleman,
it was Colonel Brandon himself. Now she could hear more; and she
trembled in expectation of it. But – it was *not* Colonel Brandon – neither
his air – nor his height. Were it possible, she must say it must be Edward.
She looked again. He had just dismounted; – she could not be mistaken; –
it *was* Edward'.[272]

When Edward Ferrars arrives to 'awaken' Elinor to the truth that he is
not in fact already married to Lucy Steele, but has instead conceded that
pleasure – alongside his inheritance – to his younger brother, he is
described indulging in an unusually unconscious 'metonymic' act:

> 'Perhaps you mean – my brother – you mean Mrs – Mrs *Robert* Ferrars.'
> 'Mrs Robert Ferrars!' – was repeated by Marianne and her mother in
> an accent of the utmost amazement; – and though Elinor could not
> speak, even *her* eyes were fixed on him with the same impatient won-
> der. He rose from his seat and walked to the window, apparently from
> not knowing what to do; took up a pair of scissars that lay there; and
> while spoiling both them and their sheath by cutting the latter to
> pieces as he spoke, said, in a hurried voice,
> 'Perhaps you do not know – you may not have heard that my
> brother is lately married to – to the youngest – to Miss Lucy Steele'.[273]

Since this is an act of 'spoiling' both the instrument of 'cutting' and its
protective 'sheath' or cover, the unusually extraneous detail might express
the narrative 'break' in Edward's narrative 'cover', and the mechanism for
'cutting' is itself shown to be spoilt in the act. Metonymy is quite literally the cutting up of a whole into representative parts, expressive of the

loss of totality, and characteristic of realism: its 'sheath', following Barthes, consists of the functional sequences – or 'cover' – which themselves 'cut up' and postpone the completion of the 'whole story'. The specific message given by Edward here – that he is *not* married, that he is no longer the 'first' brother – releases the final obstacle to Elinor's otherwise inconceivable happy ending. In so doing a metonymic identity (first brother) is revealed to be contingent, temporary, and discardable in favour of the function of romance hero.

Edward then leaves for a walk in the village, and our attention is drawn to the unexpectedness of this outcome for all involved, including at this stage the reader: 'leaving the others in the greatest astonishment and perplexity on a change in his situation, so wonderful and so sudden'. The trick is that these 'wonderful' transformations of misery into happiness, of despair into hope, are achieved without strain on the realist credentials of the narrative. The descent and ascent of romance: through exile, exposed to the trickery of strangers, near-mad with grief, paralysed by misery, the heroines are brought back from the brink to new lives of reasonable and harmonious happiness. At what point – if anywhere – does this narrative stop making claims to verisimilitude? At what point does the 'wonderful' causality of romance overtake the grim determinants of realistic and plausible representation? How do we pass from *what is* to what *should be*?

Northanger Abbey's play on the 'final determinant' of 'subject–object' relations as a harmonisation of a 'determinate subject–object polarity' returns in the question of 'individual experience' and 'collective' totality in *Sense and Sensibility*'s sliding between metonymy and metaphor. Since the final unions are achieved only once the 'whole story' is known, and even the Byronic Willoughby is forgiven once his own 'whole story' is reviewed as one of socially determined outcomes, we can approach Austen's happy endings as 'prophetic' as much as 'imaginary' resolutions, which situate the agency for change in reversals between diachronic and synchronic frames.

What do these female actants actually *do* to achieve such implausible, but convincing, harmony out of empirically documented discord? It would seem that they 'do' very little, but occupy the space of agency for the 'undoing' of the distortions of an otherwise reified realism. Elinor's restraint from acting on her feelings is precisely the model for Marianne's awakening. Catherine's adolescent inability to act, to hide her feelings for Henry also operates as a negative action. Since the structural contradictions inherent in any given mode of production, and emphasised in the 'structural polarity of capitalism' itself, constitute the very material that poses as 'potential content for the work of art', Austen's work, which mediates successfully between realist and romance modes, offers a means to consider the question of 'a collective totality which fails to have any existential equivalent in individual experience'.[274] This insolent breach of the subject–object polarity – where hope infuses the scene of representation, and alters the narrative's outcome – is precisely Austen's domain in the works which founded her subsequent claim as a narrative artist. The ending of *Sense and Sensibility* seems awkward, perhaps, because her 'prophetic' analysis 'of the idea' has not yet achieved 'its truth in the lived reality of social history.'

3
Pride and Prejudice: 'Lydia's gape'

In the face of the two possibilities which might seduce the imagination – an eternal summer or a winter just as eternal, the former licentious to the point of corruption, the latter pure to the point of sterility – man must resign himself to choosing equilibrium and the periodicity of the seasonal rhythm. In the natural order, the latter fulfils the same function which is fulfilled in society by the exchange of women in marriage and the exchange of words in conversation, when these are practised with the frank intention of communicating, that is to say, without trickery or perversity, and above all, without hidden motives.

Claude Lévi-Strauss, 'Incest and Myth'[275]

The simplest way out of the sacrificial situation, for the story-teller, is the Proserpine solution.

Northrop Frye, *Secular Scripture*[276]

8.50 am
Mmm. Wonder what Mark Darcy would be like as father (father to own offspring, mean. Not self. That would indeed be sick in manner of Oedipus)?

Bridget Jones, *Bridget Jones' Diary: The Edge of Reason*[277]

Terry Castle asked us recently to look seriously at the question: 'How bad are most of the novels produced by English women writers in the decades before Jane Austen?'[278] Since Jane Spencer demonstrated that Austen did not emerge fully formed from the mists of women's pre-literate history, we have been rightly preoccupied with documenting the relatively long and complex history of women's writing prior to Austen. Perhaps this has drawn our attention from acknowledging the specific nature of her achievement in the context of that history.

Castle finds in women's narrative writing prior to Austen a literary 'autism' which leads the reader to lose 'faith in the shaping consciousness behind the fiction'.[279] She finds evidence of a 'psychic compartmentalization', 'splitting up', or 'psychic trauma' in women's narrative writing prior to Austen. Her conclusion is that while of course socially 'empowering', women's historical acquisition of literacy 'inevitably brings with it self-division, ambivalence, and an infantile element compounded of fear and rage: fear that one's words may offend those who own writing already, rage at being cut off from discourse for so long'.

Austen 'somehow' overcomes this literary 'autism', which manifests as precisely that 'murderous, estranging hostility to parental figures' or 'Oedipal rage' evident in Wollstonecraft's work. It is in the absence of an aesthetic failure common to women's writing preceding Austen, that Castle identifies the 'miracle about which we know little': she 'invariably looks her reader in the eye'. But Castle's sense of what was specific to Austen and enabled such a literary 'miracle' to arise is provocatively discreet: 'the touch of grace, the inability to feel frightened, either of past or future', which has 'something' to do with her father. She answers her own question with an image of idealised father–daughter relations: 'the admirable Reverend Austen, whose love for his brilliant daughter shines forth in all of her compositions, had something to do with this grace', and we can only conclude that he 'did something well enough to make writing seem the most natural thing in the world'.[280]

This seems to be a turn to nostalgic biography to account for Austen's miraculous transcendence of literary distortions otherwise apparent in eighteenth-century women's literary narrative, and as a result easy to take lightly. The point remains, however: Austen is quite unique in her abiding status as the first 'great' woman novelist. She not only captures a moment of self-consciousness in the unprecedented evolution of women's (particular) narrative tradition, but also stands as a defining figure in the 'canon' of 'English Literature' itself, and more specifically the history of 'the Novel'. Castle's point is an odd one, since autism as a condition is widely believed to be an extreme form of masculinity, and the mother's positive contribution to her daughter's literary consciousness is sidelined.[281] However, the point remains that Austen achieves a narrative transcendence unavailable to her literary predecessors, and as a woman writer this *does* seem to indicate the absence of an otherwise common foreclosure of literary intelligence, which would seem to be associated with paternal power. Women writers' early attempts to achieve literary expression could be expected to have incorporated a cultural encoding of masculinity over femininity. Austen overcomes this tendency.

In the new Millenium, Austen's star continues to rise. The year 2002 witnessed the landmark opening of Chawton House Library: a unique and beautiful, material and scholarly resource to further the study of women's writing; purchased, renovated, and maintained by a private patron in Austen's name. *Pride and Prejudice* topped a poll to find women's favourite novel, and was runnerup in the recent poll to find 'the Nation's favourite literature' (The Big Read). Mr Darcy emerged triumphant, as if from Pemberley lake in a wet shirt, in a recent BBC vote to find the most fancied fictional figure of women's desire – leaving James Bond and all his bedroom skills and gadgets in second place. These three very contemporary examples of Austen's exponential appeal, within which her particular appeal to women readers is central, document the high and rising market asset of her Regency fictions, which exists in parallel to an abiding academic fascination with the highly specific aesthetic achievement the work represents. One way to appreciate the sheer scale of Austen's historical and aesthetic achievement is by contrast with her famous near-contemporary, Mary Wollstonecraft.

Mary Wollstonecraft's writing life overlaps with Austen's: Wollstonecraft lived from 1759 to 1797, Austen from 1775 to 1817. Wollstonecraft was 16 when Austen was born: the year she seems to have first made friends with Fanny Blood, who became her most intimate female companion, and whose death provoked Wollstonecraft to write her first novel (*Mary, A Fiction*, 1788). Austen had just finished the first draft of 'First Impressions', which would later become *Pride and Prejudice*, and was about to begin revising 'Elinor and Marianne' into *Sense and Sensibility*, when Wollstonecraft died in September 1797, and – according to Tomalin's biography – would have probably heard of Wollstonecraft's attempted suicide in the Spring of 1796 through a mutual family friend (Sir William East).[282] We can assume that Austen, as an intelligent literate woman, and not averse to a scandal, would in any case have become aware of Wollstonecraft's radical writings, unusual life story, and unseemly death. There is also internal evidence for considering that Austen's narratives incorporate a response to the very questions that Wollstonecraft was famous for making conscious: questions concerning women, reason, and – of course – writing.

Austen seems to refer to Wollstonecraft's work in *Pride and Prejudice* in particular.[283] This work initiated around October 1796, and was sent to Cadell publishers by Austen's father in November 1797. Rejected for publication, the manuscript was substantially rewritten around 1810–12 (Tony Tanner notes that its chronological structure is analogous to the 1811 almanac), and published in 1813. Rachel Brownstein has shown how Elizabeth Bennet echoes the tone of Wollstonecraft's *Vindication of the Rights of Woman* (1792) when she insists that her rejection of Mr Collins's proposal of convenient marriage is the utterance of 'a rational creature speaking the truth from her heart'.[284] The middle Bennet sister – Mary – is bookish and theoretical, and may figure an early version of Wollstonecraft as younger intellectual woman, living through her bookshelves: 'What say you, Mary? For you are a young lady of deep reflection I know, and read great books, and make extracts'.[285]

Mr Collins attempts to read aloud from James Fordyce's *Sermons to Young Women* (1761) for the Bennet sisters, but is undercut by Lydia's tremendous 'gape' and outburst of trivial gossip. Collins remarks in turn that it 'amazes' him 'how little young ladies are interested by books of a serious stamp, though written solely for their benefit'.[286] This scene echoes Wollstonecraft's open scorn of Fordyce's proclamations in her own 'book of a serious stamp', also written for the 'benefit' of those very young ladies. Wollstonecraft's critique of Fordyce sounds very much like one of Mary's moralising discourses: 'Dr Fordyce's sermons have long made a part of a young woman's library; nay, girls at school are allowed to read them; but I should instantly dismiss them from my pupil's, if I wished to strengthen her understanding.'[287] Wollstonecraft's sheer disdain of Fordyce's moralising strictures on female behaviour, shared by the feminist critical tradition which follows from her work, is dramatically embodied by Lydia's 'gape'.

These references to Wollstonecraft allow us to consider Austen's narrative work as a response to questions concerning women, reason, and writing that Wollstonecraft's life and work embodied. As a writing woman, I find these questions compelling, and still largely unanswered. Austen's unprecedented literary 'greatness', and her continuing popularity with women readers inside and outside the cloistered debates of the academy, begs us to consider her particular answers, as well as their longevity, carefully in our own consideration of those questions. The aesthetic 'failure' of Wollstonecraft's novels can be read as an unconscious realisation of the 'failure' of women's historical subjectivity. Wollstonecraft's narrative anti-romances offer an inverted version of the relationship of content to form exhibited by Austen. Wollstonecraft's radical argument for women's 'independence' ends in the misery, madness and/or death of her own fictional heroines, Mary and Maria. Read historically, Wollstonecraft's brilliantly broken novels capture the logical anxiety that arises when women make direct claim to reason – including a narrative claim – in the already masculine context of eighteenth-century literary culture.

Cora Kaplan has come to identify the 'instability of "femininity" ' as both 'a specific instability, an eccentric relation to the construction of sexual difference', and as a marked encounter with the 'fractured and fluctuant condition of all consciously held identity, the impossibility of a will-full, unified, and cohered subjectivity':

> Rather than approach women's difficulty in positioning themselves as writers as a question of barred access to some durable psychic state to which all humans should and can aspire, we might instead see their experience as foregrounding the inherently unstable and split character of all human subjectivity.[288]

Wollstonecraft's painful self-definition in her theoretical writing rests on the disembodiment of her rational self, in order to avoid effeminisation in the work. Femininity is explained away as a false consciousness specific to women: a humiliating dependency and resulting lack of subjective autonomy that maps onto Lacanian ideas of 'castration' as well as Kant's notion of active and passive citizenship. The articulating 'female subject' is left with no choice but to dis-identify with femininity in order to become an intelligible subject of discourse. This dis-identification reveals itself as a primary contradiction in her claim to reason, and can be traced in some detail through the fault-lines of Wollstonecraft's self-identification as a 'rational' woman.

Austen, by contrast, seems to enter signification *sans lack*, suffers no apparent symptoms of the 'humiliation' attendant on her embodiment, and makes a unique and powerful intervention in the emerging generic form of modern capitalism (the Novel). She manages this without deviating from a feminocentric style and content, and apparently without breaking sweat. The point is not so much that Austen was a better writer than Wollstonecraft, or that Austen's harmonious aesthetic implies a healthier model for female subjectivity, but that her aesthetic achievement avoids the pitfalls of cultural masculinisation. Something that is broken in Wollstonecraft's encounter with narrative remains untouched in Austen's.

If most women really do still want what Austen made Elizabeth Bennet realise she wanted two hundred years ago, as recent polls indeed imply, then as serious readers of Austen it behoves us to sit up and listen. This may not simply mean that what we/they want is Colin Firth in a Regency wet shirt (although I can think of worse ways to spend a Sunday evening). Both Wollstonecraft and Austen could be said to be engaging the problem that is rational female subjectivity under less than ideal social conditions. Wollstonecraft's theoretical paradigm tends finally towards a repudiation of the humiliations attendant on femininity under 'capitalist-patriarchy', and results in the claim to a problematically disembodied rationality for woman. This position is inevitably plagued by the 'eternal return' of the repressed feminine-maternal, which can be read as a hysterical symptom operating as counter-rhythm to the theoretical text claiming rationality for the female subject. Austen's work indicates an (admittedly unfashionable) alternative *narrative* route to rational autonomy.

Austen's six complete novels offer tantalising glimpses of the subtle range of feminine agency within the lesser or greater material and proprietal constraints of domestic existence. These narratives work through variations on the harmonic realisation of domestic tableaux disordered by the social demands of courtship, as experienced and understood through the consciousness of a young woman between adolescence and marriage. It is significant, given her eye for living detail and her realist tone, that Austen gives all her mature heroines a happy ending. The problem of the Austen happy ending for autonomous female subjectivity is pronounced in feminist interpretation. As Rosalind Coward reminds us, Austen's work situates itself in a field of reference 'where significant events may happen, after which [the heroine's] choices and identity are lost for ever'.[289]

Or are they? Under the revision of 'choices' offered by the dialectical structure of Austen's narrative work, we are brought to consider plausible routes towards positive agency, embodied in female characters, to reform and transform the otherwise degraded social context. The happy ending, after all, is only satisfactory if it offers the heroine rational autonomy as well as domestic bliss. Emma Woodhouse, Elizabeth Bennet, Anne Elliot, Catherine Morland, Elinor and Marianne Dashwood, and even Fanny Price, epitomise recognisable characteristics of rational female subjectivity finally unmarked by 'hysteria' or 'neurosis'. Their respective engagements in negotiation of the dangerous waters of possible outcomes, once faced with a common rite of passage from daughter to autonomous subject, map out abstract routes for positive resolutions of the social fate of women in the necessary transition from child to adult: a feminocentric focalisation of the 'quest' narrative.

Critical frustration with Austen's happy endings seems founded in a belief that the heroine can only be a heroine in isolation, or at best in female community. But Austen's narrative model of the possibility of objective freedom for autonomous feminine subjectivity, unmarred by hysteria or neurosis, is embedded in a conclusion centred specifically on her desire to be wed. The marital ending registers an overcoming of difference, a meeting of minds, a breach – through love – of the terms of individuation and sexual difference that otherwise seem to govern realist representation.

The common resolution offered to Austen's heroines, providential marriage, works explicitly to align individual and social destiny. Elizabeth and Darcy's union at one and the same time signals the positive reform of the female character, of the male suitor, and of the social world in which they figure. Austen's marriages consistently satisfy the conditions for narrative closure by harmonising otherwise contradictory demands on the novelistic field of reference: the heroine's need for rational autonomy, self-regulation, and freedom from undue restraint (which demands at some level a satisfactory exit from the realm of the family); the male partner's need for (re)connection to the affective domain signalled by the ethics of love (mutuality, moderation of desire, and open communication of feeling); the unbending material determinants (represented as precise – 'concrete' – economic forces determining the happy endings) that must mediate the union; as well as the formal liter- ary determinants of the romance paradigm. Each parallel series must find its proper completion before conditions make the happy ending necessary, sufficient, and hence inevitable.

By far the most popular example, *Pride and Prejudice* (1813), presents these competing demands as incommensurate, but shows them brought into harmonious relation as the key characters approach their union. Elizabeth Bennet, when forced to speak on the subject late in the narra- tive, makes a startling declaration of autonomy: 'I am only resolved to act in that manner, which will, in my own opinion, constitute my hap- piness, without reference to you, or to any person so wholly uncon- nected with me'. This scene famously inverts Elizabeth's earlier refusal of Darcy's unexpected first proposal of marriage, when he asserts that she 'must allow me to tell you how ardently I admire and love you'.[290] The narrative route offered by Darcy's first proposal, if then accepted by the heroine, would doubtlessly have answered her material and perhaps – eventually – her romantic needs. But at this point in her nar- rative sequence, the proposal is directly against her will; she does *not* wish to allow him to tell her.

The narrative turn between first and second proposals, during which Elizabeth and Darcy are both awakened to new perceptions of their situ- ations, allows precisely for the conditions attendant on her autonomy of will to be established. 'You could not have made me the offer of your hand in any possible way that would have tempted me to accept it', is finally shown to have precluded the one possible way of offering and receiving that the narrative then makes possible.[291] Between Elizabeth's arch rejection of the first proposal and easy acceptance of the second, Austen simply reverses the context. The first proposal illuminates a scene in which what we might call Wollstonecraft's paradigm dominates, where marriage is oppressive and in spite of the heroine's will. The second illuminates an alternative that testifies to the healing agency of 'love', as represented through the providential marriage, which – as the culmination of 'full identity' – reaches the limit of narrative representability: 'removed from society so little pleasing to either, to all the comfort and elegance of their family party at Pemberley'.[292] It is easy to assume that the heroine has undergone a great change in character to allow for this reversal, but her stance in both scenes is identical with regard to her claim to autonomy. The specific difference illuminated by reversal between the parallel scenes is in her perception of Darcy, now a collaborator in her narrative of possible freedom.

The heroine's threatened absence of freedom is narrated through the sequence of unwilled or imposed proposals, painfully observed in Mr Collins' truly creepy assertion that 'now nothing remains for me but to assure you in the most animated language of the violence of my affection'.[293] Elizabeth's only available action here is to insist that her own will must be consulted: 'Accept my thanks for the compliment you are paying me. I am very sensible of the honour of your proposals, but it is impossible for me to do otherwise than decline them.'[294] This assertion is overlooked by Collins, and interpreted by Mrs Bennet as 'headstrong', then highlighted as beside the point by her further plea to Mr Bennet: 'come and make Lizzy marry Mr Collins, for she vows she will not have him'.[295]

Mr Elton's proposal to Emma, and Thorpe's to Catherine, underline the same 'logical anxiety' of absence of feminine desire in an economically or sexually approvable union. Mr Collins' proposal also answers the founding narrative anxiety posed by the 'entail' on the Longbourne estate, and would elevate Elizabeth to her mother's place as Lady of the house. In fact Charlotte Lucas takes this place in an ironic recasting of Mrs Bennet's own conquest of her husband. A similar solution is posed to Anne Elliot, when Mr Elliot offers her the opportunity to revive her mother by marrying the heir to her own estate, otherwise lost to an entail. The heroine's strongest action in these narratives, given the codes of civility that prevent a sharp knee to the groin, is to assert her will by saying 'no'. This rejection preserves the condition of her availability to the providential marriage that connotes her happy ending.

The heroine's negation seems to be the hinge on which the narrative transformation that establishes the conditions for a happy ending turns.

More dangerous yet are instances where the heroine's will is temporarily inclined to say 'yes' to the wrong suitor; exhibited in Elizabeth's open attraction to Wickham, as well as Marianne's 'passion' for Willoughby, Emma's flirtation with Frank, and Anne's close encounter with Mr Elliot. Each present a fork in the heroine's narrative path, or a near-miss, that – if taken – would have found her relatively well-married, or relatively free, but lost to her own final salvation or objective freedom.

For Barthes, these near-misses illuminate the narrative sequence as 'made up of a small number of nuclei' which 'always involves moments of risk'. 'At every one of these points, an alternative – and hence a freedom of meaning – is possible.'[296] The heroine's avoidance of the wrong marriage is as important to her happy ending as her final recognition and acceptance of the right one. When the heroine finds herself positioned within a narrative sequence leading to a mistaken marriage, her only available agency is negation. The denials and refusals uttered at these moments forge a break between the redeemable and the delusional, subject to correction later in the narrative. In Frye's analysis, these moments of denial represent the 'recognition of the demonic and its separation from the progressive or surviving elements'.[297]

Marriage in spite of female will is as dangerous to Austen's heroines as it is to Wollstonecraft's, and always connotes rape. But Austen goes on to propose a reinterpretation of marriage as an appropriate object of a rational feminine desire, and a reinterpretation of rational femininity that is centred on the possibility of love. *Pride and Prejudice* contextualises the providential marriage of Elizabeth and Darcy against the incomplete conditions of a range of unsatisfactory unions. Mr and Mrs Bennet's marriage, founded on Mrs Bennet's 'youth and beauty', is warped by the absence of her husband's '[r]espect, esteem, and confidence'; Charlotte Lucas accepts Mr Collins, and wins a relative domestic truce, but at the sacrifice of intimacy; Elizabeth is warned off 'an affection [for Wickham] which the want of fortune would make so very imprudent'. Most dramatically, Lydia demonstrates the dangers of female will unrestrained by 'the periodicity of the seasonal rhythm', regulated by civility, in allowing herself to be abducted by the same man.[298]

This last pairing is particularly contrasted with Elizabeth and Darcy's providential union, at a moment when that union seems most unlikely: 'But no such marriage could now teach the admiring multitude what connubial felicity really was. An union of a different tendency, and precluding the possibility of the other, was soon to be formed in their

family.'[299] The providential marriage is carefully marked out by its negation in these examples of inadequate relations. Lydia's tremendous gape
in response to Mr Collins' attempt to read from Fordyce's *Sermons*,
which aims primarily to teach young ladies the importance of modesty,
takes on a remarkably sexual connotation in the light of her subsequent
'licentious' marriage.[300]

> If the female sex thus represents, in Sartre's words 'the obscenity … of
> everything which gapes open', then men seem to be justified in their
> instrumental attitude to women and to everything, including nature,
> which has been 'feminised' and which must therefore be distanced,
> controlled, aestheticised, subdued.[301]

Elizabeth and Darcy's 'frank' exchange of words in conversation, by contrast, establishes their union as a site of moderated exchange conducive
of 'equilibrium'. This argument is usefully inverted in Arielle Eckstut's
brilliant imagining of Austen's 'lost sex scenes':

> Both were in the throes of desire; and desire had outstripped
> sense. Elizabeth took advantage of their weakened state and pulled
> Mr. Darcy down to the ground. A quick glance over her shoulder con-
> firmed that the Gardiners were deep in conversation with a cow at
> least a mile off. She arranged him on the grass and with an unex-
> pected gesture sat square on his middle with her muslin gathered
> round her knees. With leisurely determination she advanced her
> hands up his chest. She slowed and prolonged the anticipation of
> their first kiss to a near halt until at last her lips just brushed his.
> 'I hope the weather has not been too wet for you while at Rosings,
> Mr Darcy?' The warm breath of each of Elizabeth's words was felt
> upon his lips.
> 'No, I am rather partial to all things wet, Miss Bennet. It makes
> going inside all the more pleasant.'[302]

This return of the repressed during the fateful visit to Pemberley is imagined specifically under conditions of the absence of the usual terms of
their intense conversation: 'They did not speak for some time, and both
luxuriated in the pleasant and, to them, unique sensation that nothing
at all needed to be said: that the only necessity was to restore the appearance of their clothes, which had been so enthusiastically disturbed.'[303]

Darcy's two proposals mark his own split identity: divided between
the objective weight of 'claims of duty, honour, and gratitude', and a

more unfamiliar, subjective, inclination inspired by the heroine, and expressed in terms of 'feelings' and 'inclination'. Darcy's 'feelings' literally breach the demands of social and familial 'duty'; they 'will not be repressed', leading him to blurt 'how ardently I love and admire you', in spite of his 'sense of her inferiority – of its being a degradation – of the family obstacles which judgment had always opposed to inclination'.[304] Elizabeth is rational enough to find this scene at the time 'gratifying' – but it is only in the context of a narrative reinterpretation of her autonomy of will, simultaneous with a narrative reinterpretation of Darcy's 'abominable pride', that she can maintain her rational autonomy and accept his second proposal: 'her sentiments had undergone so material a change, since the period to which he alluded, as to make her receive with gratitude and pleasure, his present assurances'.[305]

Her 'sentiments', because the context for Darcy's proposal has by now reversed: where her autonomy was under the earlier conditions preserved by the virginal 'no', now it can be realised through the bridal 'yes'. This is the Prosperpine solution of Frye's account of the Romance: while marriage has been convincingly demonstrated by the narrative to work against the relative claims to freedom of its female characters (Wollstonecraftian hell), it might *also* offer an image of specifically Austenian freedom, but only when Elizabeth has realised that union with Darcy is her own will after all.

Darcy has meanwhile shifted seamlessly, through the eyes of Elizabeth whose vision we are invited to share, from representing a possibility of relative material well-being for the heroine, a preoccupation since the novel's famous opening scene, to acting as agent of 'vertical transcendence'. Georg Lukács understands the 'irony of the novel' as 'the self-correction of the world's fragility: inadequate relations can transform themselves into a fanciful yet well-ordered round of misunderstandings and cross-purposes, within which everything is seen as many-sided'.[306] Elizabeth experiences a transformation of consciousness, which allows for a reinterpretation of her context: she literally sees things differently by the time of Darcy's second proposal. Darcy is both the catalyst for that transformation, and the transformed object of its new vision. Since the reader is given access to the heroine's consciousness, a successful reading experience will be one that shares in this transformation of 'no' into 'yes'.

A key moment in the narrative transformation of consciousness occurs through Elizabeth's reading of Darcy's letter, which follows his rejected proposal and reviews the narrative events to date from a new perspective. We read the letter with Elizabeth; it is reproduced directly and forms a long digression. She shifts, under the burden of reinterpreted evidence it presents, from 'a strong prejudice against everything he might say' to her recognition that 'I have courted prepossession and ignorance, and driven reason away, where either were concerned. Till this moment I never knew myself.'[307] This is Frye's restoration of memory, where partial perception gives way to complete knowledge: 'The theme of restoring the memory is, naturally, often an element in the recognition scene itself, as the action then normally returns to the beginning of the story and interprets it more truly than the previous account has done.'[308] The 'more true' understanding of events seems to imply the overcoming of subjective prejudices, or partiality, in the heroine's view of her object and the world in which he figures.

While Bingley is generally applauded for being a 'single man of large fortune; four or five thousand a year', Darcy offers transcendence of materiality itself with his perfectly aestheticised status as land-owning gentry. His first introduction to the narrative is as Bingley's friend: 'another young man' with his 'fine, tall person, handsome features, noble mien; and the report which was in general circulation within five minutes after his entrance, of his having ten thousand a year' and a 'large estate in Derbyshire'.[309] The full narrative significance of Pemberley remains indistinct until reinterpreted as the proper, and inevitable, context for the heroine's freedom, at which point it takes on the aura of a world governed by 'authentic value':

> The park was very large, and contained great variety of ground. They entered it in one of its lowest points, and drove for some time through a beautiful wood, stretching over a wide extent. ... They gradually ascended for half a mile, and then found themselves at the top of a considerable eminence, where the wood ceased, and the eye was instantly caught by Pemberley House, situated on the opposite side of a valley, into which the road with some abruptness wound. It was a large, handsome, stone building, standing well on rising ground, and backed by a ridge of high woody hills; – and in front, a stream of some natural importance was swelled into greater, but without any artificial appearance. Its banks were neither formal, nor falsely adorned. Elizabeth was delighted. She had never seen a place for which nature had done more, or where natural beauty had been so little counteracted by an awkward taste. They were all of them warm in their admiration; and at that moment she felt, that to be mistress of Pemberley might be something![310]

As experience and reflection correct the false perceptions of pride and prejudice in all the parties, the heroine's marriage can finally be offered as an event that harmonises and heals the degenerate world in which she has found herself, as well as healing her own partial and mistaken knowledge:

> She began now to comprehend that he was exactly the man, who, in disposition and talents, would most suit her. His understanding and temper, though unlike her own, would have answered all her wishes. It was an union that must have been to the advantage of both; by her ease and liveliness, his mind might have been softened, his manners improved, and from his judgement, information, and knowledge of the world, she must have received benefit of greater importance.[311]

The social healing of the union is figured as the moral reform of key characters, achieved by the resolution of mistaken narratives and misperceptions of character between Elizabeth and Darcy: 'But think no more of the letter. The feelings of the person who wrote, and the person who received it, are now so widely different from what they were then, that every unpleasant circumstance attending it, ought to be forgotten. You must learn some of my philosophy. Think only of the past as its remembrance gives you pleasure.'[312] Austen's heroines display a dialectical self-consciousness which transforms objective problems into subjective solutions of negation or acceptance. The heroine's transformation from fallen (degraded) subject via 'vertical transcendence' to objective freedom is clearly marked, but in terms that remain recognisable as belonging to the world of plausible reality. The union that forms the apex of the heroine's transcendence is also the smallest possible unit of collectivity, signalling a harmonisation of irreducible difference. Frye notes how 'original identity' is figured in romance by 'symbolism of the garden of Eden', in which the 'social' is 'reduced to the love of individual men and women within an order of nature which has been reconciled to humanity'.[313] It is interesting, then, that the bold adaptation of this narrative into contemporary Bollywood represents Elizabeth and Darcy's relationship as analogous to colonised/coloniser under postcolonial conditions.[314]

The impact of the marriage, once settled, and its causal history thoroughly reviewed by Elizabeth and Darcy, is detailed character by character in the last three chapters following the proposal. These chapters follow the impact of the news of the marriage on widening circles of characters, repeating the moment of reinterpretation in the light of its fact through various scenes of Elizabeth re-narrating the story of their mutual shift from mistaken dislike (pride and prejudice) via revelation to love: first Jane, then Mr Bennet, then Mrs Bennet, Mrs Gardiner, Lady Catherine, Mr Collins, Miss Darcy, Miss Bingley, Sir William Lucas and finally Wickham and Lydia, are shown in their respective reactions to the news of the marriage, and judged in the light of it, according to their acceptance of the 'authenticity' of its value in spite of the apparent mismatch it formerly represented. The reader's own relief at news of the marriage implies that the reinterpretation of 'world', characters, and events, made possible by this providential union, extends beyond the confines of the fiction and into the consciousness of the reader. This direct engagement of readerly desire might explain why a member of the BBC panel discussing the shortlist of the 'Big Read' poll recently described *Pride and Prejudice* as 'better than Prozac'. It might also contextualise the fact that Austen's novels have been dispensed as therapy for shell-shocked soldiers in times of war.

Narrative is argued to hold a privileged relationship with identity, and the movement of romance narrative comprises a pattern oscillating between loss, forgetting, or confusion of identity and regaining, remembering, or understanding of 'original identity'. 'Identity' has, since Freud at least, been understood within a frame of reference adapted to abstract masculinity. The quest narrative that seems to underlie narrative formations is centred on a hero searching for a lost object, of which he remains unconscious, but in perpetual search of which he is driven by an unnamed, or displaced, desire. This narrative is captured in the Oedipal myth, and as Barthes notes: 'without wanting to strain the phylogenetic hypothesis, it may be significant that it is at one and the same moment (around the age of three) that the little human "invents" at once sentence, narrative, and the Oedipus'.[315]

The question begged by Austen's narratives is, at its most abstract, 'how might things change for the better?' Jameson returns to the romance as a past genre of providential causality, externalised residue of 'necessity', through which we can glimpse something significant about the present. He notes that Frye's religious frame of reference aligns with the Marxist notion of 'final determination':

any comparison of Marxism with religion is a two-way street, in which the former is not necessarily discredited by its association with the latter. On the contrary, such a comparison may also function to rewrite certain religious concepts – most notably Christian histori-cism and the 'concept' of providence ... as anticipatory foreshadow-ings of historical materialism within precapitalist social formations in which scientific thinking is unavailable as such.[316]

For Jameson, romance 'does not involve the substitution of some more ideal realm for ordinary reality', but 'a process of transforming ordinary reality'. As a result, the quest that centres romance narrative form is 'the search of the libido or desiring self for a fulfillment that will deliver it from the anxieties of reality but will still contain that reality'.[317] Austen's novels turn on just such a 'magical' transformation of misery into joy, separation into union, limitation into freedom; and without sacrificing the terms of 'realist' verisimilitude and mimesis.

The subjective desire initiated and satisfied by Austen's narratives is specifically and decidedly feminine; and apparently still recognisable to contemporary women. Is this really desire for a Regency gentleman to come and make it all better that has endured feminist analysis of the 'false consciousness' of women's romance fantasies? A real dream of sexual harmony? Another bloody ideology? We might rather consider it a manifest desire for the transformation of an 'ordinary reality'.

Raymond Williams understands 'the realist tradition in fiction' as work which 'creates and judges the quality of a whole way of life in terms of the qualities of persons'. The key works of this tradition subor-dinate neither individual nor social context, but maintain a vision that allows us to consider 'a whole way of life, a society that is larger than any of the individuals composing it' without losing sight of the creative agency of 'human beings who, while belonging to and affected by and helping to define this way of life, are also, in their own terms, absolute ends in themselves.' Crucially, 'neither the society nor the indi-vidual, is there as a priority', and 'society is not a background against which the personal relationships are studied, nor are the individuals merely illustrations of aspects of the way of life.' It is precisely the inter-penetration of individual and collective consciousness, then, that cen-tres the narrative tradition in which Austen figures: '[e]very aspect of personal life is radically affected by the quality of the general life, yet the general life is seen at its most important in completely personal terms'.[318]

Jane Austen is not the first writer to centre this cultural ambition on a female individual. Samuel Richardson and Daniel Defoe are famous for focalising novelistic consciousness through a socially marginal female character (Pamela and Moll Flanders), and Austen clearly builds on the earlier narrative work of Frances Burney in particular. But Austen's work offers certainly the most successful – in terms of complete – alignment of feminine subjectivity and narrative consciousness in the Anglophone tradition. The individual in society is the 'content' of the novel as a literary mode. Put simply: if the individual is feminine, then the 'quality of the general life' exhibited cannot be straightforwardly generalised to the level of the human, without a transformation in the definition of 'human' that goes well beyond gender.

If 'a substantial work of literature is always about how one way of life is yielding to another', we can read the world of characters and problems presented in Austen as a literary swansong.[319] The intensity of these narratives is centred on a subjective transformation, or yielding, which produces a distinctively happy ending for the heroine. This internal, narrative transformation does not, however, align with external, social, factors known to be the context for Austen's writing. In fact, it reverses the movement, so that optimism is restored to the reader in spite of the irreversible decline of the world she celebrates as well as satirises (or celebrates in satire). This is why Austen never really fits the history-of-female-oppression model that is the bedrock of feminist analysis, but also why she is considered a 'great' novelist. Her work is not so much of mournful retrospective, although taken up as exemplary heritage literature: rather, a narrative study of the novels reveals a striking trajectory for feminine consciousness, which implies a social agency outside of the familiar rhetoric of 'oppression' and 'struggle'.

It has become axiomatic that women in the affluent West are progressing through a chronology from greater to lesser 'oppression': emerging slowly from social conditions which have generally denied them full access to educational, economic, material, sexual, and cultural forms of agency and self-expression. Rosi Braidotti identifies herself writing 'as a woman' in terms of writing as 'a subject emerging from a history of oppression and exclusion'.[320] The implications of this argument for the literary critic are clear: remove these forms of oppression, as tending to social exclusion, and women can achieve levels of aesthetic and social expression previously only seen in the work of men. The point can lead to Austen's biography to find what was different about *this* particular woman: if the argument concerning women's historical oppression are correct, then Austen simply should not have been able to do what she seems to have done. The problem with this argument seems to be that it positions aesthetic realisation itself as a craft, or skill, to be acquired under specific material conditions which women have traditionally been denied. In a more positive light, Terry Castle's suggestion that 'women always lag about a century behind in the history of major cultural shifts', allows us to consider a similar 'lag' in their incorporation by an increasingly totalised system of ideology. Women might turn out to have known more than should by now be known, and be hiding it as well as they can. The romance seems a good place to begin to look for this otherwise lost knowledge.

The historical oppression-of-women argument identifies 'patriarchy' as the overarching context for women's aesthetic work. The concept of patriarchy has been defined as 'a strategy which will eliminate not men, but masculinity, and transform the whole web of psycho-sexual relations in which masculinity and femininity are formed'.[321] More recently, patriarchy has become the context for feminist cultural analysis and activism:

> Feminists have taken up the struggle over the production, distribution, and transformation of meaning in a number of specific cultural practices as a focus of political intervention and opposition in order to challenge the forms of representation which constrain and oppress them.[322]

Patriarchy, it could be argued, oppresses feminists more than anyone else, in the way that capitalism particularly oppresses Marxists: both concepts certainly oppress me when I stop to think about them. The 'oppression' of women under 'patriarchy' has been evidenced in a myriad of ways since women 'seized the means' of literary and social criticism. Everywhere I now turn to think through the questions posed by women's writing, I am reminded that I am of an historically oppressed sex, and should feel humiliated and angry at my oppression, often in language raised to incite oppositional 'struggle':

> On every side we see women troubled, exhausted, mutilated, lonely, guilty, mocked by the headlined success of the few. The reality of women's lives is work, most of it unpaid and, what is worse, unappreciated. Every day we hear of women abused; every day we hear of new kinds of atrocities perpetrated on the minds and bodies of women; yet every day we are told that there is nothing left to fight for. We have come a long way, but the way has got steeper, rockier, more dangerous, and we have taken many casualties. We have reached a point where the way ahead seems to have petered out. The old enemies, undefeated, have devised new strategies; new assailants lie in ambush. We have no choice but to turn and fight.[323]

Everywhere, that is, but in the romance: where the struggle is between subjective desire and objective determinants, and one which can only be resolved by an apparently impossible, or empirically implausible, synthesis between these. One question raised by the persistence of Austen's romance, then, is whether – given the apparently ongoing alienation of feminine consciousness – we should spend our remaining energies in a struggle with oppressive material conditions, or in a struggle with our own 'ideological' desires. Neither struggle seems particularly conducive to a peaceful life at the level of the individual or the collective. The point is not so much that artistic synthesis is preferable to political struggle, but that political struggle *participates in* social disharmony, and that true harmony – social or aesthetic – cannot really be founded on struggle, except perhaps the struggle to awaken from a nightmare. Synthesis depends on a true relationship between the subject and its objects; struggle has nothing to do with this truth.

Austen's narratives of the triumph of feminine consciousness do not treat of oppression as much as of liberation: the resurrection over the cross, the comedic over the tragic, the happy ending in spite of carefully designated empirical odds. Romance is in Austen's hands a comedic formation: wish-fulfilment towards restoring the fallen world otherwise apprehended in myth. It cannot be avoided that the feminine romance tends to represent this wish for restoration, the quest of myth itself, in figures of idealised courtship.

Women's particular, and lasting, contribution to the novel is to embody the hero of the mythic quest for the sheer possibility of an unfallen world, in which social necessity is shown to give way to objective freedom, in figures of feminine agency. But if feminine romance is recognised only as outmoded fantasy, subjective wish-fulfilment, 'false consciousness', which has to give way to the more tragic forms of 'social realism' as a more appropriate and accurate mode of narrative representation, then this tendency remains a curiosity. I want to claim instead that Austen's narrative art manifests the kind of power described by Adorno:

> the greatness of works of art lies solely in their power to let things be heard which ideology conceals. Whether intended or not, their success transcends false consciousness.[324]

Recent critical thought understands the structural position of the feminine subject as inherently ambiguous. This ambiguity is productive of significantly different truth claims which would be expected to contradict – or at least speak back at – social hegemony, understood from this perspective as 'patriarchy'. Feminine romance, then, might claim an epistemic specificity, but only after considerable work:

> Perhaps the central paradox running through the [debate concerning female epistemology] has been that any attempt to define a feminist epistemology requires an acknowledgement that we seek recognition of a gendered identity that has itself, in Patricia Waugh's words, 'been constructed through the very culture and ideological formations which feminism seeks to challenge and dismantle'.[325]

So we cannot claim that Austen's work embodies a peculiarly female 'stimmung', without acknowledging that the very concept of 'femaleness' on which this claim rests has been externally defined, or 'constructed', and cannot really evidence anything but its own necessarily false consciousness. Accepting this, it remains nonetheless that the happy-ending-in-spite-of-empirical-odds common to Austen's mature narrative work, when understood as a 'socially symbolic act', can take us some way towards apprehending a particular tension between material determinants (captured at the level of realist content) and feminine desire (captured at the level of 'romance' form). Expressed another way: we love Austen because she effectively mediates the gap between the feminine imaginary and the masculine symbolic, in such a way as to suggest that things may not turn out as badly as current coordinates might seem to threaten.

Austen's particular 'substitution' for the 'magical causality' available to Medieval romances is a knowing narrative providence that works through form to harmonise discord between desires and their objects; in the process converging the various levels of determination towards the 'happy ending' that emerges in spite of realist obstacles and interruptions.[326] Austenian providence speaks back at the 'necessity' of her social context, and the work continues to speak of a providential consciousness to an enthusiastic audience. But there is less religious than economic determination in Austen's work, perhaps because her faith has been displaced onto narrative causality itself. Mr Bennet responds in a characteristically interesting way to Mrs Bennet's excitement for 'our girls' on news that '[a] single man of large fortune' is moving into their neighbourhood:

> 'How so? How can it affect them?'
> 'My dear Mr Bennet,' replied his wife, 'how can you be so tiresome! You must know that I am thinking of his marrying one of them.'
> 'Is that his design in settling here?'
> 'Design! Nonsense, how can you talk so!'

Jane is described to Charlotte Lucas by Elizabeth as 'not acting by design' in her relationship with Bingley, and Charlotte suggests that she might add a little design to her actions if she means to catch him in the end.[327] 'Design' is an interesting term in both cases, with possible connotations ranging through 'intention', 'meaning', 'planning' to 'creation', it implies a narrative consciousness of 'design' as providential in the hands of the narrator, but as wilful manipulation in the hands of human agents.

Each novel waits on the moment of self-consciousness in the heroine before the degraded perception of a fallen world and its objects turns (back) towards the paradisal: we never see beyond this indication of direction, the unfallen world is crucially not subject to direct representation. The lesson is in the turn itself. Elizabeth and Darcy recede from our view under cover of the narrative summary which sees them released to 'all the comfort and elegance of their family party at Pemberley'. Their union signals the beginning of something beyond the terms of narrative representability. Richardson, in going beyond this point and documenting Pamela's marital experiences, following her miraculous conversion of Mr B, maintains her at the status of mere wife, rather than allowing her to ascend to the realistically impossible terms of the romance heroine. Austen's work, by contrast, incorporates the 'generic message' of the structural principles of romance as 'a mediatory or harmonizing mechanism' in itself. This move effectively appropriates the comedic potential of the romance for feminine consciousness.

The 'romance' mode is shown by Austen to be structurally conducive to feminine wish-fulfilment. This alignment of what we might term abstract 'femininity' with the distinct narrative mode recognisable as 'romance' displaces the tragically inclined tropes demanded by a realism already solidifying in the fires of industrialisation. The feminisation of romance? But the form itself has always had the potential to gather into its representational content material conducive to feminine self-representation, as both Frye and Doody demonstrate in different ways.[328] Austen's specific intervention in this long narrative tradition is to make explicit the mediation of the plausible with the nonetheless possible. The 'truth' universally denied remains an unreasonably romantic desire.

4
Mansfield Park:
'she does not like to act'

Give us grace to endeavour after a truly Christian spirit to seek to attain that temper of forbearance and patience of which our blessed saviour has set us the highest example; and which, while it prepares us for the spiritual happiness of the life to come, will secure to us the best enjoyment of what this world can give.

Jane Austen, Prayer III[329]

We are quite unable to tell whether the language of mysticism resulted from a materialization of the spiritual – in which event the latter would be a first cause – or on the contrary from a sublimation of physiological phenomena – in which case these phenomena must underlie what is being expressed. But one thing is certain: we are confronted with two factors which never exist singly. That should content everyone, although in fact it contents no one.

Denise de Rougemont, Love in the Western World[330]

Let other pens dwell on guilt and misery. I quit such odious subjects as soon as I can, impatient to restore every body, not greatly faulty in themselves, to tolerable comfort, and to have done with all the rest.

Jane Austen, Mansfield Park[331]

It has already been noted by Michael Giffin that Austen works within a paradigm of orthodox Georgian Anglican ideology, representing 'soteria' in a way that situates her characters and their problems in relation to the possibility of salvation in a fallen world.[332] I would extend that argument to claim that Austen's narratives mediate between the apparently incommensurable domains of material and ideational worlds, refigured in the more abstract structuring principles of romance finally overcoming the resistance of realism, and figuring in turn the salvational logic of feminine wish-fulfilment; incrementally mediating the fallen with the paradisal. Some literary heroine. And the 'persistence' of Austen in the twenty first century suggests that there remains a desire for just such a 'transformation of the reader's subjective attitudes'.[333] Austen writes explicitly of the possibility of salvation in concrete terms of particular, still recognizable, incarnations of feminine desires and the conditions for overcoming their obstacles. Since the abstractions of desire that she captures transfer across starkly different historical and cultural conditions, her work remains a vehicle for this abstract salvational equation which shapes the narrative form.

The historical Jane Austen bears traits of the virginal romance heroine herself: never married, and never consummating her own desires (which at one level might explain their capacity for persistence). She was infamously overlooked in her own time, and lived a life of what would now be considered humiliating domestic servitude for a professional woman writer, but has since ascended to the highest terms of cultural recognition. Her virginity aligns with one pole of the terms of romance heroine, functioning in her own life-narrative to represent 'a lifelong sublimation expressing itself as a commitment, or spiritual marriage, to something impersonal, such as religious devotion or a political cause', and which itself coincides with belief in 'a world above that of the main action of the story'.[334]

In spite of at least one serious offer, Austen remained unmarried, remained a daughter, and never achieved the successful transition into autonomous subjectivity she imagines so well for her heroines. In 1802, the story goes, she received a proposal from Harris Bigg-Wither, a respectable gentleman of considerable property in Hampshire and an old acquaintance of the family. She accepted his offer, only to change her mind following a night's reflection (to the mortification of both families).[335] Jane Austen could have been very well married, then, and one can't help but wonder what would have become of the six narratives we know so well if she had produced as many children as her own mother. At one level this helps us to understand her insistent narrative idealisation of marriage as an exit to another world, in which the female character achieves economic and sexual autonomy and power, but of which she seems to have no direct representational power. At another level we might consider that she had known personal versions of a beginning to this story, and well understood the various paths towards a middle and an end, but experienced in her own life no completion of the romance equation she nonetheless knew so well.

We might say that Austen was working on realising the necessary and sufficient conditions for her own transformation from object to subject, and that she wove her experience of (realist) beginnings into (fantasy) romance narratives of dangerous middles and idealised endings. But she remains very precise about the conditions for transformation of the ground for completion of the heroine's romance cycle: the heroine must first realise that she has been mistaken – subjective reversal – and be overtaken by the truth of her context, which reveals a happy ending – objective transformation – she could not have dreamt of before its occurrence. This may indeed be an example of Christian humanism, but it is one with strong consequences for the feminine subject imagined as its key narrative agent. Frye is keen to stress that the 'redemptive female' is a 'pre-Christian' narrative figure.[336]

Austen showed herself entirely *capable* of producing powerful narratives centred on female characters who achieved their desires without reference to *any* notion of restraint: her early experiments in narrative including the remarkable *Lady Susan* (w. 1793–34?) confirm this. This complete epistolary study of manipulative, wilful, unfeeling maternal subjectivity is marked by the sudden intervention of a narrative voice at some distance from Lady Susan's consciousness:

> Whether Lady Susan was, or was not happy in her second choice – I do not see it can ever be ascertained – for who would take her assurance of it, on either side of the question? The world must judge from probability. She had nothing against her, but her husband, and her conscience.[337]

It is all the more striking, then, that her six famous narratives forward an equation for feminine agency, and the fulfilment of desire, that would situate what we commonly take for assertion of female will as the 'illusion' to be dispelled on the way to objective freedom. The Wollstonecraftian inversion of romance – that women's 'true' identity is precisely 'lost' in heterosexual marriage and the subordination of feminine will this involves – can itself be characterised as the swallowing whole of a 'representational fallacy' forged in the fires of capitalist exchange, and tending to the reification of reason. Austen offers an alternative account of the 'subjection' of heterosexual marriage that recasts 'subjection' itself as a salvational femininity, and this is the generative seed of the 'irony' for which she remains most famous.

Understood through the Christian notion of humility that is most familiar to her, the subjugation of will to a higher ordinance *is* the healing of identity. Faced with the consciousness – differently realised in Wollstonecraft – that feminine submission under patriarchy is humiliation and loss of identity, evident of a symbolic rape that silences female will and objectifies female being, the path taken up by Austen faces two directions: femininity (as masochism) or feminism (as disavowal). Austen answers this dilemma by reformulating feminine submission in a romance quest narrative that points in another direction altogether; one in which identity is already complete, but forgotten. This demands an act of subjective faith on the part of the heroine, that – if accepted – is transformative of the objective world. Austen's 'irony', from here, can be read as a mediation between two otherwise divergent possibilities, or knowledges: one embedded in and determined by the empirical world (recognisable as representational realism and empirical verisimilitude); one gesturing towards something beyond this (recognisable as archetypal significance and providential causality). Hence the comedy. Narrative shows the transition, as temporally realised transformation, between the debased world and the idealised, by a process of incorporation and displacement. It also, by completing the process in the consciousness of a reader, performs the same movement each time it is read anew.

The most openly 'providential' of the six narratives, *Mansfield Park*, is also the most directly engaged with a religious consciousness. The narrative's estimation of the heroine's object, Edmund, is centred precisely on his destined religious service: 'the character of Edmund, his strong good sense and uprightness of mind, bid most fairly for utility, honour, and happiness to himself and all his connections. He was to be a clergyman'.[338] While Edward, Brandon, Darcy, and Knightley are destined to be disinterested gentlemen, and Wentworth a self-made naval officer, Edmund is the only figure of narrative desire in Austen to represent a strong religious calling. Henry Tilney is also a clergyman, but his motivations are left unclear. Other clergy figures (Mr Collins, Mr Grant, Mr Elton) are shown to be less than ideal, often functioning as agents of the unwanted proposal which initiates the heroine's 'no'. Edward undergoes a narrative transformation that aligns him finally with the second-son who becomes a clergyman as the result of his changed circumstances. Edmund's calling is by contrast one of spiritual and social duty. It is this which is threatened by his relationship with Mary Crawford, and finally confirmed in his alliance with Fanny.

This is also the work which evidences a noticeable level of biblical discourse. Miltonic references have been identified by Jocelyn Harris, who reminds us of the textual parallels between Sotherton grounds and Milton's garden: 'Details read with Milton in mind become newly important when Mary and Edmund speak of the labyrinth as an emblem of deception, or when Mary's mind is led astray and bewildered ... Mary and Edmund take "a very serpentine route" that leads them away from "the first great path".'[339] Indeed, but Fanny remains *within* the grounds and is not led into transgression by characters motivated by greed, lust, or jealousy. All those who break out of the garden at this point in the narrative end relatively badly, while Fanny's timidity produces the final outcome of her impossible dream of marriage to Edmund, and in the process the 'world' of *Mansfield Park* is also transformed.

Yet Fanny is a notoriously difficult heroine to take seriously, perhaps best summarised by Kingsley Amis's description of her 'cringing self-abasement'.[340] While Elizabeth runs and laughs, is 'lively' and enjoys a good joke, Fanny has no such appealing characteristics. Her problematic passivity is brought into relief by contrast with the accomplished traits of worldly freedom exhibited by Mary Crawford. Fanny's abject humility makes her a problematic representative for feminine subjectivity: the displaced and traumatised object of capital, accepting of her marginal status, and submissive to the patriarchal forces of Mansfield Park itself. Displaced against her will from her birth family to the unfamiliar context of the Park at the age of ten, she has no choice but to comply with the external forces which exchange her as an object of indifferent charity (she is not chosen for any positive reason). Overtly, these forces are a combination of Mrs Norris's selfish interference and Lady Bertram's almost complete apathy, which collectively translate her mother's plea for support from these more fortunate sisters into the selection of Fanny as eldest daughter to be removed from her 'superfluity of children' and resettled at Mansfield Park.[341] It is striking that Fanny only meets her mother again some seven years following her departure, and only receives letters from her favourite brother, William.

The deeper narrative conditions for Fanny's displacement lie in the significantly different fates of the three sisters 'thirty years' earlier. Maria Ward, now Lady Bertram, has the 'good luck' to 'captivate' Sir Thomas Bertram, and thereby be 'raised to the rank of a baronet's lady'. Apparently the eldest, Miss Ward settles on 'the Rev. Mr Norris' who has 'scarcely any private fortune'. The youngest, Frances, now Mrs Price, marries 'to disoblige her family', and does this 'very thoroughly' by attaching herself to a 'Lieutenant of the Marines, without education, fortune, or connections'.[342] An 'absolute breach' between the sisters follows, again initiated by Mrs Norris's interference and Lady Bertram's inactivity, so that Mrs Price and her children are consigned to the unhappy fate of a 'large and still increasing family, an husband disabled for active service, but not the less equal to company and good liquor, and a very small income to supply their wants'. Mrs Norris translates Mrs Price's later plea for support into a plan to relieve her 'from the charge and expense of one child entirely out of her great number'.[343]

Fanny's overdetermined passivity (both a quality of her character, and structurally reinforced by circumstances beyond her control) carries over into her role at Mansfield Park as the orphan cousin. She spends much of her time 'listening, trembling, and fearing to be sent for'.[344] Yet she manages a happy ending nonetheless, and the terms of that ending are a direct outcome of her fundamental refusal to 'act'. Her key moments of narrative agency are specifically negative. She quite literally refuses to 'act' in the private performance of *Lover's Vows* which is planned following Sir Thomas Bertram's exit to Antigua: 'No, indeed, Mr Bertram, you must excuse me.'[345] When the dashing Henry Crawford subsequently offers 'himself, hand, fortune, every thing to her acceptance', she can only negate the idea: ' "No, no, no".'[346] Her reiterated refusal, her 'no' to Sir Thomas Bertram's acceptance of the arrangement, highlights the particular narrative agency of Fanny as a negation of apparently pre-determined outcomes:

> 'And now, Fanny, having performed one part of my commission, and shewn you every thing placed on a basis the most assured and satisfactory, I may execute the remainder by prevailing on you to accompany me down stairs ...
>
> There was a look, a start, an exclamation, on hearing this, which astonished Sir Thomas; but what was his increase of astonishment on hearing her exclaim – 'Oh! no, Sir, I cannot, indeed I cannot go down to him.'

Fanny's timidity, then, is transformed into a powerful negation, which is both within and quite beyond her usual range of actions: ' "This is very strange!" said Sir Thomas, in a voice of calm displeasure. "There is something in this which my comprehension does not reach." '[347]

Her unwillingness to 'act' is captured in her pausing between rooms following Sir Thomas Bertram's sudden return from Antigua:

> Too soon did she find herself at the drawing-room door, and after pausing a moment for what she knew would not come, for a courage which the outside of no door had ever supplied to her, she turned the

lock in desperation, and the lights of the drawing-room and all the collected family were before her.[348]

The narrative conundrum of *Mansfield Park* is precisely: how can this trembling mouse of a character, faced by powerful forces which threaten to overwhelm her wishes at every turn, manage to find the conditions for realisation of her desire?

Fanny does very little but listen to others and subordinate her own feelings to those of others, as in the scene where Edmund asks for her 'approbation' of his plan to act in the play opposite Miss Crawford in place of a 'young man very slightly known to any of us', and on her return to the Park following Maria's disappearance with Henry Crawford: 'To talk over the dreadful business with Fanny, talk and lament, was all Lady Bertram's consolation. To be listened to and borne with, and hear the voice of kindness and sympathy in return.'[349] But it is precisely in this absence of willed activity, acceptance of – and accommodation to – context, this yielding to the needs of others, situated *between* Norris's 'spirit of activity' and Lady Bertram's 'tranquil feelings', that conditions emerge for the outcome which sees Fanny achieving her wishes:

> I purposefully abstain from dates on this occasion, that every one may be at liberty to fix their own, aware that the cure of unconquerable passions, and the transfer of unchanging attachments, must vary much as to time in different people. – I only intreat everybody to believe that exactly at the time when it was quite natural that it should be so, and not a week earlier, Edmund did cease to care about Miss Crawford, and became as anxious to marry Fanny, as Fanny herself could desire.[350]

The final conditions for Fanny's happy ending are set in motion by Maria's fall from an unloving marriage into an unloving affair, both born of jealousy. This crisis triggers Fanny being recalled from a prolonged visit to her dismal family home in Portsmouth, and leaves her 'in the greatest danger of being exquisitely happy, while so many were miserable'. She struggles to remember '[t]he evil which brought such good to her!'[351] Maria's 'guilt' and Julia's 'folly' indirectly grant Fanny's wish of leaving the misery of her family home at Portsmouth and resuming her desired intimacy with Edmund. She is collected by Edmund himself, now safe from being 'duped' by her rival. Henry's open liaison with the recently married Maria, his fall from public grace, vindicates her previous refusal of him and makes her safe from any further attentions.

Her escape back to Mansfield Park, from the uncomfortable surroundings of her parental home, is improved further by permission to take her favourite sister with her, for her 'support'. Fanny's narrative salvation is produced in the wake of a prior narrative punishment of those who had previously mistaken her passivity for weakness. This is indeed a narrative agency beyond the comprehension of a man like Sir Thomas Bertram (and, one might add, of influential Freudian notions of agency, centred as these are on libidinal 'activity').

On return to the Park, Fanny's aunts and cousin Tom have all already been crucially transformed by the 'evil' of Maria's abandonment of her new husband with Henry Crawford. Lady Bertram, previously indifferent to all but her own immediate needs, now openly welcomes her niece 'with no indolent step; and, falling on her neck, said, "Dear Fanny! Now I shall be comfortable".' Mrs Norris is by contrast pacified: 'an altered creature, quieted, stupified, indifferent to every thing that passed', and soon removed from the Park for ever.[352] Tom's illness and 'self-reproach' for establishing the grounds for Maria's and Julia's illicit liaisons, had corrected his faults as eldest son by making 'an impression on his mind which, at the age of six-and-twenty, with no want of sense, or good companions, was durable in its happy effects'. He had learnt to be 'useful to his father, steady and quiet', no longer 'living merely for himself'.[353]

Finally, Edmund is awakened to the truth that 'it had been the creature of my own imagination, not Miss Crawford, that I had been too apt to dwell on for many months past'. Mary Crawford's 'cool' response to her brother's transgression finally breaks the 'charm' he has been under: 'My eyes are opened.' Not too long after ('exactly at the time when it was quite natural that it should be so') Edmund is further enlightened to the 'whole delightful and astonishing truth' of 'knowing himself to have been so long the beloved of such a heart'.[354] Even Sir Thomas Bertram is changed for the better: he learns 'the advantages of early hardship and discipline, and the consciousness of being born to struggle and endure'. These are strong terms indeed when applied to a man directly engaged in the slave economy. He also finds a new happiness in the removal of Mrs Norris to accompany the disgraced Maria in retirement, and one which again offsets the 'evil' that is its catalyst:

> He had felt [Mrs Norris] as an hourly evil, which was so much the worse, as there seemed no chance of its ceasing but with life; she seemed a part of himself, that must be borne for ever. To be relieved from her, therefore, was so great a felicity, that had she not left bitter remembrances behind her, there might have been a danger

of his learning almost to approve the evil which produced such a good.[355]

Here again is Frye's 'Proserpine solution', whereby 'some heroines may symbolise not only a descent from a higher world but a permanent return to it', providing on the way 'near-miraculous powers of healing': 'more than simply a representative of human integrity'. Fanny is shown to 'exert a certain redemptive quality by her innocence and goodness'.[356] Her irritating lack of resistance is precisely the point: this willingness to accept the humiliations of her situation with 'forbearance and patience' positions her to receive – and perhaps more to the point to appreciate – her unexpected happiness when it finally arrives.

If we follow through Jameson's analysis, which allows us to consider Austen's romance narratives as projections of solutions to historically determined problems, then Fanny's peculiarly passive agency takes on an argument concerning the realisation of feminine will. From this slant she becomes a lot more interesting, but I am afraid the argument itself is difficult to swallow.

It is, then, precisely Fanny's negation of mutuality with Henry Crawford, her 'no' when everyone assumes a 'yes', that is highlighted as the key to these closing scenes of correction, where everybody finds an appropriate place. Mrs Norris explicitly blames Fanny for Maria's disgrace, thinking her 'the daemon of the piece. Had Fanny accepted Mr Crawford, this could not have happened.'[357] Mary Crawford similarly asks 'Why, would not she have him? It is all her fault. Simple girl! – I shall never forgive her. Had she accepted him as she ought, they might now have been on the point of marriage, and Henry would have been too happy and too busy to want any other object'.[358] But Fanny's passive agency is itself emptied of all subjective consciousness and attributed quickly to the work of 'Providence'.

'Providence' is openly credited for Fanny's ultimately powerful refusal of Henry: 'It seems to have been the merciful appointment of Providence that the heart which knew no guile, should not suffer.'[359] Even the narrator later reminds us that, had Henry Crawford 'persevered, and uprightly, Fanny must have been his reward – and a reward very voluntarily bestowed – within a reasonable period from Edmund's marrying Mary'.[360] The narrative key, then, to the specific terms of the happy ending here lies in the providential pre-attachment of Fanny to Edmund; precisely that which she had earlier denied when Sir Thomas Bertram hints that her 'affections' were already engaged as the only reason he might understand for her refusal of Henry. 'He paused and eyed her

fixedly. He saw her lips formed into a *no*, though the sound was inartic-
ulate, but her face was like scarlet.'[361] This providential pre-attachment
is specifically that which Sir Thomas fears on her first entering the
household, and Mrs Norris brushes aside as 'the least likely to happen'.[362]
The least likely remains possible for Austen's heroines.

From exile to home-coming the heroine safely reaches the happy end
of her journey. From orphan to 'indeed the daughter that he wanted',
from cousin to sister to wife, Fanny ends up exactly where she wants to
be: her subjective desire and her objective determinants are brought into
accord.[363] Or, more precisely, a narrative 'Providence' releases the conditions for completion of her will, which coincides with completion of
poetic justice: 'Let no one presume to give the feelings of a young woman
on receiving the assurances of that affection of which she has scarcely
allowed herself to entertain a hope.'[364] Fanny's own final happiness is
unspeakable ('no description can reach'), beyond representation, and
covered by narrative summary. It finds an indirect register in the Edenic
scenery of the Park that meets her return:

> It was three months, three full months, since her quitting [the Park];
> and the change was from winter to summer. Her eye fell everywhere
> on lawns and plantations of the freshest green; and the trees, though
> not fully clothed, were in that delightful state, when farther beauty is
> known to be at hand, and when, while much is actually given to the
> sight, more yet remains for the imagination.[365]

But this peculiar narrative resolution is precisely *against* the by now
established pattern of successful exit of the daughter from the family.
Mansfield Park is special for its inversion of the exogamic narrative
imperatives established in Austen's other mature works; an inversion
repeated differently in *Emma*. While Emma's happy ending finds her
exactly where she began, with a different consciousness of her context,
Fanny's finds her returning to where she did not wish to be, having
found that her desire lies where she had been placed against her will.
Emma's apotheosis is reforged around her new consciousness: Fanny's is
forged in her dawning recognition that her happiness is pre-determined
by external forces, acting against or at least overlooking her will, which
bring her precisely where she would be. She is brought to happiness in
spite of her explicit inability to 'act' in her own interests. Her exit from
the family has already occurred before she engages in the dangerous
journey of courtship, and she ends the journey long before she comes to
realise her own desire.

In the inverted world of Mansfield Park, the near becomes the distant, exit becomes entrance, and the 'auxiliary' becomes the 'daughter'. Fanny's return to the 'home' from which she has been transported as a child makes Mansfield Park her 'home'; her recognition by Sir Thomas Bertram as 'the daughter he wanted' makes her all the more desirable to his son. This is the metamorphosis that centres Fanny's story: one which reveals her *true* identity as *above* the terms of *Mansfield Park*, although she is misperceived there as belonging to the world *below* it: 'At the lowest point of such a heroine's career, when her innocence and gentleness are most strongly contrasted with the malignancy of the powers arrayed against her, she gives the impression of someone living in a world below the one she ought to be living in.'[366]

Her status as object of exchange with no regard to her own will is precisely that which brings her to the realisation of an otherwise unconscious will. Fortuneless, except by the benevolence of Sir Thomas Bertram, she even saves him the expense of a settlement, by entering ever more closely *into* the Bertram family: becoming the daughter. Being of so numerous a birth family in Portsmouth, she leaves no trace of her removal by providing a sister as 'auxiliary' to 'substitute' her place by Lady Bertram. And this sister closes the logical sequence of Fanny's unwilled displacement by being 'delighted to be so! – and equally well adapted for it by a readiness of mind, and an inclination for usefulness, as Fanny had been by sweetness of temper, and strong feelings of gratitude'.[367]

As romance heroine, Fanny's only narrative action is to become awake to the truth of her providential identity: true and beloved daughter of a father she can now respect, rather than foundling orphan. She is indeed exiled from home; but experiences her home as itself an exile from her true self newly discovered.

> At the beginning of a romance there is often a sharp descent in social status, from riches to poverty, from privilege to a struggle to survive and even slavery. Families are separated and the hero may ... find himself falling in love with his sister.[368]

Mansfield Park is famously bordered by incestual implications: Fanny's love for her real brother, William, is transplanted onto her love for her 'brother' and cousin, Edmund; her 'father' sexualises her on his return from Antigua and in his attempts to bring her 'out' socially; Henry Crawford courts Fanny but then indulges in a 'guilty' relationship with her adoptive sister, while his sister courts her adoptive brother and wished-for lover. In fact the narrative closure is achieved by somehow side-stepping these multiple incestual markers: her adoptive brother transforms into her providential husband, and in so doing dislodges her real brother to the more appropriate second place in her affections.[369]

The providential condition for the happy ending of *Mansfield Park*, then, is precisely Fanny's loyalty to her first attachment to Edmund, in spite of temptation in the form of the flattering addresses of Henry Crawford. This inexplicable loyalty – and I would like to find a reader who had not balked at her rejection of Henry prior to his fall on first reading – in the face of the improbability of reciprocation, marks her 'virginity ... or married loyalty' as 'her normal state during the endurance, suffering, suspense, and terror which precede her real life after the story'.[370] It is not a desire likely to be returned, which suggests it is not a desire for satisfaction or sensation, since it endures and remains unaltered by the lack of complete reciprocation. The 'two poles of [Fanny's] career' are clearly demarcated in relation to her desire: her 'eventual triumph' includes 'marriage and the recovery of her identity' and 'the point of her lowest fortunes' sees her 'threatened with rape' in the form of an unwanted marriage. She is an embodiment of the 'sacrificial virgin' exposed to danger by a 'foolish or inattentive father', in the form of Sir Thomas Bertram.[371]

Fanny completes the narrative function of subjective consciousness passing between 'the polarization of ideal and abhorrent worlds'. She is also represented as functioning the completion of 'the cycle of nature, in which the solar and seasonal cycles are associated in imagery with the cycle of human life,' in that her new-found happiness on return to the Park is represented as the budding of early summer. She is finally the 'heroine who becomes a bride, and eventually, one assumes, a mother': 'the structural principle of the cycle and of accommodation to it'. On the romance register, her marriage is precisely *not* the final loss of an already indistinct identity, but the regaining of it, so that once married she 'has accommodated herself to the cyclical movement' and so 'completes the cycle and passes out of the story'.[372] The implication here is not so much that women like Fanny will be happier married, but more that achieving a place *in* the story is not all it has been made out to be, and certainly not an end in itself.

Fanny's timid passivity is an embodiment of femininity; expressed as modesty, reserve, caution, stasis, inaction, yielding to authority and self-sublimation. These qualities can also be understood through the register of comic heroism. Tragic heroism 'is associated with an often invulnerable strength', usually male-embodied, and 'yet the heroism ends in death and the strength is after all not invulnerable'. Comic heroism 'often takes the form of a triumph of a slave or maltreated heroine, or other figure associated with physical weakness'. Fanny's physical weakness and lack of power is emphasised throughout, and contrasts particularly with Mary Crawford's more robust corporeality, in spite of similar stature, particularly her more assured 'riding'. Fanny cannot spend time in the sun cutting roses without feeling unwell afterwards. Nonetheless she is shown to achieve her 'triumph' through 'suffering, endurance, and patience, which can coexist with such weakness, whatever other kinds of strength it may require'. This is, as Frye notes, 'the ethos of Christian myth'.

This implies an isomorphism between femininity and romance heroism: the kind of heroism embodied by Fanny Price means that she takes on 'a redemptive role' parallel to 'her divine counterpart in the Christian story'.[373] Fanny Price can be – and has been – read as a plausible and recognisable representation of specifically oppressed femininity: objectified, powerless, self-abnegating and generally overlooked. She also functions as uncanny *figura* for a distinctively feminine salvational agency that is shown to emerge triumphant over her more worldly adversaries.

The romance epistemology at play here is re-signified in Fanny's dream of 'the Island', ridiculed by Maria and Julia as a sign of her lack of proper knowledge:

> But, aunt, she is really so very ignorant! – Do you know, we asked her last night, which way she would go to get to Ireland; and she said, she should cross to the Isle of Wight. She thinks of nothing but the Isle of Wight, and calls it *the Island*, as if there were no other island in the world.[374]

'The Island' calls directly on the mythic imagination of romance: beautifully realised in Shakespeare's *Tempest*, which offers a deep source-text for Austen's *Mansfield Park*. In place of Prospero the magician, however, we have Austenian narrative determination, which works its transformations through exchanges between apparently parallel series. Fanny functions seamlessly as realist individual; but taken under Jameson's second interpretive horizon as representative of the 'class' of 'woman', she offers a strong intervention in questions concerning women's knowledge and agency under explicit forms of 'patriarchy', where that is understood to refer to conditions established in spite of feminine will. Neither masochistic nor in disavowal of femininity; neither raped nor dead; she finds her patient desire realised by a transformation in her objective determinants, which metamorphose before her and our eyes. Her naïve and ridiculed dream of reaching 'the Island' is a figure for her discrete stepping out of the frame of narrative itself in her desired union with Edmund.

The passage concerning Fanny's 'ignorance' tells us more. Fanny cannot 'put the map of Europe together', 'tell the principle rivers in Russia', and has not heard of 'Asia Minor'. By contrast, Julia and Maria have long since been able to 'repeat the chronological order of the kings of England, with the dates of their accession, and most of the principle events of their reigns!' They also claim knowledge of 'the Roman emperors as low as Severus', 'a great deal of Heathen Mythology, and all the Metals, Semi-metals, Planets, and distinguished philosophers'.[375] But Fanny is the only one in her ignorance to 'ask him about the slave trade' on Sir Thomas's return from Antigua.[376]

Maria and Julia's socially superior 'knowledge' is finally found to have been centred on 'a deficiency' which the reformed Sir Thomas 'could scarcely comprehend to have been possible': 'Something must have been wanting *within*.'[377] Fanny provides the 'something', and in the process insists that it is indeed 'within', rather than to be learnt from external coordinates; since she cannot – by the logic of the narrative itself – be expected to have acquired this 'something' as herself the product of a union between a vicious father and weak-minded mother. Fanny's knowledge, like her dream of 'the Island', derive from elsewhere; in explicit contrast to Mary Crawford's specifically *worldly* education. Her birth mother, Mrs Price, is revealed to be as embedded in – although more overcome by – worldly concerns as Mary Crawford:

> a partial, ill-judging parent, a dawdle, a slattern, who neither taught nor restrained her children, whose house was the scene of mismanagement and discomfort from beginning to end, and who had no talent, no conversation, no affection towards herself; no curiosity to know her better, no desire of her friendship, and no inclination for her company that could lessen her sense of such feelings.[378]

Fanny is, after all, removed from the influence of her parents at a young age: perhaps something is shown to be conserved in this removal that is normally lost.

If the feminist problematic, represented by the aesthetic fissures in Wollstonecraft's socially committed art, is how to insert female will into the subject – object relation without being scuppered by the hysterical return of a displaced femininity this necessarily engenders, then Austen overcomes the problem by simply treating it as the first step towards an answer. If we cannot claim rationality without defeminisation – and hence the 'loss' or at least displacement of a claim to a specifically female identity – then we cannot do so. We might, rather, accept the apparent dichotomy between femininity and an instrumental rationality, but this in turn demands a 'reasonable' position from which to look back at ourselves doing so. Fanny is deemed 'unreasonable' by the other characters when she denies their particular, immediate, desires. Her knowledge is explicitly represented as improper, she cannot repeat the chronology of crowns or the accepted geography of the world, a geography that would interpret the map put together by Maria and Julia in terms of accelerating British economic interests fuelled by the slave economy. Her way of understanding the world, and therefore her place in the world, does not align with increasingly hegemonic principles of instrumental rationality, expressed here as empirical mapping.

Fanny's odd dream of 'the Island' specifically echoes Austen's own words: 'Charles leaves us on Saturday, unless Henry should take us in his way to the Island, of which we have some hopes'; 'This scheme to the Island is an admirable thing'; 'I do not at all regard Martha's disappointment in the Island.'[379] This represented contrast between the kind of knowledge that can locate and name 'an' island, and the kind of knowledge that knows of only 'the Island' suggests an imaginary field of reference not yet limited to the terms of the Atlas. '*The* Island' is simply the only one within imaginative and actual reach from Austen's home, the only one with which she would have need to concern herself. This resonance between Fanny's geographic ignorance and Austen's unguarded letters seems important given the 'worldly' understanding of this character's marginality as inherent powerlessness. Fanny's apparent marginality, her 'auxiliary' status and attendant lack of 'active' agency explicitly align with abstract femininity. However, she overcomes, and finally corrects, the more powerful figures representing a much stronger grasp on 'worldly' knowledge. Without straining the analogy too far, this tension echoes the romance/realism dissonance itself, pitting apparently naïve romance fantasy against a more realist mapping of objective determinants.

Austen here raises the question of feminine agency in a way that is unusually explicit. Fanny does not fight for her rights, does not demand equality, does not even argue her case particularly well when wronged, and is entirely governed by 'the obligation and expediency of submission and forbearance'.[380] Yet, without the slightest assertion except towards sublimating her feelings, and managing only a quiet 'no', the world she inhabits transforms itself in accordance with her soft desire. The one activity she persists in throughout her trials, the one that is least popular with her current editors and critics, is the act of prayer. It is worth pausing on an example of this:

> He would marry Miss Crawford. It was a stab, in spite of every long-standing expectation; ... But he was deceived in her: he gave her merits which she had not; her faults were what they had ever been, but he saw them no longer. Till she had shed many tears over this deception, Fanny could not subdue her agitation; and the dejection which followed could only be relieved by the influence of fervent prayers for his happiness.[381]

This turn from the disappointment of self-interest in favour of the 'happiness' of the loved object is crucial to our understanding of Fanny's outcome. She consciously aligns her 'intention' with her 'duty': 'to try to overcome all that was excessive, all that bordered on selfishness in her affection for Edmund'. This stabs indeed at the heart of the feminist argument, when understood through the Wollstonecraftian tradition, which is founded on a mistrust of the selflessness associated with traditional femininity; the promotion of care for others over care for the self; the ethic of disinterested love, now understood as pure ideology. Austen's position here has traditionally been considered 'conservative', in the sense of underpinning the status quo on the basis of women's unpaid domestic and affective labour. As Emily Auerbach notes:

> Austen seems deliberately to present Fanny Price as a blend of all the characteristics her era found desirable in women: modesty, delicacy, piety, and submissiveness. ... The Reverend Fordyce would have approved of Fanny Price, as he calls in his frequently reprinted *Sermons for Young Women*, 1761, for 'meekness and modesty ... soft attraction and virtuous love,' as well as the capacity to be 'agreeable and useful'.[382]

Fanny is crucially devoid of irony, and an imaginative alliance between this character and her creator is sealed in the reference to the 'amber cross' brought by William from Sicily, a direct incarnation of the topaz crosses bought for his sisters by Charles Austen.[383] We find Austen's written prayers asking God to dispose her own heart to 'fervent prayer':

> We feel that we have been blessed far beyond any thing that we have deserved; and though we cannot but pray for a continuance of all

these mercies, we acknowledge our unworthiness of them and implore thee to pardon the presumption of our desires.[384]

What gets lost in the conservative/radical debates surrounding Austen's narrative ambivalence is the astonishing power of the self-abnegation here claimed through an abject femininity.

It may not be something we can stand being told by the Reverend Fordyce, but there is a claim to truth in Austen's mode of representation that perhaps deserves closer attention. The contrast between Fanny and Mary Crawford is a contrast between different aspects of potential modes of womanhood. Mary Crawford's assertive negotiation of her own desires might attract us temporarily, but we are asked to review our own fascination with her through Fanny's smiling triumph at the end. This package of Christian femininity is in itself quite offensive to current critical sensibility (including my own), but Austen's final approval of the outcome that sees the attractive and tempting Crawfords overthrown, and the serious, spiritual cousins happily united is devoid of any trace of irony that would let us off the hook:

With so much true merit and true love, and no want of fortune and friends, the happiness of the married cousins must appear as secure as earthly happiness can be.[385]

The gesture of self-abnegation that centres Fanny's subjectivity as well as Austen's own voice in prayer transcends the cultural and historical characteristics associated with Christian humanism. Found in ancient sources as diverse as the *Tao te Ching* and Buddhist Sutras, it is in itself anathema to current cultural preoccupations with self-assertion, competition, survival of the fittest, and material accretion (expressive of the capitalist economic mode): 'I will endure words that hurt in silent peace as the strong elephant endures in battle arrows sent by the bow, for many people lack self-control.'[386] Fanny's happy ending is explicitly karmic: she gets it because she has deserved it at a level that can still make us deeply uncomfortable.

It is no surprise, ultimately, that the object of narrative desire expressed through Austen's work (the peaceful achievement of autonomy in such a way as to heal the social) is still desired, if only under cover of romance, by a contemporary audience. As Jung puts it: 'I have not been able to avoid recognizing certain regularities.'[387] We might say that it is equally difficult to avoid recognizing certain regularities in Austen's narratives of salvational feminine agency: an initial disjunction between the heroine's desire and her objective determinants, or a disjunction between her will and her objective needs, or indeed both; an 'inversion' following a denial (the heroine's 'no' initiates a reversal); the heroine's 'awakening' which contrasts her past knowledge with her present in such a way as to produce a new perspective on her objective conditions, represented through her recognition of the object of her (now explicitly marital) desire. This offers the core structure of the peculiar daydream narrated in feminine romance. Žižek notes in the most provocative terms what is at stake in the material under study in Austen's narrative experiments:

> From this fantasy structure springs the near panic reaction – not only of men, but also of many a woman – to a feminism that wants to deprive woman of her very 'femininity'. By opposing 'patriarchal domination', women simultaneously undermine the fantasy-support of their own 'feminine' identity.[388]

Mansfield Park implies that there is more than a gendered representation in play here, rather a fundamental meditation on spiritual truth through a compelling and intriguing realist narrative that invites us to participate directly in the meditation. It might help to consider this femininity through Lévi-Strauss's intriguing sense of the fundamental passivity, or emptiness, in the place of what we think of as the subject: 'Each of us is a kind of crossroads where things happen. The crossroads is purely passive; something happens there'.[389] One of the things that 'happens there' is the daydream of romance. Jameson reminds us that 'daydreaming and wish-fulfilling fantasy are by no means a simple operation':

> they involve mechanisms whose inspection may have something further to tell us about the otherwise inconceivable link between wish-fulfilment and realism, between desire and history.[390]

Mansfield Park suggests a novel reinterpretation of that inconceivable link, one which reverses its normally conceivable relation, and centres that reversal on a mode of femininity we perhaps would still rather overlook.

5
Emma: 'the operation of the same system in another way'

> If there is one belief (however the facts resist it) that unites us all ... it is this conviction that somehow, in some occult fashion, if we could only detect it, everything will be found to hang together.
>
> Frank Kermode, *The Genesis of Secrecy: On the Interpretation of Narrative*[391]

> Seldom, very seldom, does complete truth belong to any human disclosure; seldom can it happen that something is not a little disguised, or a little mistaken; but where, as in this case, though the conduct is mistaken, the feelings are not, it may not be very material.
>
> Jane Austen, *Emma*[392]

> 'Beauty is truth, truth beauty', – that is all
> Ye know on earth, and all ye need to know.
>
> John Keats, *Ode on a Grecian Urn*[393]

The question of the nature of feminine agency cuts to the core of Austen's work, but is expressed in a distinctive way in her last two complete narratives, *Emma* (1816) and *Persuasion* (1818). We find her late heroines in opposing circumstances: the privileged Emma, who rarely finds her will crossed either by an indulgent and weak father or a loving governess, and whose economic independence makes marriage unnecessary to her; and the already static Anne, whose inert condition at the opening of her narrative of revival is reinforced by the absence of her direct voice. We hear Emma speak early, but Anne is only indirectly registered by the narrator until a passing reference to the navy brings her into the present of the scene: 'here Anne spoke'.[394] The movement of *Persuasion* turns

Anne's stasis into a revised concept of freedom in its final un-mooring of her character from its 'landed' determinants: 'She gloried in being a sailor's wife.'[395] This contrasts directly with *Emma*, when this is read as a study in the implications of ungrounded female will.

Emma's transformation is achieved through a curbing of her wilful activity, her romancing, coupled with her acceptance of a narrative authority beyond her own free will:

> The first error and the worst lay at her door. It was foolish, it was wrong, to take so active a part in bringing any two people together. It was adventuring too far, assuming too much, making light of what ought to be serious, a trick of what ought to be simple. She was quite concerned and ashamed, and resolved to do such things no more.[396]

She ends where she began, at the feminine centre of her father's house, but with the transformative supplement of a loving husband. Anne exits on a bold abandonment of her father's house, escaping to sea. Both heroines are faced with the discovery, or rediscovery, of desire; and both are utterly transformed as a result. Emma is freed from an excess of subjectivism, while Anne is freed into a late and unexpected subjectivity. This analysis of *Emma* reveals a text thoroughly preoccupied with the possibility of a final comic turn, associated with a late and crucially unexpected realisation of 'the truth'. At the same time, it reveals a representation of the feminine subject's parallel realisation of a thoroughly marital desire beyond any social or economic demands.

Emma is unique as an Austen heroine, since marriage is simply unnecessary for her; she is already economically secure, has no fear of spinsterhood, and her father would rather that she remained unchanged as his daughter: 'I have none of the usual inducements of women to marry.'[397] She is conscious of her own powers, and enjoys her independence. But the narrative reveals a new experience – focused through Mr Knightley as its object – that reaches consciousness at the moment the object's loss is threatened. Emma early on makes the narrative catalyst conscious by denial:

> 'Were I to fall in love, indeed, it would be a different thing!' and 'without love, I am sure I should be a fool to change such a situation as mine. Fortune I do not want; employment I do not want; consequence I do not want: I believe few married women are half as much mistress of their husband's house, as I am of Hartfield; and never,

never, could I expect to be so truly beloved and important; so always first and always right in any man's eyes as I am in my father's.'[398]

Emma's quest, and the quest of the feminine subject of history that I take her to represent is to find and secure her own desire. This desire, unconscious to the heroine for most of the narrative, but increasingly conscious for the reader, calls on recognition of a 'truth' beneath appearances. Its absence in the earlier parts of the novel is reinforced by images of a distorted surface reflection: Emma imagines herself 'in love' with Frank Churchill; Mr Elton imagines himself 'in love' with Emma; and Harriet imagines herself 'in love' with Mr Elton and, later, Mr Knightley, before remembering her experience of love with Martin Smith.

The narrative works to reveal, in the full sense of revelation, an *experience* of love that is qualitatively different from these *concepts* of love. In the course of this reveal we are brought to consciousness of the difference between the appearance and the truth of things. This distinction is made manifest in relation to the act of narrative representation itself, and incorporated into the material of the novel as a discussion of the productive failure of realism. The narrative is woven from a number of incommensurable gazes, which in their combination suggest that realism *has* to fail simply because it *is* a representation, but this failure finally gives way to an expression of 'the real thing'.

Paul Ricoeur's work claims a 'deep' manifestation in narrative of an otherwise inexpressible, but apparently universal, relationship between human consciousness and time. Hayden White makes a related claim for narrative: 'far from being one code among many that a culture may utilize for endowing human experience with meaning, narrative is a meta-code, a human universal on the basis of which transcultural messages about the nature of a shared reality can be transmitted'.[399] Barthes's narrative analysis turns its attention explicitly away from chronology, focalised through the foregrounded consciousness, expressive of liberal individualism, towards an abstract (synchronic) 'logic' of narrativity; a laudable move. But Ricoeur asks us to consider a second path away from the insistence on the chronological characteristic of a reified realism:

> The struggle against the linear representation of time does not necessarily have as its sole outcome the turning of narrative into 'logic,' but rather may deepen its temporality.[400]

Ricoeur reminds us that narrative turns on two principle axes: the 'paradigmatic order of action' and the 'syntagmatic order of narrative'.[401]

Actions, as emploted in narrative, contain a 'synthesis of the heteroge-neous that brings narrative close to metaphor'.[402] Through narrative emplotment 'goals, causes, and chance are brought together within the temporal unity of a whole and complete action'. In this 'grasping together' of a 'whole and complete story' we find 'multiple and scattered events' organised in such a way that we *grasp* the 'intelligible significa-tion attached to narrative as a whole'.[403] Ricoeur's frame of reference gives us a new way to consider Austen's seaming of realism to romance followed through the previous chapters. The metaphoric resonance of narrative finally interpellates a figurative, or romance register.

Margaret Homans has argued that 'the relative valuation of figurative and literal language, and of figuration and literalization, is at the heart of gender difference in language', since 'literalization suggests a move in the direction of mother–daughter language' and 'figuration suggests a return to the paternal symbolic'.[404] *Emma's* movement from the figura-tive to the literal, in this insistence on the difference between the *concept* of love and the *experience* of love, centres on the problem for the daugh-ter of the absence of the maternal that Homans finds at the heart of Western cultural myths. Emma's mother is quite literally absent, and the mother's absence establishes the conditions for the daughter's wilful romancing. The experience of love that closes the narrative offers Emma a renewal of her relation to the maternal that is otherwise unconscious to the narrative and its heroine, at the same time that it makes literal the figurations of love that have occupied her.

Susan Greenfield finds that *Emma* 'marks a turning point in the repre-sentation of the mind, enabling Austen to fashion one of the most precise early models of the unconscious'. Since there is a clear 'division between Emma's self-understanding and the actual cause of her behav-iour', we become aware of unconscious material associated with 'endur-ing sorrow about her mother's death'.[405] This analysis accepts Greenfield's account of the novel as an expression of maternal melancholia, but extends the point with reference to the insistence on the 'truth', associ-ated with the experience of love that characterises Emma's particular happy ending.

Ricoeur's account of narrative gives us a further conceptual frame through which to consider the peculiarly 'feminine' agency captured in Austen's work. Narrative agents may 'act and suffer in circumstances they did not make', but these circumstances 'circumscribe the inter-vention of historical agents in the course of physical events and offer favourable or unfavourable occasions for their action'. Action is always 'interaction', 'to act "with" others', and this takes 'the form of cooperation or competition or struggle'. The final 'outcome of an action may be a change in fortune towards happiness or misfortune'.[406] *Emma* represents a realisation of the transformative power of the thoroughly feminine action of yielding to love, which is shown to produce a late change in narrative fortune towards 'happiness' over 'misfortune'. *Persuasion* goes on to suggest that this experience is still available even under the most unfavourable conditions.

While structural analysis of narrative is rooted in 'an implicit phenomenology of "doing something" ', narrative itself is not 'limited to making sense of our familiarity with the conceptual network of action'. The relationship between the 'conceptual network of action' and 'the rules for narrative composition' is made by Ricoeur with reference to the paradigmatic/syntagmatic polarity:

> With regard to the paradigmatic order, all terms relative to action are synchronic, in the sense that the relations of intersignification that exist between ends, means, agents, circumstances and the rest are perfectly reversible. The syntagmatic order of discourse, on the contrary, implies the irreducibly diachronic character of every narrated story.

Plot is the 'literary equivalent of the syntagmatic order that narrative introduces into the practical field'.[407] Ricoeur's analysis of narrative centres on Aristotle's apprehension of 'recognition and reversal' as the core condition of narrative in its paradigmatic form as tragedy. This raises an important question for Austen's work: 'whether what we are calling narrative can draw this surprising effect from other procedures than those of tragedy'.[408] *Emma* provides strong narrative evidence that it can. That evidence has some interesting implications for the wilful feminine subject it imagines as its central concern – it is Austen's *Taming of the Shrew*.

Recognition and reversal are understood as core symptoms of dialectical progression along the diachronic register: but can narrative only achieve this when the outcome is 'suffering'? The agency at work in completion of the narrative action that is *Emma* makes us conscious that plausible conditions for a reversal of fortune towards tragedy might be nonetheless finally productive of 'happiness'. This work openly expresses the possibility of a very late reversal bringing recognition that leads to *release from* suffering without damaging the terse realist conditions of what Ricoeur calls the 'cultural constraints of acceptability'. That possibility, central to *Emma*, is further insisted upon in *Persuasion*, where the tragic outcome has already been realised prior to, and is effectively reversed by, the narrative action.

Austen had certainly never read Ricoeur, but the Aristotle and Augustine out of whose thoughts on narrative and time he turns his conclusions would be a feature in an Oxford-educated clergyman's library. Ricoeur's particular understanding of narrative as a mediation of the relationship of consciousness to time would by definition have to credit Austen's *narrative* formula as a fuller, more complete, and more effective expression of something otherwise intangible. It strikes me as interesting, then, that she chose to insist on the possibility of a happy ending for her feminine narrative subject, and that she chose to associate this happy ending with the realisation of 'true' love.

What is important here is the extent to which this grand theory of narrative as 'the product of a universal human need to reflect on the insoluble mystery of time' associates an apparently 'universal' experience of human time with the tragic mode: 'the symbolic content of narrative history, the content of its form, is the tragic vision itself'.[409] *Emma* offers strong – and beautifully realised – evidence that the same empirical determinants that seem to produce the inevitability of suffering expressed by tragedy might also, when feminised, offer grounds for a profoundly unexpected comic turn. For Frye, the 'comic' inevitably follows the 'tragic' in the 'higher' romance narrative cycle. For Austen, the comic turn that is the first stage of the realisation of romance is associated precisely with the arrival of a hitherto unconscious truth. And there's the irony – implying an inversion of conscious and unconscious knowledges in relation to the same manifest evidence.

Frye's romance narrative movement runs from a figure of descent through the lowest point in the heroine's fortunes through a twist or reversal that initiates an ascent and final apotheosis. He identifies one 'central image of descent' as 'that of being involved with pictures or tapestries or statues or mirrors in a way that suggested the exchange of original identity for its shadow or reflection'.[410] Emma's infamous 'picture' of Harriet is discussed here as an indeterminate object highlighting the indivisible but unstable relation between what we have since come to call the 'signifier' and the 'signified'.

Elton's misreading of the picture corresponds to a preoccupation with the 'signifier' as the pre-eminent aspect of the sign: it is no coincidence that he also functions under the narrative signature of the absence of love. In a revision of affection only outstripped by Mr Collins of *Pride and Prejudice*, he soon finds a more suitable object for his superficial desire for a wife in the morally vacuous, and surface-oriented, Mrs Elton: all form and no content. By contrast, the *experience* of love that resolves the narrative problems initiated by Emma's interference in the *appearance* of love is so far below the surface of the narrative as to be unconscious for most of the story. It is this association between otherwise unconscious material, the heroine's realisation of the truth of her desire, and the late narrative turn towards a happy ending, that this analysis explores.

Emma, when taken as a narrative message, is centred on a proliferation of encoded messages. Each message is both a material object – letter, word, instrument, 'charade', signifier – and its signification in a network of communication. The same thing can be said about the narrative text in which these messages appear. Harriet's picture; Frank's word games, imputed dream, and private correspondence; Jane's mysterious pianoforte; Mr Elton's charade – each concretise the narrative function of misdirection, misreception or misunderstanding of significant, but thoroughly ambigious, material. This narrative movement revolves around a startlingly clear apprehension of an otherwise unconscious relation between appearance and reality, or signifier and signified.

The multiple misunderstandings and misreadings that form the texture of the action give way to a final realisation of truth that reverses an otherwise inevitable tragedy. Miles has already shown how Austen adapted 'the narrative structure of tragedy to her comic plots'.[411] Austen's late works perform this adaptation without disturbing the realist conditions of the narrative. The entirely plausible alternative outcome – the story of Emma losing her object of desire, at the moment of recognising this desire, to her protégé – is shown to be the result of our heroine's excess of subjectivism: 'what could be increasing Emma's wretchedness but the reflection never far distant from her mind, that it had all been her own work?'[412] The rather beautiful happy ending we get in place of this is only achieved once she begins to participate in, rather than determine, the romance.

When ambiguous objects, gestures, and words are misread, these misreadings have real effects. Austen shows the moment of tragic recognition whereby Emma's fortune seems to have been reversed by her own 'blind' actions, but she also allows further narrative opportunities to follow which 'somehow' ensure that the intended message of love reaches its destination after all. If we follow Emma as the focal centre of this web of misunderstandings, misdirections and misreadings, the larger narrative movement takes the form of an exchange between unconscious and conscious knowledge. Emma only knows herself, and therefore the full meaning of the objects that surround her and determine her happiness, when she gives up her powerful illusion of narrative power. She learns that she does not write the romance at the centre of the narrative, but is written into it. This remains a difficult lesson.

Having decided to 'make [Mr Elton] marry [Harriet]', Emma runs into her first round of mistaken interpretation when Mr Elton 'seconded a wish of her's, to have Harriet's picture': 'Pray, pray attempt it. As you will do it, it will indeed, to use your own words, be an exquisite possession.'[413] The desired object is offered by Emma as representative of the sitter, but received by Mr Elton as representative of the 'hand' of the artist: 'she had great confidence of its being in every way a pretty drawing at last, and of its filling its destined place with credit to them both – a standing memorial of the beauty of one, the skill of the other, and the friendship of both; with as many other agreeable associations as Mr Elton's very promising attachment was likely to add'.[414]

When the likeness is complete, it is critiqued by Emma's circle in characteristic ways: ' "Miss Smith has not those eye-brows and eye-lashes. and you have made her too tall, Emma." ' But Mr Elton 'was in continual raptures, and defended it through every criticism'.[415] 'The next thing wanted was to get the picture framed' and 'it must be done in London'. Mr Elton is eager to 'be trusted with the commission, what infinite pleasure should he have in executing it!': ' "What a precious deposit!" said he with a tender sigh, as he received it.'[416] The dissonance between Emma's offer of the likeness, and Elton's reception of it, marks an antinomy between the perceptions of these characters, which reaches consciousness at last when Emma is 'completely overpowered' by Elton 'perfectly [knowing] his own meaning':

> I protest against having paid the smallest attention to any one else. Everything that I have said or done, for many weeks past, has been with the sole view of marking my adoration of yourself. You cannot really, seriously, doubt it. No! – (in an accent meant to be insinuating) – I am sure you have seen and understood me.[417]

A 'logical anxiety' concerning the misreception of a 'message' of love – offered to and accepted by Emma in the course of her handing it to Harriet – is recapitulated through the discrete functional series of Harriet's collection of 'all the riddles of every sort that she could meet with, into a thin quarto of hot-pressed paper, made up by her friend, and ornamented with cyphers and trophies'.[418] On being invited to contribute 'any really good enigmas, charades, or conundrums', Mr Elton 'called for a few moments, just to leave a piece of paper on the table containing, as he said, a charade, which a friend of his had addressed to a young lady, the object of his admiration'.[419] In spite of recognising that 'he rather pushed it towards me than towards you', Emma pushes the paper on to Harriet: ' "Take it," said Emma, smiling, and pushing the paper towards Harriet – "it is for you. Take your own." '[420] This sequence of misdirected messages expresses an incommensurability between Elton's and Emma's view of objects and their intended meaning. The dual narrative strands this initiates cannot be seen in full relation until Elton finally does indeed 'marry' Emma: to Mr Knightley.[421]

It is this fundamental 'logical anxiety' that centres the narrative's layered reversals between signification and its interpretation. Emma mistakes Frank Churchill's ambiguous messages as intended for her; she misreads the sender – and therefore the meaning – of Jane Fairfax's pianoforte; she misinterprets Mr Knightley as a 'brother', and misreads the signs of attention he pays towards Harriet on her behalf; her relationship with Frank Churchill is in turn misunderstood by Mr Knightley, and Mr Knightley's civility mistaken as the distinctions evident of love by Harriet. At the heart of the narrative movement is Emma's romancing of Harriet's original identity: she misinterprets the evidence of her mysterious parentage as an aristocratic origin designating Harriet for a romance outcome.

Fortunately for Emma, Harriet's parentage turns out to be more obviously 'natural', in the sense of all too plausible, and she ends with the providential partner designated for her prior to Emma's interventions:

> 'any message to Miss Smith I shall be happy to deliver; but no more of this to *me*, if you please'. 'Miss Smith! – Message to Miss Smith! – What could she possibly mean!'[422]

These parallel sequences of misinterpreted signification, taken together, give this narrative a 'higher' (more general) 'message': each case involves the ambiguity of the signifier, and the active misunderstanding of the recipient of the exchange as condensed and suggestive as any purloined letter: 'addressing myself to Miss Smith'![423] One wonders, in the midst of these layers of incommensurable messages, how suffering is to be avoided.

Emma is conscious of a structural alignment between her subjective desire and its apparent conjunction in Mr Elton's perceived 'courtship' of Harriet:

> really it is very strange; it is out of the common course that what is so evidently, so palpably desirable – what courts the pre-arrangement of other people – should so immediately shape itself into the proper form. ... There does seem to be a something in the air of Hartfield which gives love exactly the right direction, and sends it into the very channel where it ought to flow.[424]

Emma's active desire for a happy ending finds significant resistance in the material it seeks to 'pre-arrange', even though that material does finally 'shape itself into the proper form', but not through her shaping. The problem raised in these striking examples is precisely that of the relation between form and content (where the signifier holds the form, the signified is the promise of content). Emma is being shown to lack consciousness of the 'proper form' for 'what is so evidently, so palpably desirable', to the degree that she openly encourages Mr Knightley to think of Harriet as his own future wife: 'Were you, yourself, ever to marry, she is the very woman for you.'[425] The 'likeness', the 'charade', and the proposal, can together be taken as an account of Austen's mature aesthetic vision.

In the brief episode of Harriett's 'likeness', we find a desire for the potential expression of 'realism' in representation:

> Here is my sketch of the fourth, who was a baby. I took him, as he was sleeping on the sofa, and it is as strong a likeness of his cockade as you would wish to see. He had nestled down his head most conveniently. That's very like. I am rather proud of little George. The corner of the sofa is very good.[426]

The last sketch shown is of 'my brother, Mr John Knightley', 'a very good likeness'. This is unfinished, bearing a 'fault on the right side': '*very* like ... only too handsome – too flattering'.[427] Harriet's likeness has the same 'fault': 'as she meant to throw in a little improvement to the figure, to give a little more height, and considerably more elegance, she had great confidence of its being in every way a pretty drawing at last'.[428] Mr John Knightley's 'likeness', while being approved by Mrs Weston, meets with 'cold approbation' from his wife, Isabella, who asserts that it 'did not do him justice'.[429]

The tension between these different receptions of a common representation marks the incommensurability of perspective as determined by the particularity of relationship between subject and object. Isabella, as the one who has married John Knightley, and borne several children by him, while remaining a 'devoted wife', would be expected to perceive him differently to the artist and another party, who find the representation 'flattering'.[430] Isabella's ties to her husband and family are described as 'higher' than her attachment to her sister and father. Emma finds that John Knightley's 'temper was not his great perfection', but Isabella rates his 'temper' as 'equal' to his brother, and even to the excessively good-humoured Mr Weston.[431] Elton's presumed reference to 'Harriet's ready wit' in the 'charade' is met with Emma's 'Humph –', and ascribed to a man 'very much in love indeed, to describe her so'.[432] In *Persuasion*, Anne Elliot is pleased to recognise that Wentworth's assertion of her continuing beauty following eight years of separation ('to my eye you could never alter') is 'the result, not the cause of a revival of his warm attachment'.[433]

The artist's representation, as much as the lover's perception of her or his beloved object, is shown to be relative to the relationship between perceiving subject and the object it aims to represent. This returns us to Barthes, who concludes that '[c]laims concerning the "realism" of narrative are therefore to be discounted' because 'imitation remains contingent'.[434] Austen takes the point to its limit – perception remains contingent:

> He had found her agitated and low. – Frank Churchill was a villain. –
> He heard her declare that she had never loved him. Frank Churchill's
> character was not desperate – She was his own Emma, by hand and
> word, when they returned into the house; and if he could have
> thought of Frank Churchill then, he might have deemed him a very
> good sort of fellow.[435]

Ruth Ronan defines 'incommensurability', through early Kuhn and Feyerabend, as the particular relationship between 'language (or method or theory) that aims to represent a cosmology through its formal "stylistic" features' and 'the object' itself. Any method 'shapes the world according to its own suppositions' while 'the world itself is at the same time viewed as, to some extent at least, prior to its particular theoretical shaping'.[436] Emma's 'likeness' of Mr John Knightley represents 'an object of represen-tation': 'shaped but not created through a particular mode of representa-tion'. Incommensurability will express itself in 'lexical, epistemic and ontological' dissonance as a 'comprehensive split between theories'.

Emma's 'theory' concerning Harriet and Mr Elton is incommen-surate with Mr Elton's own theory concerning himself and Emma. Incommensurability occurs 'when one theory resists a divergent point of view so that conditions of meaningfulness for the terms used for articulating this point of view are not available'. Emma cannot accept the 'conditions for meaningfulness' demanded by Mr Elton's open expressions of attachment to her:

> She was vexed. It did appear – there was no concealing it – exactly
> like the pretence of being in love with her, instead of Harriet; an
> inconstancy, if real, the most contemptible and abominable![437]

At the same time, Elton is wondering what Emma could 'possibly mean!', and – more disturbingly – implies that she has 'long understood me'.[438] Indeed she has at one level 'understood' the 'charade' which 'means' 'courtship' ('plain as can be'), but has redirected rather than received the encoded message according to her own interpretation: 'There can be no doubt of its being written for you and to you. ... You are his object – '.

The word game of chapter five reframes the narrative puzzle in a single condensed scene concerning the circulation of language. The key characters are situated around a table with a box of alphabet letters left behind by Emma's nephews:

> Frank Churchill placed a word before Miss Fairfax. She gave a slight glance round the table, and applied herself to it. Frank was next to Emma, Jane opposite to them – and Mr Knightley so placed as to see them all.[439]

Frank's word for Emma is 'Dixon', referring to a private joke at Jane Fairfax's expense, which is then passed on to Jane herself. His word for Jane's private amusement is 'blunder': referring back to his earlier 'blunder' in asking Mrs Weston for information concerning 'Mr Perry's plan of setting up his carriage' that can only have come through a secret correspondence with Jane Fairfax. His explanation for the excess of information is that it must have come to him in a dream: 'of course it must have been a dream. I am a great dreamer'.[440]

This association of dreaming with the illicit relationship hints directly at unconscious material. The illicit – because covert – correspondence between Frank and Jane is indirectly raised in an odd outburst asserting that 'the post-office is a wonderful establishment!':

> So seldom that any negligence or blunder appears! So seldom that a letter, among the thousands that are constantly passing about the kingdom, is even carried wrong – and not one in a million, I suppose, actually lost! And when one considers the variety of hands, and of bad hands too, that are to be deciphered, it increases the wonder![441]

This image of a system of endlessly circulating messages, in perpetual danger of misdirection, concretises for a moment the narrative system at work. The chiming of 'blunder' between this passage and the word-game suggests a deep current of thought concerning the sending, receiving, and exposure of private messages.

In the end, according to Barthes as well as Ricoeur, narrative itself functions as an indirect message. The ambiguous relation between form and content is brought directly to the question of language by Frank's alphabetic game of covert communication. Mr Knightley does not like Frank's 'hand': 'it is too small – wants strength. It is like a woman's writing'.[442] Miss Bates also elides the 'hand' with the 'content' of Jane Fairfax's letters, and we should be reminded of Fanny Price's strong attachment to Edmund's hastily scribbled note on the day she fears she has lost him to Mary Crawford: 'The enthusiasm of a woman's love is even beyond the biographer's. To her, the handwriting itself, independent of anything it may convey, is a blessedness.'[443] Throughout these examples the 'hand' of the author remains clear, and we tend to receive Austen's story as confirmation of her brilliant skills as a narrative artist. However much she asks us to consider the content (the objects of her representation and their relations) as the point, we are still preoccupied by the authorial signature.

Once we are considering 'cultural phenomena that proclaim an explicit aspiration to represent as accurately as possible a picture of reality', epistemic questions 'arise with particular force'.[444] Indeed. Literary realism emerges 'from the idea that art can represent reality without distorting it in any significant manner'. The 'realist mode' is distinguished by its 'aim at mimeticism', and itself is subject to 'an incommensurability between realist and non-realist modes of representation'.

The history of literary realism can be read through evidence of emerging techniques for representing 'the inner world of character (i.e., mental states, associative sequences, thoughts and fantasies) as we move from earlier forms of the novel to the stream-of-consciousness novel'.[445] But 'no text of narrative fiction can show or imitate the action it conveys, since all such texts are made of language, and language signifies without imitating'.[446] This is only true unless language aims to represent language. Tony Tanner believed Jane Austen had realised that 'language itself might be the origin of what we talk about – i.e. that language is the origin of what we think of as reality'.[447]

We could go further, and claim that Austen precisely represents an awareness of the problems of incommensurability. Her realist representation of representational realism emphasises the contingency of perspective ('it was very like', *and* 'it did not do him justice'). Her work is a conduit for this meta-narrative of literary 'progress' through the novel's 'earlier forms' towards interior realism as 'stream-of-consciousness'. The transition is marked in Austen, leaving a trace in her realisation of the potential in *Free Indirect Discourse* (FID) as a realist representational device.

FID, or 'narrated monologue', is one of the key techniques for literary realism in general. It refers to the 'linguistic device that can record the random flow of inner thoughts because it reproduces, by means of language, the effect of inner processes' resulting in a 'claim to transparency, which conditions any claim to know the thing represented' and which 'in fact characterizes all artistic realisms'. FID is to narrative realism what 'perspective' is to visual realism: the former fails to 'represent the way people think' as much as the latter fails to achieve an 'objective representation of visual reality'. These are, rather, 'signifiers that determine an object by other means than by reproducing knowledge about it'. Realism, then, can be defined as an 'artistic aim' which can never be satisfied by 'artistic practice': 'Realism is what cannot ignore the presence of the artistic signifier (or image) and the absence of the object of representation yet aims to overcome their non-identity.'

Representation demands the distortion of the object, since the object is not itself a representation: 'realist representation is characterized by the inevitable split it creates between the signifier (the artistic image) and the object which art aims to represent'. This is the 'relation of impossible representation' which Ronan terms 'incommensurability'.[448] The problem of the incommensurable, once recognised, tends to lead to the rejection of 'claims of universal truth and principle', and an insistence upon the 'irremediably local nature of truth, validity and knowledge': 'the irreducible difference of a plurality of incommensurate worlds'.[449] This is the logical anxiety that is subject to narration in *Emma*.

Since a 'severance of the subject from the object of representation, is immanent to any system that wishes to ... represent an object as accurately as possible', this severance is the very condition for representation, and is highlighted by the mimetic desires of literary realism. It is precisely the terms of severance between representation and object that is reflected by representation. This inherent severance is simultaneously 'denied' by realist representation: 'linguistic signifiers function as if they replicate the workings and mechanisms characteristic of the inner flow of thoughts'. FID is a discrete mode of discourse functioning *as if* a replication of 'the inner flow of thoughts' and its narrative presence implies psychological realism, or 'depth' of interiority. Ronan concludes that '[i]ncommensurability inheres in every moment of representation'.[450]

Barthes describes the 'function' of narrative as 'not to "represent" ' but to 'constitute a spectacle still very enigmatic for us but in any case not of a mimetic order'. 'The "reality" of a sequence lies not in the "natural" succession of the actions composing it but in the logic there exposed, risked, and satisfied.'[451] This is a claim to 'reality' over and above the accuracy of empirical detail in mimesis. Realism, in aiming to overcome the incommensurability between the object and its representation, reveals in various patterns the inevitability of failure. These patterns are subsequently apprehended as form: the mediation of the particular failure of the particular artistic subject in the aim of perfectly representing its object. Elton finds Harriet's likeness 'exquisite' and wishes to 'possess' it, not because it refers to Harriet, but because it refers also to Emma's desire to represent her friend in a 'pretty picture'. Emma wants only the object to be 'seen and understood', but Elton insists on seeing in the representation something of the desire of the artist to display herself indirectly to him: 'No, madam, my visits to Hartfield have been for yourself alone; and the encouragement I received.'[452]

If the 'object' is the desired 'content' of the 'likeness', and the 'desire of the artist' is its mediation as form, Emma's relation to her objects is analogous to her narrator's relation to her own imaginary objects, including Emma. Both aim to improve on the empirical data referring to their object in their representation of it, in such a way as to reveal a relatively consistent desire. Austen's insistence on romance simply refers to a desire to show 'it should be otherwise'. This improving consciousness is aesthetically realised ('a pretty picture'), so that a narratively expressed desire to make things as they *should* be tends in practice to make them more beautiful:

> Miss Woodhouse has given her friend the only beauty she wanted. ... The expression of the eye is most correct, but Miss Smith has not those eye-brows and eye-lashes. It is the fault of the face that she has them not.[453]

Romance seems to suggest that truth is signified by beauty.

Since the realist tension between form and content can be referred to the incommensurate relation between subject and object, mediated through infinite degrees of failure to represent, Austen's proliferation of FID as a narrative strategy can be taken as a concrete realisation of an otherwise unconscious wish for synthesis between subject and object. FID emerges from a blurring of linguistic boundaries between direct and indirect discourse. It represents an 'empathetic' attitude between narrator and character, while producing conditions for 'ironic distance' between the documented tone of the character's discourse and the narrative stance which is still distinguishable from it.[454]

FID 'permits us to see the fictional characters moving ... against the background of the narrator's consciousness' as well as 'within their own worlds of perception and understanding'. Its presence in realist narrative insists on the prior presence of a narrative consciousness 'even if only through the syntax of the passage, the shape and relationship of sentences, and the structure of and design of a story'. FID finally underlines 'the agency that brings multiple and complex events into relationship with one another and leads them to an end that establishes, even without explicit comment, an all-embracing meaning'.[455] This is achieved as a reading-effect of the 'dissonance between narrative voice and focalisation', which 'always maintains a potential position of greater knowledge and worldliness from which the stylistic contagion, that is the character's consciousness, can be evaluated'.[456]

Skinner recognises this 'specific formal advance by which she elided the distinction between first- and third-person narrators' as 'the most radically original aspect of Austen's writing'.[457] Austen could not be claimed to have *invented* FID, as it appears at isolated moments in – for example – Richardson and Wollstonecraft. However, as a mode of narrative writing, FID is not captured as a self-conscious novelistic technique until later in the nineteenth century, and not categorised until Charles Bally's linguistic analysis in 1912.[458] As Roy Pascal's landmark study notes, FID is deployed by Austen at the end of the eighteenth century with 'a precise intuitive understanding of its syntax', of which she could have had 'no theoretical consciousness', since it was – prior to her lasting modulation of the technique as a specific mode of narrative fiction – quite grammatically incorrect in itself.

Beth Newman has credited Virginia Woolf with the 'technical innovation' of FID, and aligns this with a feminist dispersal of the narrative gaze.[459] But Austen had already inaugurated this narrative breach of the subject by a consciousness that is not its own, in a way that exposes deep relations between the cultural imperative of the absent maternal, the making unconscious of forbidden material, and the oscillation between literal and figurative language that seems to mark representations of femininity.

FID is a specifically realist trope that signals access to the consciousness of a separate individual: it does this by performing a linguistic breach in the subject–object relation. This breach is apprehended critically as a 'contamination' of narrative voice by the consciousness of the character. In psychoanalytic terms, this would be apprehended as introjection and projection. In common experience, it is experienced in a number of quite ordinary activities; including gossip, prayer, falling in love, and reading. All of these actions seem to involve a heightened relationship to unconscious material, and they all feature in Austen's literary landscape.

Gossip for Austen is incarnated in the shifting sands of social, collective discourse in which one is always already inserted as an object, and has a special place in these narratives. Catherine's shifts between the poles of realism and romance are initiated by becoming the object of a social exchange of opinion, particularly between Thorpe and the General. The collective gossip of 'London' had already outed Marianne's indiscreet private relationship with Wickham before the scene at the ball in which she finally confronts him. The 'truth universally acknowledged' which initiates *Pride and Prejudice* resides in the collective noun of accepted opinion, and is embodied in Mrs Bennet's mistaking of external for internal fears and desires. Henry Crawford's fall is in relation to public opinion, and Mary Crawford's 'error' is to concur with the 'cool' wave of its reception as accommodating to the 'world'. Collective opinion runs through *Emma* like tragic chorus, reflecting back the actions and changing status of characters. Emma and Mr Knightly 'had calculated from the time of [their engagement] being known at Randall's, how soon it would be over Highbury; and were thinking of themselves, as the evening wonder in many a family circle, with great sagacity'.[460]

Gossip is for Austen an external, collective, public, extra-subjective realm of discourse in which the heroine's fate is at least partly implicated. The myriad of local conversations combine as a tissue of social opinion – registered in *Emma* as 'Highbury' – in which the heroine is inserted along with everyone else as an object of interest and judgement. This is language as the property of others, which 'exists independently' of the subject: that from which the subject 'is excluded but in which it is represented'.[461] Gossip performs the permeation of the subject by the 'objective', and in Austen the stress goes both ways. This extra-subjective realm of language is associated with unconscious material. It is also, of course, a highly feminised discourse, and not normally associated with true statements.

Prayer offers a different instance of a similar problem for representation. In prayer, the solitary voice expresses its private hopes and fears in silence. One possible explanation for Austen's heightened exploration of FID is that there is no other way to represent for realism the discourse of silent prayer. Prayer demands an interlocutor, functioning at a 'higher' level than the subject, which corresponds in Austen to the extradiegetic narrator. The recent film adaptation of *Emma* resolves the problem of representing FID in relatively realist film through the intrusion of Mrs Elton's voice as narrative presence, having Emma keep a journal, and simply listening in on her private prayers. Journal writing as an adaptive mode peaks in the *Bridget Jones' Diaries*, which we read in terms of abstracted FID. 'Dear diary' and 'Oh Lord' trigger discursive spaces in which FID is received; an imputed interlocutor justifies the otherwise purely subjective utterance. Speaking to oneself and speaking to God seem to be structurally identical to Austen.[462]

A breach in the isolation of the narrative subject is represented in the scraps of private FID that occur at the darker moments of Austen's narratives. These offer the effect of the most intensely private, interior, wordless reflection overheard as if directed to a listening authority: isolated FID connotes a listening authority in the same way that narrative connotes its reader. This is interesting for this study in particular to the degree that FID is recognised by narratology to constitute 'in some sense, a miniature reflection of the nature of both mimesis (in the broad sense of representation) and literariness'.[463] Austen's extensive deployment of FID offers a discrete body of evidence for considering her mimetic and literary consciousness more generally. Rimmon–Kenan refers the literariness of FID to the claim that '[i]t is perhaps because of the difficulty a speaker would experience in trying to perform orally the co-presence of voices characteristic of FID that the phenomenon seems more congenial to the silent register of writing'.[464]

Some of Austen's more striking examples of FID derive from the collective oral register of gossip:

> Miss Nash had been telling her something, which she repeated immediately with great delight. Mr Perry had been to Mrs Goddard's to attend a sick child, and Miss Nash had seen him, and he had told Miss Nash, that as he was coming back yesterday from Clayton Park, he had met Mr Elton, and found to his great surprize that Mr Elton was actually on his road to London, and not meaning to return till the morrow, though it was the whist-club night, which he had been never known to miss before; and Mr Perry had remonstrated with him about it, and told him how shabby it was in him, their best player, to absent himself, and tried very much to persuade him to put off his journey only one day; but it would not do; Mr Elton had been determined to go on, and had said in a *very particular* way indeed, that he was going on business which he would not put off for any inducement in the world; and something about a very enviable commission, and being the bearer of something exceedingly precious.[465]

This is the narrator's version of Harriet's narration of material she has been 'told' by Miss Nash, but that tale itself incorporates and circulates oral material told to Miss Nash by Mr Perry, who was reporting something he had earlier seen and heard regarding Mr Elton. The narration is generally conditioned by Harriet's naïve style of telling a story; it is delivered in one complete, breathless, sentence of discrete clauses linked by addition. Her highly personalised style of telling incorporates traces of Mrs Nash's voice intermingled with Mr Perry's. The statement that 'Mr Perry could not quite understand him, but he was sure there must be a *lady* in the case' originates in Mr Perry's words to Miss Nash and is carried intact into Harriet's words to Emma. Mr Elton's voice is captured in the reported 'enviable commission' and his self-importance as 'bearer of something exceedingly precious' (which chimes with his earlier description of the picture as 'precious possession').[466] This commingled clatter of gossip appears again in *Persuasion* as Mrs Smith's narratively transformative 'authentic oral testimony' concerning Mr Elliot's true character:

> it does not come to me in quite so direct a line as that; it takes a bend or two, but nothing of consequence. The stream is as good as at first; the little rubbish it collects in the turnings, is easily moved away.[467]

Or, as Žižek has it, the 'truth is out there' in spite of the distortions of ideology:

> It is as if an ideological edifice, in order to function 'normally', must obey a kind of 'imp of perversity' and articulate its inherent antagonism in the externality of its material existence.[468]

After all, the received opinion that 'there must be a *lady* in the case' is true in a way that Emma cannot understand, and the story is interpreted accurately as it is passed on.[469] This unlikely stream of popular knowledge contains an unexpected, because for the most part unconscious, truth claim.

Emma's happy ending rests on realisation of a 'truth' that has remained unconscious for most of the narrative. Her particular revelation is given as the sudden lifting of layers of prior blindness ('I seem to have been doomed to blindness'):

> He never wished to attach me. It was merely a blind to conceal his real situation with another. – It was his object to blind all about him; and no one, I am sure, could be more effectually blinded than myself – except that I was *not* blinded–that it was my good fortune–that, in short, I was somehow or other safe from him.[470]

Emma and Mr Knightley quite literally come to a shared and open 'understanding' over half an hour in the shrubbery: their eyes are 'open' to each other. With 'all the wonderful velocity of thought' Emma's 'most busy mind' is able to 'catch and comprehend the exact truth of the whole', a truth which entails her own present and future 'perfect happiness'.[471] At the moment of Emma's realisation of the 'complete truth' the narrator discreetly draws the curtain on her consciousness, to generalise about the rarity of 'complete truth' revealed through 'human disclosure': 'seldom can it happen that something is not a little disguised, or a little mistaken'. Quite true, but this narrative – in conjunction with *Persuasion* – hints that the 'complete truth' cannot finally be prevented from revealing itself in spite of the 'the little rubbish it collects in the turnings', and however overdue its realisation seems to be. Emma's 'blindness' chimes with that of Oedipus, but she is somehow made 'safe' from the unconscious return to incestuous relationship with the father which it threatens, and which is hinted at early on: 'never, never, could I expect to be so truly beloved and important; so always first and always right in any man's eyes as I am in my father's'. Her alternative ending delivers her at the same time from participating in the murder of the mother: she does not simply take her mother's place, but finds a new and productive relationship to the maternal at the close of her narrative.

If the achievement of this peculiarly satisfying happy ending is in indifference to the feminine subject's conscious will, but in synthesis with her unconscious desire, we are brought to a bold narrative message concerning the achievement of objective freedom out of the determinants of social necessity. Emma is shown to gain her 'perfect happiness' by first learning to subjugate her 'vain' reason to Mr Knightley's judgement. Since his judgement involves Emma as an object, she only recognises her true value once she accepts his authority to judge as well as hers. She has to learn that she has been in error, before she can learn to understand her own place in the narrative. Accepting that she has been mistaken in her solitary romancing does not damage her autonomy, but saves and reinforces it.

The various obstacles to the heroine's complete happiness are represented as an entirely plausible resistance in the realist material (Mr Woodhouse's subjective fears, and Harriet's disappointment), but speedily overcome by events unconsciously, rather than wilfully, brought about by Emma. Mr Knightley spectacularly gives up his masculine autonomy to join Emma's household.[472] Harriet bumps into Robert Martin during her stay in London, which has been prompted by Emma for other reasons, and they speedily resolve any difficulties.

Finally, even the staunchly anti-marital Mr Woodhouse learns not only to accept but openly to desire his daughter's marriage, following the redirection of his subjective fears towards the danger of 'house-breaking' on receiving news of the 'pilfering' of Mrs Weston's 'poultry-house':

> In this state of suspense they were befriended, not by any sudden illumination of Mr. Woodhouse's mind, or any wonderful change of his nervous system, but by the operation of the same system in another way.[473]

No unnatural events disturb the meticulous realism in the turn from tragedy to comedy. Emma's happy ending is produced by a force beyond, and in correction of, 'her own work'; by 'the operation of the same [narrative] system in another way'. One symptom of the working out of this 'system' is that she literally incorporates Mr Knightley's view of objects (including herself) and their relations. At the same time, she corrects errors in his subjective perception: they simply come to see each other more clearly than they can see themselves alone. Mr Knightley alone is equally 'blind' to his own narrative role:

> I have no idea that she has yet ever seen a man she cared for. It would not be a bad thing for her to be very much in love with a proper object. I should like to see Emma in love, and in some doubt of a return; it would do her good. But there is nobody hereabouts to attach her.[474]

The 'happy determinant' allowing their mutually transformative recognition to happen is, of course, an exchange of the *appearance* of love for *the real thing*.

Tony Tanner identifies the variously articulated 'problem' for Austen's characters, of 'private communication in a predominantly public world in which various taboos on certain forms of direct address between the sexes are still operative'. He marks this endemic 'problem' as 'of hermeneutics'. At one level this is a 'historical' problem: 'social conditions and codes made this particularly difficult in Jane Austen's period'. But in that case, why should we care, since as a local inhibition it has surely been more than solved, in the affluent urban West at least, by our rapid development of 'less inhibited and less formal modes of achieving sexual and marital *rapprochements*'.[475]

If Catherine, Elinor, Lizzy, Fanny, Emma, Anne – and even Marianne – could have simply *told* the men they fancied what was troubling them, or *asked* what they needed to know, we would not have Austen's work to worry about. We might then claim that the historical problem at the heart of Austen's narrative complexity – under what conditions can women realise their desire – has already been resolved by increasingly open and direct forms of inter-sexual communication and agency available to 'modern' young women today. If the problem *had* been objectively resolved, however, Austen's novels would now represent a minor footnote to the history of immature forms of Western consciousness, and we would all have found 'perfect happiness', and have very little time for reading as a probable side-effect. The continuing fascination with Austen is evidence that this is not yet the case. Telling the 'truth' about one's desire is no straightforward matter when we consider that the necessary conditions for its realisation include *consciousness* of that desire.

In *Emma*, the conditions for the working out of a narrative 'force' or happy determinant associated with the 'truth' is associated with two kinds of metaphor. Emma's fortune finds a correlative in the 'weather' ('everybody feels a north-east wind'):

> The evening of this day was very long, and melancholy, at Hartfield. The weather added what it could of gloom. A cold stormy rain set in, and nothing of July appeared but in the trees and shrubs, which the wind was despoiling, and the length of the day, which only made such cruel sights the longer visible.
>
> ...
>
> The weather continued much the same all the following morning; and the same loneliness, and the same melancholy, seemed to reign at Hartfield – but in the afternoon it cleared; the wind changed into a softer quarter; the clouds were carried off; the sun appeared; it was summer again.[476]

The improbable-but-entirely-plausible happy ending of the Frank Churchill sequence highlights the workings of a happy determinant under the sign of 'good fortune':

> Frank Churchill is, indeed, the favourite of fortune. Every thing turns out for his good. – He meets with a young woman at a watering-place, gains her affection, cannot even weary her by negligent treatment – and had he and all his family sought round the world for a perfect wife for him, they could not have found her superior. – His aunt is in the way. – His aunt dies. – He has only to speak. – His friends are eager

to promote his happiness. – He has used every body ill – and they are all delighted to forgive him. – He is a fortunate man indeed![477]

Emma is judged, and equally forgiven, by a common narrative judgement: 'the sweetest and best of creatures, faultless in spite of all her faults'. This unexpected and equally undeserved happiness in turn transforms her experience of the familiar objects that surround her:

> They sat down to tea – the same party round the same table – how often it had been collected! – and how often had her eyes fallen on the same shrubs in the lawn, and observed the same beautiful effect of the western sun! – But never in such a state of spirits, never in anything like it; and it was with difficulty that she could summon enough of her usual self to be the attentive lady of the house, or even the attentive daughter.[478]

Nature and 'good fortune' are again strongly associated in *Persuasion*, where Mrs Smith is described as entering her 'spring of felicity', and Anne learns to hope 'to be blessed with a second spring of youth and beauty'.[479] This yoking of seasonal metaphors to the happy narrative outcomes of these characters hints at the turn from potential 'tragedy' to the possibility of 'comedy' that the works imagine through an association between narrative and nature which asks us to consider a 'natural' causality for the action. Comedy is shown to follow the apparent inevitability of tragedy in the way that dawn follows night and spring follows winter.

A further important seasonal reference occurs in *Emma* during the strawberry-picking excursion to Donwell Abbey. This takes place 'at almost Midsummer', and it is in this already mythic temporal zone that we find the 'sweet view – sweet to the eye and mind', subsequently recognised as 'Jane Austen's most lamentable landscape-painting error': 'prosperity and beauty ... rich pastures, spreading flocks, orchard in blossom, and light column of smoke ascending'.[480] John Sutherland has noted that 'there is not one "error" in the description (blossom in June), but two, and possibly three':

> Surely, on a sweltering afternoon in June, there would not be smoke rising from the chimney of Abbey-Mill Farm? Why have a fire? And if one were needed for the baking of bread, or the heating of water in a copper for the weekly wash, the boiler would surely be lit before dawn, and extinguished by mid-morning, so as not to make the

kitchen (which would also be the family's dining-room) unbearably hot. The reference to the ascending smoke would seem to be more appropriate to late autumn. And the reference to 'spreading flocks' would more plausibly refer to the lambing season, in early spring.

He finds in this passage a 'precise description, in the form of a miniature montage, of the turning seasons', since Emma believes herself at this moment secure that '[m]onths may come and months may go, but Harriet will not again succumb to a mere farmer'.[481]

We might also find in this comingling of seasons the still-distant narrative intimations of a second 'spring', here associated with Harriet and Robert Martin's narratively secure future union, which itself opens the final door to Emma's 'perfect happiness'. Anne Elliot associates Autumn and the 'analogy of the declining year' with 'declining happiness, and the images of youth and hope, and spring, all gone together'.[482] By the spring following the Donwell-Abbey strawberry-picking party of 'Midsummer', Harriet and Robert Smith are happily married, and their orchard is indeed in blossom, as their flock presumably spreads.

The view 'sweet to the eye and mind' is the shimmer of a potential outcome, and collapses in one scene the nine-month gestation associated with distinctively human creation, breaching the gap between the present and future. A similar breach of tenses between the present and future occurs in Anne and Wentworth's revelation scene:

> the power of conversation would make the present hour a blessing indeed; and prepare it for all the immortality which the happiest recollections of their own future lives could bestow.[483]

Emma's happy present and future are secured by the very events that seem to threaten their loss, against her conscious will, until her will is revised in line with a hitherto unconscious desire. All the struggle and the resistance, all the potential and real suffering, are recast as symptoms of Emma's mistaking of her own desire, her displacement of romance heroism onto another. The break between her false romancing and her true desire occurs in the dark, cold days of Christmas following Mr Elton's exposure of his unexpected meaning: 'But with all the hopes of cheerfulness, and all the comfort of delay, there was still such an evil hanging over her in the hour of explanation with Harriet, as made it impossible for Emma to be ever perfectly at ease.'[484] By aligning the turn in Emma's consciousness with the turn in the natural narrative of the seasons, we are asked to consider the release of the heroine from suffering towards happiness as the outcome of an equally 'natural' process. The arrival of spring/summer following her winter, and the return of summer following its apparent ruination by an unseasonal interruption, align with the return of narrative possibilities for happiness out of the determinants of tragedy.

These seasonal metaphors act as a literalisation of the absent maternal that conditions the narrative movement. The reaching for a spring/summer metaphor hails the return of the daughter to the mother, Proserpine to Ceres, displaced onto the cycle of nature. When the apparent death of winter still gives way to the creative miracle of spring, we should be reminded of a mythic return of matrilineal relations. In this symbolic convergence, the maternal is literalised as the living causality of nature, rather than its diverse forms. The return of signs of summer makes Emma long to be 'in' nature, where she encounters Mr Knightley, and the crucial revelation scene takes place:

> With all the eagerness which such a transition gives, Emma resolved to be out of doors as soon as possible. Never had the exquisite sight, smell, sensation of nature, tranquil, warm, and brilliant after a storm, been more attractive to her.[485]

This apprehension of being *in* nature as the literalisation of an otherwise unconscious maternal ideal makes of Austen's realism a feminised Platonism. We can find this otherwise slightly odd idea concretised in Fanny Price's meditation on nature and art, which owes something to Anne Finch's attempt to capture the same mood in a poem:[486]

> Fanny agreed to it, and had the pleasure of seeing him continue at the window with her, in spite of the expected glee; and of having his eyes soon turned like her's towards the scene without, where all that was solemn and soothing, and lovely, appeared in the brilliancy of an unclouded night, and the contrast of the deep shade of the woods. Fanny spoke her feelings. 'Here's harmony!' said she. 'Here's repose! Here's what may leave all painting and all music behind, and what poetry can only attempt to describe! Here's what may tranquillize every care, and lift the heart to rapture! When I look out on such a night as this, I feel as if there could be neither wickedness nor sorrow in the world; and there certainly would be less of both if the sublimity of Nature were more attended to, and people were carried more out of themselves by contemplating such a scene'.[487]

This makes Fanny a romantic, of course, in her turn to nature for a guarantee of a truth associated with social healing: 'wickedness' and 'sorrow' in the world can be overcome by contemplation of the wonders of nature. *Emma* intensifies the idea that Austen offers a realism that is not centred on the heightened detail of empirical consciousness – which must always fail because it remains mere representation – but in a narrative entroping of the mystery of the thing itself. The natural *cycle* is the deep model for her narratives: spring follows winter as dawn follows night, we need only be a little patient.

Persuasion emphasises this point by again placing Anne's narrative crossroads precisely at Christmas, the darkest time of the year, which parallels the lowest point of the heroine's narrative quest. Following Christmas, the web of narrative strands begins to pull together into the revised pattern of a future 'happiness'. Christmas is traditionally the season of turning despair into hope through forgiveness. This is a cyclical thought as much as a religious one: but if we did not all learn to think cyclically, we would despair each Autumn, if not each evening. Rituals imagining and welcoming the return of the life-giving light and warmth of the sun have been developed and transmitted throughout human history to remind us that the turning of night into day, winter into spring, is an act of cosmic generosity beyond anything in our power: '*it* was summer again'.[488] Given that such rituals are no longer an integral part of our collective consciousness – elided as superstitious, mythic, commercialised, romantic, or arbitrary – Austen's narratives might simply offer a gentle corrective.

This corrective takes the form of imaginative evidence that it is possible, if not plausible, that narratives which seem to be ending – or already to have ended – very badly indeed, may nonetheless turn out for the good. Accepting this at the level of realist narrative invites an imaginative possibility concerning grounds for renewed hope in the face of empirical evidence pointing towards despair. It is a lesson we still seem to desire, in our fictional if not in our historical narratives. It is also a narrative philosophy that seems to depend on the workings of a feminine agency *in* nature, a capacity to endure in the face of potential hopelessness, and a preoccupation with the endurance of love, that is perhaps most fully captured in Austen's last complete work.

6

Persuasion: 'loving longest, when existence or when hope is gone'

What if the 'original' subjective gesture, the gesture constitutive of subjectivity, is not that of autonomously 'doing something', but rather that of the primordial substitution, of withdrawing and letting another do it for me, in my place. Women, much more than men, are able to enjoy by proxy ... in this precise sense, the Hegelian 'cunning of reason' bears witness to the resolutely feminine nature of what Hegel calls 'Reason'.

Slavoj Žižek, 'The Supposed Subjects of Ideology' *CQ*[489]

What is love? Ask him who lives, what is life; ask him who adores, what is God. [...] – the meeting with an understanding capable of clearly estimating the deductions of our own, an imagination which should enter into and seize upon the subtle and delicate peculiarities which we have delighted to cherish and unfold in secret, with a frame whose nerves, like the chords of two exquisite lyres strung to the accompaniment of one delightful voice, vibrate with the vibrations of our own [...] this is the invisible and unattainable point to which love tends, to attain which it urges forth the powers of man to arrest the faintest shadow of that without the possession of which there is no rest or respite to the heart over which it rules.

Percy Bysshe Shelley, 'On Love'[490]

I must speak to you by such means as are within my reach. You pierce my soul. I am half agony, half hope. Tell me not that I am too late, that such precious feelings are gone for ever. I offer myself to you again with a heart even more your own, than when you almost broke it eight years and a half ago.

Jane Austen, *Persuasion*[491]

It has to be said that Emma and Anne achieve their narrative function as pretty passive recipients of the 'complete truth' – and the truth of their present and future 'perfect happiness' – in the form of an unexpected message of love. Their particular narrative purpose, the one that is 'risked' and found safe in the end, is to receive and 'understand' the message that they are loved: 'On the contents of that letter depended all that this world could do for her!'[492] They are quiet recipients in their scenes of revelation.[493] Yet Anne's receptivity is productive of one of the most plausible and beloved happy endings available in the realist tradition. This ending turns on the possibility of the endurance of love against all the odds, and the key to Anne's release is a message of love that has been risked and then found safe after all.

Persuasion provides the clearest and most concise example of Austen's mature realist vision. The consolations of romance appear in a new form, untied from the material determinants of landed property, since the final dissolve is literally oceanic:

> Anne was tenderness itself, and she had the full worth of it in Captain Wentworth's affection. His profession was all that could make her friends wish that tenderness less; the dread of a future war all that could dim her sunshine. She gloried in being a sailor's wife.[494]

The sea fascinated Austen, and we know she returned to it as often as possible in an age of difficult travel: one letter enjoys 'the prospect of spending future summers by the Sea', another greatly prefers 'the sea to all our relations'. *Persuasion*'s narrator pauses to note that Anne's party in Lyme 'soon found themselves on the sea shore, and lingering only, as all must linger and gaze on a first return to the sea, who ever deserve to look on it at all'.[495] It seems fitting, then, that Austen's last complete heroine is freed to a life at sea.

The highly desirable young Wentworth embodies a positive vision of oceanic masculinity, to the extent that a contemporary adaptation of the novel might well recast him in the guise of a sea-tanned surfer:

> Captain Wentworth had no fortune. He had been lucky in his profession, but spending freely, what had come freely, had realized nothing. But he was confident that he would soon be rich; – full of life and ardour, he knew that he should soon have a ship, and soon be on a station that would lead to every thing he wanted. He had always been lucky; he knew he should be so still. – Such confidence, powerful in its own warmth, and bewitching in the wit which often expressed it, must have been enough for Anne.[496]

It is quite plausible, then, that the eight pre-narrative years of separation following the end of their brief engagement leaves Anne 'altered' by disappointment ('years which had destroyed her youth and bloom'), but unaltered in her feelings: 'Alas! With all her reasonings, she found, that to retentive feelings eight years may be little more than nothing.' Eight years of naval action have by contrast 'only given him a more glowing, open look, in no respect lessening his personal advantages. She had seen the same Frederick Wentworth.'[497]

This is a new narrative condition, in which the heroine has already fallen 'rapidly and deeply in love' with a 'remarkably fine young man, with a great deal of intelligence, spirit and brilliancy', but has been talked into refusing his proposal, and long regretted her refusal. The last complete Austen narrative is a condensed treatment of desiring a second chance, for the seeds of new hope under the apparently entrenched conditions for despair:

> She was persuaded that under every disadvantage of disapprobation at home, and every anxiety attending his profession, all their probable fears, delays and disappointments, she should yet have been a happier woman in maintaining the engagement, than she had been in the sacrifice of it.[498]

Nonetheless, Wentworth's return is an excruciating event for Anne, and made the more painful by his insistence on flirting with every attractive younger woman in range:

> Any body between fifteen and thirty may have me for asking. A little beauty, and a few smiles, and a few compliments to the navy, and I am a lost man.[499]

It is an exquisitely uncomfortable situation for our heroine, fully realising her mistake as the object she was persuaded to reject returns to haunt her and flaunt its indifference to her lingering desire. He is, of course, now possessor of a substantial fortune, having achieved everything promised in his youth:

> All his sanguine expectations, all his confidence had been justified. His genius and ardour had seemed to foresee and to command his prosperous path.[500]

They are now 'worse than strangers', since 'they could never become acquainted': 'it was a perpetual estrangement'.[501]

The early stages of the narrative emphasise Anne's powerlessness, which makes the painful re-encounter both a passive event that returns the object against her will and entirely unavoidable:

> They were in the drawing-room. Her eye half met Captain Wentworth's; a bow, a curtsey passed; she heard his voice – he talked to Mary; said all that was right; said something to the Miss Musgroves, enough to mark an easy footing; the room seemed full – full of persons and voices – but a few minutes ended it.[502]

This impressionistic scene is given in heightened FID, presenting the first encounter between Anne and Wentworth since she had 'deserted and disappointed him' eight years earlier, through Anne's very partial view.[503] The narrative focus for this work mostly limits itself to Anne's isolated perspective, leaving the reader as desiring of evidence concerning Wentworth's feelings as our heroine must be: 'What might not eight years do?'[504]

FID offers access to the private consciousnesses of Anne, locked into separation since the severance of their apparently long-forgotten love: 'She would have liked to know how he felt as to a meeting.'[505] This example occurs the first moment Anne is aware that, after 'so many, many years of division and estrangement', Wentworth is 'only half a mile distant':

> Perhaps indifferent, if indifference could exist under such circumstances. He must be either indifferent or unwilling. Had he wished ever to see her again, he need not have waited till this time; he would have done what she could not but believe that in his place she should have done long ago, when events had been early giving him the independence which alone had been wanting.[506]

The narrator slips quietly from direct quotation and indirect description to interior FID the instant Anne is left alone:

> They were gone, she hoped, to be happy, however oddly constructed such happiness might seem; as for herself, she was left with as many sensations of comfort, as were, perhaps, ever likely to be hers. She knew herself to be of the first utility to the child; and what was it to her, if Frederick Wentworth were only half a mile distant, making himself agreeable to others![507]

Interior FID is also representative of Emma's lowest moment:

> The picture which she had then drawn of the privations of the approaching winter, had proved erroneous; no friends had deserted them, no pleasures had been lost. – But her present forebodings she feared would experience no similar contradiction. The prospect before her now, was threatening to a degree that could not be entirely dispelled – that might not be even partially brightened. If all took place that might take place among the circle of her friends, Hartfield must be comparatively deserted; and she left to cheer her father with the spirits only of ruined happiness.[508]

Both characters are brought from these dark introspections, expressed through a quiet empathy between narrative and character consciousness, yet marked by a profound isolation, to their particular versions of 'complete happiness', manifest in *Emma* as an open acknowledgement of union and community, and in *Persuasion* as a release from the sterile determinants of land, property, and rank. What in fact happens at Hartfield, following Emma's moment of despair, is not only an avoidance of what it seems 'might take place' at this moment, but its inversion. *Persuasion* is a study in the reversibility of fortune in the form of the unlikely endurance of love.

Emma and Anne, then, share a powerful transition from potential despair and 'ruined happiness' to the 'perfect happiness' which overcomes them before the close of their narratives, represented in terms of accepting an unexpected message of love. Anne is finally, and completely, enlightened to Wentworth's 'precious feelings' by a secretly written and cunningly delivered 'silent' message: 'I must speak to you by such means as are within my reach.'[509] This phrase resonates with Austen's more general purpose. She communicates 'by such means as are within [her] reach' the possibilities released by a comedic state of mind, in which the apparent turn of history towards the petrification of the subject is revealed from a different angle, through irony, with a tendency to make us laugh ourselves awake.

Frye notes that the comedic movement of 'ascent' – the movement narrated through Anne Elliot's experience of the gradual realisation that she is still loved – is conceived through 'themes and images' of 'escape, remembrance, or discovery of one's real identity, growing freedom, and the breaking of enchantment'.[510] The immobilising spell finds expression in Lady Russell's explicit 'persuasion' and Anne's loss of 'bloom', which we can read as the creeping paralysis of the sexual subject.

Sir Walter Elliot's proliferation of mirrors and preoccupation with appearance signals his immersion in the reflections of the dream world, his loss of the 'real'. Anne's movement out of the frame of representation into the oceanic signals the potential for reversal, associated with a return to an idealised maternal and with the unconscious.[511].

The intense 'recognition scene' between Anne and Wentworth sparks a 'reversal of movement which is both a surprise to the reader and yet seems to him an inevitable development of events up to that point'. This is the 'logical anxiety' common to all romance narratives: the possibility of a happy ending exposed to risk, but shown to be safe after all. A crossroads of causal implications is revealed to be split between diverging paths promising possible outcomes emerging from identical causal conditions: '*If* all took place that *might* take place among the circle of her friends ...'.

Frye believes this 'ideal' effect of romance has, however, 'never been attained by any work of literature', since 'a completely successful comic resolution depends upon an ideal reader or listener, which means one who has never encountered a comedy or romance before, and has no idea of literary convention'.[512] As a result, we merely recognise its formulaic qualities: 'the cyclical movement of the story, down through the threatening complications and up again through the escape from them' rather than 'the particular mystery by which this movement may be operated'. But this re-enactment of the 'particular mystery' of the 'movement' to which Frye refers seems to remain compelling to readers and viewers of contemporary romance.

The top two titles in the recent poll for the 'nation's favourite book' were Austen's *Pride and Prejudice* and Tolkein's *Lord of the Rings*. Both can be taken as 'romances' in the complete sense of the word, narrating the quest for the final undoing of 'evil' as somehow inextricably entwined with the quest for 'love' expressed through the providential union of a man and woman (or man and Elvin princess who enters mortal life as a condition of the successful quest). As I write, a new 'romantic comedy' is making claims to be the 'most successful' British film of all time.

The romance trope of petrification (immobility, loss of power and voice, objectification, turning to stone, under a spell, under the power of others, abduction, rape, death) refers us back to the problem of feminine agency under an increasingly totalised synchronic 'structure'. It should by now also remind us of the Christian notion of Providence. The narrative struggle of the heroine to awaken to the truth can be read for its incarnation of a particularly feminine subject under the constraints of an all-determining mode: Anne finds that her broken 'attachment' to

Wentworth and her 'regrets' following its severance 'had, for a long time, clouded every enjoyment of youth; and an early loss of bloom and spirits had been their lasting effect'.[513] She had been 'forced into prudence in her youth', and 'learned romance as she grew older'. Learning romance is explicitly tied to yielding to 'Providence' in this passage, and given as a 'natural sequel of an unnatural beginning.'[514]

It is worth noting that Louisa Musgrove is said to be 'determined' to make the fateful second jump from Lyme Cobb: 'I am determined I will.'[515] She boasts to Wentworth of not giving in to the persuasion of others: 'What! – would I be turned back from doing a thing that I had determined to do?'[516] Emma mistakes Harriet as equally 'determined' not to have Robert Martin. Anne Elliot has no say in, and actively opposes, the economic conditions which bring her into Wentworth's social circle, and can finally only receive with gratitude the salvation from a life of perpetual frustration and constraint he offers: 'On the contents of that letter depended all which this world could do for her'![517] The final awakening of Emma is an awakening to what has always already been true, but completely mistaken: nothing significant changes, except that she realises a narrative power working beyond her subjective will, but corresponding with a 'deeper' desire of which she becomes conscious as it is answered. The formal inevitability of her happy ending is painfully delayed, but not 'ruined', by what Knightley describes as her abuse of reason. Her own attempt to write romance onto her materials is corrected by an extradiegetic narrative power, one which knew her proper ending all along. Anne learns to trust to the apparently ossifying effects of 'Providence', and becomes a romance heroine in the process, representing in her release the sheer possibility of a new life of freedom which is offered in spite of all the realist determinants threatening her final petrification.

Since romance connotes an understanding of the sexual relationship which is not merely 'breeding', the difference turns on the definition of romance as the structuring power of 'love' – which itself transforms the providential union from base worldly marriage to a 'higher' register. *Persuasion*, in particular, distils this problem and its extradiegetic answer into a question regarding the very possibility of love in a world that seems to deny its presence. It is in *Persuasion* that we find perhaps the most compelling and complete reversal of the heroine's loss of 'power' in relation to her own desires: it is Austen's *Winter's Tale*. Anne Elliot functions along the mythic sequence of petrification and resurrection, which at the level of narrative correspond to figures of objectification and subjectivation. Her initiating mistake is that she has been offered a providential transformation prior to the beginning of the narrative, but has already rejected this with reference to the voice of reason.

It is significant that the voice of reason in this case, Lady Russell, is described as bearing 'almost a mother's love, and mother's rights'.[518] The difference marked by that 'almost' is crucial. We cannot help but wonder what Anne *would* have done eight years ago with her mother as an adviser, and the absence of this relationship is the common narrative denominator for Anne and Emma. In *Persuasion*, its absence is lightly referenced:

> 'it was only in Anne that [Lady Russell] could fancy the mother to revive again';
>
> 'she had never, since the age of fourteen, never since the loss of her dear mother, known the happiness of being listened to';
>
> 'No, except when she thought of her mother, and remembered where she had been used to sit and preside, she had no sigh of that description to heave.'[519]

Mr Elliot offers Anne the neat marital opportunity for maternal identification, as marriage to him would allow her to occupy her 'dear mother's place, succeeding to all her rights, and all her popularity, as well as to all her virtues'. Anne is 'bewitched' by the 'idea of becoming what her mother had been'.[520] Lady Russell and Mrs Weston, as substitute mothers, both mistake their step-daughters' true needs, and aim to have them married to objectively suitable partners (Mr Elliot, Frank Churchill). The *true* mother is absent as a narrative condition of understanding: her absence determines the 'fall from grace' of the heroines, and the absence of her perspective – particularly in matters of 'love' – allows these daughters to wander into their particular 'nightmare from which one can [only] escape by waking up'.[521]

Of course, for the young woman engaging in courtship of any kind, the absent mother is the ideal mother, in every sense of the thought. Since she is also idealised, we might expect her to return at the level of abstraction. Austen's imagining of the conditions for a plausible happy ending bespeaks the return of the ultimately idealised mother at the level of a formal synthesis, associated with compassion and forgiveness that makes everything alright after all. Since the narrative 'force' that releases the heroine is also shown to operate in spite of her objective 'faults', as best exemplified by Emma, the romance form acts as the narrative spirit of forgiving love and results in the healing of discord between the feminine subject and her objects. It is an odd thought, but one which emerges from a close analysis of Austen's late narratives, that the romance narrative mode might idealise a matrilineal relation, daughter as heroine and mother as narrative 'force', otherwise absent from the social equation. Doody's apprehension of the Goddess as the divinity that governs novelistic representation is another way of noting this narrative force. Romance is in these terms governed by the Goddess, projection of the archetype of the Great Mother, returning to put all in order that has been disordered in her long absence.

This return of an *idealised* maternal consciousness, read historically, denotes acceptance and understanding of a 'wordless message' captured and delivered at the level of the work's form, which acts to harmonise and heal its social content. The message is not difficult to decode, since it appears as the organising principle to which the referential material out of which these narratives have been woven is patterned: it regards the *possibility* of 'true' love. At this point, the contemporary association between romance and feminine wish-fulfilment can be illuminated as a historical coincidence between the cultural absence of matrilineal forms of communion, and the more general social absence of ideal relations.

The romance quest at its most abstract is a narrative of finding one's lost object without a map, or a clear sense of what that object might be in reality. The trick is to recognise it when it stands before you, and that recognition demands a kind of knowledge now as thoroughly debased as the feminine romance form in which it makes most sense. Moreover, Austen finds continuity between the experience of matrilineal love and the recognition of romantic love. Anne has 'never since the loss of her dear mother' found herself the object of loving attention, and as a result 'had been always used to feel alone in the world': never, that is, 'excepting one short period in her life' that was her brief acknowledgement of love with Wentworth.[522] Anne's first inkling of her awakening, and the subsequent regaining of her power, is in response to two early experiences of a 'wordless message' associated with 'the state of being released'. In the first, she is literally released from the grip of an unruly toddler.

In another moment, however, she found herself in the state of being released from [Walter]; some one was taking him from her, though he had bent down her head so much, that his little sturdy hands were unfastened from around her neck, and he was resolutely borne away, before she knew that Captain Wentworth had done it.[523]

In the second, she is selected to be given rest by the same 'will and hands':

> Yes, he had done it. She was in the carriage, and felt that he had placed
> her there, that his will and his hands had done it, that she owed it to
> his perception of her fatigue, and his resolution to give her rest.[524]

In both slight instances Anne is indirectly freed from worldy discom-
forts, and finds herself 'in the state of being released' when she is in no
position to be able to release herself. I take this as rather pure example of
Austen's imagining of the awakening of feminine consciousness to the
freedom of enlightenment. Austen's final narrative preoccupation is
with the terms of release from the world, and she documents this 'movement' in figures of believable action. The work is at this level so Gnostic
as to have slipped into tropes more characteristic of Buddhism than traditional Christianity. We can read Wentworth's return to save the heroine from the material determinants of her world under either system of
belief: he concretises a desire for salvation when all hope has already
been lost. Crudely stated, he embodies a narrative desire for the second
coming and the release from history this idea entails.

The particular material and civil constraints on feminine agency
are foregrounded in Anne's sense of what she *would* have done in
Wentworth's place, and again in the recognition of incommensurate
sexual difference in her overheard conversation with Captain Harville:
'We shall never agree I suppose upon this point. No man and woman
would, probably.'[525] This essential disagreement is understood by Anne
to be predetermined by conditions:

> It is a difference of opinion which does not admit of proof. We each
> begin probably with a little bias towards our own sex, and upon that
> bias build every circumstance in favour of it which has occurred
> within our own circle.

Anne further rejects claims to documentary evidence of any kind to
resolve the argument:

> no reference to examples in books. Men have had every advantage of
> us in telling their own story. Education has been theirs in so much a
> degree; the pen has been in their hands. I will not allow books to
> prove anything.

Her argument, made in 'the spirit of analogy', is that women suffer the
'privilege' of 'loving longest, when existence or when hope is gone'.[526]

This powerful claim can be read as analogous to the argument made at the historical level by these works: that women as a class are marked by the 'privilege' of holding out for 'love' after all, in spite of a wealth of empirical evidence directed towards proving its absence from the 'real' world.[527]

This argument seems to be borne out by evidence of an abiding feminine taste for romance in popular narrative forms. That taste, we should recall, remains largely unshaken by a grinding contemporary scene of, to name but a few: continuous wars, recurring famine, immunodeficiency epidemics, exponential evidence of murderous paedophilia as *the* modern social pathology, the vulgarisation and relativisation of sexual relations, ongoing deconstruction of heteronormativity, the apparently irreversible ecological and environmental decay threatening the survival of the planet, the almost complete triumph of capitalist exploitation of human labour and natural resources, and the decimation of entire living cultures in the name of democracy, religious purity, or progress. It is in this sense that women tend to be openly associated with the 'romantic': as a subjective escapism, or sanctioned – because apparently powerless – 'opiate'. We still dream of the possibility of a happy ending after all.

Frozen by objective determinants, and powerless to release herself, the last complete Austen heroine is nonetheless released to objective freedom by the very conditions which seem to act in opposition to her subjective desire prior to narrative transformation. If incommensurability conditions relations between subject and object, and between subjective representations of objective conditions, and is reiterated in further dissonant relations between men and women, realism and romance, high and popular culture, fallen and salvational perspectives, and between metonymy and metaphor, then Austen's final mediation of incommensurability performs what can be described as a narrative miracle. FID offers mediatory moments where change occurs, through the interpenetration of consciousness between narrator and character. This interpenetration is re-enacted at the level of narrative itself: offered by a narrator and received by a narratee. Austen's narrative mediation works through an alignment of consciousness between reader, narrator and character, which side-steps the 'subject-object determinant' by simply overlooking its determining conditions. It is this action that the work calls by the name of love.

Two powerful moments of transformation of character consciousness occur in Austen's work following the receipt of a letter: Wentworth's letter to Anne and Mr Darcy's letter to Elizabeth. In both cases, the letter is reproduced as direct discourse, read and understood by the reader in the same narrative moment that its message is delivered to the heroine. Elizabeth receives the letter of explanation from Darcy which, in spite of comprising 'two sheets of letter paper, written quite through, in a very close hand' in an envelope which 'itself was likewise full', is reproduced in full in the text, interrupting the narrative movement with a lengthy and detailed recapitulation of events up to this moment from Darcy's perspective.[528] Her experience of reflecting on the contents of the letter mirrors the reader's on first reading, as up until this moment only Elizabeth's perspective is implied. So when she decides the letter 'must be false! This cannot be! This must be grossest falsehood!', we follow her rapid comprehension of her previous 'prejudice' to the point where she realises that her judgement until this moment had in fact been completely misguided.

The letter produces 'a turn which must make him entirely blameless throughout the whole', even though she had previously believed not even an 'apology to be in his power'. Her judgement of Wickham is similarly reversed, and her 'amazement' that 'she could remember no more substantial good than the general approbation of the neighbourhood, and the regard which his social powers had gained him in the mess', would be mirrored by a reader who had unsuspectingly followed her perspective thusfar: 'How differently did every thing now appear in which he was concerned!' Her recognition that she 'had been blind, partial, prejudiced, absurd' is also a judgement the reader is invited to make regarding their own understanding of events and characters represented so far. The resulting 'just humiliation' she experiences leads her to revise her understanding of objects and their relations, and in the process catalyses a new understanding of herself: 'Till this moment, I never knew myself.'[529]

This particular narrative crossroads is marked by an attempt to deliberate 'on the probability of each statement', but her rational 'impartiality' is met with 'little success'. The letter more effectively opens the way for 'compassion' towards a previously despised object, and finally a recognition that 'never had she so honestly felt that she could have loved him, as now, when all true love must be vain'. This experience is realised through an analogous readerly desire, raised to awareness, then completely satisfied in chapter 58: 'If your feelings are still what they were last April, tell me so at once. *My* affections and wishes are unchanged, but one word from you will silence me on this subject for ever.'

This readerly experience of recognised and risked wish-fulfilment is intensified in *Emma* by the lateness of the realisation, giving an urgency to the last-minute communications. That lateness is further intensified in *Persuasion* by situating the loss of the providential object as *already* experienced as a prior condition for the narrative itself. It is only the *return* of the object that produces effects leading to Anne's full recognition of her original loss, and this is a quite new experience of the subject–object problem for the reader. A reversal of conditions tending to despair is shown to be possible, if not inevitable.

If FID is the narrative resolution of subject–object incommensurability through consciousness of an extradiegetic narrative 'force', which turns a system of representation towards an immanent object of knowledge, Austen's irony can be seen as the recognition of incommensurability and its resolution at a higher level in language itself. As with FID, which seems to proliferate in Austen's hands until it becomes the representational condition for literary realism itself, we know Austen *is* 'ironic' but have difficulty pinpointing the local operations of her irony. Verbal irony literally 'states the opposite of what its speaker or writer means'.[530] We would then need somehow to *know* what Austen 'means' before we can tell if her work is *being ironic* or not.

Persuasion is the least ironic, or at least, the narrative in which irony has become so merged with representation as to be imperceptible. The tone of *Persuasion* is such that even the more serious forms of momentary irony are banished: the foolish characters are overtly and continually foolish, the good are early recognised, and there is little self-irony in Anne's creeping despair. Some examples from Austen's work stand out as exemplary: 'It is a truth universally acknowledged, that a single man in possession of a good fortune, must be in want of a wife.' This 'truth' is 'so well fixed in the minds of the surrounding families, that he is considered as the rightful property of some one or other of their daughters'.[531] Peter Childs finds this 'one of her most famous uses of irony'. The 'truth universally acknowledged' is both merely a 'local attitude' and a genuinely universal truth; it depends on signifying contexts for the words 'truth', 'fortune' and 'want'. If the 'truth' is misread as 'local opinion', or vice versa, irony arises in the ridiculous distance between the absolute and particular signifieds.

Yet the novel shows by the end that this same 'truth' is also assumed by even the most sophisticated reader in the course of making sense of the narrative, and becomes a determinant of the final happy ending, itself opening up our sense of 'fortune' (as material and providential at the same time), and finding that the 'want' works precisely in relation to desired structural outcomes, in the sense of 'lack'. Austen's irony in fact never rests until it finds its object arrested in the literalism of interpretation: when we try to arrest any apparently solid, material, 'realist' object, the joke is squarely on us.

Four material objects in particular stand out: Edward's 'spoiled' scissors in *Sense and Sensibility*; Betsey's knife in *Mansfield Park*; Wentworth's forgotten gloves in *Persuasion*, and the 'hazel nut' he holds as analogous to his desire for firmness of character. Each object seems for a moment to hold the narrative in reference to specific temporal and spatial determinants; when little girls with bad tempers were given knives; when men could 'spoil' a pair of scissors or 'forget' a pair of gloves without fear of over-interpretation; when one might happen upon a hedgerow full of nuts on a beautiful autumn day. Of course, each object also falls on the representational side of instrument of 'cutting' or 'penetration' and 'container', and as such are over-invested objects at that moment of the narrative (when Edward declares himself no longer the 'first son'; when Fanny realises she has been cut loose from her former self; when Wentworth becomes fully conscious of his providential 'constancy' to Anne, and returns to her). For the irony to be recognised, 'the listener or reader must "get it" – but must already have grasped enough of something to realise that something does need to be got'.[532]

The hazel-nut opens a particularly condensed scene of overheard conversation. The party of characters has gone for a long walk, which results in a renewal of affection between Harriet Musgrove and her cousin, Charles Hayter, whose farm is the object of their walk. While Harriet and Charles Musgrove walk on to the farm, Anne, Mary, Louisa Musgrove and Wentworth are left 'at the top of the hill'. Louisa 'drew Captain Wentworth away' to look for nuts in the hedgerow, and Mary follows as she 'was sure Louisa had found a better seat somewhere else', while Anne rests on 'a dry sunny bank, under the hedge-row' in which Louisa and Wentworth are 'making their way back, along the rough, wild sort of channel, down the centre'. Anne overhears Wentworth in conversation with Louisa concerning the difference between her 'decisive' character and her sister's more yielding temper:

> 'To exemplify, – a beautiful glossy nut, which, blessed with original strength, has outlived all the storms of autumn. Not a puncture, not a weak spot anywhere. – This nut,' he continued, with playful solemnity, – 'while so many of its brethren have fallen and been trodden under foot, is still in possession of all the happiness that a hazel-nut can be supposed capable of.' Then, returning to his former earnest tone: 'My first wish for all, whom I am interested in, is that they should

be firm. If Louisa Musgrove would be beautiful and happy in her November of life, she will cherish all her present powers of mind.'[533]

All well and good, as Louisa's 'determination' to pursue an action in spite of the persuasion of others sees her endanger her life in the fall from Lyme Cobb. But the same determinants that make her jump the second time also ensure Wentworth's release from her affections, turning her desiring gaze towards Captain Benwick. And the second overheard conversation (when Wentworth hears Anne speak of her constancy) is initiated by a representation of Benwick and reflection on his capacity to overcome a lover's grief for Harville's dead sister, and develop a new love for Louisa Musgrove:

> 'Look here,' said [Captain Harville], unfolding a parcel in his hand, and displaying a small miniature painting, 'do you know who that is?'
> 'Certainly, Captain Benwick.'
> 'Yes, and you may guess who it is for. But (in a deep tone) it was not done for her. Miss Elliot, do you remember our walking together at Lyme, and grieving for him? I little thought then – but no matter.'[534]

It is the case of Louisa and Benwick that leads to Anne's claim that 'we do not forget you, so soon as you forget us'. This claim is offered in terms of a pointed enlightenment aphorism: 'If the change be not from outward circumstances, it must be from within.'[535] Wentworth's nut is equally indeterminate: it functions as a simple metaphor for the 'firmness' of mind he seeks in a woman, but taken literally has the more mysterious function of harbouring new life in its apparently impermeable self-enclosure. It is also a signifier of autumn, which is the specific context for the scene:

> Her *pleasure* in the walk must arise from the exercise and the day, from the view of the last smiles of the year upon the tawny leaves and withered hedges, and from repeating to herself some few of the thousand poetical descriptions extant of autumn, that season of peculiar and inexhaustible influence on the mind of taste and tenderness, that season which has drawn from every poet, worthy of being read, some attempt at description, or some lines of feeling.[536]

Austen is well aware that she is 'worthy of being read' and gives her own 'attempt at description' through Anne's consciousness of the 'thousand poetical descriptions' that colour her perception of the scenery. But her memory is disrupted by overheard remarks between Wentworth and Louisa:

> 'If I loved a man, as she loves the Admiral, I would always be with him, nothing should ever separate us, and I would rather be overturned by him, than driven safely by any body else.'
> It was spoken with enthusiasm.
> 'Had you?' cried he, catching the same tone; 'I honour you!' And there was silence between them for a little while.
> Anne could not immediately fall into a quotation again. The sweet scenes of autumn were for a while put by – unless some tender sonnet, fraught with the apt analogy of the declining year, with declining happiness, and the images of youth and hope, and spring, all gone together, blessed her memory.[537]

Faced by the fact of her now impossible desire, Anne finds resonance with the poetic analogy of autumn with decay, decline, and loss. But a different figuration of autumn is also available from the scene:

> another half mile of gradual ascent through large enclosures, where the ploughs at work, and the fresh-made path spoke the farmer, counteracting the sweets of poetical despondence, and meaning to have spring again.

Austen's narrative purpose here is in line with the farmer's more narrative than poetic activity: 'meaning to have spring again'. The farmer's plough drives through enclosed land, so his non-poetic activity is associated with a modern 'progress' as much as a romantic rural idyll: the writer also means 'to have spring again', and her writing is at least partly an economic activity. Nature is one thing, the productive participation in nature by human cultivation is another. Autumn can signify death, decay, loss and decline, but it can also signify the moment to prepare for the return of spring that naturally follows. The hazel-nut also functions as a concretised figure of the cycle of nature which fruits in autumn, as a sign that *it* also means 'to have spring again'. It grows in hedgerows that mark the boundaries of enclosed fields, ploughed for profit: nature continues to produce its wonders in spite of the economic determinants of human activity.

For Carter and McRae, Austen's 'irony' is central to her representation of 'universal' concerns. In opposition to critics who 'speak of her delicacy and irony, her femininity and lack of scope' as critical devaluations of the writer and her work, these critics foreground Austen's 'gentle irony' in the place of 'great didactic, moral, or satiric purpose'. Her 'small-scale' perspective in the face of 'the wars being waged outside the limits of the village' is inverted in the 'universality' of her characters and narratives.[538] Lukács aligns irony with the 'self-recognition and, with it, self-abolition of subjectivity' of the novel. Irony resides in the dissonance between 'a subjectivity as interiority' and 'a subjectivity which sees through the abstract and, therefore, limited nature of the mutually alien worlds of subject and object' and sees 'their limitations as necessary conditions of their existence'.

> At the same time the creative subjectivity glimpses a unified world in the mutual relativity of elements essentially alien to one another, and gives form to this world. Yet this glimpsed unified world is nevertheless purely formal; the antagonistic nature of the inner and the outer worlds is not abolished but only recognised as necessary; the subject which recognises it as such is just as empirical – just as much part of the outside world, confined in its own interiority – as the characters which have become its objects. Such irony is free from that cold and abstract superiority which narrows down the objective form to a subjective one and reduces the totality to a mere aspect of itself; this is the case in satire. In the novel the subject, as observer and creator, is compelled by irony to apply its recognition of the world to itself and to treat itself, like its own creatures, as a free object of free irony.[539]

For Riley, '[i]rony is the mark of such an active nonidentity' between representation and its objects.[540] Irony is the inevitable response – in the face of despair – of a realist aim to the incommensurate nature of subject–object relations, replicated in the mimetic aim of realist representation. Knowing an object demands at some level its incorporation: FID shows this to be possible at the level of language. Discursive incorporation is a point of identification, which is reversed in the irony implied by the relative difference between incorporated material and the extradiegetic force at work in the process. Subject-object determinants are nonetheless breached by this evidence of a dialectic between subjective and objective discourses. It is significant, then, that the three discursive fields in which this breach can be most commonly experienced and recognised (gossip, prayer, love) are central to Austen's narrative work. Reading is a fourth arena for FID to be found in common experience: when we read Austen's novels, just as when Elizabeth reads

Darcy's letter, we incorporate the writing consciousness's words and perspective.

While gossip captures recognisable aspects of the language that belongs to others, in which we only circulate as objects; prayer captures recognisable aspects of the language that is withheld from others. The former solidifies into a reified objectivity, whether or not it aligns with the 'truth'; the latter solidifies into an equally reified solipsism. Love, on the other hand, denotes an ideal condition in which apparently insurmountable boundaries between subject and object dissolve, and desire is met with no resistance in the material, since for a moment at least, it is mutually realised. In Austen, the full experience of love has a powerful effect on otherwise determined relationships, leading to her key characters' release into freedom and associated with perception of an enhanced beauty in the world and its objects:

> It is something for a woman to be assured, in her eight-and-twentieth year, that she has not lost one charm of earlier youth: but the value of such homage was inexpressibly increased to Anne, by comparing it with former words, and feeling it to be the result, not the cause of a revival of his warm attachment.[541]

We all love a happy ending, and Anne's is thrown into relief by comparison with the false ending she thought she had already experienced eight years earlier:

> There they returned again into the past, more exquisitely happy, perhaps, in their re-union, than when it had been first projected; more tender, more tried, more fixed in a knowledge of each other's character, truth, and attachment; more equal to act, more justified in acting. And there, as they slowly paced the gradual ascent, heedless of every group around them, seeing neither sauntering politicians, bustling house-keepers, flirting girls, nor nursery-maids and children, they could indulge in those retrospections and acknowledgments, and especially in those explanations of what had directly preceded the present moment.[542]

Love seems to be a critically unfashionable concept that has been theorised out of the social equation, and relegated to private fantasy, escapism, romance: 'Love is impossible because love is a disguised form of self-love: when one is a man, one sees in one's partner what can serve, narcissistically, to act as one's own support.' Anthony Easthope adds: 'When one is a woman, likewise. Love is impossible because, as far as Lacan is concerned, the sexes are completely asymmetrical in their desires.'[543] But what has it got to do with symmetry? In the end it depends what you think love is, and what you think it is that loves, or what was 'there' to love in the first place: if we can accept the experience of love over and above the theorising of the impossibility of love, this point becomes easier to digest. The plenitude of love is more than worth the exchange of the illusion of the self.

The 'wisdom of love' is precisely that which Luce Irigaray finds lacking in the tradition of Western thought. Her prophecy ('from a solipsistic love, from a certain reason dominated by logical formalism, philosophy passes to a wisdom of love') chimes eerily with Austen's narrative movement.[544] Of course, this is all romancing the argument, but there is just a possibility, unlikely as it seems, that it is also true. Narrative at its most general is the diachronic mediation of otherwise incommensurable synchronic modes. What seems to stand in the way of objective freedom simply shifts, in order to become a condition for objective freedom: Austen's comedic irony implies a late and unexpected dialectical reversal on the horizon. If this is possible in realist narrative – and Jane Austen is rather persuasive in her demonstration that this is the case – it is, by the argument of analogy she seems to enjoy, also possible in other kinds of narrative. Perfect happiness? But that would be against all the empirical odds available.

Conclusion: 'such an alternative as this had not occurred to her'

> The point is rather that the Enlightenment *must examine itself*, if men are not to be wholly betrayed. The task to be accomplished is not the conservation of the past, but the redemption of the hopes of the past.
>
> Theodor Adorno and Max Horkheimer,
> *Dialectic of Enlightenment*[545]

> Art deals not with the real but with the conceivable; and criticism, though it will eventually have to have some theory of conceivability, can never be justified in trying to develop, much less assume, any theory of actuality.
>
> Northrop Frye, 'The Archetypes of Literature'[546]

> In Prudie's dream, Jane Austen is showing her through the rooms of a large estate. Jane doesn't look anything like her portrait. She looks more like Jocelyn and sometimes she is Jocelyn, but mostly she's Jane. She's blond, neat, modern. Her pants are silk and have wide legs. [...]
>
> Jane arrives again. She is in a hurry now, hustling Prudie past many doors until they suddenly stop. 'Here's where we've put your mother,' she says. 'I think you'll see we've made some improvements.'
>
> Prudie hesitates. 'Open the door,' Jane tells her, and Prudie does. Instead of a room, there is a beach, a sailboat and an island in the distance, the ocean as far as Prudie can see.
>
> Karen Joy Fowler, *The Jane Austen Book Club*[547]

Women seem so far to have survived their disconnection from the 'higher' realms of knowledge, but remain at a tangential relationship to 'objective' knowledge today:

> The sciences – as the paradigm of modern academic disciplines – maintain the self-serving and misleading pretense of 'dispassionate objectivity,' an attitude which promotes a sense of separation between self and other, observer and observed, scientist and nature.[548]

This 'sense of separation' has been associated with 'certain emotions alleged to be especially characteristic of males in certain periods, such as separation anxiety and paranoia or an obsession with control and fear of contamination'.[549]

Feminist epistemology emphasises the fact that '[g]eneralizing the activity of women to the social system as a whole would raise, for the first time in history, the possibility of a fully human community, a community structured by connection rather than separation and opposition'. Furthermore, '[i]f the community of exchangers (capitalists) rests on the more overtly and directly hostile death struggle of self and other, one might be able to argue that what underlies the exchange abstraction is abstract masculinity'. When female-centred experience is theorised, we find that 'continuity and relation – with others, with the natural world, of mind with body' are recognised as central to human life.[550] It isn't such a startling realisation when you think about it.

The claim to objectivity in knowledge rests on the accumulation of empirical evidence, and a particular strain of empiricism characterises the capitalist world view. Incidentally, it is not obvious that our individual or collective experience of the world has particularly improved as a result of exponentially increasing the *quantity* of empirical data about it since the rise of the empirical sciences through the eighteenth century. Austen's narratives invite us to bring to light the determinants of our *interpretation* of the data, and ask us to consider the remarkable implications of a change of mind. In some ways this brings her closer to Blake than Locke:

> 'What', it will be Question'd, 'When the Sun rises, do you not see a round disk of fire somewhat like a Guinea?' O no, no, I see an Innumerable company of the Heavenly host crying 'Holy, Holy, Holy is the Lord God Almighty'.[551]

It brings her closest to the properly dialectical principles of feminist epistemology. Austen was audacious enough to take those principles to their logical conclusion, and her narrative offers the imaginative means for communicating an enduring vision of the feminine alternative to what has come to be understood as an 'abstract masculinity' that expresses itself through the death struggles of capitalism. We have already acknowledged that the knowing subject and the object of knowledge always exist in dynamic inter-relationship, and that we cannot abstract one from the other without distorting both. 'All human knowledge serves ... a defensive function', and the 'unhappy consciousness' finds evidence for its unhappiness in the world it has constructed. Jane Flax has very convincingly analysed the 'roots' of the particular form of 'unhappy consciousness' underpinning the capitalist world view in terms of a narcissistic reaction to 'the discovery of separateness', 'in which the outside world is seen purely as a creation of and an object for the self':

> Underlying the narcissistic position, the fear and wish for regression to the helpless infantile state remains. The longings for symbiosis with the mother are not resolved. Therefore, one's own wishes, body, women and anything like them (nature) must be partially objectified, depersonalized and rigidly separated from the core self in order to be controlled. Once this position is established, the relationship between the self (subject) and object (other persons, nature, the body) becomes extremely problematic, perhaps unresolvable. This frozen posture is one of the social roots of the subject–object dichotomy and its persistence within modern philosophy. It is an abstract expression of a deeply felt dilemma in psychological development under patriarchy and thus cannot be resolved by philosophy alone.[552]

Furthermore, the 'apparently irresolvable dualisms of subject–object, mind–body, inner–outer, reason–sense, reflect this dilemma' since 'only certain forms of the self and of philosophy can emerge under these conditions'. Austen's narrative outcomes compel us to recall other kinds of philosophy, and other kinds of self, alongside other kinds of endings to the narrative.

The common resolution of Austen's realist narratives in idealised marriages points unflinchingly at the sheer imaginative possibility of a happy ending, in spite of the careful documentation of the determinants of tragedy. Elizabeth only gets her Darcy (and her Pemberley) when she realises that this is what she wants, given the opportunity to think about it properly. Getting what she wants follows recognition that she had previously been wrong about her own desire. All roads seem to lead to Mr Darcy, but what does he really represent? Well, the name is likely to have been borrowed from the engineer who oversaw the 'new' building of the Cobb at Lyme in the 1790s. The plaque marking his work remains in place, but is no longer 'new'. The Cobb reaches out to sea in an arc that shelters the harbour and its village. The sea is parted by the Cobb, but also encloses it. One can still walk on the Cobb, and attempt the precarious steps that lead from the Upper to the Lower levels. It is an indeterminate structure, both joining land and sea and separating land from sea; allowing an experience of direct access to the sea from a position of relative security. The Cobb is an ironic object, and unusually beautiful as a result. It also invites one to jump one way or the other – or maybe that's just me. If it is a phallic structure, it is a friendly one that lies in a relaxed curve in the embrace of the sea.

More generally Darcy stands as the object of a quintessentially feminine desire to be *somehow* saved from the inevitability of suffering that seems to be the historical condition. He embodies this in a form readily available to Austen: a handsome, masculine, powerful, aristocratic presence that remembers how to live well in nature and culture. He does not exploit, claims less than he deserves, gives more than he is asked to, and will not suffer fools. His foil, Wickham, represents the lure of the dangerous object, one that – in Colonel Brandon's words – has not learnt to 'feel for' an other. Darcy embodies an idea that can be loved without fear or shame by the feminine subject, a masculine power that will not colonise her desire.

Austen's other kind of philosophy foregrounds the role of love in the social equation. This is a difficult point to take seriously, in a world where love seems to exist only incidentally, if at all, in the scraps of 'private' domestic space we have managed to protect from the increasing instrumentalisation of human experience. Love is a difficult thing to write about outside of literature, and does not seem to belong in theory at all. An illusion, a dream, a figment of popular myth, love increasingly eludes the subject, or worse – threatens to draw the subject to its doom in the cycle of desire and despair that seems to constitute the social life of the urban West.

All our popular songs and the most enduring works of literature and film are of love. What is it that makes something as fundamental to the survival of the individual and the species seem a chimera, an ideology, a myth? Furthermore, why is it that the eighteenth century seems marked by the demise of love into ideology at the very moment that capitalism gained ground: 'Much of patriarchal history has been a history of patriarchy: its wars, its politics, a progressive journey toward professionalized, urbanized, bureaucratic capitalist or socialist states'.[553] Not that life before this was necessarily better, just that we can see the contour of this specific loss in cultural documents most removed from the political or historical arena. Is it always the eighteenth century somewhere? The 'European Enlightenment', and the empiricism that inflects its English manifestation, might best be characterised by the loss of love in the face of efficiency. Austen's *insistence* on love as the key causal agent for a happy ending becomes remarkably significant from this perspective. Love is not an empirically observable object: it is a dynamic process, occurring *between* two subjects, that initiates a new and distinctive inter-subjective rhythm, and that reveals more of the thorough emptiness of the self than any deconstructive methodology will find possible:

> Something deeply embarrassing and truly scandalous abides in this reversal by means of which the mysterious, fascinating, elusive object of love discloses its deadlock, and thus acquires the status of another subject.[554]

But Elizabeth Bennet thinks it better:

> The respect created by the conviction of his valuable qualities, though at first unwillingly admitted, had for some time ceased to be repugnant to her feelings; and it was now heightened into somewhat of a friendlier nature, by the testimony so highly in his favour, and bringing forward his disposition in so amiable a light, which yesterday had produced. But above all, above respect and esteem, there was a motive within her of good will which could not be overlooked. It was gratitude – Gratitude, not merely for having once loved her, but for loving her still well enough, to forgive.

What changes Mr Darcy from an object of Elizabeth's disdain to an agent of her extraordinary happiness? The experience of love: 'for to love, ardent love, it must be attributed'.[555]

Austen's idea of love mediates between the individual and the social, and again between the material and the spiritual. The public assembly and the private party, central to Austen's study of what is possible in human relationships, represent the permeation of 'public' and 'private' boundaries. Bringing the social community into one's private space or entering the social community, women move freely within and even dominate these productive social spaces. Dances are traditional ('every savage can dance') and performed each time anew. They crystallise an encounter of the individual in the social. Dance is a synchronic expression (wordless pattern) manifested over time:

> Rhythm, or recurrent movement, is deeply founded on the natural
> cycle, and everything in nature that we think of as having some anal-
> ogy with works of art, like the flower or the bird's song, grows out of
> a profound synchronization between an organism and the rhythms
> of its environment, especially that of the solar year.[556]

Austen's narratives engage in a dance of their own: Elizabeth is snubbed
by Darcy, then she refuses him, but they dance well together in the end.
Mr Knightly and Emma dance to affirm that they are not 'brother and
sister'. Lydia exposes herself in her eagerness to dance with *all* the
officers. Mary is never asked, and takes her consolation in rational philosophy. Mr Elton won't dance with Harriet, while Mr Knightley and
Mr Darcy turn out to be fine dancers after all. For the dance to be successful each must know their part, subordinate their movements to
the whole, without being able to appreciate that whole in its entirety.
Partnership between a masculine and feminine couple centres the dance,
and its formal movements emphasise this elemental pair. One of the
things that makes the brilliant adaptation of *Pride and Prejudice* into
Bride and Prejudice so successful is the centrality of social dance, and
romance, to the Bollywood genre. Dance and narrative are both metaphors
for the rhythm of the natural cycle of life.

Denise de Rougemont has described the contemporary tendency to
understand metaphor as an imaginative expression of a material condition as 'another instance of the eagerness of the contemporary mind to
settle a question in favour of whatever is lower'. It is, according to him,
'impossible for anybody who thinks that the physical came first to give
reasons for his opinion':

> Nobody has found out that the 'material' meaning of every word
> has actually preceded the 'mental' meaning. The opinion that it
> has is merely based on a presumption – that the physical is *more
> true and more real* than the mental, and hence that the physical
> is at the foundation of all things and is the principle of all
> *explanations*.[557]

The alternative, that the material is an *expression* of imagination, or mind,
according to the spirit of analogy, is an ancient idea. Austen allows Anne
Elliot authority to speak of the specificity of 'women's feelings' in

'the spirit of analogy'. Addressing men in general through Captain Harville, she gives her opinion:

> I believe you capable of every thing great and good in your married lives. I believe you equal to every important exertion, and to every domestic forbearance, so long as – if I may be allowed the expression, so long as you have an object.[558]

If we turn to Jameson to account for the critical questions posed by Austen's romance we find another argument 'in the spirit of analogy'. Marxian political analogy represents history as a partially understood narrative, the ending of which is yet to be realised, and which 'only Marxism' can ever adequately interpret:

> Only Marxism can give us an adequate account of the essential *mystery* of the cultural past, which, like Tiresias drinking the blood, is momentarily returned to life and warmth and allowed once more to speak, and to deliver its long-forgotten message in surroundings utterly alien to it. This mystery can be reenacted only if the human adventure is one; only thus – and not through the hobbies of antiquarianism or the projections of the modernists – can we glimpse the vital claims upon us of such long-dead issues.[559]

Marxian analogy establishes abstract modes of production and exchange as prior to culture and productive of history itself. A mode is a highly abstract idea: determining and inclusive, producing effects in the cultural domain, but always just out of sight to those whose lives are structured by and through it; 'the Real' apprehended at the level of the economic. Under the 'mode' we understand as capitalism, it has been infamously claimed an inevitability that 'the collective consciousness gradually loses all active reality and tends to become a mere reflection of the economic life and, ultimately, to disappear'.[560] Has it disappeared yet? Do we still know the dance?

Women's writing has always offered the potential for such questions to arise. When engaged in the representation of feminine desire and its objects, women writers straddle the subjectivation/objectification of language, and literally take representations of themselves and their desires to market. What gets imported with them is an impression of the 'object' as constructed *through* feminine desire. Women may well have been symbolically objectified by kinship exchange, fetishised and reified in themselves. However, if it is *true* that the exchange of women as symbolic objects overcomes incestual desires, it remains the case that we are in all likelihood better off as symbolic objects than as objects of incestual desire. Objectification may simply be a strand of human connectivity and collectivity, and aligned with a particularly masculine gaze because 'the pen has been in their hands'. Mr Darcy is objectified by the narrator and reader as well as by Mrs Bennet, indeed by the 'universal opinion' that initiates the narrative in which he takes form. He clearly expects to find this objectifying desire already at work in Elizabeth Bennet's gaze: 'I believed you to be wishing, expecting my addresses.'[561] Elizabeth's rising consciousness of desire for Darcy follows on from his first, unexpected, proposal and seems to interpellate a parallel desire in the reader.

Gazes are an important index for this powerful narrative. Elizabeth first becomes an 'object of some interest in the eyes' of Mr Darcy, and his attention is initiated by the 'beautiful expression of her dark eyes'.[562] The reader is invited to join in a more general narrative gaze that apprehends Darcy as the prime object of feminine desire, and – when the narrative works – the shift in our perception of him occurs following recognition that he desires Elizabeth against his own will, without her knowledge, and at least in part in response to her *resistance* to his desiring gaze:

> Elizabeth looked archly, and turned away. Her resistance had not injured her with the gentleman, and he was thinking of her with some complacency, when thus accosted by Miss Bingley.
> 'I can guess the subject of your reverie.'
> 'I should imagine not … I have been meditating on the very great pleasure which a pair of fine eyes in the face of pretty woman can bestow'.[563]

The 'fine eyes' are both beautiful to the observer and beginning to observe an unexpected beauty in return. Austen's narratives seem determined to direct her readers' gaze with breathtaking confidence at the possibility of a more beautiful 'prospect', another possible outcome, or imaginary 'world', implicit in the transformation of the object of Elizabeth's gaze.

I want to bring the discussion to a close on this note of the possibility of a happy ending as expression of a more general 'comic vision'. The romance closure of Austen's realist narratives brings into focus an indirect representation of an 'innocence which sees the world in terms of total human intelligibility', and can also be recognised as a specific 'vision of the unfallen world or heaven in religion'.[564] This account of Austen's work helps to explain the repetition-compulsion it seems to inspire, both in the sense of multiple re-reading, and in the sense of its ongoing adaptability. As the members of the *Jane Austen Book Club* realise, 'in three or four years it would be time to read Austen again'.[565] The question I am left with is whether these famous romantic closures, which articulate the persistent dream of *true* love, social harmony, and respectful intersubjectivity, are pure 'romance' in the sense of sheer wish-fulfilment, feminine pornography, or escapism. The alternative is an engaging thought. The works might offer a narrative representation of a feminine desire for 'good fortune', working a dialectical reversal of the more plausible 'objective' conditions for suffering available from empirical evidence, and centred on forgiving actions and a healing laughter. Here is agency indeed.

Elder Olsen defines the poetics of comedy as 'not so much a question of laughter as of the restoration of the mind to a certain condition ... a pleasant, or rather an euphoric condition of freedom from desires and emotions which move men to action'.[566] This 'condition' is achieved 'through a special kind of relaxation of concern: a katastasis': 'the annihilation of the concern itself ... by the conversion of the grounds of concern into absolutely nothing'. This is the movement of feminine enlightenment: a subjective reversal that inaugurates objective revision. It is also the narrative movement of romance. For the outcome to be comedic, there must be plenty to smile about in the end, and the journey itself can be forgotten: 'You must learn some of my philosophy. Think only on the past as its remembrance gives you pleasure.'[567]

In 'orthodox structuralism' romance might exemplify one of a number of 'deep permanent structures of which the observed variations of languages and cultures are forms'. The formal qualities of romance can be apprehended as 'permanent constitutive human formations: the defining features of human consciousness and perhaps of the physical human brain'.[568] The romance as an essentialist fantasy comes into focus when we consider this highly particularised imaginative structure as reference back to the materiality of *the* 'human brain'.

Austen's worlds and characters have been *real* to millions of readers and viewers, and continue to be so, but they only exist in the material world as a stream of print on the pages of books. And Austen reminds us of this as soon as we are tempted to believe in the imaginary universe she invites us to share: 'my reader, who will see in the tell-tale compression of the pages before them, that we are all hastening together to perfect felicity'.[569] The rest is down to the reader's desire and imagination: 'the most charming young man in the world is instantly before the imagination of us all'.[570] Fay Weldon comments on the imaginary universe available through reading Jane Austen: 'Novelists provide an escape from reality: they take you to the City of Invention. When you return you know more about yourself. You do not read novels for information, but for enlightenment.'[571] Austen's narratives seem to suggest that this very experience of subjective enlightenment can be transformative of the subject's relationship with its objects and context.

There is no wonder this idea is only obscurely available today, preoccupied as we are with the astonishing mess we have made in *this* world, but it is preserved as a fair prospect in Hegelian and Marxian, as well as Christian, analysis. Perhaps this is the very 'representational fallacy' that Austen was exposing in her own turn to symbolic answers to ideological problems. Her body of work remains a compelling source of recognition and fascination today because we all really still want the same thing – even if only unconsciously. The desire for a happy ending *is* a universal.

If narrative is an organisation of the subject in desire, the feminine subject is held by Austen to desire objective freedom, and she shows how to begin from where one finds oneself, in the most subjective place of all. Acknowledging desire for a happy ending is the first step, acknowledging that the agency for such an ending is vastly beyond individual will is the second, and the rest follows. Fay Weldon hints at Austen's work as conduit to 'That Other Place': 'One could leave this world easily enough and take up one's existence over there.'[572] But of course it isn't really as easy as that, and we close the book to find ourselves where we have always been, but with the slightest hint that we might be able to know it differently.

Austen's work incorporates its context and hands it back transformed. The British government's 'General Land Enclosure Act' of 1801 marks the culmination of a long and profound paradigm shift in our relationship to, and conceptualising of, the land. The eighteenth century sees an ancient intuition of 'commonality' finally giving way to the now simply more 'realistic' principle of enclosed areas of land as property (fenced off, measured out, economically more efficient):

> So much of the land was in some way shared. You could walk across the parish land from one end to the other along common track and banks without fear of trespass. Your children could seek out bits of lane grass and river bank for the geese or pigs; they could get furze or turf, go berrying or nutting in the woods or on the common.[573]

Land since the eighteenth century only seems to make sense when it is in the legal hands of a named freeholder. The elusive principle of commonality (what Neeson calls 'possession without ownership') that is lost in this very broad cultural shift is also the principle of a collectively meaningful understanding of an elemental materiality, now reduced to a market commodity.

This shift is not spoken directly in Austen's work, but manifests indirectly: in anxieties over the 'whole' estate (*Persuasion*); narrative implications of primogeniture and the entail (*Sense and Sensibility, Pride and Prejudice, Persuasion*); unspecified concerns over the purchasing power of 'new' money (*Emma*); fear of the disruption to traditional relationships between family and land (*Sense and Sensibility, Persuasion*); awareness of the new intensive farming methods and fashion for 'improvements' to the estate (*Mansfield Park, Emma*); narratives interested in the possibility of being exiled from one's home (*Northanger Abbey*, Sense *and Sensibility*). Austen's narratives are structurally implicated in a broader logical anxiety concerning the individual, the dyad, the social community, and the world. This anxiety manifests as the romance/realism tension. Commonality as a legitimate relationship to land, and to the community through shared responsibility for and ownership of land, has also become a sheer 'romance', associated with a lost past:

> We know relatively little about common rights, and less about commoners, and even that is disputed among historians. There are many reasons, but one of them is a failure of the imagination. For good reason: imagining something that has disappeared is difficult; after all loss *is* loss.[574]

Enclosure of common land is simply a more 'realistic' way to deal with the world: 'imagining how commoners lived off the shared use of land is difficult in an age such as ours when land is owned exclusively, and when enterprise is understood to be essentially individual not co-operative'.[575] It also an act of literalising metonymy: cutting a theoretical whole into discrete parts (market stocks operate in a similar way). Austen refuses the cut, and we love her for that.

The estate is also a metaphor. Not just the literal estates of existing land owners, but the social estate; a principle of primal order, apparently always under threat, but finally and inexplicably saved in new formations centred on the activation of a feminine consciousness. Something is made safe in the course of Austen's narratives, and their enduring appeal illuminates that elusive 'something' as still precious, a lost object silently mourned, and perhaps misread as a nostalgic desire for guilt-free fantasies of an escape from the ossifying demands of 'realism' into the revivifying embrace of a handsome, powerful, and very well-endowed gentleman.

The providential union of irreducible difference that centres each narrative finally represents the synthesis of a heterogeneous pair, and also finds unity in apparently dichotomous possibilities: marriage that is economically and ethically perfect *is* romantic. This records a questing for the possibility of true love under conditions that speak directly of its impossibility (except as fantasy). This final union of the realistic and the romantic can be understood as an indirect representation of a synthesis between the empirical and the ideal. If this remains possible, nothing *has* been lost, fears *are* unfounded, and we are invited to shrug off the shadow of the inevitability of tragedy in the light of a final comedic narrative inversion. The comedic outcome becomes romance proper when the social reality under representation is reframed by a metaphysical intelligence: a shift from a temporal to an eternal frame of reference.

The point is reviewed well at the close of the infamous BBC adaptation of *Pride and Prejudice*: the concluding double marriage is represented visually through a voice-over of the traditional Christian marriage service, with cut-aways to couples standing for the various forms of marriage available to the world of the representation. Marriage to avoid fornication (Lydia and Wickham); marriage for mutual companionship (Mr and Mrs Gardiner); marriage not to be undertaken lightly (Mr and Mrs Bennet); and, finally, marriage as analogous to the relationship between Christ and his church (Darcy and Lizzy). The metaphysical frame is never very far from Austen's narrative purpose.[576]

Eighteenth-century English empiricism has come to dominate the contemporary world view: we insist on believing what we see and seeing what we believe. Faith in empiricism seems to be what saves us from the illusory scenes of ideology, from false consciousness, and from fantasy, as Dr Johnson's famous sore toe still testifies. But it is highly likely that what we currently accept as common sense is also thoroughly ideological: we see what we are shown, or have already decided must be there before we even look. Like Elizabeth Bennet, however, we can still have experiences which suggest that everyone to some extent has 'courted prepossession and ignorance, and driven reason away'. What we make of empirical evidence depends on the determinants of the senses, and currently it would seem those determinants have little real purpose beyond confirming the detail of (usually tragic) causal inevitability. This is a cold return for the investment of belief, since – for example – knowledge of the detailed causal factors in the loss of a loved one does nothing to alleviate the pain of losing them or reversing the loss. Naming of parts is simply not enough.

But what is it that remains to guarantee the increasingly hegemonic truth claims of a secularised empiricism, given that the rise of this critical and perceptual paradigm neatly parallels the narrative of the instrumentalisation of human experience under capitalism? Perhaps only the fear that there is nothing to know if we look too hard, other than the ungrounded nature of our claims to know anything securely, particularly through the senses. And isn't it better in the long run to be honest and open about these things?

At the moment Austen was writing her sweet tales of courtship and consummation, Hegel was working on his argument for the pheonomenology of spirit: 'Its task is to run through, in a scientifically purged order, the stages in the mind's necessary progress from immediate sense-consciousness to the position of a scientific philosophy.'[577] This is a (much harder to read) work that identifies a phenomenological intelligence *preshaping* empirical judgement. It also argues that this intelligence – spirit or mind – understands itself through a process of negation in relation to objects of consciousness. A parallel argument is at the heart of Austen's narrative movements, expressing itself through a fundamental contradiction between feminine knowledge and feminine desire: or the dialectic between what women have been able to know and do, and what they still seem to want nonetheless. Feminine knowledge has traditionally been dissociated from institutions of knowledge (the University, Literature, and Science), perhaps it has also remained at one step removed from the reification of knowledge as instrumental rationality: 'I will not allow books to prove anything.'

Marxian critics have turned to the romance for evidence of a 'body of knowledge' at one remove from reified realism and its attendant disciplines. I only want to add that the dissociation of the *feminine* romance from any serious claim to knowledge is a core aspect of the dialectical negation of romance as feminised, popular, commercialised false consciousness. The proper response to this is to consider very hard indeed the relationship between romancing and knowing. Reading feminine romance through feminist epistemology, there appears a body of knowledge so consistent with itself that one only has to pause for a moment to be hit by the oddness of arguments that credit the dream of romance as false consciousness. This book has attempted to begin an alternative account of the sheer bloody-minded persistence of a feminine dream of romance, and to bring to light the cultural logic that is exposed, risked, and found safe in that very particular mode of narrative representation.

Structuralism asked us explicitly to consider 'certain regularities' across the plenitude of narrative instances. These regularities, once recognised, are either *impressed upon* consciousness by homogenising external forces (the mode argument, which understands mind as *tabula rasa*, or the subject as a discursive construct), or they exist as the inherent determining boundaries *of* consciousness (the phenomenological argument, which understands mind as structuring intelligence). Austen's work suggests there is little between these alternatives. Setting the goal of a happy ending seems to demand giving up the tropes of tragedy, or at least remembering that tragedy was a literary trope before all else, and has been projected out of the 'imaginary' onto the 'external' world to give meaningful shape to otherwise possibly meaningless social and personal experiences. My encounter with Austen has left me with the thought that we might pause and consider what difference it would make to favour the tropes of romantic comedy for making sense of the world and our place within it. How do we *want* the narrative to end?

Notes

Preface

1. Margaret Anne Doody, *The True Story of the Novel* (London: Fontana, 1998), p. 5.
2. Nancy C.M. Hartsock, 'The Feminist Standpoint: Developing The Ground for a Specifically Feminist Historical Materialism', in Sandra Harding and Merrill B. Hintikka (eds), *Discovering Reality: Feminist Perspectives on Epistemology, Metaphysics, Methodology, and Philosophy of Science* (Dordrecht: Kluwer Academic Publishers, 2003), pp. 302–3.
3. Jane Austen, *Northanger Abbey* (ed.) Claire Grogan (Ontario: Broadview, 2002), p. 124.
4. Jane Spencer, *The Rise of the Woman Novelist: From Aphra Behn to Jane Austen* (Oxford: Basil Blackwell, 1986), p. 181.
5. But see Alex Woloch for an interesting example of narrative analysis of Austen's minor characters, 'Narrative Asymmetry in *Pride and Prejudice*', in *The One and the Many: Minor Characters and the Space of the Protagonist in the Novel* (Princeton: Princeton University Press, 2003), pp. 43–124.
6. Erich Auerbach, *Mimesis: The Representation of Reality in Western Literature* (Princeton: Princeton University Press, 1974), p. 122.
7. *Ibid.*, pp. 135, 141.
8. Raymond Williams, *Keywords: A Vocabulary of Culture and Society* (London: Fontana, 1988), pp. 274–5.
9. Spencer, p. 182.
10. Juliet Mitchell, 'Introduction 1', in Juliet Mitchell and Jacqueline Rose (eds), *Feminine Sexuality: Jacques Lacan and the école freudienne* (tr.) Jacqueline Rose (New York: Norton, 1985), p. 25. I would strongly recommend the brilliant introductory essays by Juliet Mitchell and Jacqueline Rose to anyone wanting to grasp what is at stake in our understanding of femininity.
11. Julia Byrne, *Ravensdene's Bride* (Surrey: Harlequin's Mills and Boon, 1999), pp. 277–8. This is one of the Mills and Boon 'Regency Collection': 'where rogues find romance'.
12. In a study of 100 Hollywood films made before 1960, it was found that 95 per cent 'involved romance in at least one line of action', while 85 per cent 'made that the principle line of action'. David Boildwell, Janet Staiger, Kristin Thompson, *Classic Hollywood Cinema: Film Style and Mode of Production to 1960* (London: Routledge, 1985), p. 16. Thanks to Helen Hanson for pointing this out.
13. Adrienne Rich, 'Compulsory Heterosexuality and Lesbian Existence', in Sandra Kemp and Judith Squires (eds), *Feminisms* (Oxford: Oxford University Press, 1997), p. 322.
14. Alison Light, ' "Returning to Manderley" – Romance Fiction, Female Sexuality and Class', in Kemp and Squires (eds), *Feminisms*, p. 336.
15. Madeleine Bunting, 'Not Shrill Like Sybil or Silly Like Bridget', *The Guardian*, Wednesday December 31st 2003, p. 18.

16. Carl Gustav Jung, *Four Archetypes: Mother, Rebirth, Spirit, Trickster* (London: Routledge, 2004), p. 11, 12.
17. Fredric Jameson, *The Political Unconscious: Narrative as a Socially Symbolic Act* (London: Methuen, 1983), p. 132.
18. Jameson, *Political Unconscious*, pp. 119–23; Vladimir Propp, *Morphology of the Folk Tale*, (trans.) L Scott (Austin: University of Texas Press, 1968), pp. 21–3.
19. Woloch, p. 122.
20. Jameson, *Political Unconscious*, p. 127.

Introduction: The Persistence of Jane Austen's Romance

21. Jameson, *Political Unconscious*, pp. 109–10.
22. Slavoj Žižek, 'There is no Sexual Relationship', in Elizabeth Wright and Edmond Wright (eds), *The Žizek Reader* (Oxford: Blackwell, 1999), pp. 194–5.
23. Jane Austen, *Persuasion* (ed.) Linda Bree (Ontario: Broadview, 2000), p. 69.
24. Austen's biography is widely available: see, for example, Claire Tomalin, *Jane Austen: A Life* (Harmondsworth: Penguin, 2000); Carol Shields, *Jane Austen* (London: Phoenix, 2003); Emily Auerbach, *Searching for Jane Austen* (Wisconsin: University of Wisconsin Press, 2004). The excellent Broadview editions of the novels contain useful timelines of the works in relation to Austen's life and her wider context. Robert Mack made the point on reading this chapter recently, that having a relative arrested and executed in revolutionary France would have been as unavoidable an introduction to the reality of contemporary politics as having a relative kidnapped and executed in Iraq today.
25. Norma Clarke, *The Rise and Fall of the Woman of Letters* (London: Pimlico, 2004), p. 343.
26. Austen, *Pride and Prejudice* (ed.) Robert P. Irvine (Ontario: Broadview, 2002), p. 384.
27. Austen, *Pride and Prejudice* (ed.) Tony Tanner (Harmondsworth: Penguin, 1972), p. 399, n4.
28. Hartsock, 'The Feminist Standpoint', p. 297.
29. John Skinner, *An Introduction to Eighteenth-century Fiction: Raising the Novel* (Houndmills: Palgrave, 2001), p. 238.
30. Andrew Sanders, *The Short Oxford History of English Literature* (2nd edition) (Oxford: Oxford University Press, 2000), p. 370.
31. Sanders, p. 370.
32. Edward Said, *Culture and Imperialism* (London: Chatto and Windus, 1993).
33. Marilyn Butler, *Jane Austen and the War of Ideas* (Oxford: Oxford University Press, 1975); Margaret Kirkham, *Jane Austen: Feminism and Fiction* (Sussex: Harvester Press, 1986); Isobel Armstrong, ' "Conservative" Jane Austen? – Some Views', in Isobel Armstrong (ed.), *Mansfield Park*, Penguin Critical Studies (Harmondsworth: Penguin, 1988), pp. 94–104; Claudia Johnson, *Jane Austen: Women, Politics and the Novel* (Chicago and London: University of Chicago Press, 1990).
34. Tony Tanner, *Jane Austen* (London: Macmillan, 1986), p. 3.
35. Oliver Goldsmith, *The History of England from the Earliest times to the Death of George II* was published in 1771. Jane Austen, *The History of England from the*

Reign of Henry the 4th to the Death of Charles the 1st (written 1791) (ed.) A.S. Byatt (Chapel Hill, NC: Algonquin Books, 1993).

36. Antoinette Burton, ' "Invention is What Delights Me": Jane Austen's Remaking of "English" History', in Devoney Looser (ed.), *Jane Austen and Discourses of Feminism* (Basingstoke: Macmillan, 1995), p. 35.
37. Burton, p. 40.
38. *Ibid.*, p. 45.
39. Johnson, p. xxiii.
40. *Ibid.*, p. xxiv.
41. Judith Lowder Newton, 'Power and the ideology of "Woman's Sphere" ', in Robyn R. Warhol and Diane Price Herndl (eds), *Feminisms: An Anthology of Literary Criticism and Theory* (New Brunswick: Rutgers University Press, 1991), pp. 769–10.
42. Jameson, *Political Unconscious*, 'On Interpretation: Literature as a Socially Symbolic Act', pp. 17–102.
43. Gregory L. Lucente, *The Narrative of Realism and Myth: Verga, Lawrence, Faulkner, Pavese* (Baltimore and London: Johns Hopkins University Press, 1981), p. 45. According to Lucente, 'realism's irony protects the validity of the pursuit of knowledge by building essential uncertainty into its program from the beginning' (p. 46).
44. Anthony Easthope, *Englishness and National Culture* (London: Routledge, 1999), p. 69.
45. Easthope, *Englishness*, pp. 88–9. He is referring to Edward Thompson, *The Poverty of Theory* (London: Merlin, 1978).
46. Robert Miles, *Jane Austen* (Tavistock: Northcote House, 2003), p. 28.
47. Jameson, *Political Unconscious*, p. 39.
48. Miles, p. 30.
49. *Ibid.*, p. 31.
50. Easthope, *Englishness*, p. 97, citing Linda Hutcheon, *Irony's Edge: The Theory and Politics of Irony* (London: Routledge, 1994), p. 12.
51. Michael McKeon, *The Origins of the English Novel 1600–1740* (London: Radius, 1988), pp. 45–6.
52. Ian Watt, *The Rise of the Novel: Studies in Defoe, Richardson and Fielding* [1957] (London: Hogarth Press, 1987), p. 12.
53. Pam Morris, *Realism* (London and New York: Routledge, 2003), p. 77.
54. Austen's letter to Anna Austen, Wednesday 10 August 1814. See R.W. Chapman (ed.), *Jane Austen's Letters to her Sister Cassandra and Others* (London: Oxford University Press, 1959), letter 98, p. 393.
55. McKeon, p. 39.
56. Woloch, pp. 124, 123.
57. McKeon, p. 38.
58. *Ibid.*, p. 39.
59. Ruth Salvaggio, *Enlightened Absence: Neoclassical Configurations of the Feminine* (University of Illinois Press: Urbana and Chicago, 1988), p. xi.
60. Susan Sontag, 'Against Interpretation', in Susan Feagin and Patrick Maynard (eds), *Aesthetics* (Oxford: Oxford University Press), pp. 250–1.
61. Doody, *The True Story of the Novel*, p. 294.
62. *Ibid.*, p. 472.
63. Johnson, *Jane Austen*, p. 75.

64. Miles, pp. 41–3.
65. Patricia Meyer Spacks, 'Energies of Mind: Plot's Possibilities in the 1790s', *Eighteenth-century Fiction*, 1,1 (October 1998), p. 2.
66. Northrop Frye, 'The Archetypes of Literature', in David Lodge (ed.), *Twentieth-century Literary Criticism: A Reader*, (London and New York: Longman, 1985), p. 431.
67. Austen, *Pride and Prejudice*, p. 227; *Mansfield Park* (ed.) June Sturrock (Ontario: Broadview, 2003), p. 439; *Sense and Sensibility* (ed.) Kathleen James-Kavan (Ontario: Broadview, 2001), p. 366; *Persuasion* (ed.) Linda Bree (Ontario: Broadview, 2000), p. 245; *Emma* (ed.) Kristin Flieger Samuelian (Ontario: Broadview, 2004), p. 366.
68. Frye, 'Archetypes of Literature', p. 429.
69. Austen, *Persuasion*, p. 87; *Emma*, p. 405.
70. Johnson, p. 74.
71. Janice Radway, 'The Institutional Matrix of Romance', in Simon During (ed.), *The Cultural Studies Reader* (London and New York: Routledge, 1994), pp. 447–8.
72. Radway, p. 439.
73. *Romantic*stats: <http://www.theromancereader.com/hyper5.html> (correct at 30 September 2003).
74. Radway, p. 445.
75. See <www.likesbooks.com/top100y2k.html> and <www.writepage.com/others/austenj.htm> (correct at 6 October 2003); <http://news.bbc.co.uk/go/em/fr/-/1/hi/entertainment/arts/4256613.stm> (correct at 14 October 2005).
76. Terry Eagleton, 'Towards a Science of the Text' [1976], in Terry Eagleton and Drew Milne (eds), *Marxist Literary Theory: A Reader* (Oxford: Blackwell, 1996), pp. 302–3.
77. See Tomalin, *Jane Austen: A Life*, pp. 8–9, 18–19, 49–50.
78. The quote is from Austen's *Letters*, 3rd edition (ed.) Dierdre Le Faye (Oxford and New York: Oxford University Press, 1995), p. 306; quoted by Isobel Grundy, 'Jane Austen and Literary Traditions', in Edward Copeland and Juliet McMaster (eds), *The Cambridge Companion to Jane Austen* (Cambridge: Cambridge University Press, 2002), p. 191.
79. D.W. Harding, 'Regulated Hatred: an Aspect of the Work of Jane Austen' [1940], in David Lodge (ed.), *Twentieth-century Literary Criticism: A Reader* (London and New York: Longman, 1972), p. 263.
80. Johnson, p. 117; and see Glenda A. Hudson, *Sibling Love and Incest in Jane Austen's Fiction* (Hampshire: Macmillan, 1999).
81. This argument is made in detail in *Mary Wollstonecraft and the Accent of the Feminine* (Houndmills: Palgrave, 2002).
82. McKeon, *Origins of the English Novel*, p. 28.
83. BBC News <wysiwg://109/http://news.bbc.co.uk/1/hi/entertainment/arts/3019637.stm> (correct at 12 May 2003).
84. Julia Kristeva, *Powers of Horror: An Essay in Abjection* (trans.) Leon S. Roudiez (New York: Columbia University Press, 1982), p. 1.
85. See Jane Spencer, *The Rise of the Woman Novelist*.
86. Ashley Tauchert, 'Writing Like a Girl: Revisiting Women's Literary History', *CQ*, 44,1 (2002): pp. 49–76.

87. Northop Frye, *The Secular Scripture* (Cambridge: Harvard University Press, 1976), pp. 28–31.
88. Quoted by Norma Clarke, *The Rise and Fall of the Woman of Letters*, p. 100. Clarke's account of the literary achievements of women writers through the eighteenth century is fascinating, and provides a useful and detailed survey of what happened to the female literary tradition behind Austen. She describes Reeve's *Progress of Romance* as 'a well-informed literary history dealing with what was, at the time, the more or less untheorised subject of fiction and its origins. The book was the first to address the relationship between the old romance and the new novel and to make explicit some commonplace gendered prejudices, to wit: that there was "literature", which men were having important conversations about, and "romance", a lower form, traditionally the province of women. Romance was "popular" while "literature" belonged to the learned' (p. 102).
89. Doody, *The True Story of the Novel*, p. 5.
90. See, for example, Alison Jagger, 'Love and Knowledge: Emotion in Feminist Epistemology', in Kemp and Squires (eds), *Feminisms*, pp. 188–93; Nancy C.M. Hartsock, 'The Feminist Standpoint', pp. 283–310.
91. Jane Flax, 'Political Philosophy and the Patriarchal Unconscious: A Psychoanalytic Perspective on Epistemology and Metaphysics', in Harding and Hittika (eds), *Discovering Reality*, p. 269.
92. Woloch, p. 124.
93. *Ibid.*, p. 111.
94. Mary Poovey, *The Proper Lady and the Woman Writer: Ideology as Style in the Works of Mary Wollstonecraft, Mary Shelley, and Jane Austen* (Chicago: Chicago University Press, 1984), p. 229. Quoted by Woloch, p. 96.
95. Poovey, p. 205; Woloch, p. 96.
96. Jameson, *Political Unconscious*, p. 103.
97. *Ibid.*, p. 104.
98. Spencer, p. 183.
99. Jameson, *Political Unconscious*, p. 105, pp. 19–20.
100. Frye, 'Archetypes of Literature', p. 428.
101. Austen, *Persuasion*, p. 243.
102. My emphasis. Wayne Booth, *The Company We Keep: An Ethics of Fiction* (Berkeley: University of California Press, 1988), p. 423; quoted by Laura Mooneyham White, in her excellent summary of the 'injuriousness of romance plots' as argued through Austen criticism. 'Jane Austen and the Marriage Plot: Questions of Persistence', in Devoney Looser (ed.), *Jane Austen and Discourses of Feminism*, p. 75.
103. Jameson, *Political Unconscious*, p. 96.

1   *Northanger Abbey*: 'hastening together to perfect felicity'

104. Raymond Williams, *The Long Revolution* (Harmondsworth: Penguin, 1980), p. 69.
105. Jameson, *Marxism and Form: Twentieth-Century Dialectical Theories of Literature* (Princeton, NJ: Princeton University Press, 1971), p. 50.

106. Margaret Homans, *Bearing the Word: Language and Female Experience in Nineteenth-Century Women's Writing* (Chicago: University of Chicago Press, 1986), p. 15.
107. Laura M. White, p. 83.
108. *Ibid.*, p. 80.
109. Woloch, p. 97.
110. Frye, *Secular Scripture*, p. 35.
111. Lucente, *The Narrative of Realism and Myth*, pp. 44, 40.
112. *Ibid.*, p. 42.
113. *Ibid.*, pp. 41, 44.
114. Roman Jakobson, 'On Realism in Art' [1921] (trans.) Karol Magassy, in *Readings in Russian Poetics: Formalist and Structuralist Views* (ed.) Ladislav Matejka and Krystyna Pomorska (Cambridge, Mass.: MIT Press, 1971), pp. 38–46.
115. J.A. Cuddon, *Penguin Dictionary of Literary Terms and Literary Theory*, 4th edition, revised by C.E. Preston (Harmondsworth: Penguin, 1998), p. 327.
116. Jameson, *Marxism and Form*, p. 313.
117. Lucente, p. 40.
118. Frye, *Secular Scripture*, p. 133.
119. *Ibid.*, p. 38, 15, 24.
120. Doody, *The True Story of the Novel*, p. 480.
121. McKeon, *Origins of the English Novel*, p. 59.
122. Deborah Ross, *The Excellence of Falsehood: Romance, Realism, and Women's Contribution to the Novel* (Kentucky: University Press of Kentucky, 1991), p. 206.
123. Lucente, p. 37.
124. Frye, *Secular Scripture*, pp. 35, 36, 39, 40.
125. Jameson, *Political Unconscious*, p. 129.
126. *Ibid.*, pp. 130–1.
127. *Ibid.*, pp. 131, 141
128. Ross, pp. 3–4.
129. Frye, *Secular Scripture*, p. 104.
130. *Ibid.*, p. 54.
131. Laura M. White, p. 76.
132. Frye, *Secular Scripture*, pp. 76–7.
133. Austen, *Sense and Sensibility*, p. 380.
134. Jameson, *Political Unconscious*, p. 76.
135. *Ibid.*, pp. 76–7.
136. *Ibid.*, pp. 80–1.
137. *Ibid.*, p. 80.
138. *Ibid.*, pp. 84, 85, 87, 89, 76.
139. *Ibid.*, pp. 89, 90.
140. *Ibid.*, p. 91.
141. *Ibid.*, pp. 95, 97, 141.
142. Frye, 'Archetypes of Literature', p. 429.
143. Lucente, *The Narrative of Realism and Myth*, p. 39.
144. Miles, *Jane Austen*, p. 75, pp. 48–9.
145. Austen, *Northanger Abbey*, p. 195.
146. Lucente, p. 41.
147. *Ibid.*, p. 30.

148. Roland Barthes, 'Structural Analysis of Narratives', in *Barthes: Selected Writings* (ed.) Susan Sontag (Oxford: Fantana, 1983), p. 253, n2.
149. Hayden White, *The Content of the Form: Narrative Discourse and Historical Representation* (Baltimore and London: Johns Hopkins University Press, 1990), p. 36.
150. This is a very complex area of legal and social history, which I am raising here as a recognisable instance of the broad context for Austen's narrative preoccupation with singularity and universality. The rights of commonality have been obscured by centuries of land-ownership clauses, and are only indirectly available from the instances of common law that have survived this long process. See, especially, J.M. Neeson, *Commoners: Common Right, Enclosure and Social Change in England, 1700–1820* (Cambridge: Cambridge University Press, 1995); W.E. Tate, *A Domesday of English Enclosure Acts and Awards* (ed.) M.E. Turner (Reading: Reading University Library Publications, 1978).
151. Roy Porter, *Enlightenment: Britain and the Creation of the Modern World* (Harmondsworth: Penguin, 2001) pp. 308–9.
152. *Brooke's Gazeteer*, Hampshire, 1815: reproduced on-line at <http://geog.port.ac.uk/webmap/hantsmap/hantsmap/brookes1/brk1txt16.ht> (correct at 9th March 2005).
153. Porter, p. 385.
154. Austen, *Northanger Abbey*, p. 37, 40.
155. *Ibid.*, p. 41.
156. *Ibid.*, pp. 195, 196, 197.
157. *Ibid.*, p. 218.
158. *Ibid.*, p. 233.
159. *Ibid.*, p. 240.
160. *Ibid.*, p. 240.
161. *Ibid.*, p. 233.
162. *Ibid.*, p. 238.
163. *Ibid.*, p. 240.
164. Blanford Parker, *The Triumph of Augustan Poetics: English Literary Culture from Butler to Johnson* (Cambridge: Cambridge University Press, 1998), pp. 89, 125.
165. Frye, *Secular Scripture*, pp. 103–4.
166. Austen, *Love and Friendship: Deceived in Friendship and Betrayed in Love*, foreword by Fay Weldon (London: Hasperus Press Ltd, 2003), p. 32.
167. Austen, *Northanger Abbey*, p. 239.
168. *Adaptation* (Dir.) Spike Jonge, Screenplay by Charlie Kauffman and Donald Kauffman, Sony Pictures Entertainment, Columbia Pictures, 2002.
169. Frye, *Secular Scripture*, p. 163.
170. Lucente, *The Narrative of Realism and Myth*, p. 40.
171. Frye, *Secular Scripture*, p. 139.
172. Raymond Williams, 'Formalist', in *Keywords*, p. 139.
173. Raymond Williams, *The Long Revolution* (Harmondsworth: Penguin, 1980), p. 64.
174. Jameson, *Political Unconscious*, p. 118.
175. Jameson, *Marxism and Form*, p. 385.
176. Jacob Torfing, *New Theories of Discourse: Laclau, Mouffe and Zizek* (Oxford: Blackwell, 1999), pp. 18, 19.

177. Slavoj Žižek, 'The Spectre of Ideology', in *The Zizek Reader* (ed.) Elizabeth Wright and Edmund Wright (Oxford: Blackwell, 1999), p. 74.
178. Lucian Goldmann, 'Introduction to the problems of a Sociology of the Novel', in Terry Eagleton and Drew Milne (eds), *Marxist Literary Theory*, pp. 213–4.
179. Roland Barthes, 'Structural Analysis of Narrative', in *Barthes: Selected Writings* (Oxford: Fontana Paperbacks, 1983), p. 278.
180. Jameson, *Marxism and Form*, p. 342.
181. Hartsock, 'The Feminist Standpoint', in Harding and Hintikka (eds), *Discovering Reality*, p. 292.
182. Barthes, p. 270.
183. Lucente, p. 1.
184. *Ibid.*, p. 33.
185. Claude Lévi-Strauss, *L'Origine des manieres de table* (Paris, 1968); quoted by Hayden White, *The Content of the Form: Narrative, Discourse and Historical Representation* (Baltimore and London: Johns Hopkins University Press, 1987), p. 34.
186. Lucente, p. 33.
187. Jameson, *Marxism and Form*, pp. 322, 50.
188. Austen, *Northanger Abbey*, p. 240.
189. Ross, *The Excellence of Falsehood*, p. 209, n18.
190. Jameson, *Marxism and Form*, p. 55.
191. *Ibid.*, pp. 307–8.
192. *Ibid.*, pp. 311, 312.
193. *Ibid.*, pp. 319, 327, 328.
194. Ross, p. 169.

2 *Sense and Sensibility*: 'her opinions are all romantic'

195. Žižek, 'From "In-itself" to "For-itself" ', in Wright and Wright (eds), *The Žizek Reader*, p. 227.
196. Doody, *The True Story of the Novel*, p. 472.
197. Austen, *Sense and Sensibility*, p. 364.
198. *Ibid.*, p. 366.
199. Barthes, p. 255, quoting Martinet.
200. *Ibid.*, pp. 256–7.
201. *Ibid.*, p. 260.
202. *Ibid.*, p. 293.
203. *Ibid.*, pp. 261, 264.
204. *Ibid.*, pp. 264–5, 272–3.
205. *Ibid.*, p. 255.
206. Unsigned review, *British Critic* (May 1812), reproduced in Austen, *Sense and Sensibility*, p. 384.
207. *Sense and Sensibility* (Dir.) Ang Lee, Columbia Pictures, 1995.
208. Austen, *Sense and Sensibility*, pp. 53, 73. Kathleen James-Cavan's footnote indicates that the first edition has 'furniture' rather than 'jointure' here. She notes that Ros Ballaster 'points out that the change "highlights Mrs Jennings lack of autonomy over inheritance" ' since '[a] widow could bequeath

furniture to whomever she chose; however, upon her death her jointure went to her children'. See 'Textual Variants', in Austen, *Sense and Sensibility* (Harmondsworth: Penguin, 1995), p. 330.

209. Austen, *Sense and Sensibility*, p. 41.
210. *Ibid.*, p. 131.
211. *Ibid.*, p. 42.
212. *Ibid.*, p. 42.
213. Barthes, p. 279.
214. Austen, *Sense and Sensibility*, p. 42.
215. Austen, *Persuasion*, p. 52.
216. Austen, *Sense and Sensibility*, p. 43. My emphasis.
217. *Ibid.*, p. 52.
218. *Ibid.*, p. 43.
219. *Ibid.*, pp. 47, 49.
220. *Ibid.*, p. 46.
221. Barthes, pp. 270, 271.
222. *Ibid.*, p. 269.
223. Austen, *Sense and Sensibility*, p. 91.
224. *Ibid.*, p. 242.
225. Porter, *Enlightement*, p. 386.
226. Austen, *Sense and Sensibility*, p. 225.
227. *Ibid.*, p. 226.
228. *Ibid.*, p. 227.
229. *Ibid.*, p. 227.
230. *Ibid.*, p. 100.
231. *Ibid.*, p. 230.
232. *Ibid.*, p. 100.
233. *Ibid.*, p. 102.
234. *Ibid.*, pp. 329, 44.
235. *Ibid.*, pp. 44, 230.
236. *Ibid.*, p. 54.
237. *Ibid.*, p. 44.
238. *Ibid.*, pp. 42, 43.
239. *Ibid.*, pp. 248, 249, 57, 265.
240. *Ibid.*, p. 337.
241. *Ibid.*, p. 337.
242. *Ibid.*, pp. 338, 328.
243. *Ibid.*, p. 329.
244. *Ibid.*, p. 228.
245. *Ibid.*, pp. 327, 328, 329, 330, 335.
246. *Ibid.*, p. 356.
247. *Ibid.*, pp. 329, 370.
248. Barthes, 'Structural Analysis of Narratives', p. 272.
249. Austen, *Sense and Sensibility*, pp. 90, 91.
250. *Ibid.*, pp. 379–80.
251. *Ibid.*, p. 315.
252. *Ibid.*, pp. 349, 350, 351.
253. *Ibid.*, p. 380.

254. *Ibid.*, p. 327.
255. Williams, *Keywords*, pp. 280–3. See also Janet Todd, *Sensibility: An Introduction* (London and New York: Methuen), 1986: *'Sense and Sensibility, which, in the stories of Marianne and the shadowy Elizas, comes close to invoking the *Clarissa* plot, mocks and stifles the agony of the female victim; ultimately it socialises the near scream of Marianne into sensible rational discourse'* (pp. 144–5).
256. Lucente, p. 16.
257. Austen, *Sense and Sensibility*, p. 44.
258. *Ibid.*, p. 375.
259. *Ibid.*, p. 262.
260. *Ibid.*, pp. 261, 250, 321.
261. Barthes, p. 273.
262. Austen, *Sense and Sensibility*, p. 64.
263. *Ibid.*, p. 65.
264. *Ibid.*, pp. 78, 79.
265. *Ibid.*, pp. 74, 342.
266. *Ibid.*, p. 221.
267. *Ibid.*, pp. 275, 253.
268. *Ibid.*, p. 302.
269. *Ibid.*, p. 322.
270. *Ibid.*, pp. 322–3.
271. *Ibid.*, p. 339.
272. *Ibid.*, pp. 360, 361.
273. *Ibid.*, p. 363.
274. Jameson, *Marxism and Form*, p. 354.

3 *Pride and Prejudice*: 'Lydia's gape'

275. Lévi-Strauss, 'Incest and Myth', in David Lodge (ed.), *Twentienth-century Literary Criticism*, p. 550.
276. Frye, *Secular Scripture*, p. 87.
277. Fielding, *Bridget Jones' Diary: The Edge of Reason* (London: Picador, 2004), p. 5.
278. Terry Castle, 'Sublimely Bad', *Boss Ladies, Watch Out! Essays on Women, Sex, and Writing* (London and New York: Routledge, 2002), p. 137.
279. Castle, p. 140.
280. *Ibid.*, pp. 141, 142, 143.
281. Simon Baron-Cohen, 'The extreme-male-brain theory of autism', in H. Tager-Flusberger (ed.), *Neurodevelopmental Disorders* (Cambridge, Mass.: MIT Press, 1999).
282. Claire Tomalin, *Jane Austen: A Life* (Harmondsworth: Penguin, 2000), p. 160.
283. Min Wild has drawn to my attention the strains of Robert Bage, *Hermsprong: or Man as He is Not* (1796) in Austen, and Claire Tomalin mentions the fact that Austen owned a copy of the novel (p. 125). Bage was an admirer of Wollstonecraft's work.
284. Rachel Brownstein, '*Northanger Abbey, Sense and Sensibility, Pride and Prejudice*', in Edward Copeland and Juliet McMaster (ed.) *The Cambridge Companion to Jane Austen* (Cambridge, 2002), p. 53.

285. Austen, *Pride and Prejudice*, p. 47. But I have been reminded by Jane Spencer that Mary is not particularly 'Wollstonecraftian' in her proclamations, particularly when she comments on Lydia's elopement: 'we must stem the tide of malice, and pour into the wounded bosoms of each other, the balm of sisterly consolation' (*Pride and Prejudice*, p. 298). Mary's tone here seems to derive from an allusion to Mr Tyrold's epistolary conduct advice to his daughter in Frances Burney, *Camilla* (1796). See also Fordyce's *Sermons to Young Women*, the relevant sections of which are included in Appendix B to Irvine's edition of the novel; and Hannah More's *Strictures on the Modern System of Female Education, with a view of the principles and conduct prevalent among women of rank and fortune* (London: T. Cadell Jun. and W. Davis, 1799), pp. 53–5 (included in Irvine's edition, Appendix D).

286. Austen, *Pride and Prejudice*, p. 103.

287. Mary Wollstonecraft, *Vindication of the Rights of Woman* (London: Everyman, 1995), p. 105.

288. Cora Kaplan, 'Speaking/.Writing/Feminism', in Kemp and Squires (eds), *Feminisms*, p. 42.

289. Rosalind Coward, 'The True Story of How I Became My Own Person', in Catherine Belsey and Jane Moore (eds), *The Feminist Reader*, p. 37.

290. Austen, *Pride and Prejudice*, p. 210.

291. *Ibid.*, p. 214.

292. *Ibid.*, p. 382.

293. *Ibid.*, p. 137.

294. *Ibid.*, p. 138.

295. *Ibid.*, p. 141.

296. Barthes, 'Structural Analysis of Narratives', pp. 273–4.

297. Frye, *Secular Scripture*, p. 145.

298. Austen, *Pride and Prejudice*, p. 250, 172.

299. *Ibid.*, p. 318.

300. *Ibid.*, p. 103.

301. Patricia Waugh, 'Modernism, Posmodernism, Gender: The View from Feminism', in Kemp and Squires (eds), *Feminisms*, p. 211. She is quoting from Jean Paul Sartre, *Being and Nothingness* (New York: Philosophical Library, 1956).

302. Arielle Eckstut, *Pride and Promiscuity: The Lost Sex Scenes of Jane Austen* (Edinburgh: Canongate Books, 2003), pp. 25–6.

303. Arielle Eckstut, *Pride and Promiscuity*, p. 29.

304. Austen, *Pride and Prejudice*, pp. 210–41.

305. *Ibid.*, p. 366.

306. Georg Lukács, *The Theory of the Novel* (tr.) Anna Bostock (London: Merlin Press, 1971), p. 75.

307. Austen, *Pride and Prejudice*, pp. 223, 227.

308. Frye, *Secular Scripture*, p. 145.

309. Austen, *Pride and Prejudice*, p. 49.

310. *Ibid.*, p. 259.

311. *Ibid.*, p. 318.

312. *Ibid.*, p. 368.

313. Frye, *Secular Scripture*, p. 149.

314. *Bride and Prejudice* (Dir.) Gurinder Chadha, Miramax Films, 2004.

315. Barthes, p. 295.
316. Jameson, *Political Unconscious*, p. 285.
317. *Ibid.*, p. 110.
318. Raymond Williams, 'Realism and the Contemporary Novel', in David Lodge (ed.), *Twentieth-Century Literary Criticism*, p. 584.
319. John Peck and Martin Cole, *A Brief History of English Literature* (Houndmills: Palgrave, 2002), p. 149.
320. Rosi Braidotti, 'Cyberfeminism with a difference', in Kemp and Squires (eds), *Feminisms*, p. 523.
321. Sally Alexander and Barbara Taylor, 'In Defence of "Patriarchy" ', in Mary Evans (ed.) *The Woman Question: Readings on the Subordination of Women* (Oxford: Fontana Press, 1982), p. 80.
322. Elizabeth Wright, 'Thoroughly Postmodern Feminist Criticism', in Kemp and Squires (eds), *Feminisms*, p. 180.
323. Germaine Greer, *The Whole Woman* (London: Anchor, 2000), p. 19.
324. T.W. Adorno, 'Lyric Poetry and Society' (trans.) Bruce Mayo, *Telos*, 20 (Spring 1974), p. 58.
325. Kemp and Squires, 'Epistemologies', in Kemp and Squires (eds), *Feminisms*, p. 145. See Patricia Waugh's excellent piece in the same collection, 'Modernism, Posmodernism, Gender: The View from Feminism', pp. 206–12: 'The concept of a "woman's identity" functions in terms both of affirmation and negation, even within feminism itself. There can be no simple legitimation for feminists in throwing off "false consciousness" and revealing a true but "deeply" buried self. Indeed, to embrace the essentialism of this notion of "difference" is to come dangerously close to reproducing that very patriarchal construction of gender which feminists have set out to contest as *their* basic project of modernity' (pp. 206–7).
326. Jameson, *Political Unconscious*, p. 131.
327. Austen, *Pride and Prejudice*, pp. 44, 60.
328. And as Jane Spencer reminded me in a corridor conversation – the return of romance, rather than its inauguration at this moment.

4 *Mansfield Park*: 'she does not like to act'

329. Austen, prayer III, first printed in R.W. Chapman, *The Works of Jane Austen* (Oxford: Clarenden Press, 1923), reprinted as Appendix B, in Austen, *Mansfield Park*, (ed.) June Sturrock (Toronto: Boradview Press, 2003), p. 480.
330. Denise de Rougemont, *Love in the Western World* (Princeton: Princeton University Press, 1983), pp. 164–5.
331. Austen, *Mansfield Park*, p. 457.
332. Michael Giffin, *Jane Austen and Religion: Salvation and Society in Georgian England* (Houndmills: Palgrave, 2002). Also, see Gary Kelly, 'Religion and Politics', in Edward Copeland and Juliet McMaster (eds), *The Cambridge Companion to Jane Austen* (Cambridge: Cambridge University Press, 2002).
333. Jameson, *Political Unconscious*, p. 152.
334. Frye, *Secular Scripture*, p. 84.
335. Carol Shields, *Jane Austen* (London: Phoenix, 2001), pp. 98–9.

336. Frye, *Secular Scripture*, p. 88.
337. Jane Austen, *Lady Susan/The Watsons/Sanditon* (ed.) Margaret Drabble (Harmondsworth: Penguin, 1974), p. 103.
338. Austen, *Mansfield Park*, p. 51.
339. Jocelyn Harris, 'Jane Austen and the Burden of the (Male) Past: The case Reexamined', in Devoney Looser (ed.), *Jane Austen and Discourses of Feminism*, pp. 90–1.
340. Kingsley Amis, *What Became of Jane Austen? And Other Questions* (New York: Harcourt Brace Jovanovich, 1970), p. 16.
341. Austen, *Mansfield Park*, p. 36.
342. *Ibid.*, p. 35.
343. *Ibid.*, pp. 36, 37.
344. *Ibid.*, p. 317.
345. *Ibid.*, p. 166.
346. *Ibid.*, p. 308.
347. *Ibid.*, pp. 320, 321.
348. *Ibid.*, p. 195.
349. *Ibid.*, pp. 174, 447.
350. *Ibid.*, p. 465.
351. *Ibid.*, p. 441.
352. *Ibid.*, pp. 445, 446.
353. *Ibid.*, p. 458.
354. *Ibid.*, pp. 455, 453, 465, 466.
355. Austen, *Mansfield Park*, pp. 468, 461.
356. Frye, *Secular Scripture*, pp. 86–7.
357. *Ibid.*, p. 446.
358. *Ibid.*, p. 453.
359. *Ibid.*, p. 453.
360. *Ibid.*, p. 462.
361. *Ibid.*, p. 322.
362. *Ibid.*, p. 38.
363. *Ibid.*, p. 467.
364. *Ibid.*, p. 466.
365. *Ibid.*, p. 445.
366. Frye, *Secular Scripture*, pp. 85–6.
367. Austen, *Mansfield Park*, p. 467.
368. Frye, *Secular Scripture*, p. 104.
369. There is a structural resonance between this story and the infant Austen's own experiences on returning to the family parsonage after being sent out to a village wet-nurse around 3–4 months old. Claire Tomalin's biography imagines the experience in terms of a 'painful experience [...] an exile or abandonment' (pp. 5–6). The infant Austen's return from the familiar poverty of her foster home and nurse to her now unfamiliar true home and family, already busy with older children and marked by its economic and cultural difference, positions her around the age of acquiring language as entering her true home as if in exile, and meeting her birth brothers as if they were distant relatives. From here we can only speculate as to where romance and realism coincide.
370. Frye, *Secular Scripture*, p. 80.

371. *Ibid.*, pp. 82, 81.
372. *Ibid.*, p. 83, pp. 79–80.
373. *Ibid.*, pp. 87–8.
374. Austen, *Mansfield Park*, p. 49.
375. *Ibid.*, pp. 48, 49.
376. *Ibid.*, p. 214.
377. *Ibid.*, p. 459.
378. *Ibid.*, p. 392.
379. Austen's letters, 20th November 1800; 26th June 1808; 30th June 1808. See *Jane Austen's Letters to her Sister Cassandra and Others* (ed.) R.W. Chapman (London: Oxford University Press, 1959), pp. 92, 199, 207.
380. Austen, *Mansfield Park*, p. 399.
381. *Ibid.*, p. 274.
382. Emily Auerbach, *Searching for Jane Austen*, pp. 171–2.
383. Austen, *Mansfield Park*, p. 265; see Austen's letter dated 26th May 1801: '[Charles] has received 30£ for his share of the privateer & expects 10£ more – but of what avail is it to take prizes if he lays out the produce in presents to his sisters. He has been buying gold chains & Topaz crosses for us; – he must be well scolded.' See Chapman (ed.), *Jane Austen's Letters*, p. 137.
384. Austen, prayer III, first printed in W. Chapman (ed.), *Works of Jane Austen*, reprinted in Austen, *Mansfield Park*, p. 478 (appendix B).
385. Austen, *Mansfield Park*, p. 468.
386. *Buddha's Teachings* (tr.) Juan Mascaró (Harmondsworth: Penguin, 1995), p. 63.
387. Jung, quoted by Lucente, p. 34.
388. Žižek, 'Courtly Love, or Woman as Thing', in *The Žižek Reader*, p. 168.
389. Lévi-Strauss, *Myth and Meaning* (London: Routledge and Kegan Paul, 1978), pp. 3–4.
390. Jameson, *Political Unconscious*, p. 182.

5 *Emma*: 'the operation of the same system in another way'

391. Frank Kermode, *The Genesis of Secrecy: On the Interpretation of Narrative* (Cambridge: Harvard University Press, 1979), p. 72.
392. Austen, *Emma*, p. 367.
393. John Keats, 'Ode on a Grecian Urn' [1820], 5, pp. 49–50.
394. Here Anne spoke, – 'The navy, I think, who have done so much for us, have at least an equal claim with any other set of men, for all the comforts and all the privileges which any home can give. Sailors work hard enough for their comforts, we must all allow' (Austen, *Persuasion*, p. 59).
395. Austen, *Persuasion*, p. 258.
396. Austen, *Emma*, p. 154.
397. *Ibid.*, p. 116.
398. *Ibid.*, pp. 116–17.
399. Hayden White, *The Content of the Form*, p. 1.
400. Ricoeur, Paul, *Time and Narrative*, vol. 1. (trans.) Kathleen Mclaughlin and David Pellauer (Chicago: University of Chicago Press, 1984), p. 30.

401. Ricoeur, Paul, *Time and Narrative*, p. 56.
402. *Ibid.*, p. ix.
403. *Ibid.*, p. x.
404. Homans, *Bearing the Word*, pp. 29–30.
405. Susan C. Greenfield, *Mothering Daughters: Novels and the Politics of the Family Romance, Frances Burney to Jane Austen* (Detroit: Wayne State University, 2002), p. 34.
406. Ricoeur, p. 55.
407. *Ibid.*, p. 55.
408. *Ibid.*, pp. 42–3.
409. White, p. 181.
410. Frye, *Secular Scripture*, p. 155.
411. Miles, *Jane Auston*, p. 41.
412. Austen, *Emma*, p. 361.
413. *Ibid.*, pp. 83, 84.
414. *Ibid.*, p. 87.
415. *Ibid.*, p. 87.
416. *Ibid.*, p. 88.
417. *Ibid.*, pp. 150, 149.
418. *Ibid.*, p. 103.
419. *Ibid.*, pp. 104, 105.
420. *Ibid.*, pp. 111, 105.
421. This particular logical anxiety concerning the subject of marriage is repeated beautifully in the BBC sit-com, *The Vicar of Dibley*, when the female vicar opens her door on a lonely Christmas Eve to find the man of her dreams asking her to marry him. Of course she says yes, and of course he then goes back to the car to fetch his beautiful fiancé.
422. Austen, *Emma*, p. 149.
423. *Ibid.*, p. 151.
424. *Ibid.*, p. 108.
425. *Ibid.*, p. 99.
426. *Ibid.*, p. 85.
427. *Ibid.*, p. 85.
428. *Ibid.*, p. 87.
429. *Ibid.*, p. 86.
430. *Ibid.*, p. 122.
431. *Ibid.*, pp. 122, 124.
432. *Ibid.*, p. 106.
433. Austen, *Persuasion*, p. 250.
434. Barthes, 'The Structural Analysis of Narratives', p. 295.
435. Austen, *Emma*, p. 368.
436. Ruth Ronen, 'Incommensurability and Representation', *AS/SA* 5: <http://www.chass.utoronto.ca/french/as-sa/ASSA-No5/RR2.htm>, pp. 294–6. (Correct at 6 December 2004.)
437. Austen, *Emma*, pp. 145–6.
438. *Ibid.*, pp. 149, 150.
439. *Ibid.*, p. 305.
440. *Ibid.*, p. 303.
441. *Ibid.*, p. 267.

442. *Ibid.*, p. 268.
443. Austen, *Mansfield Park*, p. 275.
444. Ronen, p. 296.
445. *Ibid.*, p. 296, n3.
446. Shlomith Rimmon–Kenan, *Narrative Fiction: Contemporary Poetics* (London: Routledge, 2002), p. 109.
447. Tony Tanner, *Jane Austen* (Houndmills: Macmillan, 1986), p. 243.
448. Ronan, p. 300.
449. Morris, *Realism*, pp. 135–6.
450. Ronan, p. 301.
451. Barthes, p. 295.
452. Austen, *Emma*, p. 151.
453. *Ibid.*, p. 87.
454. Rimmon–Kenan, pp. 112, 115.
455. Roy Pascal, *The Dual Voice: Free Indirect Speech and its Functioning in the Nineteenth-century European Novel* (Manchester: Manchester University Press, 1977).
456. Morris, p. 117.
457. Skinner, *An Introduction to Eighteenth-Century Fiction*, p. 264.
458. A Tobler, 'Eigentümliche Mischung direckter und indirekter Rede', T. Kalepky, 'Vershleierte Rede', in *Zeitschrift für Romanische Philologie*, XXI 1897 and XXIII 1899. C. Bally, 'Le Style Indirect Libre en Française moderne' and 'Figures de pensée et formes linguistiques', *Germanishce-Romanische Monatsschrift*, IV 1912 and VI 1914. Pascal gives a detailed account of the linguistic debate following Bally's claims for *Style Indirect Libre* in *The Dual Voice* (Manchester: Manchester University Press, 1977). Pascal's remains the fullest analysis to date of FID in prose fiction.
459. Beth Newman, ' "The Situation of the Looker-on": gender, narration, and gaze in *Wuthering Heights*, Robyn' R. Warhol and Diane Price Herndl (eds), *Feminisms: An Anthology of Literary Theory and Criticism* (New Jersey: Rutgers University Press, 1997), p. 461.
460. Austen, *Emma*, p. 394.
461. Colin MacCabe, Introduction to Sigmund Freud, *The Schreber Case* (Harmondsworth: Penguin, 2003), p. xii.
462. *Emma* (Dir. and screenplay) Douglas McGrath, Miramax Films, Matchmaker Films, 1996.
463. Rimmon–Kenan, p. 115.
464. *Ibid.*, p. 116.
465. Austen, *Emma*, p. 102.
466. *Ibid.*, p. 88.
467. Austen, *Persuasion*, p. 218.
468. Slavoj Žižek, 'Fantasy as a Political Category', in Eagleton and Milne (ed.) *Marxist Literary Theory*, p. 89.
469. Austen, *Emma*, p. 102.
470. *Ibid.*, pp. 362, 364.
471. *Ibid.*, p. 366.
472. I still find this unprecedented narrative solution breath-taking: it testifies to the gap between the real effects of social determinants, and what remains nonetheless possible.

473. Austen, *Emma*, p. 405.
474. *Ibid.*, p. 82.
475. Tanner, *Jane Austen*, pp. 235, 238, 239.
476. Austen, *Emma*, pp. 360, 361.
477. *Ibid.*, p. 364.
478. *Ibid.*, p. 368.
479. Austen, *Persuasion*, pp. 258, 147.
480. Austen, *Emma*, pp. 313, 315.
481. John Sutherland, *Is Heathcliffe a Murderer: Great Puzzles in 19th -century Literature* (Oxford: Oxford University Press, 1996), pp. 16, 18, 19.
482. Austen, *Persuasion*, p. 115.
483. *Ibid.*, p. 248.
484. Austen, *Emma*, p. 156.
485. *Ibid.*, p. 361.
486. Anne Finch, 'A Nocturnal Rêverie' [1713]: 'When a sedate Content the Spirit feels, / And no fierce Light disturbs, whilst it reveals; / But silent Musings urge the Mind to seek / Something, too high for Syllables to speak; / Till the free Soul to a compos'dness charm'd, / Finding the Elements of Rage disarm'd, / O'er all below a solemn Quiet grown, / Joys in th'inferiour World, and thinks it like her own: / In such a *Night* let me abroad remain, / Till Morning breaks, and All's confus'd again; / Our cares, our Toils, our Clamours are renew'd, / Or Pleasures, seldom reach'd, again pursu'd.' See David Fairer and Christine Gerrard (eds), *Eighteenth-Century Poetry: An Annotated Anthology* (Oxford: Blackwell, 2004), pp. 33–35.
487. Austen, *Mansfield Park*, p. 135.
488. Austen, *Emma*, p. 361.

6 *Persuasion*: 'loving longest, when existence or when hope is gone'

489. Žižek, 'The Supposed Subjects of Ideology', *CQ*, 39, 2, p. 53.
490. P.B. Shelley, 'On Love' [1818], in Duncan Wu, *Romanticism: An Anthology* (Oxford: Blackwell, 1994), pp. 860–1.
491. Austen, *Persuasion*, p. 245.
492. Austen, *Persuasion*, p. 245, and see p. 247 where Anne 'received' Wentworth's 'look'.
493. Harding notes that the revised revelation scene of *Persuasion* has the effect of increased agency in Anne, but the agency is still enmeshed with the risk concerning her receipt of the message; the 'truth' that she brings to the narrative is 'wordless' or indirectly understood. See Harding, 'Regulated Hatred: an Aspect of the Work of Jane Austen' [1940], in Lodge (ed.), *Twentieth-century Literary Criticism*, pp. 263–75. The deleted scenes are included in Linda Bree's excellent Broadview edition of the novel, pp. 259–69.
494. Austen, *Persuasion*, p. 258.
495. Letters to Cassandra, dated Saturday 3 January 1801, Sunday 25 January 1801, in R.W. Chapman (ed.), *Jane Austen's Letters*, pp. 103, 118; Austen, *Persuasion*, p. 125.
496. Austen, *Persuasion*, p. 66.

497. *Ibid.*, pp. 94, 95.
498. *Ibid.*, p. 68.
499. *Ibid.*, p. 96.
500. *Ibid.*, p. 68.
501. *Ibid.*, p. 97.
502. *Ibid.*, p. 94.
503. *Ibid.*, p. 95.
504. *Ibid.*, p. 94.
505. *Ibid.*, p. 93.
506. *Ibid.*, p. 248.
507. *Ibid.*, p. 93.
508. Austen, *Emma*, p. 360.
509. Austen, *Persuasion*, p. 245.
510. Frye, *Secular Scripture*, p. 129.
511. Wentworth's feminisation of his 'old' ships is interesting in this context: 'But, Captain Wentworth,' cried Louisa, 'how vexed you must have been when you came to the Asp, to see what an old thing they had given you.'
    'I knew pretty well what she was, before that day'; said he, smiling. 'I had no more discoveries to make, than you would have as to the fashioning and strength of any old pelisse, which you had seen lent about among half your acquaintance, ever since you could remember, and which at last, on some very wet day, is lent to yourself. – Ah! She was a dear old Asp to me. She did all that I wanted. I knew she would. – I knew that we should either go to the bottom together, or that she would be the making of me' (Austen, *Persuasion*, pp. 98–9).
512. Frye, *Secular Scripture*, p. 131.
513. Austen, *Persuasion*, p. 67.
514. *Ibid.*, p. 69.
515. *Ibid.*, pp. 137–8.
516. *Ibid.*, p. 117.
517. *Ibid.*, p. 245.
518. *Ibid.*, p. 66.
519. *Ibid.*, pp. 48, 83, 149.
520. *Ibid.*, p. 180.
521. Frye, *Secular Scripture*, p. 134.
522. Austen, *Persuasion*, p. 83.
523. *Ibid.*, p. 111.
524. *Ibid.*, p. 120.
525. *Ibid.*, p. 243.
526. *Ibid.*, pp. 242, 244.
527. Jameson argues for four 'levels' to interpretation, in a revision of the medieval model: (1) Literal; (2) Allegorical; (3) Moral; (4) Anagogical. The anagogic reveals – or posits – a point at which 'the text undergoes its ultimate rewriting in terms of the destiny of the human race as a whole'. (*Political Unconscious*, p. 31).
528. Austen, *Pride and Prejudice*, pp. 216–22.
529. *Ibid.*, p. 227.
530. Riley, Denise, *The Words of Selves: Identification, Solidarity, Irony* (Stanford: Stanford University Press, 2000), p. 147.

531. Peter Childs, *Reading Fiction: Opening the Text* (Houndmills: Palgrave, 2001), p. 29.
532. Riley, p. 147.
533. Austen, *Persuasion*, pp. 116–17.
534. *Ibid.*, p. 241.
535. *Ibid.*, p. 242.
536. *Ibid.*, p. 114.
537. *Ibid.*, p. 115.
538. Ronald Carter and John McRae, *The Routledge History of Literature in English: Britain and Ireland* (London: Routledge, 2001), p. 238.
539. Lukács, *The Theory of the Novel*, p. 75.
540. Riley, p. 163.
541. Austen, *Persuasion*, p. 250.
542. *Ibid.*, p. 248.
543. Lacan, *Feminine Sexuality: Jacques Lacan and the 'Ecole Freudienne'* (trans.) Jaqueline Rose (London: Macmillan, 1982). See, also Lacan's argument that 'Love is essentially deception', in Jacques Lacan, *The Four Fundamental Concepts of Psychoanalysis*, trans. Alan Sheridan (London: Hogarth, 1977), p. 268. Quoted in Anthony Easthope's discussion, *The Unconscious* (London and New York: Routledge, 1999), pp. 67–8.
544. Luce Irigaray, *The Way of Love* (London: Continuum, 2002) introduction.

Conclusion: 'such an alternative as this had not occurred to her'

545. Theodor Adorno and Max Horkheimer, *Dialectic of Enlightenment*, (trans.) John Cumming (London: Verso, 1992), p. xv.
546. Frye, 'Archetypes of literature', p. 431.
547. Karen Joy Fowler, *The Jane Austen Book Club* (Harmondsworth: Penguin, 2005), pp. 115–16.
548. Michael Gross and Mary Beth Averill, 'Evolution and Patriarchal Myths of Scarcity and Competition', in Harding and Hintikka (eds), *Discovering Reality*, p. 82.
549. Alison Jaggar, 'Love and Knowledge: Emotion in Feminist Epistemology', in Kemp and Squires (eds), *Feminisms*, p. 190.
550. Hartsock, 'The Feminist Standpoint', p. 305, pp. 302–3.
551. William Blake, 'A Vision of the Last Judgement', quoted by Easthope, *Englishness*, p. 103. Easthope contrasts Blake's sun with John Locke's: 'What is it, but an aggregate of those several *Ideas*, Bright, Hot, Roundish, having a constant regular motion, at a certain distance from us?' Locke, *An Essay Concerning Human Understanding*, II.23.6.
552. Flax, 'The Patriarchal Unconscious', pp. 260–1, 269.
553. Gross and Averill, 'Evolution and Patriarchal Myths', in Harding and Hintikka (eds), *Discovering Reality*, p. 82.
554. Žižek, 'Courtly Love, or Woman as Thing', in Wright and Wright (eds), *The Zizek Reader*, p. 164.
555. Austen, *Pride and Prejudice*, p. 277.
556. Frye, 'Archetypes of Literature', p. 428.

557. Denise de Rougemont, *Love in the Western World*, (trans.) Montgomery Belgion (Princeton, New Jersey: Princeton University Press, 1983), pp. 164–5.
558. Austen, *Persuasion*, p. 244.
559. Jameson, *Political Unconscious*, pp. 19–20.
560. Lucian Goldmann, 'Introduction to the problems of a Sociology of the Novel', in Terry Eagleton and Drew Milne (eds), *Marxist Literary Theory*, pp. 213–14.
561. Austen, *Pride and Prejudice*, p. 369.
562. *Ibid.*, p. 61.
563. *Ibid.*, p. 64.
564. Frye, *Secular Scripture*, p. 432.
565. Fowler, p. 249.
566. Elder Olsen, *The Theory of Comedy* (Bloomington: Indiana University Press, 1975), p. 25.
567. Austen, *Pride and Prejudice*, p. 368.
568. Williams, *Keywords*, pp. 304–5.
569. Austen, *Northanger Abbey*, p. 238.
570. *Ibid.*, p. 239.
571. Fay Weldon, *Letters to Alice: On First Reading Jane Austen* (London: Coronet Books, 1985), pp. 37–8.
572. Weldon, p. 149.
573. Neeson, *Commoners*, p. 3.
574. Neeson, p. 1.
575. *Ibid.*, p. 6.
576. *Pride and Prejudice*, adapted by Andrew Davies, (Dir.) Simon Langton, BBC in Association with the Arts and Entertainment Network, 1995.
577. G.W.F Hegel, *Phenomenology of Spirit*, (trans.) A.V. Miller, foreword by J.N. Findlay (Oxford: Oxford University Press, 1977) (p. v). The *Phenomenology* was first published in 1807. I am particularly intrigued by the resonance here of Hegel's account of the work of art where the 'Notion strips off the traces of root, branches, and leaves still adhering to the forms and purifies the latter into shapes in which the crystal's straight lines and flat surfaces are raised into incommensurable ratios, so that the ensoulment of the organic is taken up into the abstract form of the understanding [...] its essential nature – incommensurability – is preserved for the understanding' (p. 427). See also Forest Pyle, *The Ideology of Imagination: Subject and Society in the Discourse of Romanticism* (Stanford: Stanford University Press, 1995), pp. 62–6. Pyle quotes Paul de Man's intriguing note concerning Hegel and Romanticism: 'Few thinkers have so many disciples who have never read a word of their master's writings' (p. 63).

Index

Note: I have avoided the tedious listing of page-by-page references to Jane Austen, her works, characters, or her family. I have also avoided references to 'narrative', 'realism' and 'romance', as these terms recur on almost every page of the book. This index gives a broad indication of my discussion of key concepts, and of where I have made use of the work of others in building an argument.

Printed in the United States
68298LVS00001B/152

9 781403 997470